Romeo
Romeo

ROBIN KAYE

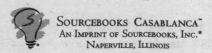

SOURCEBOOKS CASABLANCA™
AN IMPRINT OF SOURCEBOOKS, INC.®
NAPERVILLE, ILLINOIS

Published by Sourcebooks Casablanca, an imprint of Sourcebooks, Inc.
P.O. Box 4410, Naperville, Illinois 60567-4410
(630) 961-3900
FAX: (630) 961-2168
www.sourcebooks.com

Library of Congress Cataloging-in-Publication Data

Kaye, Robin.
  Romeo, Romeo / Robin Kaye.
    p. cm.
  ISBN-13: 978-1-4022-1339-7
  ISBN-10: 1-4022-1339-5
  1. Italian Americans—Fiction. 2. Brooklyn (New York, N.Y.)—Fiction.
I. Title.
  PS3611.A917R66 2008
  813'.6—dc22
                                        2008022497

Printed and bound in the United States of America
OPM 10 9 8 7 6 5 4 3 2 1

*For my grandparents, Anna Maria
and Antonio Orlando*

Chapter 1

ROSALIE RONALDI MADE A SUCCESSFUL ESCAPE FROM THE insane asylum. Okay, so it wasn't a real insane asylum; it was her parents's Bay Ridge home. But most days, it could pass for the Sicilian version of Bellevue. She pulled on her coat as the storm door snicked closed behind her, took a deep breath of cold early January air, and ran for the solace of her car.

Sitting through a typical Italian Sunday dinner at Chez, Ronaldi was always a lesson in self-control. Today it had become a lesson in avoidance—marriage avoidance.

For the life of her, Rosalie couldn't figure out why her mother would push a daughter she supposedly loved down the aisle. It wasn't as if the institution had brought Maria Ronaldi any happiness. Just the opposite.

Whenever Rosalie made decisions, she measured the odds and studied the statistical evidence—something at which she'd always excelled. With the divorce rate at 53 percent, if you added the number of unhappy marriages that wouldn't end in divorce because of religious beliefs or sheer stubbornness, which she estimated was running at about 46 percent, only 1 percent of all marriages could be considered happy. A person would have to be crazy to take a calculated risk with a 99 percent failure rate.

Rosalie was many things, but crazy wasn't one of

them. As a child, she'd made the decision never to marry, and nothing in her experience since had done anything but cement her resolve. Of course, if she said that, she'd be breaking the eleventh commandment: thou shalt marry a nice Catholic boy (preferably Italian) and have babies—or go straight to hell.

Rosalie climbed into her VW Beetle and headed toward her Park Slope apartment. Turning onto the Prospect Expressway, she heard a funny thumping noise. Never a good sign. She pulled over to find her tire was as flat as matzo, and after a marathon Italian dinner, the waistband of her pants was so tight that if she took a deep breath, she'd pop a button. God only knew what would happen when she bent down to change the tire.

Rosalie opened the trunk, expecting to see her spare tire. It was supposed to be right there, but all she saw was a big hole.

Great! Just what she needed. She stared into the trunk, turned to kick the flat tire, and called her brother the nicest name she could think of that fit him. Asshole.

"Stronzo!" She should have known better than to give him a hundred and sixty bucks to replace her spare tire. She'd told him to buy a full-sized spare, and he hadn't even gotten her one of those donuts. "He's *proprio un stronzo della prima categoria.*"

She had no problem calling Rich the world's biggest asshole in Italian. After all, God excused cursing if done in a second language. He gave bonus points for cursing in a third. Rosalie had a feeling she'd be brushing up on her Spanish.

Dominick Romeo stood in the state-of-the-art garage of his flagship dealership, the largest car dealership in all of New York. He'd built it from nothing but brains and hard work. He owned a chain of dealerships that covered most of the East Coast, but he'd be damned if he could figure out what was wrong with his Viper.

Nick checked the clock next to his private hydraulic lift and decided to call it a night. He was the only one unlucky enough to be there at five o'clock on a Sunday evening. Anyone with the sense God gave a flea was at home digesting a traditional Italian supper, but not him. His car had chosen today to act up. He slammed the hood and cringed as the noise echoed through his aching head. Wiping grime from his hands, Nick contemplated one of the world's great mysteries: why man had ever combined computers and the internal combustion engine.

The weekend had started badly and gone downhill from there. On Friday, the offer he'd made to acquire the one car dealership he'd coveted since he was a boy had been rejected. Then on Saturday night, instead of being considerate about his loss, his girlfriend Tonya started making noises about marriage, leaving him no choice but to break things off. That led to tears on her part, more than half a bottle of Jack on his, and a screaming hangover Sunday morning.

The very morning he was awakened at six o'clock by his mother's phone call reminding him it was his turn to take Nana to church. Experiencing Mass with Nana while hungover made him wonder whether Jesus really died for our sins—or because dying was less painful than listening to Nana sing. That morning, Nick had been

tempted to give the cross a try himself. His broken-down
Viper was the icing on the cake. He'd heard trouble came
in threes. He must have gotten a double dose, because
he was up to five at last count, which meant he had one
more to look forward to.

Nick put a socket wrench away and switched off the
lights. At least he knew he'd find a cold beer and a warm
bed at home. But unless he wanted to drive a wrecker,
he'd have to search the key box and move the cars block-
ing the entrance of the dealership to take a demo.

Nothing brought out the neighbors faster than parking a wrecker in front of his Park Slope brownstone.
The dirty looks didn't bother him—at least not enough
to spend half an hour searching for keys and moving
cars. Hell, he'd lived in the same house since his birth
thirty-one years earlier, back when Park Slope had almost as bad a rep as Bedford Stuy. If he wanted to park
a garbage truck in front of his house, it was no one's
business but his.

Nick wore his coveralls so he wouldn't get his clothes
dirty sitting on the greasy bench seat of the wrecker and
took off for home. He was almost there when he came
across a disabled vehicle on the shoulder. A woman was
kicking the shit out of a flat tire, paying no attention to
the cars and trucks careening by at high speeds.

He flipped on the emergency lights and pulled off in
front of the lunatic's car. At least, he hoped it was her
car. If it wasn't, the owner was going to be pissed, since
the woman had missed the tire and kicked the back
fender. He backed up, figuring he might as well get
through the remaining bad thing sooner rather than later.

The deranged woman looked like a good candidate for bad thing number six.

Nick hopped out of the wrecker and walked toward the crazy lady. Over the sound of the traffic, he swore he could hear her cursing in Italian and maybe Spanish.

"Hey lady, if you're done beating on that side of the car, you might want to start on the other side. You're liable to end up as road pizza if you stay where you are." He waited for a response, but she only looked at him as if he were an alien being. He tried again, slowly this time. Maybe she *was* crazy. "Lady, if you'd pop the trunk, I'll change the tire. Then you can go home and deal with the cause of your anger in person."

"What are you, *stunad*? Don't you think if he were anywhere in the tristate area, I'd have hunted him down like the dog he is and beaten him within an inch of his life?"

Nick raised an eyebrow, content to watch the meltdown from a safe distance.

"And if he'd bought the spare with the money I gave him, I would have already changed my own tire. You'd think I'd have learned my lesson when I was five and realized Richie had been robbing me blind, trading my dimes for nickels. He said nickels were worth more because they were bigger, and I believed him. I should have killed my brother years ago. Instead, I'm standing here in twenty-degree weather talking to you."

At that moment, it must have occurred to her that she was yelling at a Good Samaritan. She took a deep breath, tucked her hands in her pockets, and gentled her tone. "Not that I don't appreciate you stopping."

"Sure." Nick had a hard time hiding his grin. He'd

always had a weakness for feisty women. He wouldn't want to piss her off, but damn, she was cute. A real lunatic, but cute as hell. "Look, lady, why don't you get out of the cold and wait in the wrecker? Just don't touch anything. I'll put your car on the flatbed and take you home. You can pick it up tomorrow at Romeo's."

She backed up. "You want me to get in the truck with you?"

Dominick narrowed his Sicilian blue eyes, wondering if he'd get credit for number six if he left her standing on the expressway. It wasn't as if he hadn't tried to help.

"You want me to tow your car to the garage or not?"

"Of course I do, but I'm not in the habit of taking rides from strange men."

He removed the cables he needed to hook up the car. "Good luck finding a cab at this hour. If you need to, you're welcome to use my cell phone. It's on the seat in the truck. I'll be another ten minutes if you change your mind." Nick heard her say someone should die in a pool of blood, but with the noise of the traffic rushing by, it was hard to tell who she was talking about. He hoped it wasn't him.

Rosalie wondered if the points she'd racked up cursing in Spanish were enough to convince God to send help, since, when she'd called, she hadn't found one garage open in all of Brooklyn when she'd called. It was nice to know her three years of high school Spanish hadn't been a complete waste, but then again, when something seemed too good to be true, it most often was. Wreckers didn't drive around looking for broken-down cars, did they?

If God had sent this guy, she must have scored major points. Okay, she knew she was staring, but how could she not? He looked like a large, dark Jude Law. The Italian in him only added to his good looks, not to mention the way he filled out those mechanic's coveralls. It should be illegal to be that dirty and still look so hot.

Under normal circumstances, she wouldn't have thought twice about having a mechanic drive her home, but something about him didn't add up. He wore coveralls with his name embroidered on them, and his hands were grimy, but his haircut was something you'd see on the pages of *GQ*, not *Mechanics Weekly*. He was wearing dress shoes that looked handmade, not oil-covered work boots. Then there was his accent—or lack of one. He had the Brooklyn speech pattern, said the right words, but the accent was missing. He sounded like a guy from Connecticut trying to sound like he was from Brooklyn. That made him either a rich man with amnesia working as a mechanic—or a mass murderer. The likelihood of either was slim, though a mass murderer was a better bet.

Rosalie dug though her pocketbook looking for the cell phone she'd thrown in after her last attempt to find an open garage. She dialed her boyfriend Joey, her parents, her best friend Gina, and even her cousin Frankie. No one was home, and it was beginning to snow. She called a cab. The best they could do was a forty-five minute wait. She'd sooner take her chances with a possible Ted Bundy than stand on the side of the road for the next hour. Besides, her favorite suede boots were fading fast, and she loved those boots. Damn.

She looked up to find Nick, if that was even his real name, walking toward her.

"Did you reach anyone?"

Rosalie shook her head.

"If you don't want me to take you home, at least let me drop you off at a restaurant or bar where you can wait for a cab."

"Why don't you have an accent?" Okay, so he thought she was crazy. At least, he was looking at her that way.

"A heavy Brooklyn accent isn't good for business, so I changed mine. Now, are you coming or not?"

His reason was plausible. Even she tried to drop the accent when working. It was strange for a mechanic, but if he were a mass murderer, he could have already thrown her into the truck. What the hell, she'd take a chance and save her boots. "Home, James."

"The name's Nick," he said, pointing to the name embroidered on his chest.

"So, is Nick short for Dominick Romeo? It would make my day to be rescued by the most eligible bachelor in New York . . . well, now that Donald Trump's married again."

Her joke fell flat. Nick's scowl made her wonder if she'd do better on the expressway, but he was already helping her into the truck.

Nick closed the door and rounded the front. He jumped in and picked up the conversation, not bothering to hide his distaste.

"So, are you looking to get lucky and land a rich man?"

"Who? Dominick Romeo?" Right, like that was going to happen. She strapped herself in, trying to ignore the grease-covered seat belt and the cleft in Nick's chin. Both made her squirm in her seat, for very different reasons. "Bite your tongue. The last thing I need is a husband, rich or otherwise. I have a hard enough time cleaning up after my dog. But if you ever tell another living soul I said that, I'll have to kill you."

He laughed, and his scowl disappeared. "Your secret's safe with me. So, they're comparing Romeo to Trump now?"

"Yeah. I've heard he's Brooklyn's version of The Donald, minus the comb-over. He might not be as wealthy, but I hear he's younger and much better looking."

Nick smiled, and she felt as if she'd been hit with a tire iron. He should register his smile as a lethal weapon and be careful where he aimed it. That smile would make any normal woman throw her arms up and scream, "Take me."

It was a good thing Rosalie wasn't normal. Hell, she wasn't even single. She was in a relationship—one of convenience, but still, it was enough. Correction, it had been enough to keep her parents off her back about marrying, until today. Today her mother had informed her that it was the two-year anniversary of her first date with Joey—a date that obviously had made more of an impression on her mother than it had on Rosalie.

Joey seemed content to let things go on the way they were. She fed him several times a week; they had occasional, albeit boring, missionary-position sex; and they both had a significant other to take to family functions. It also helped that his mother no longer questioned his sexuality. For a while there, he'd said, Mrs. Manetti would ask if he'd like to bring a boyfriend or girlfriend to dinner. She'd said that a boyfriend wouldn't upset her, although she'd looked relieved the first time Rosalie joined them for a meal. Somehow, Rosalie doubted Nick had ever had his sexuality questioned.

Nick took another look at the woman next to him. Crazy Lady was giving him the "alien arrival" stare again. Too bad the only single woman he'd ever met who wasn't looking to marry a rich man was a nut job. Though, to be fair, it could be temporary insanity. He had to admit, he'd go a little crazy if someone left him without a spare.

After getting a good look at her, Nick decided sanity was way overrated. Miss Loco was every guy's wet dream. She reminded him of the Sophia Loren pinup his Great Uncle Giovanni had hanging in the back room of his barbershop. Nick liked his women curvy and built. None of those bony women who looked more like a boy than a girl for him. Tonya was always trying to lose weight, and it drove him nuts. Her ass was so small, there was almost nothing to hold. Psycho had an ass like you read about. Damn, he should ask her out for her ass alone. Plus, a guy had to admire a woman who could curse in several languages. And she was beautiful, even without makeup. He'd never seen Tonya without makeup, not even after sweaty sex, but he'd bet she wouldn't look so good. *La Donna Pazza* wasn't drop-dead gorgeous like Tonya, but he'd lay odds she didn't get Botox injections and collagen implants—and didn't have breasts you were afraid to squeeze for fear they'd pop. Hers looked like one hundred percent natural 36Ds.

He had a real problem with her car, though. The sunflower yellow VW Beatle couldn't have been girlier if she'd painted it pink. It had a freaking bud vase built into the dashboard. If he did decide to date her, he'd have to get her a new car. He couldn't date a woman who drove a car he'd be embarrassed to be seen in.

"Are you going to give me your address, or do you want me to drop you off at a bar or something? Since I need your name and address for the work order, you might as well let me take you home."

"Huh?"

Nick was tempted to snap his fingers in front of her face. Instead, he picked up the clipboard and filled out the form.

"I need your name."

"Rosalie. Rosalie Ronaldi."

"Ronaldi? Any relation to Rich Ronaldi?"

"He's my older brother and the reason I'm missing a spare. You know him?"

Nick smiled. The less she knew about his history with her brother, the better. Even at fifteen, getting drunk and sleeping with Rich's girl had been unforgivable. Getting them both arrested for grand theft auto had added insult to injury.

The last he'd heard, Rich had been teaching at some college in New Hampshire or Vermont—one of those states that had more trees than people and way too much snow. He saw no need to alert either the delicious Rosalie or her brother that Nick Romeo was dogging her. She'd figure it out soon enough, and by the time Rich heard, it would be too late to do anything but wipe her tears. Not that Nick intended to leave his women crying, but more often than not, that's what happened. His relationships never lasted long, so why complicate things by bringing up old news? He'd be history by the time Rich came back to town. Although for some reason, the thought wasn't gratifying.

He shook it off. He was a Romeo in every sense of the word. It was a legacy and a curse. Nick came from a long line of men who married women, knocked them up, and left, never to be seen again. He'd never put a woman and a kid through what he and his mother had gone through. No, the Romeo line would end with him. It wasn't as if he did anything underhanded. All his women knew the score. He practiced serial monogamy, refused to marry, and always used condoms. The way he looked at it, he was doing women a favor.

"Rich still teaching?"

Rosalie turned to face him, pulled her leg up, and tucked it under her. "He is. It's hard to believe, I know. I can't imagine an ex-juvenile delinquent like Richie in charge of impressionable kids, though I hear he's great at it."

"It just goes to show you, we all grow up sooner or later."

"Do we?"

Rosalie looked as if she doubted it. He remembered Tonya saying he "suffered" from Peter Pan syndrome. But his definition of suffering and hers were two different things. He got to sleep with a beautiful woman until the novelty wore off or she started talking about marriage, whichever came first. He kept his place off-limits, so he never had to worry about putting the toilet seat down. And, best of all, he didn't have to be at anyone's beck and call. If he didn't want to do something, he didn't. Yeah, that was his kind of suffering.

Nick pulled into the slow lane and stole a glance at his passenger. "So, Rosalie, are you going to tell me where you live, or do I have to guess?"

"Get off at the next exit, and head toward the park. Left on 4th Street."

Rosalie tried not to stare, honest she did. She fumbled with her bag, but her eyes always returned to Nick. He must have been having a bad day. His eyes were blood-shot, and he wore a pained expression as if he had the mother of all headaches. The emotions that swept over his face were telling—anger, determination, and a cocky "I'll show you" look.

The man could grace the covers of magazines and romance novels, but if she needed eye candy, she'd buy herself a beefcake calendar. She knew they made one with guys from the NYFD. Maybe they made one with mechanics. She had no problem imagining Nick with the zipper of his coveralls pulled low, showing his muscled chest, washboard abs, and treasure trail leading down to. . .well, let's just say she wouldn't mind checking out his undercarriage.

"Well, what do you think?"

The sound of Nick's voice pulled Rosalie's mind out of the gutter. "Excuse me? I'm sorry, I wasn't paying attention. . .um, what did you say?"

"I asked if you wanted to grab lunch or a cup of coffee when you pick up your car."

"Why?" Okay, now he looked as if he thought she'd escaped from a mental ward, which, today, wasn't far from the truth. "I mean, um, I guess, okay."

"Gosh, try to contain your excitement. You got something against dating a mechanic?"

"A date? With you?" she sputtered. Great. She sounded like an idiot. "I've got a boyfriend—"

"Look, if you don't want to go out, just say so. There's no reason to lie."

"I'm not lying. I have a boyfriend."

"Yeah? Then why didn't you call him when you got stuck on the side of the road?"

"I did. He wasn't home."

"Where is he?"

"How the hell do I know? We don't check in with each other."

"You two are real close, huh?"

"My relationship with Joey is no concern—"

"So, how long have you and Joey been going out?"

"Two years. Why?"

"I see."

"You see what?"

"I see that either Joey's an idiot, or he's ready to move on. Maybe both."

"I know I'm going to regret this, but I'll ask anyway. What do you mean by that?"

"It's obvious. Joey's not concerned about some guy coming on to you and stealing you away, which makes him an idiot. 'Cause if you were mine, I'd damn sure know where you were—and you'd know how to reach me twenty-four hours a day. But maybe he's ready to move on. Then he's distancing himself, showing that you're not together, that you're out of sync and not involved in each other's lives, in which case, he's an idiot for letting you go."

She couldn't believe she was having this conversation

with Nick the mechanic . . . or anyone for that matter. She crossed her arms and turned toward him.

"Wow, you're good, aren't you? You just cut my boyfriend to shreds, made him sound like an uncaring jerk, all the while making me out to be some kind of fantasy woman. Amazing. It's hard for a girl to listen to that monologue and be angry with you. I bet it works like a charm."

The weasel had the nerve to smile. Sure it was a good old-fashioned, take-your-breath-away-and-moisten-your-panties smile, but, still, he had some nerve.

"Did it ever occur to you that I might be distancing myself? That I'm the one ready to move on?"

"I sure hope so, but it still proves my point."

"What point is that?"

"The guy's an idiot. Only an idiot would leave you unsatisfied."

She hoped he had good peripheral vision, because he had his eyes on her, not the road. The look he gave her said he knew what to do to keep a woman satisfied and that he'd be happy to demonstrate. He smirked and returned his attention to the road.

"I'm right, aren't I? The guy's an idiot. Now the question I have is this—why would you, Rosalie Ronaldi, date an idiot for two years?"

"It keeps my family from harping about me getting married, and I always have someone to take to family functions."

"So, how's that working out for you? Your family off your case?"

"What are you, a freaking psychic? It worked fine until today. It seems I've passed the uncommitted-relationship expiration date. Where in the Italian handbook does it say a girl turns into a *puttana* after dating a guy for two years?"

Nick shot her a sideways glance. "It's in the fine print below the section on arranged marriages."

"Well, no wonder I missed it. I'm not interested in marriage, never have been. Why would anyone take that kind of risk, especially a woman? Why spend her life catering to a man, only to be replaced by a new model as soon as her body starts to droop?"

"Beats me."

"Make a left on the next block. Third house on the right."

Nick double-parked in front of her brownstone and took her car key off the key chain.

"Which floor is yours?"

"Why do you want to know?"

Nick pointed to his clipboard. "I need your address."

"First floor."

He held out Rosalie's keys and then wouldn't let them go. "So, where do you want to go to lunch tomorrow?"

Tugging the keys from his hand, she found him smirking again and tried not to smile. Not an easy thing to do; he had one hell of a smirk. She started to grab the door handle, but Nick stilled her hand.

"Don't." He jumped out of the cab, walked around to open the passenger side door, and helped her out of the truck. His rough, scarred hand warmed and dwarfed hers.

Rosalie stood with him on the sidewalk in front of her apartment and had to tip her head back to look him dead in the eyes. "I never said I'd go to lunch with you. I'm seeing someone."

"You told me that you're distancing yourself from Idiot Joey, the guy who doesn't satisfy you. So I'll see you around one tomorrow."

"I can't come back to Brooklyn for lunch. I work in the City."

"Dinner then. I'll meet you at the garage. You can pick up your car before we eat."

"Nick, I told you—"

"I know. Look, pick up the car after work, and we'll grab a bite. No big deal."

"I don't even know your name."

He handed her the clipboard and a pen. "Sure you do." He pointed to his chest. "Nick."

Rosalie scribbled her signature and handed the clipboard back. Nick wrote something else before he tore off her copy and gave it to her.

"Call me if you need anything. You can reach me at Romeo's. Just ask for Nick. Everyone there knows me. The other number is my cell phone."

She took the paper and stuffed it in her coat pocket. "I won't need anything." She started up the steps of her brownstone with Nick on her heels. When she reached the door, she and Nick did another tug-of-war with her keys. He won. He unlocked the door, held it open, and stood on the stoop under the porch light. "Good night, Rosalie Ronaldi."

"'Night, Nick."

He leaned forward and for a second there, she thought he was going to kiss her. She held her breath, but he only pushed a lock of hair behind her ear and winked. Then he turned around and took the steps two at a time, whistling. Whistling!

Chapter 2

NICK JUMPED INTO THE WRECKER AND WAITED UNTIL THE light came on in Rosalie's apartment. As soon as he saw the curtains move, he knew that Idiot Joey was history. No woman watches a man drive away unless she's interested, and the way Rosalie looked at him when he touched her, she'd been plenty interested . . . and not a little disappointed that he hadn't followed through.

What had he been thinking? She belonged to someone else. Sure, the guy seemed like an idiot, but Nick didn't poach. He'd learned that lesson with Rich Ronaldi's girlfriend, no less.

With Rosalie, Nick couldn't help but want to touch and taste. Especially taste, she had a hell of a mouth on her. Yeah, Rosalie gave new meaning to the word "lush." From her black, chin-length, curly hair that felt as soft as it looked to her killer rack and world-class ass, she epitomized fantasy material. But until she broke up with Joey—the jamoke—he wouldn't touch her, no matter how cute she looked, how great her ass was, or how nice she smelled. Nick pulled into traffic and took a deep breath. The scent of her perfume lingered over the ever-present scent of motor oil. He wanted to smell her perfume again—up close and personal.

Nick had forgotten the thrill of the chase. For the last several years, he hadn't had to dog women. He had to beat them off with a stick, and he'd taken full advantage of the veritable sexual smorgasbord. Nick couldn't remember when he'd lost the taste for it, but for the last year or so, he'd had a hard time telling the difference between girlfriends.

Okay, so Rosalie watched Nick pull away. It didn't mean anything. She'd watched him because he had her car. She loved her car. Yeah, good one, Ronaldi. Dave wouldn't buy that even if you attached it to a cookie. Speaking of which. . .

"David Rufus Ronaldi, where are you?"

Dave lumbered into the living room looking confused. Damn, she should have snuck into the bedroom. She could have caught the sneaky bastard sleeping on her bed, though she hardly needed proof. All that black hair pretty much gave the mutt away.

"Expected to hear the car, didn't you, boy?" She bent down to kiss him on the head and got a wet lick on the lips. Ewww! The damn dog had impeccable aim. "Come on, let's go out."

Rosalie followed Dave to the garden and tried not to think about what Nick said, not that it worked. But really, how could she help but think about it?

After Dave watered every bush that he hadn't already killed, they went back inside. Rosalie turned on some music and went to get out of her clothes so she could breathe. She'd pulled on flannel sleep pants and a T-shirt when Dave started barking. A second later, there was a knock at the door. She had a bad feeling it was Joey.

Looking though the peephole, Rosalie spied Joey staring back at her. Damn, why did she have to be right—and how had he gotten past the security door?

Rosalie disengaged all four locks and opened the door while trying to hold back Dave, who'd been doing a realistic imitation of Cujo. Dave was half Saint Bernard. The other half looked like Black Lab, but then he hadn't come with a list of ingredients. Dave had never liked Joey, and Joey, not one to tempt fate, seldom came over, which she'd always thought was a godsend. It got her out of doing the whole clean-the-apartment-and-change-the-sheets-before-a-date thing. Rosalie would never be confused with Martha Stewart, and the major difference wasn't that she'd never worn a police-issued ankle bracelet.

After she locked Dave in the bedroom, Rosalie returned to find Joey pacing. Something must have had him pretty worked up, because Joey didn't pace. He was so laid-back, there were times when she contemplated taking his pulse to see if he was still alive. Damn. She wanted to crawl into bed and lose herself in a hot romance novel, not have a serious discussion.

"I got your message and looked for your car. Are you all right?"

Rosalie wanted to say "Duh, what the hell does it look like?" but it wasn't his fault that she'd had a flat and gotten picked up by Hot Mechanic Guy.

"Yeah, I'm fine. A wrecker happened by and took my car to Romeo's garage." Joey seemed distracted. Why hadn't he called? Rosalie tried to ignore the sound of Dave digging at the door and whining. "Is that the only reason you came by? To check on me?"

"No, I want to talk to you about something."

Could the day get any better? He wanted to talk. It would surely be a scintillating conversation. The word "idiot" blinked like a neon sign in her brain. "Do you want wine? I think I have a Cabernet open." Actually, she was the one who needed the wine.

He started pacing again. "No, um, can we sit down?"

"Sure." She pushed her briefcase and pocketbook to the side and sat on the couch, right on her hairbrush. She pulled it out from under her and stuffed it into her bag.

Joey gave her one of his disapproving looks. He got that from his mother; Rosalie saw it every time his mother asked when they were going to marry. His lips pressed together with such force, they all but disappeared. One eyebrow shot up to his hairline, which, for Joey, was pretty high, and his head shook a bit before he made a tsking sound. Talk about annoying. He had a way of making her feel as if she were five years old again and trying to explain to Mother Superior the reason she'd flushed all the pennies down the toilet.

Joey sat on her coffee table. Now, there's not a whole lot of room between the couch and the coffee table. Rosalie wanted to get up and move away, but Joey trapped her leg between his and then reached for her hands. His were cold and shaking. Oh man, she had a bad feeling.

"Rosalie, I've been thinking about my life. I talked to my parents, and we've made a decision."

"Look, Joe—"

"No, just let me get this out, okay? I practiced all day."

The phone rang. Saved by the bell. She picked it up from the table behind the sofa and thanked God for the interruption. "Hello?"

"Has he asked you yet? I got a call from Mrs. Manetti. She wants to have the wedding at her church! Do you believe the nerve of that woman? I should pay for a wedding at her church? You'll be married at St. Joseph's, I told her."

"Ma?"

"Of course. Who did you expect? The Virgin Mary?"

OhmyGod, ohmyGod, ohmyGod. "Yeah, Ma, Joey's right here. No, nothing's new."

"Oh, he's asking you to marry him, and I'm interrupting. I gotta go and say a novena to bless your marriage. *Ti amo*, you've made me very happy."

"Ma, hold the novenas, I think you're jumping the gun here."

"*Ciao, bella*. I'll talk to you tomorrow."

Rosalie stared at the phone until the damn thing beeped. She couldn't believe this was happening. Joey took the phone, pressed the end button, and rose to put it back on the cradle.

She tried to come up with an out. If she let Dave out of the bedroom, he'd kill Joey, and then at least she'd have a valid excuse not to marry him. Joey got down on one knee. The phone rang again.

"I'm sorry. I have to get this." Rosalie slid past Joey . . . well, okay, she kind of hit him and pushed him off balance in her rush to answer the phone. "Hello?"

"If you think your wedding's gonna upstage mine, you got something coming to you. How dare you get engaged before I'm married? This is my time. Mine!"

"Annabelle?" Great, first her mother, then her sister.

"Who'd you think it was? The freakin' Good Humor Man?"

"No, the Virgin Mary."

"Very funny. Look, just because you're an old maid doesn't mean you can . . . Oh my God, you got knocked up! I thought you looked bloated today."

"I do not look bloated!" Rosalie looked down. Okay, she did look a little bloated—what do you expect after eating for four hours? "Look, Annabelle, why don't you call Mama and talk to her? I gotta go."

Joey returned the phone and disconnected it. There would be no more phone calls. "Rosalie." He took her hands again but this time, thank God, he stayed on his feet. "Pop's gonna retire at the end of the year. He and Mama are moving to Florida with Nonna. I'm gonna buy them out of the butcher shop, so I think it's time we finalized our arrangement. We'll live in their apartment above the store, and you can quit your job. You'll be too busy helping me run the store to work. And once we start a family, you'll have the children to care for. Marry me, Rosalie."

Rosalie couldn't imagine how bad the proposal would have been if he hadn't practiced. No declaration of ever-lasting love, no promises of forever. Just "I'm buying out my parents' business, and I want to finalize our arrangement." His proposal was so romantic, she couldn't contain herself. She melted. Not!

Joey pulled out a ring box and opened it to show off the smallest diamond this side of a saw blade. He'd pulled out all the stops.

"Yeah, Joey, I think it's time we finalized our arrangement, too. I won't marry you. I'm sorry, but you'll just have to find someone else to help you run the store. I'm a corporate turnaround expert, and I'm damn good at it. Hell, I'm up for vice president. I didn't put myself

through school and work my butt off for the last five
years so I could run your butcher shop."

"I'd run it. You'd only help me."

"Whatever. It's not going to happen."

His jaw dropped, and then that disapproving look
resurfaced.

"Okay, you take some time to think about it. Just remember, Rosalie, you're not getting any younger. It's not
like you're going to· get a better offer. I own my own
business. I make good money. You'll have a nice home
over the shop. What more do you want?"

Rosalie's mother and aunt had told her the very same
thing between the antipasto and the manicotti. It seemed
insanity was catching. "That's the third time today I've
been called an old maid. I'm only twenty-seven, for
Christ's sake!"

His disapproving look made her want to scream. Joey
didn't believe women should curse. Well, too damn bad.
"I'm not an old maid, and though I might not know what
I want, I certainly know what I don't want. I don't want
to ever marry you. So you can take your ring and your
business arrangement and leave before I let Dave show
you to the door."

"Rosalie, calm down—"

"Don't tell me to calm down. I want you out of
here. Now."

Dave heard the shouting and started head butting the
door. Joey looked from the bedroom door to Rosalie and
slowly backed out of the living room. He had one hand
on the doorknob when he cleared his throat and squared
his shoulders.

"You'll be sorry you threw my proposal in my face. You mark my words. No one is going to want you now. Oh, and you do look bloated." He slammed the door behind him.

Rosalie let Dave out of the bedroom and noticed that all the trim around the door would have to be replaced. She figured she got off easy. She locked up and turned out the lights before going to bed. She didn't watch Joey leave.

Chapter 3

ROSALIE HAD TO FACE FACTS. THE DAY HAD BEEN A COMPLETE loss, and it was all the fault of the man who shall remain nameless. She'd spent a sleepless night asking herself why she'd dated an idiot for two years. The answer was not one she'd ever want repeated outside the hallowed halls of a shrink's office. To make matters worse, she'd missed her subway stop and was late for work, all because she'd been thinking about "him." The subway debacle also made her late for her staff meeting, where she got caught not paying attention because she'd been thinking about him. Again. *Madònne.*

Okay, so he could be described as smart and gorgeous. Too bad "complete buttinsky" fit the bill, too. Who'd asked for his opinion, anyway?

Rosalie *had* been trying to distance herself from Joey. Could she help it that Joey was too much of an idiot to notice? It's not as if her refusal to marry him had anything to do with a knight-in-shining-wrecker fantasy. She'd been unhappy in the relationship long before Mr. Buttinsky did his Dr. Phil impression.

By the time five o'clock rolled around, she'd only accomplished avoiding her mother and sister. It paid to have a pushy assistant.

Nobody got by Gina. Rosalie had never known anyone to intimidate her mother, but Gina did—and Rosalie would be indebted to her forever. Unfortunately, Gina also intimidated Rosalie.

She cringed as Gina walked into her office and closed the door. She should have known she wouldn't get away without a bit of bloodletting.

Rosalie had thought it odd when Gina hadn't pressed for information during lunch. The thought of food had her reaching for an antacid. Talk about *agita*. God forbid she should be one of those people who can't eat when they're nervous or upset. No, she became the human equivalent of a self-propelled vacuum, eating anything and everything in sight. Not only had she eaten a whole Katz's pastrami sandwich, an unbelievable feat, but she'd finished Gina's meal. Even the servers had been astounded. Rosalie was proud of herself, though—she hadn't let anything slip. She only opened her mouth to stuff food in it.

Gina tossed her short, inky hair out of her eyes and warmed up for round two. "I'm ready to leave for the day. I've turned the phone over to voice mail, so your mother's tenth call will be answered. Now you can tell me what the hell happened to make a sweet, albeit controlling, mother hen lose all her tail feathers and most of her sanity."

Rosalie stared at the floor, knowing that in a few minutes Gina would say the dreaded I-told-you-so. She and Gina worked too closely together to keep their personal lives out of their relationship. Hell, they were so close that they even had their periods at the same time. And yes, the rest of the office treaded lightly and avoided them like the plague during the nightmare PMS week, the cowards. Her boss even had it noted on his Black-Berry. Talk about embarrassing.

"Joey proposed last night, and I said no." Just because they were close didn't mean she had to go into specifics, did it?

"We'll get back to the deets of Joey's proposal in a moment. The fact you said no explains your mother's rash of phone calls, including the one asking me if you should use Benadryl or cortisone cream on hives—"

"Look Gina, I'd love to dish, but I have to pick up my car at Romeo's before it closes." She shut down her computer, gathered her things without making eye contact, and prayed she'd make it out alive. No such luck.

Gina stepped in front of the door, the one entrée to freedom. Rosalie sneaked a look out the window and wondered how bad it would hurt if she jumped. Sure, they were on the fifth floor, but maybe she'd hit an awning and break her fall.

Nah. She wasn't that lucky. If she were, she wouldn't have to consider jumping out the window in the first place.

Gina gave her the stink eye. How Gina could look down her nose at Rosalie when she stood a good eight inches shorter defied physics. Then she smiled her I'm-going-to-torture-you-and-enjoy-it smile, her golden brown eyes sparkling with anticipation.

"I'll walk with you to the subway."

Sure she would. "If you're going to pump me for information on the way, the least you could do is ply me with alcohol." She heard the definite hint of a whine in her last statement.

"I plan to."

"Oh, good. It's nice to know that some things don't change. You still anesthetize me before you open me up. It's always less painful that way."

They left the office and pushed their way into the first elevator. Once they hit the lobby, Gina continued her interrogation, as if the elevator ride hadn't happened.

"You didn't have to lie to me about your car, *chica*. I thought we were friends."

She pushed past a group of women and went out the revolving door as fast as her short legs could carry her. Gina had to be pissed off to slip into Spanish, and a pissed-off Gina was not just a little bit scary. Rosalie gave herself a virtual thump on the head when she remembered she'd learned to curse in Spanish from Gina. Three years of Spanish—wasted.

They stopped at a street corner to wait for the light to change. Rosalie straightened the strap on her purse. "It's not a lie. I got a flat tire on the way home from dinner last night."

"Since when do you take your car to a garage for a flat?"

"Since I asked Richie to get me a spare. He pocketed my money and forgot to buy it. And to think I lent him the damn car in exchange for his tire knowledge."

Traffic cleared, and Gina pushed by two nuns to jaywalk. She raised one eyebrow. "Tire knowledge?"

Rosalie said hello to the sisters and crossed herself for good measure before passing them. "All those years of Richie stripping cars with his buddies must have taught him something."

"Other than what military life was like?"

"It was a military prep school."

"It was his one chance to stay out of jail. I know the story."

"Fine. Anyway, I had no spare, so I had the car towed to Romeo's." Rosalie opened the door to their after-work watering hole. She watched as Gina—a cross between Jessica Rabbit and Tinkerbelle with a Latin twist—strode through on four-inch heels that brought her up to a whopping five feet four. Rosalie always enjoyed watching men's heads turn and jaws drop like dominoes when they saw Gina. Not that she ever noticed.

"Romeo's was open on a Sunday night?"

"I don't know. Nick drove by and stopped. He towed the car and dropped me off at home." Rosalie took a seat at the bar and tucked her briefcase behind the foot rail.

"Nick?"

"The mechanic driving the wrecker. Anyway, after I got home, Joey came over and proposed, if that's what you'd call it."

"Why? How'd he do it?"

Suffice it to say, Gina gave her a refresher course on cursing in Spanish and attracted the attention of every man in the bar. Of course, she did that by breathing. Over the years, Rosalie had gotten used to it. She knew not to have Gina sit in on any meetings with a straight man in attendance. Nothing got accomplished.

By the time they'd finished their second drink, Gina had said her "I-told-you-so's," and Rosalie had heard several new descriptions of an idiot, both in English and Spanish, but she'd yet to hear one "poor baby." Instead, she had to deal with a drunken Gina doing a happy dance over the still-warm corpse of her failed relationship.

When it came to disliking Joey, Gina and Dave were alike, though Dave was more subtle.

After pouring Gina into a cab headed uptown, Rosalie called her neighbor to ask him to let Dave out and went straight to Romeo's. In the service department, she waited for the woman with the beehive hairdo to finish talking to an old codger. Had no one ever told her that beehives went out with the '60s? She turned her blue eye-shadowed gaze toward Rosalie.

"What can I do for you?"

"I'm here to pick up my car." Rosalie dug the work order out of her pocket and smoothed the wrinkles before sliding it across the counter. She saw the woman's nametag and smiled. The name Trudy fit.

"Oh, so you're the one. Okay, I'll call the boss."

As Trudy paged Nick, her eyes never left Rosalie. Within seconds, five women came out of various doorways and crowded behind the counter to join in the stare fest while they tried to look busy.

Rosalie looked around the waiting area, trying to ignore the fact that several women were staring at her. It was nice—the waiting room, not the women staring. It had a section with desks and Internet access for customers to work while they waited, a play area for kids, and an area with TVs, magazines, and leather couches. Nick must be the service manager, since Trudy had called him the boss. Impressive.

"Hi, Rosalie."

She turned at the sound of Nick's voice. He'd snuck up on her. He wore black slacks and a white Oxford shirt with the sleeves rolled up. Nothing special, but on him it made her newly single hormones do the tango.

"Hi." Okay, not the most brilliant conversation starter, but she was happy she could utter a single syllable. Maybe she shouldn't have had that second dirty martini.

Nick shot a glance at the women gathered behind the desk, and they scattered faster than a bunch of kids after breaking a window.

"Do you have that effect on all women, or only the ones who work for you?" There, that was better.

"Only the nosy ones working for me. I don't see you running away."

"I can't. You're holding my car hostage. Speaking of which, I need to pay for it before closing."

"Don't worry about it." He handed her the key to her car. It hung from a ring with a numbered manila tag. "Let me get my coat, and we can leave."

"No. I mean thanks, but I don't want to get you in trouble, and I need to buy a spare—"

Nick moved closer and put his hand on her shoulder. She'd taken off her trench coat; the heat from his hand seeped through her suit jacket.

"I replaced the tire. The nail in it was too close to the edge to fix. And you have a new full-size spare. I won't get into trouble, so forget about it."

"Still, I can't accept, but thanks. I'll settle up with Trudy while you get your coat."

Nick shook his head and ran his hand though his hair. "Fine. I'll have Trudy charge you cost, but no labor."

Nick spoke in hushed tones to Trudy. The two of them nodded a lot and shot incredulous glances in her direction. After Nick left, it took a few minutes for Trudy to punch the information into the computer and come up with a bill.

Nick returned, wearing a leather bomber jacket. "Are you ready to go? I'll follow you home to drop off your car."

"Why?"

"We're going out to dinner."

"I'll follow you to the restaurant." Rosalie dug through her pocketbook for her wallet. After she'd found it, she noticed Nick had his jaw clenched. Trudy shoved the bill toward her and moved over to the other side of the long counter.

Nick's arms were crossed, and he didn't look like a happy camper. He spoke through clenched teeth. "I never let my dates drive."

She couldn't believe him. She should have been out-raged, but he looked so sexy, all annoyed. He got a tick by his left eye, ran his fingers though his hair, and stood with his feet apart so his slacks stretched tight across his thighs and package. Her heart raced as if she'd run five miles. Not that she ever had, but if she did, she assumed her heart would race like that. She wondered if looking at Nick could burn the same number of calories as run-ning. If it could, every woman alive would be flinging her running shoes in the trash.

"Nick, I hardly know you. I'd prefer to drive myself."

"You don't trust me? I'm a good guy. Ask Trudy. She'll vouch for me."

Nick was tall. When Rosalie wore heels, she was in the neighborhood of six feet—yeah, they were four-inch heels, and no, she didn't wear them because they make her legs look amazing—but Nick still towered over her. Well, maybe towered was an exaggeration, but in her book, if she wore heels and the guy wasn't eye level with the twins, he was a keeper.

"I don't care if the Pope himself vouches for you. I'm still going to take my car and meet you at the restaurant."

Rosalie had a few first-date rules. Rule number one—Always meet the guy in a public place in case he turns out to be a psycho. That way, she could cut out without having to walk eighteen blocks to a subway station in a bad neighborhood where even taxis feared to tread. A lesson learned by experience.

Rule number two—Never sleep with the guy on the first date, no matter what, even if her hormones told her to hurry the hell up, they wanted a cigarette.

Rule number three—If you fight on the first date, don't make a second. Damn, she hated that one. Well, right now, she pretty much hated rule number two as well.

By Rosalie's definition, a fight meant both parties had to participate. To avoid that, she came up with the perfect compromise. "How about I drive you to the restaurant?"

That way, if he turned out to be a psycho and she had to make an escape, he'd be the one stuck walking through a dangerous neighborhood, not her, thus following rule one and rule three.

Rosalie thought he'd be happy, but no, he had a look of absolute horror on his face. So much for her brilliant plan.

"Look, Nick, I appreciate you taking care of my car, but it's getting late, and I don't have much of an appetite."

"You follow me to the restaurant, and I'll follow you back to your place. No date of mine leaves without me seeing her home safe."

"Fine, whatever. Let me finish paying, and we can go."

Trudy seemed to have enjoyed every second of their debate. Rosalie studied the bill and saw that Nick hadn't charged her for towing. She wanted to point out the discrepancy, but he'd give her a hard time, and she wasn't up to avoiding another fight. It went against her nature. Rosalie liked nothing better than a good bout of verbal sparring to get the blood flowing, but she had to consider that pesky rule number three. Plus, fighting with a guy sometimes ended in hot, sweaty, make-up sex, but because of rule number two, that couldn't happen.

Nick checked the rearview mirror of the new Mustang he drove. Rosalie had no problem following him. It would be almost impossible to lose her. That neon yellow car stuck out like a sore thumb. He shuddered at the thought of riding shotgun in the Barbie Mobile. He had his reputation to consider. He'd lose his credibility and the respect of his staff in one fell swoop. Plus, he'd never live it down if someone in his family found out—and they always found out.

Nick parked a few blocks away from DiNicola's, his cousin's restaurant, hoping no one would notice she'd followed him. He had her door opened before Rosalie cut the engine. Her long leg snaked out, and he almost forgot to offer her a hand. Damn, he'd been so busy arguing with her that he hadn't noticed what she was wearing. What the hell was wrong with him? Her trench coat had fallen open to reveal one of those sinfully sexy suits with a skirt so short, the jacket almost covered it, and heels so high and spiked, they were an engineering marvel. Her legs were already long with a capital "L." He guessed she stood five-eight or nine in stocking feet, most of which was leg. Wearing those stilts made her almost his height, not that he had a problem with that. In fact, he liked tall women, and with those heels, they lined up perfectly . . . to dance.

Yeah, dancing would be good. He hated to dance, but a guy's gotta do what a guy's gotta do. Rosalie didn't seem the type to kiss, much less screw around on the first date, and he didn't think he'd last the night without at least holding her. Good thing he and his cousin Vinny had a system down since the old days when Nick brought all his dates here. But back then, Nick washed dishes Saturday night to pay for his Friday night date, and Vinny had all his hair. Nick would ask to sit in the back room, away from the crowd, and Vinny would put on Sinatra, the patron saint of single men everywhere. Nick never failed to make it to third base with Ol' Blue Eyes in his corner.

Nick opened the door for Rosalie and cringed when he saw Mona working the desk.

"Nicky!"

The bleached blonde bimbo threw herself at Nick, and he caught her. Rosalie looked for the ladies' room.

"Mona, this is a friend of mine, Rosalie. Lee, this is my cousin Vinny's wife, Mona."

Lee? "Nice to meet you." Mona shook her hand and gave her the once-over. Rosalie didn't mind, since it turned out to be a "Is she good enough for our Nick?" and not a "What's she doing with my Nick?" kind of inspection. She could tell Mona liked the shoes, wondered if the boobs were real, and if she dyed her hair. Mona's came straight from a bottle of peroxide.

Mona gave her the sisterhood look, the one designed to make you spill juicy gossip on your first trip to the ladies' room. Rosalie returned the smile and looked around for a back door to the place. She'd never be able to pull off an escape via the ladies' room with this one in front.

"Mona, tell Vinny we're here. We'll grab a table in the back."

"Tell him yourself. He's in the kitchen. Antonio's got the flu, and Vinny's cooking."

Nick had his annoyed look on. It seemed to have no effect on Mona, but it had the same effect on Rosalie it had earlier, even when aimed at someone else. Damn.

"Mona Constantina DiNicola." Nick pulled the full name gambit, which most often worked, if for no other reason than force of habit.

"Okay, but you owe me, Nick."

"No way. You're still paying up for the Rita incident."

Mona headed to the kitchen, and Nick steered Rosalie into the dimly lit bar.

"The Rita incident? Sounds intriguing," Rosalie said as Nick shuffled her past bar stools and quiet booths.

"Just the opposite. It was a nightmare blind date to her sister's wedding."

"Oh, man, she'll be paying for life." Italian weddings sometimes lasted the entire weekend, and you can't escape. "You have my sympathies."

Nick took her hand on the other side of the bar and ushered her into the small dining room beyond. One used for private parties. Small, quiet, and empty. Frank Sinatra crooned in the background; the lights were low and the feeling intimate. She turned and took in the scene he'd set. He scored points for romance but lost a few for lack of originality.

"So, does this always work for you?" said the fly to the spider.

Nick helped her out of her coat, folded it, and laid it over the back of a chair. Rosalie sensed the debate going on in his head—Should he feign ignorance, or give her a straight answer?

"Yes, it does, but if it's any consolation, I haven't used it for years."

He held her chair as she sat. "How come? Were you in a long-term relationship?"

Nick took his seat, shot her a grin, and she melted a little.

He shook his head. "No one else seemed worth the trouble."

Damn, this guy was good. He handed her a line, and her bullshit meter didn't even go off.

A busboy came in and caught Nick's eye.

"Yo, Nick."

"How's it going, Sonny?"

"Dad asked if your date was one of those vegetarians. If not, he said you should order the special. Veal saltimbocca."

Nick laughed. "Does she look like a vegetarian?"

Rosalie didn't know whether to be insulted or not. Had he just called her fat? Sonny looked at Rosalie and then away. She had a hard time seeing in the dimly lit room, but she could swear the kid blushed.

"Nope."

"Rosalie, meet Sonny, Vinny and Mona's son."

She bit back a grin. The kid looked about sixteen, and once he grew into his feet and filled out, he would be a lady-killer. "Hi."

Sonny kept his eyes averted. Nick winked at her. "Veal okay with you?"

"Sounds good."

Nick pushed his chair back and dug into his back pocket for his wallet. "How much is she paying you for spying?"

"Ma said I'd get a ten, and she'd buy me the new Xbox 360 game I want."

Nick took out a twenty. "Here's the deal. You tell her what we ate, say Rosalie was nice, and we held hands, but you didn't hear or see anything beyond that, capisce? You do that, and you can keep this and your mother's bribe. Agreed?"

"Yeah, whatever you say, Nick." Sonny pulled on the twenty, but Nick didn't let go.

"I find out you told Mona anything else, I'll stop adding to your college fund. You get me?"

Sonny nodded and stashed the bill in his pocket. "You know, if I don't get back out there, Ma will figure this out for herself, and we'll both be in deep sh—"

"Watch your language and get out of here."

Nick took Rosalie's hand. She tried pulling away, but he held on.

"You don't want to make a liar out of Sonny, do you?"

She shook her head. She didn't want to make a big deal of it. Nick held her hand and rubbed his thumb on the center of her palm. She wouldn't say it felt as if a lightning bolt shot through her, because that sounded so clichéd, but she needed to rethink her opinion on reflexology. There had to be something to it, because whatever he did to her hand had a definite effect on several other parts of her body.

Nick sat back, rocking on the back legs of the chair. "So, when did you see Joey?"

"How did you know I saw him?"

"You wouldn't be here with me if you were still in a relationship with him, and you're too nice to break up with a guy over the phone."

"You're assuming a lot."

Nick dropped her hand and slid his chair back before he stood.

"I'll take you home."

What? Confused, she asked. "What do you mean?"

"I mean, I'll take you home. I'm no saint, Lee, but I don't poach."

Rosalie's anger got the better of her. She stood, because she couldn't very well let the guy have it when she sat eye level with his crotch. "Fine, but for the record, I don't cheat. I broke up with Joey last night, but it had nothing to do with you. Second, I resent the term "poaching." It brings to mind images of hunting poor defenseless elephants. I am neither defenseless nor an elephant. And nobody calls me Lee." Rosalie turned to grab her coat.

"Whoa." Nick caught her by the arm and held her gently, but firmly. She wouldn't get away unless she struggled, and if she did, it would kill any chance of a dignified exit. He stepped closer.

"You're the one who said I assumed a lot. You can't blame me for misinterpreting your meaning."

Okay, she'd give him that. She started to tell him so, but he took both her hands in his, leaving her speechless. Rosalie had a really hard time talking without using her hands. She'd become mute. Nick, however, didn't suffer the same affliction.

"I don't see you as defenseless, and the only thing you have in common with an elephant is your ability to walk all over a guy. I'm sorry if you don't like me calling you Lee, but Rosalie is too damn long, and you don't look like a Rose or even Rosa. Lee suits you. So shoot me."

Sometime during his little speech, he'd moved closer. She didn't know what shocked her more, that she could feel his breath on her cheek or that he thought she could walk all over a guy. She put her hand on his chest to try to control the distance between them as he closed in and kissed her. He sent no silent message that said, "I'm going to kiss you now unless you back away." There were none of the typical signs. He went for it full throttle.

The word kiss didn't describe what he did to her, with her. It was too tame to express the possessive, carnal dance of mouths, tongues, teeth, and breath. It bespoke intimacy and need, and vibrated with barely controlled passion. He explored her mouth with a diligence so complete, it was almost a religious experience.

It took Rosalie a moment to realize that Nick had stopped kissing her. She had her fingers tangled in his hair, and her chest flattened against his. Nick had his knee between her legs, pushing her skirt higher than it should ever be in public, his hands were on her butt, and they were both breathing heavily. She opened her eyes and stepped back on weak legs. Nick stared at the table behind her. When she turned, she understood why. The table now held two glasses of wine, an opened bottle of Chianti, and a loaf of bread with a plate of olive oil sprinkled with cheese and cracked black pepper. She didn't know who groaned, but one of them did.

"I'm going to have to pay Sonny a lot more than a twenty to hush this one up, though maybe I should charge him for the lesson."

Rosalie wished the earth would open up and swallow her whole. She'd never been more embarrassed.

Someone knocked on the now-closed door. It opened, and a big man walked in wearing an apron and black-and-white checked pants with a soiled towel thrown over his shoulder.

"I brought the wine, in case you were wondering. Sonny's too young to serve alcohol."

"Thanks, Vin." Nick looked equal parts relieved and embarrassed.

"Eh? You two goin' somewhere before dinner? Sit down."

Nick held Rosalie's chair. She had no choice but to sit.

Vinny put a plate of antipasti on the table. "*Buon appetito.*"

She reached for her wine and drank it down. Nick went for his water. From the looks of it, water hadn't worked any better than wine to stop the flames shooting between them, but the wine definitely helped the embarrassment factor.

She couldn't believe she'd been humping his leg!

Her face got hot all over again, thinking about it. He looked at her, she looked at him, and neither one of them seemed to know what to say, so they ate.

Rosalie stomach suddenly felt as if her throat had been cut. It must have been the embarrassment. The more wine she consumed, the easier the dinner conversation flowed. Unfortunately, her newfound ease didn't reduce her appetite. At least, their clean plates made Vinny happy.

After dinner and two bottles of wine, they drank demitasse spiked with sambuca and ate an exceptional cannoli, one of her all-time favorites. She took a bite of the delectable dessert and eyed Nick as she licked powdered sugar off her top lip. Nick cleared his throat. He'd been doing that all night.

She had a smile on her face, but how could she not, when she ate cannoli? She was having a great time, and it wasn't because of the food, though she had to admit, great food helped. Nick had turned out to be a lot of fun. She wanted to see him again, so she needed to warn him. She knew it wouldn't make a difference. Guys don't listen, but never let it be said she hadn't been straight from the get-go. She put down her cannoli and looked him square in the eye.

"You know, you're making me break one of my rules."

He raised an eyebrow. "You have rules? About what?"

"About dating. Dating rules."

"Should I ask what they are?"

"I'm breaking rule number three. If you fight on a first date, don't make a second."

"I haven't asked you out on a second date."

"After that kiss, if you hadn't asked me out, I would have asked you."

He wiped his mouth with his napkin and pushed his plate aside. Then he rested his elbows on the table and leaned toward her. "Really?"

"Yeah, but don't let it go to your head. Now, before I do something like ask you out—"

"You know, I don't think I've ever been asked out. I've been propositioned, but never asked out. Why do you think that is?"

"Maybe because you never let a girl get a word in edgewise?"

Nick smirked and she melted more, but then she'd kinda been melting like a Fudgsicle at the beach ever since she'd set eyes on him.

Rosalie cleared her throat. "As I was saying, before I ask you out—"

"Do you think I'll accept?"

"Nick, if you don't put a sock in it, it will never happen, believe me." She rushed on before he could comment yet again. "We have to get a few things straight. First and foremost is that I'm not looking for marriage, and I'm not one to change my mind. If that's a problem, you might want to pull a Barbara Bush and just say no."

"Nancy Reagan."

"Nancy Reagan what?"

"She coined the phrase 'Just Say No.' Do most men say no?"

"No, most men smile and nod, and two years later they're down on one knee."

"This happens often?"

"Well, twice now."

"I see. Two out of how many?"

"Three."

"What happened to number three?"

"He was number one, and well, he ranoffand-joinedtheseminary."

"Excuse me?"

"I said, he ran off and joined the seminary."

"Was this before or after you . . . um, spoke to him?"

"After. Anyway, back to the point. I like being single. I like having my own place. I like my job, and I like doing what I want to do when I want to do it. I'm not looking for a man to take over my life. So, unless you're looking for a monogamous, commitment-free, no strings relationship, do us both a favor and just say no."

"What about the others?"

"What others?"

"The other men you've dated. Come on, you're what, twenty-five?"

"Twenty-seven. What's your point?"

"You're twenty-seven, and you expect me to believe you've only dated three men? Come on, Lee, I wasn't born yesterday."

"I never said I'd only dated three men. I dated plenty. I meant I've only had three relationships."

"Now, I don't want to misinterpret your meaning again, so let me see if I understand. You told me you did-n't want a 'relationship,' because the word relationship implies commitment, which, if my hearing is correct, you want no part of."

She nodded.

"I don't understand what you're talking about."

"Christ, Nick." He smiled, one of those smiles again. She watched as the dimple in his left cheek popped out, or in, really, and the skin around his eyes crinkled. Then his mouth did this amazing twisty thing before his lips curved up and opened enough to show off a beautiful set of white teeth. They were perfect, she thought, except his right front tooth slanted over the other. Not that a person would notice, unless she looked close or kissed him, both of which she'd done. But, like everything else about him, Rosalie mused, it screamed sexy. She remembered how it felt when her tongue slid over it and . . . A shiver ran its way up her spine.

"Lee? Are you okay? You're shivering."

"Oh, I'm fine." She rubbed her arms and tried to catch her train of thought—it must have slipped out of the station without her. Oh, yeah, she remembered. "Anyway, I meant . . . um, a sexual relationship."

"Oh, so you *are* propositioning me." He smirked again as he leaned back in his chair, turning toward her. He crossed his arms and looked so damn smug.

"I never said . . . You know, forget I said anything." She took a sip of her demitasse and the last bite of her dessert. She didn't look at him, but felt him watching her. She brought her fingers to her mouth to lick off the cannoli cream, but remembered her manners and refrained, even though the thought of wiping the cream on her napkin almost killed her. What a waste.

She was reaching for her napkin when Nick caught her hand. Great, cream would get all over him. For the life of her, she didn't see how he could miss such a big glob of the stuff. She obsessed over it while Nick brought her hand to his mouth and licked off the cream. He proceeded to suck on every one of her fingers while keeping his eyes locked on hers.

She'd heard guys sucked on fingers and toes and other things. But not any of *her* guys. She was no virgin, but it was as if the guys she'd been with had gotten directions from the same book—*How to Get Off in Ten Minutes or Less*—and took it as a challenge. They all beat it.

Nick knew how to take his time. She didn't know how long he'd spent sucking on her fingers, but she wouldn't be surprised if they were pruny. He only stopped because Vinny came to tell them to lock up on their way out.

Nick helped Rosalie up—and she needed help. In her quest to drown her embarrassment, they'd finished two bottles of wine and had sambuca with their demitasse. It worked like a charm. Nick held on to her and smiled. She felt so good, tucked under a guy's arm and held close to his side, especially a big guy like Nick. She felt all warm and toasty and slightly buzzed. Okay, maybe more than slightly.

The next thing she knew, they were face-to-face and moving, but not going anywhere. He held her so close, she felt the vibration of his humming in her chest.

"What are we doing?"

"We're dancing." He kissed her temple, and she rested her head on his shoulder. Frank sang "I've Got You Under My Skin," and she couldn't help but chuckle at the warning, but like Frank, she couldn't resist. She kissed him.

She brushed her lips over his when "Night and Day" began, and they didn't come up for air until well after the song ended. Nick held her, and she wondered how he could kiss like that and dance at the same time. She had a hard time standing.

"I'm taking you home."

His words may have said "I'm taking you home," but his eyes said, "I'm taking you."

So much for rule number two.

Chapter 4

"YO, VIN, IT'S NICK."

"Nick? What the hell time is it? Five? Who died?"

"Nobody. How come you're not up?"

"It's Tuesday. Nino always opens on Tuesday."

"Oh, sorry."

"Yeah, well, I'm up now. What do you want, and who the hell is snoring like a freakin' freight train?"

"Dave."

"Who the fuck is Dave?"

"Rosalie's dog."

"Ah, so that's why you're whispering. I can't believe you get laid after you give 'em your first-date talk. I guess Sinatra's still your lucky charm, eh? So, is she as hot as she looks?"

"Lee's a nice girl."

Nick had promised himself a long time ago he wouldn't do anything he'd regret the next morning. No matter how badly he'd wanted to take the delicious Rosalie up on her offer last night, he knew he couldn't have taken the look he'd have seen when she remembered she'd gotten drunk and allowed him, no, *begged* him, to take advantage. That was the reason he was on the phone with his cousin while he had an erection hard enough to pound rock salt. The same problem he'd had since he undressed her and put her to bed—alone.

"And for your information, Lee gave *me* the first-date talk. If I hadn't been so surprised, I would have taken notes. Her style was ingenious."

"No shit. She must know your rep and be pullin' that reverse psychological shit. I tried it on Mona—didn't work."

"Vin, she doesn't know who I am. I picked her up on the way home the other night. I drove a wrecker, and her car had broken down on the expressway. She thinks I'm a mechanic."

"Ha! You're shittin' me!"

"No, man. She thinks I'm Joe Schmoe. It's nice."

"Yeah, she looked real nice wrapped around your leg."

"Watch your mouth, Vin."

"You're lucky Sonny didn't catch the same show I did."

"Yeah, I know. I wasn't thinking." He couldn't remember a time when he'd had so little control. Okay, there was that time with Rich's girlfriend, but hell, he'd been a drunk kid. When a hot older woman promised to show a fifteen-year-old boy his way around a custom king, there's no way he'd say no. Hell, if Janet Reno had propositioned him, he'd have thought twice before turning her down. Nick hadn't turned Rich's girlfriend down, and he lived to regret it.

"Look, Vin, I need you to do me a favor. We left Lee's car in front of Mrs. Ragusa's house. Could you bring it to the dealership today? The keys are in the register drawer at the bar."

"Sure, but it's gonna cost ya."

"Okay, what'll it be this time? Are you going to borrow the new Chrysler, or are you going for the Mustang? I've been driving one lately. It's pretty hot."

"What about the Viper?"

"No way you're driving my Viper."

"No, why aren't you driving it?"

"I'm a mechanic, remember? Mechanics don't drive Vipers."

"Oh, right. Okay, I'll bring her car in. What does she drive?"

"It's a yellow Beetle."

"Christ, Nick, I can't drive that. I'll never live it down."

"Ask Mona. She'll drive it over. It's a girly car—she'll love it."

"Yeah, that's what I'm afraid of. She already wants one. If I let her drive Rosalie's, I might as well have you special order a pink one for Mona. There's no way I'm gonna buy a freakin' fairy car. Why don't you have one of the shop guys drive it in?"

"Can't. It'd be the talk of the dealership. I'm sure Trudy's already having a field day telling everyone how we argued last night. Lee insisted on paying for the tire and spare I replaced."

"No shit? She's the independent type, huh?"

"Yeah, I never met a girl who didn't want a guy to take care of her. I thought independent women were an urban legend. Turns out it's no legend—it's a pain in the ass."

"I'll get the car to the shop for ya, but you owe me big. Tell Ronny I want a Chrysler 300C with all the bells and whistles."

"Done."

Nick put the phone back on the sofa table. Stepping over the pile of stuff he'd had to move off the couch to make room to lie down, he went in search of aspirin.

Christ, the place was a mess. He walked to the bedroom and checked on Rosalie. She still slept hard, and so did Dave, from the sound of him. Nick had no trouble finding the glasses in the immaculate kitchen, though he cursed when he saw she only had a non-aspirin painkiller. He poured himself a glass of orange juice, popped a couple, and looked around. Weird, you could eat off her kitchen floor, but it looked as if a bomb had gone off in the rest of the place. Not many things surprised him when it came to women, but Rosalie—she was a freak of nature.

He went back to the couch to lie down, wondering why he'd chosen to stay. He pushed Dave off the pillow he'd snagged from Rosalie's bed when he poured her into it last night. Clearing his throat, he tried to erase the vision of Rosalie in bed, all warm and wanton, teasing him while he did his damnedest to behave. It didn't help that she wore lingerie that would tempt a eunuch, or that she filled it out better than anyone had a right to.

He turned the pillow over to avoid dog slobber, and ignoring his raging hard-on, tried to get some sleep.

Rosalie thought she was going to die, but she was sure that surviving was worse. Her head pounded, her tongue felt like a shag carpet, and it hurt to focus her eyes. She should never have had that last sambuca, but Nick had looked so cute playing bartender, she'd had it anyway.

After finger combing her hair, she tried to remember what had happened the night before. She remembered Nick kissing her—a lot, and really, really well. But after that last drink, everything got fuzzy. She didn't know how she'd gotten home and into bed, wearing nothing but her bra and panties, without her knowledge.

Rosalie knew that Dave must have his legs crossed, since she couldn't remember taking him for a walk last night, either. She stumbled out of bed, happy she could stand without her head exploding. It was unfortunate that she stood on the spiked heels she'd worn the day before. Ow. Stepping on them hurt even more than wearing them. She didn't call them Benito Mussolinis instead of Bruno Maglis for nothing. They might make everything look great, but they did it by using torture.

She groaned and wondered where Dave hid. Both he and her nightshirt were absent. She found her nightshirt under a pillow and pulled it over her head, wanting nothing more than to return to her nice warm bed. She hoped Dave wouldn't mind watering the garden by himself, because she *so* wasn't up for a trek outside.

Rosalie went to look for her furry friend and found more than one. Dave slept on one side of the sectional sofa, sharing a pillow with none other than Nick, who looked like he slept naked—not that she could tell for sure, more's the pity. The quilt she'd left thrown over the back of the sofa covered everything below the waist. Even feeling as if she should be on her way to the mortuary, looking at him stirred her imagination. Fantasies took shape—the very shape of Nick. She didn't know how long she stared at his broad, flat chest. His muscles were ripped, but not bulging, and he had a dusting of dark hair that trailed over six-pack abs and disappeared beneath the damn quilt. She imagined how it would feel to tangle her hands in his chest hair, to feel the scrape of his stubbled chin against her skin, her breasts. Oh, and his mouth. What the man could do with his mouth.

She must have groaned aloud, because Nick awoke in an instant. She'd never seen anyone awaken so quickly and totally. She pulled her nightshirt down to cover her big butt and backed up a step.

"Sleep well?" He pushed the quilt down and stood with his back to her. He wore boxers. Damn, foiled again. He stretched, the muscles of his back and shoulders rippling, then pulled on his pants and shirt, turned, and looked at her as if he expected something. Um . . . oh, right, an answer.

"Yeah, I think." That was the best she could do, considering she remembered nothing.

He nodded. God, what could he be doing here, and how could he look so incredible first thing in the morning? There should be a law against it.

He walked though her apartment as if he owned the place, got a glass out of the kitchen cupboard without having to search, filled it with water he knew she kept in the fridge, and took out the painkillers she had stashed over the sink. What? Had he done an inventory of her kitchen while she slept?

Nick strode barefoot toward her, his shirt hanging open and the waistband of his pants unbuttoned. After having seen him shirtless and wearing only boxers, she didn't know whether to cringe or celebrate her good fortune. The man didn't have an ounce of fat on him. There were no love handles, no rolls, nothing but skin, bone, and muscle. He was the picture of male perfection . . . well, except for that pushy attitude, but looks-wise, yeah, pretty much perfect. She wished she could say the same for herself. She tugged her shirt down again as he placed the tablets in her hand.

"Take these and drink all the water. It'll help. You'll survive, though you might not want to."

Yup, there was that pushy attitude. She would have said so, if she hadn't needed something to stop the pounding in her head.

"Thanks." Rosalie backed down the short hallway toward her room. "I . . . I'll get dressed."

"Lee? Do you remember anything from last night?"

Oh, God, what had she done? "Um, yeah, I remember dinner, that last shot of sambuca, dancing, and um . . ."

"Coming home?"

She shook her head. Mistake, big mistake. She groaned, ducked into her room, and closed the door. Nope, she didn't remember a thing.

Rosalie walked past her dresser on the way to the bathroom. She needed a shower, oh, and about a gallon of coffee to clear her head. As she passed the mirror, her reflection caught her eye, and she stifled a scream. As a rule, she wasn't a vain person. She always tried to look her best, but once she had the prerequisite makeup on, she didn't powder her nose every five minutes. She couldn't believe Nick had seen her looking like this and hadn't run screaming from the apartment.

She groaned. "Note to self: never go to bed without removing makeup."

Rosalie took the world's fastest shower and brushed her teeth for five minutes while obsessing over how one should act when she doesn't know what happened the night before—a first for her. By the time she realized she couldn't hide the fact that she was clueless as to what had happened, she'd dressed in the only clean suit she'd found in her closet and made a mental note to hit the dry cleaners on the way home. Before facing Nick again, she took a deep breath to prepare herself. She had no idea what she'd done, but she prepared to be embarrassed to no end. She remembered she'd left her shoes in the dining area. She pictured them under the table . . . the table covered with mail, newspapers, and the stuff she needed to take to the post office but never got around to. Shit! Her place was a wreck. How long had it been since she'd cleaned? Rosalie couldn't remember, and she had a very good memory, which meant it had been a long, long, long, long time.

Sign her up at the local community college. She now qualified to give lessons on how to impress a man. On your first date, fight with him, make out in a public place, get caught by a member of his family while you're humping his leg . . . oh, yeah, and let's not forget the all-important get drunk so he has to drive you home. But don't let it end at the door . . . somehow, make sure he comes inside your pigsty, um, place. That's the ticket. Works every time.

Both Nick and Dave were gone. Rosalie thanked God for the temporary reprieve, though she felt even worse. Poor Nick not only had to take her home, but he also walked her dog.

After stepping into her purple pumps, she started straightening the apartment when a thought hit her. Nick had already seen the disaster she lived in, and there was no way, in the time it took to walk Dave, she could make a noticeable improvement without the use of a front-end loader. She'd be better off spending the time hiding the ravages of too much alcohol, too little sleep, and abject embarrassment. She needed all the help she could get.

Ten minutes later, Dave ran into the bathroom as she finished applying mascara. She tried not to wince or poke herself with the wand, a difficult feat on her best day. The throbbing of her head kept time with Dave's tail banging against the built-in metal clothes hamper, sounding like a big brass drum.

She kissed Dave's head, fluffed her hair, and followed him to the kitchen. Nick had bought coffee and pastry from the bakery down the street, Fiorentino's.

Rosalie looked at the box of pastry and couldn't help but wonder what she'd done last night to deserve breakfast . . . oh, and coffee. Yes, Nick had great taste in baked goods, as well as being the picture of male perfection. And let's face it, a man who gave her coffee scored big points. Coffee and chocolate were her weaknesses, and he'd brought both.

Any man worth his salt knew the fastest way into a woman's pants was the combination of chocolate and a legal addictive stimulant—caffeine. Hmm, maybe she hadn't done anything after all, well, at least, nothing sexual. If she had, he wouldn't be trying so hard. All's fair in lust and war, but why, of all the bakeries in Brooklyn, did he have to pick Fiorentino's?

Mrs. F. and Rosalie's mother had gone to Erasmus High School together. Erasmus High School not only produced musical legends the likes of Paul Simon, Barbra

Streisand, and Neil Diamond, but also gossip legends the caliber of which were unparalleled outside the borough of Brooklyn.

The phone rang.

Rosalie didn't have to look at her caller ID to know it was her mother. She knew it instinctively. Just as she knew Mrs. Fiorentino had waited on Nick and called Mama the second he'd left.

She'd have rather eaten glass than speak with her mother, but listening to the phone ringing was worse. Plus she wanted to make sure Nick didn't hear the message her mother was bound to leave.

"Morning, Ma."

Nick turned and raised an eyebrow.

"Rosalie Angelina Ronaldi, you should be ashamed of yourself! You spit on the good name of your family. One day after breaking the heart of a fine man, you're sleeping with a bum."

"Ma, this isn't a good time." Nick handed her coffee and smiled. She took a fortifying sip as Mama continued her spiel.

" . . . ungrateful, *puttana* of a daughter. I thank God my sainted mother is dead, God rest her soul, because if she saw what you've become, it would have killed her. As it is, she's rolling over in her grave."

"Ma, I can't talk now. I gotta go to work."

"You'll come to dinner so I can talk sense to you. Maybe Joey Manetti will forgive you and take you back."

"Sorry, Ma, I can't. I've got a date."

"A date with who? The bum who walked that big horse of yours? The bum who bought you breakfast and coffee at Fiorentino's bakery? The bum who doesn't shave? That *cafone?* He's more important than making peace with the family?"

"Mama, I refused Joey's proposal. If you'd heard it, you'd have refused, too. It has nothing to do with the family, and you know it. I have no need to make peace with anyone, and I would sooner die an old maid than marry Joey Manetti."

Rosalie sipped her coffee while Mama said a prayer to the Virgin Mother and sighed. "Is this *cafone* gonna give you a home, children? You're so smart with your college degree and big office. Think about what you do, Rosalie. Think hard. And for God's sake, go to confession."

"I will. 'Bye, Ma."

Nick had somehow unearthed the dining table. A plate of pastry and bagels sat in the center. He'd even poured orange juice. Rosalie had never had a man serve her. Now she was sure she hadn't done anything involving Tab A and Slot B . . . or Slot A for that matter—well, kinda sure, anyway, since Nick wasn't just any man. No, typical he was not.

Nick pulled out a chair and took the box of tampons off the seat. Damn, she'd wondered where those went. He nudged her into the chair and put the tampons on top of the pile of stuff he'd taken off the table. Could a person die of embarrassment?

"*Mangia tutto.* Eat, it'll make you feel better."

Sitting at her table with Nick across from her was strange, intimate. This was as strange to Dave as it was to her. She'd never had guys stay over. If for some reason they ended up at her place, they took off after the obligatory five minutes of cuddling. Not that she minded. Who wanted to sleep with a guy who snored and hogged all the covers and most of the bed? And don't even mention the nightmare of sharing a bathroom. If she and Nick had sex, why had he slept on the couch? No guy she'd ever known would leave a comfortable bed and move to a couch unless he was forced. But if they hadn't had sex, why had he stayed? Rosalie took a sip of juice. "Thanks for breakfast."

"It was the least I could do."

That second sip of juice went down the wrong pipe. She turned red, but it wasn't only due to the coughing fit, and Nick, the smug bastard, knew it. There was a reason she never had men spend the night. She caught her breath and started to recover.

"So, where are we going?"

Rosalie took a slow sip of her coffee and wiped tears from her eyes. Great, her eye makeup was now all over the napkin. "Excuse me?"

Nick licked cream cheese off his finger, which invoked indecent memories. Indecent memories were the only memories she had of last night. Damn him.

"Where are we going on the date you told your mother about? You know, the one with the *cafone* you're sleeping with. The bum who doesn't shave and walks that big horse of yours."

Nick's eyes twinkled like the devil. Oh, yeah, he was enjoying the hell out of that.

"Didn't your mother ever tell you it's not nice to eavesdrop?" Rosalie had intended to sound sarcastic, something she hadn't had a problem with until now, but even to her own ears, she sounded cranky, petulant, and, perhaps, the slightest bit whiny.

Rosalie went for the dark chocolate-covered dough-nut, and when she bit into it, she was pleasantly surprised to find it filled with Bavarian cream.

"No. I don't think so. But don't worry about it, Lee, I've been called worse. Besides, she didn't say anything that wasn't true at one time or another."

"She didn't?"

Nick finished his juice, wiped his mouth, and smiled. Darn him. He knew she didn't have the foggiest idea what had happened after that last sambuca.

"Don't look so upset. I was a gentleman. Or, is that why you're upset?"

"Not likely. Um . . . were you really?" She took an-other bite, trying to seem as if she could care less and was simply asking to make conversation.

"Was I really what?"

"Were you really a complete gentleman?"

"No. Not a complete gentleman. You can't blame a guy for looking, can you? I never said I was a freakin' saint, Lee, and I sure as hell don't bat for the other team." He waggled his eyebrows. "Nice undies, by the way."

She met his laughing eyes with defiance—at least she hoped it looked more like defiance than extreme embar-rassment. He'd undressed her and seen her naked. Well, except for a little bra and . . . Oh, God, she'd been wear-ing a thong. He'd seen all of her.

Now, Rosalie was as delusional as the next girl, but even she couldn't believe he'd somehow missed seeing her butt. It'd be like going on the Staten Island Ferry and not seeing the Statue of Liberty.

Nick was having way too much fun at her expense, so she threw her napkin at him.

Dave barked, making her wince. Rosalie patted Dave's big head to calm him. He groaned when she started rubbing his ears. Dave's, not Nick's, but if she wasn't mistaken, Nick looked jealous. Good.

"Aw, Lee. It wasn't as bad as all that. It's not like I took off *all* your clothes, just most of them."

The worst part was she didn't remember a thing. Usually, when she got naked with a guy and had to live with the embarrassment, she got a little enjoyment out of it. Very little in her experience, but still, it sometimes made the mortification worthwhile. She had no problem imagining how much she'd have enjoyed herself with Nick. He was watching her as if he could read her mind, and she felt sure he could. His eyes drifted to her chest. She followed his gaze, only to find her bra did nothing to hide her reaction to those fantasies. Rosalie crossed her arms.

"I couldn't have done any more even if I'd wanted to." He nodded at Dave. "You've got quite the chaperone there. I brought you home, helped you undress, and tucked you in. I was barely able to grab a pillow before he started growling. He all but herded me out of the room."

"You're lucky that's all he did. He always wanted to tear Joey limb from limb."

"You weren't joking about Joey proposing to you, huh?"

"You didn't miss much of my conversation with Mama, did you?"

Nick threw her a smug smile and shook his head. "So, you okay with this?"

"With what?"

"Us seeing each other."

They were seeing each other? When did that happen? "Why shouldn't I be?"

"Good. So, I'll pick you up here at seven?"

"Damn, you're smooth."

Nick stood and nudged Dave out of the way. He leaned over Rosalie, his hands on the arms of her chair, their noses close to touching.

"I usually get what I want."

Rosalie tried not to ask, really she did. But he was so close, and he had that whole morning-after, sexy as hell, stubble thing going on. And those clear blue eyes. She felt herself falling right into his trap. She was in trouble.

"Yeah, and what do you want?" she asked, barely recognizing the husky voice emanating from her.

"You."

He cupped her face and stared at her as if he were trying to make a decision. Then, after a long pause, his lips whispered over hers. He kissed her. Soft and light and seductive. Slowly, he deepened the kiss, but only in movement and pressure. There was no thrusting of tongues, no roaming of hands other than threading his fingers though her hair and massaging her scalp and neck. He hit a hot button . . . well, the one above her waist, anyway. Then the kiss became a wide-open, mouth-to-mouth exchange of breath, slow and sensual. It went on forever, and when at last he touched his tongue to her bottom lip, she imploded. She'd never experienced anything like it. The man should write a book for the good of all womankind.

She groaned in frustration and tried to wrap her arms around him, but his hands cupped her shoulders, holding her in place as he ended the kiss. She opened her eyes and tried to focus on his. They'd turned gray, like the color of the sky before a violent storm. Nick returned to his seat, as if nothing had happened, leaving her dazed and confused. It took a moment to gather her wits, what little she had left, considering her condition—hungover and horny. Her mouth still tingled—in fact, quite a few of her two thousand and one parts tingled.

Rosalie tried to figure out what had happened, why Nick had pulled away. How could he kiss her like that and be insensitive to the unbridled sexual tension arcing between them? Well, except for that stormy eye thing.

Nick pushed his chair back and disturbed her musings. "Do you take the Broadway Express in?"

She nodded.

."I'll drive you to your stop."

"Okay, thanks."

"Do we need to do anything with Dave?"

Dave who? Oh, right, Dave . . ." I need to feed him."

Nick rose. "Where's his food? I'll feed him."

"By the door to the garden, but you don't have—"

"How much does he eat?"

"Three scoops."

He nodded and started out of the room. "Drink your juice."

Nick disappeared. Hearing the telltale sound of kibble

hitting stainless steel, Dave ran toward his bowl. Rosalie prayed Nick would get out of the way before Dave ran him over. She heard a grunt. She couldn't tell if it was Nick or Dave, but either way, poor Nick hadn't been quick enough.

"When was the last time he ate? He practically tackled me."

"I had Henry feed him last night. Henry's my neighbor. He feeds Dave and walks him for me when I can't get home." She rose and took the dishes to the kitchen.

"So this Henry, he's a teenager?"

"No, he's a graphic designer. Why?"

"An old graphic designer?"

"No, he's my age. . ."

"And he's got a key to your place?"

"Well, yeah. It's not as if Dave can let him in. Why are you so interested in my neighbor?"

"I'm not."

"I'm sure Wayne will be happy to hear that. If Henry so much as looks at another man, Wayne gets all weird and possessive. I don't know how Henry stands it."

The lightbulb switched on in Nick's head. What was it with men and the whole proprietary thing? She'd kissed Nick a few times, and now he was checking out the competition? Rosalie knew she should have been mad, but the girl in her could only sigh.

"Are you ready to go?"

So much for the warm fuzzies her reflection brought about. Nick helped her on with her coat, stuck an umbrella in her briefcase, and led her out the door. Was he going to tuck lunch money in her pocket, too? Rosalie was about to ask him when she noticed it.

"Where's my car?"

"It's at the shop. You were in no shape to drive."

"Oh, right. Um, thanks for getting my briefcase."

He opened the door of the white convertible Mustang and handed her in. The drive to the subway was only a few blocks.

When Nick pulled up to the station, she unbuckled her seat belt and started to get the door. His hand came around the nape of her neck; he pulled her close and kissed her. His rough beard rubbed against her skin like sandpaper, and his lips were velvet soft. His hold was gentle, but his kiss was raw. She held on, her fingers anchored in his hair, and all thought of being late for work, of Gina's questions, of everything except her and Nick in the cocoon of the car fled. She took in the smell of Nick mixed with new car and leather, the feel of his tongue against hers, the press of his mouth, the sharpness of his teeth, the brush of his beard against her skin, and his arms banded around her. She reveled in it. Rosalie sank into him, and he pulled away.

Nick's hands held hers, nicely but firmly, extracting them from his person while she reeled from his kiss. She wondered if he had a catalog of kisses. Each one he planted on her was different, although they all seemed to have the same effect. He, on the other hand, went from hot and heavy to casual and offhanded in the blink of a stormy eye. It was downright unnerving.

"I'll be by about seven to pick you up."

She nodded and picked up her briefcase as he reached across her to open her door. She was unable to put words together.

"Call me if you need anything. You have my numbers."

She nodded again, thinking she needed to do something. A taxi behind them laid on the horn . . . right. She had to leave.

What a difference a day made. One day she got the world's most insulting marriage proposal, and the next she had a date with the hottest guy she'd ever seen in boxers . . . yeah, including the Calvin Klein underwear models.

Rosalie slid out of the car and held onto the door, half expecting to ooze onto the pavement before she could close it.

It took several moments for the realization to hit her. When it did, she tripped on the curb. Nick saw the show and winked before he drove off, but she was too dumbfounded to be embarrassed. Damn, Nick had done it again. He'd said he usually got what he wanted, and he was right—he'd gotten a date. But that wasn't all he wanted.

Oh, yeah, what a difference a day made. Rosalie was one lucky girl, except for the nasty hangover. A date wasn't all she wanted, either. She found herself singing on the way to work. "Tonight, tonight, tonight. . ."

Chapter 5

ROSALIE STEPPED OFF THE ELEVATOR AND FOUND GINA waiting.

"Somebody had fun last night." Gina said in a singsong voice, which was the last thing Rosalie needed to hear.

She took a deep breath and decided to make Gina run for it. Sometimes an eight-inch height difference had its advantages. Rosalie power walked down the hall singing " . . . She knows when I am sleeping. She knows when I'm awake. She knows when I've been bad or good . . ." She stopped singing. "It's annoying as hell."

Gina fell behind. She was not a good runner. Her breasts bounced so much, it was a wonder she didn't blacken both eyes.

"Oh, and you're hungover." Gina gasped, breathless, as she turned the corner into their office suite. "I can't wait to hear all about it. I had a few drinks, but I'm not hungover, and you're twice my size."

"Thanks for the news flash." Rosalie glared as she pushed open the door.

"I thought you were going to pick up your car."

"I did." Rosalie took the last swig of her latte. There was nothing like mainlined caffeine to increase the irritant factor of nosy assistants. Gina closed the door behind her. It was unfortunate that she was on Rosalie's side of the door when she did.

"So, spill." Gina made herself comfortable in the leather chair in front of the desk, slipped off her shoes, and sat with one leg pulled up underneath to make herself look taller.

Rosalie sat at her desk, took out the files she hadn't had the chance to look over the night before, and got down to work.

"Gina, I have a lot to catch up on, and I have to get ready for our move to Premier Motors—"

"I've already made the arrangements for our move to the dealership. I've requisitioned computers, scheduled the IT installation, ordered supplies, and hired and scheduled a service to move the files we have here uptown. The only thing I haven't done is scope out the area for restaurants and a good bar. You're all caught up, thanks to me. Now, what did you do last night and with whom?"

"How do you know I was with someone?"

"Hmm . . . maybe it's the whisker burn all over your face, but it could be the glow."

"What the hell are you talking about?"

Gina's brows furrowed, and her eyes narrowed to slits, squinting as if Rosalie had the answer written in fine print on her face. If Gina kept that up, she'd need Botox before she was thirty.

"You have that glow—the one you get when you're in lust. Stop stalling, and tell me his name."

"Nick."

"Nick what?"

"Nick, the mechanic at Romeo's . . . well, he's the service manager. We went out to dinner." Rosalie didn't meet Gina's eyes. She needed no encouragement.

"And?"

"And we had a nice time."

When Rosalie got the guts to look, Gina was leaning forward, sitting on the edge of her seat. Damn.

"And?"

"And Dave likes him." She might as well get the inevitable over with while she still felt sick. There was no way the situation could get worse.

"You took him home?"

"No, he took me home. I had too much to drink."

"Rosalie, how long have we known each other?"

"Close to four years."

"In all that time, I've never seen you hungover, and I've never known you to introduce Dave to any of your boyfriends on purpose—not after that unfortunate emergency room visit. Come to think of it, I've never seen you with whisker burn, either. Did you break rule number two?"

"No." Rosalie shook her head and regretted the movement. Beating back nausea, she took a deep breath. "Nick slept on the couch."

"Sure . . ."

"Gina, if you don't believe me, that's your problem. I don't need grief from you, too."

"What's that supposed to mean?"

Rosalie rested her elbows on the desk, dropped her head into her hands, and rubbed her forehead with her fingertips, hoping they'd erase the headache rooted there. "Nick took Dave for a walk and stopped to buy breakfast at Fiorentino's. Mrs. F. called my mother, and then Mama called me. . ." She'd been going for a boring shopping list tone, not that it helped. Gina's eyes widened and shone like new pennies.

"Oh, to have been a fly on the wall."

"Yeah, well, Nick was. He must have exceptional hearing, because he repeated several parts of our conversation verbatim." Rosalie slid the top drawer of her desk open and searched for something to stop the banging in her head. Rubbing wasn't cutting it.

Gina padded out of the office and returned with a bottle of water and a handful of pills.

One look at Gina told Rosalie the inquisition was not over. "Cyanide?"

"You wish." Gina handed Rosalie the medication.

"I hate pills. I already took three. They didn't help."

"This is aspirin mixed with caffeine—it's the perfect hangover remedy."

Rosalie popped them in her mouth and swallowed a half-bottle of water. "Thanks."

"So, what does this Nick look like?"

"He's a big, tall, Italian, Jude Law with the same blue eyes, a phenomenal chest, and an incredible ass."

"Sounds like he's got the physical attraction part of the love equation covered. How about personality and intellect? Is he dumb or something?"

"No. He's smart and funny. I had a nice time."

"As evidenced by your whisker burn. I hope you're not on the rebound."

"How can I be on the rebound, when I was never bound in the first place?"

Gina slid forward in her seat with her toes planted firmly on the floor, ready to take off at any moment. With her little body erect, she looked like all she needed was the countdown. Ten, nine, eight . . . Rosalie knew it was time to take cover.

"Are you sure he's single? Did you check for the telltale wedding ring tan line?"

"He took me to his cousin Vinny's restaurant. He wouldn't do that if he were married."

"Where does he live?"

Rosalie shrugged. "I never asked."

"You didn't ask. Okay, what's Nick's last name? You did ask his name, didn't you?"

"I forget. Maybe DiNicola. That's his cousin's last name, I think."

"You slept with a man, and you don't even know his last name?"

"I didn't sleep with him. He slept on my couch."

"Semantics—he could have been a mad rapist."

"Oh, and knowing his last name would have been a big help if he were."

Gina stood and wiggled into her shoes. Shit, she was going to pace. Rosalie hated when she did that. And she was off . . . hand on hip, she strutted back and forth in front of Rosalie's desk, her back slightly arched, making her miniature JLo butt stick out more than usual.

"Rosalie, you're too damn trusting. Have I taught you nothing? Haven't I told you about all those nice girls Sam's pulled out of the East River?"

Rosalie didn't follow Gina's double-time march. She couldn't muster enough energy to move her eyeballs.

"Gina, ever since your sister married a homicide detective, you've been obsessed with murder. I'm not an idiot. I'm careful. I met him at the restaurant, and I know he's the service manager at Romeo's."

"How do you know he didn't slip something in your drink?"

"Leave it alone, Gina. Nick's a nice guy."

"Fine, but don't blame me when you find out he's a married serial rapist with six kids living on Long Island." She muttered something in Spanish and stormed out, slamming the door behind her.

Rosalie winced. Neither the conversation nor the slamming door had helped her hangover. Damn, she felt like shit.

Nick sat in the Mustang parked across the street from Rosalie's under the wash of a streetlight, missing his Viper. He killed the engine and wondered if a night with Rosalie was such a good idea. Sure, she said she wasn't interested in a relationship, and on the surface, she seemed like the perfect playmate—for lack of a better term. But women always said what he wanted to hear in the beginning. The only difference was that Rosalie had said it first. Strange.

Something nagged at him in the deepest recess of his mind, yet he couldn't get a grip on it. It was a sense of anticipation, but not the same anticipation he felt about taking over another dealership or seeing the preliminary P&Ls. This was more turbulent, nervous. The thought of being nervous astonished him.

Something about Rosalie was different, or maybe it was that he felt different when he was with her. He wasn't used to not knowing his own mind, and he didn't like it. It might take time, but he'd figure it out. He always did.

He scrubbed his hands over his face and got out of the 'stang. At least he was comfortable in his clothes. Being someone else meant he no longer had to live up to his image or his status. It felt great to be out of a suit and tie. He pulled the sleeves of his Henley down and shrugged on his old leather jacket before skipping up the steps of Rosalie's brownstone. He rang her apartment, and she buzzed him in.

"Door's open. Come on up."

What was she thinking, not even asking who it was— and then leaving her door open? Nick pushed his way past the guy getting mail out of his box, strode down the hall, and slipped into her apartment, determined to give her a lecture on safety.

"What are you—"

Dave barked and jumped, slamming Nick against the closed door. The dog's beefy paws knocked the air out of Nick with a whoosh, and he struggled for his next breath.

"Oh, sorry, Nick." Rosalie rushed to the door, grabbed Dave by the collar, and yanked. "Down, Dave. You remember Nick, don't you, boy? He fed you your nummies this morning."

Damn, she looked good. She had on a lipstick-red, wraparound sweater that his fingers itched to untie, over some kind of satin and lace lingerie top that skimmed her hips and brought to mind sweaty sex and the sound of ripping fabric. Her black jeans made her legs look long and hot as a summer day. Pink polished toenails peeked out beneath the hems of her jeans. Nick cleared his throat.

"Hi."

She smiled, and he fought the urge to grab her and kiss her like he'd been thinking of doing all damn day. He couldn't do that. It would look as if it was natural to want to kiss her. Which, he guessed it was for other guys, just not for him. He hadn't had the urge to kiss his other girlfriends when he saw them, though they usually kissed him. He'd never understood it. They'd put on all that damn lipstick, and then they'd kiss him. He always ended up wiping the stuff off his face and hoping he got it all. Rosalie had painted her mouth to match her sweater, all red and glossy, and for the first time, wiping off lipstick didn't seem like that big a deal.

He'd wanted to kiss Rosalie the first time he set eyes on her and every time after that—even that morning, when she'd looked green. She didn't look green now. Her dark eyes were sparkling, an improvement on the bloodshot looks she'd thrown him earlier. Her curly hair was sexy and tousled, the same as that morning, when he awoke to find her staring at him. The sight of her in nothing but a nightshirt had him thinking of little else all day. Well, that and the memory of how she looked out of the nightshirt.

"Hi." Nick was staring at her. What was she supposed to do? Kiss him? No. That'd be too much of a "Hi, honey, welcome home" moment, and Rosalie didn't want to give him any ideas. The sound of stainless steel being kicked—Dave's way of saying, "Hurry the hell up, I'm hungry"—broke the silence. You'd think Nick would have said something. Maybe he was struggling with the same dilemma—to kiss or not to kiss. It was time for her to make a quick exit and regroup.

"Um, I'll go feed Dave, and then we can leave."

"There's no rush."

She pushed her hair back and walked barefoot to the alcove/mudroom behind the kitchen. She should have straightened up the apartment, or at least, put away the damn box of tampons sitting on top of a pile on the buffet, but she hadn't had time. She'd had less than an hour to change out of her work clothes. As it was, she'd gone through a dozen outfits, because he hadn't told her what they were doing or where they were going. Come to think of it, he hadn't even asked her out. He'd taken the lie she told her mother and held her to it.

"Make yourself at home. I'll only be a minute." Rosalie walked away, knowing he was watching her. The hair on the back of her neck stood up. She hated that, especially since she didn't know if her jeans made her butt look big. The one day she really needed them, her personal fashionistas, Wayne and Henry, were both unavailable for consultation.

When she returned, Nick was looking around the apartment as if he'd been cataloging changes and saw none for the better. Oh, well. It's not as if she could do anything about it now.

Nick turned his gaze back to her and cleared his throat. He ran his hands through his hair as if frustrated, then stuffed them in the pockets of his jacket.

"Um . . . I was going to lecture you. You buzzed me in without even asking who it was, and your door was open."

He'd spoken. Well, that was a relief. They'd gotten past the awkward greeting deal.

"I don't need to ask. Nobody gets by Dave, although I do try to keep him from jumping. I was looking for my boots and. . ." She was still looking for her boots. She made a slow turn, hoping she'd see them under the coffee table or maybe in the corner by the door. She didn't want him to think she didn't know where her clothes were, which she didn't, but that was beside the point.

One second she was trying to figure out where her boots were, and the next, she had two hundred pounds of man wrapped around her, kissing her. Oh, and what a kiss. This was no "hello, good to see you" kiss. It was more of an "I want to taste you all over, starting with your mouth, and moving on from there" kind of kiss. Not that she'd ever had one of those before, but she was sure enjoying having one now.

He was all over her. He seemed bigger, harder, and well . . . determined. Not that she was complaining, but damn, give a girl a minute to catch up.

Oh, yeah, Rosalie caught up fast. She wrapped her arms around his neck. God, he tasted good. Minty, like he'd brushed his teeth before he came over. She had, too, but that was before she'd snagged a few dark chocolates. There were worse things to taste like . . .

She tasted of dark chocolate and hot spice. Nick traced her lips with the tip of his tongue. He couldn't tell if it was flavored lipstick or if she'd eaten something sweet, dark, and rich. Hot, soft, small, she seemed shorter. Right, no shoes. Her arms looped around his neck before she nipped his lower lip and sucked it into her mouth.

Damn, she kissed like a porn star. Her scent, her taste, her soft moans had his heart beating hard enough to crack a rib, and that wasn't the only thing going hard. He felt like he had the time he'd flown in an F-14. The G-force slammed into him and stole his breath. In this case, it was the Lee-force.

He grabbed a handful of world-class ass, drawing her closer. Her chest flattened against his, and he straightened, pulling her to her toes. She tightened her hold around his neck and rocked her pelvis against his while she explored his mouth. She played tag with his tongue and then ran hers along every tooth and recess, as if she were mapping it for a future invasion.

Nick couldn't get enough. He reached for more with every stroke of his tongue, delving deeper. Needing to be closer, he spun them around and pressed her back against the wall.

His heart hammered against his ribs. She swallowed his groan as he lifted her off her feet. Rosalie wrapped her legs around his waist so tight, he could feel her heat through his jeans. He cursed the layers of denim separating them.

Nick pulled his mouth from hers, trying to catch his breath and slow the passion that was escalating out of control. It didn't help that she was writhing against him. No, slowing down was not an option.

Rosalie's dark eyes swam with desire. Her swollen lips were now free of lipstick, and her skin flushed. He buried his face against her neck. Her perfume changed with the heating of her skin, to a dark, intoxicating scent—a mixture of deep woods, something oriental, vanilla, and aroused woman. Rosalie's pulse raced beneath his lips as he untied her sweater, searching for skin, needing to feel it beneath his fingertips. Frustration escalated. His hand slid over heated satin as he explored the body he'd fantasized about since he first saw her.

"Nick, hurry, bedroom."

With one tug, Rosalie had his jeans unbuttoned and unzipped. In his next ragged breath, her hand slid inside his boxers.

He hadn't thought he could get any harder. He'd been wrong.

"No. Too far. Couch." He groaned as he squeezed his eyes shut, trying to regain control.

"Dave—"

"Okay. Bedroom."

He stumbled through the living room and into the bedroom, kicked the door shut, and sat on the edge of her unmade bed. Her knees found purchase as she worked the jacket off his shoulders. Nick slid it off without ever taking his mouth off hers.

He considered ripping the lacy top keeping him from his intended destination, but he wasn't sure if she'd appreciate his haste. Before he could find its hem, she pulled his shirt over his head and shoved him down on the mattress. He was more than willing to accommodate her. She straddled him, her hands running over his chest, her pelvis fitting onto his just right. When her hot, wet mouth opened over his chest and sucked his flat nipple, he almost came off the bed.

Nick was fine with give-and-take. He didn't mind women having their way with him, but he wanted his way, too. Now. He flipped her onto her back with little struggle, captured both of her hands, and pinned them above her head.

"My turn."

Nick straddled her hips and slid the satin top over the lace of the bra that barely covered her nipples. He traced the lacy edge of the pale green material with his tongue and nibbled her breasts. He teased her but left her nipples craving attention. The more he teased, the more she writhed beneath him.

"Nick, please. . ."

He unhooked the front clasp before sliding the works over her head, creating a pair of cashmere, satin, and lace handcuffs. Sitting back with a wicked smile, he held her wrists with one hand and drank in the sight of her.

"Perfect." His tongue followed his fingers as he traced her swollen lips, caressed her jaw, and kissed a path down the column of her neck. Rosalie's pulse skittered beneath his lips, her breathing ragged, her skin flushed. He continued to take his time, making her wait. Anticipation built with every impatient move she made. He took a detour to explore a collarbone, nibbled on her shoulder, and continued at his leisurely pace to the valley between her breasts.

Rosalie squirmed, making it difficult not to get caught up in the feel of her beneath him. He slid to her side, not yet ready to give up control.

Rosalie's stomach muscles tensed, and she gasped as he thrummed her ribs and dipped his tongue into her navel before unfastening her jeans. She lifted her hips as he slid her pants off.

Capturing her thong with his teeth, he uncovered all the pink bits he'd been thinking about ever since he'd met her. He dragged the slip of fabric down her long legs and kissed his way back up her inner thigh.

He tuned into her, concentrating on her breathing, the little noises she made, her quivering muscles, her sweet scent. He passed the juncture of her thighs and let his hands roam the area without touching. Her breath turned into shallow pants scattered between soft sighs that drove him mad.

He kissed the underside of her breast.

"Nick . . . please, just . . . oh, please."

Her body tightened when he took her breast in his mouth. Her back arched, and her pelvis rose to meet his hand. His finger parted her and slipped inside. Her muscles clamped down around him as he slid his thumb higher, separating her damp curls, teasing her.

Everything increased—her volume, her scent, her groans. Her hips rose with every tug of his mouth on her breast. Her muscles tightened around his finger.

"More?" Nick asked.

"Nick? Oh, God, if you don't stop. . ."

Rosalie struggled to free her hands as Nick moved lower, his mouth now between her thighs. He grasped her ass tightly, keeping her from moving. She tasted hot, sweet, and oh man, so good.

Her gasp and the tension that flowed through her revealed her shock. She tried to pull away in panic and then she lost herself in the feeling of his mouth on her, in her, licking, laving, and sucking. Her groans turned to muffled sobs.

Nick explored the curve of her ass with his fingers, and they joined his mouth in pleasuring her.

She whispered a breathless plea, "Oh, don't. Stop."

Her hands pulled his hair, bringing him closer, telling him she meant "Don't stop." He couldn't have if he'd wanted to, at least, not without losing half his hair. He focused on her muscles tensing, her gasps, and he concentrated on the tiny nub of flesh, alternately sucking and stroking.

The fine thread of his control slipped as she cried out. Her body shuddered, her thighs quivered, and her muscles tensed as the lightning strike of orgasm crashed through her, through him, leaving him closer to the edge than he could ever remember being while still dressed. He held her as she quieted, grateful for time to regain his self-control.

Nick didn't want to stop touching. His fingers skimmed her hip and dipped down to her waist and over the curve of her belly. Rosalie curled into him as her breathing slowed. Her limbs melted against his. He felt like a cat with a mouthful of feathers. Though it wasn't as if he'd discovered something new. Oral sex was just one way to ensure his partner got off before he did.

She kissed his chest and looked him in the eye. "I think you're overdressed."

Nick placed a soft kiss on her lips, then stood and removed his wallet from his back pocket. After taking out the condoms, he threw the works on the nightstand and stepped out of his shoes, pulling off his jeans, boxers,

and socks along with them. Rosalie watched him, un-
abashed. She looked as if she were ready to make a meal
of him. She knelt on the bed, her body so lush and beautiful that Nick wondered what he'd ever seen in those
bony girls he'd always dated.

Rosalie cleared her throat and scooted toward him,
holding out her hand. He took her small hand in his, sat
beside her, pulled her into his arms, and kissed her as
they lay down together. She slid her leg over his as she
kissed a path from his neck to his chest.

Nick drew in a lung full of air and held back a groan.
Her hands ran over his chest while her mouth kissed and
nipped along the muscles of his abdomen. Nerves twitched
beneath her lips. When her fingers wrapped around his
erection, he groaned and pushed up onto his elbows. Her
hair, her lips, her breath whispered over his skin, soft but
tantalizing. He ground his teeth together "God, Lee. . ."

When her tongue touched the head of his erection, he
caught her hair in his hands and concentrated on breathing. He tucked a pillow beneath his head so he could
watch. Her hand moved to a rhythm, and her tongue
licked and teased. "So good. . ."

Every muscle tensed and every nerve short-circuited
when she opened her mouth and took him in. He gasped
for air as she closed her lips around him. Her hair teased
his belly and thighs. His groin tightened when she
sucked, taking him deep. Her fingers dug into his thigh
muscle as his buried themselves in the mass of her curly
hair, clenching against her scalp.

Nick tried to control the urge to push deeper. He tried
to keep his hips on the mattress, when every nerve in his

body was signaling him to buck. The vibration of her moan ran through him, and he almost lost it. He struggled with his need to come—and the desire to be inside her when he did.

"Lee, stop."

He wondered if his plea sounded as halfhearted as hers had.

Nick tugged on her hair, and she released him.

"What?"

"Guys shouldn't come until their partner's satisfied."

"Since when?" she mumbled before he rolled them both over. He plunged his tongue into her mouth, tasting a heady mixture of himself and her, while he reached blindly for the condoms he'd left on the nightstand.

She took him in hand and managed to flip around. Her hand worked in tandem with her mouth. The suction, the flick of her tongue, the gentle teasing of his balls had him so tied up in knots, he couldn't stop her. He was going to come, and when he did, he wanted her to come, too.

He threw the condoms aside and slid his hand over her body, into her heat. God, she was so wet. He buried two fingers inside her and felt her body tighten around them, sucking them in deeper. He circled her clit with his thumb and flicked it lightly. Her mouth went lax, and she pulled away, her cheek rested against his thigh, her hand still encircling him. Pumping.

"Oh God, Nick . . . Yes. . . ." For a moment, she seemed to forget what she was doing. He slid his fingers in and out of her and continued to stroke her. She vibrated with excitement, her body tightening around him. Her hand following his rhythm, she screamed as her orgasm took hold. Her body milked his fingers. He pressed them deeper, and when he felt her orgasm explode, he followed her over.

Nick locked eyes with hers, and she watched his face as he came. He looked as shocked as she'd been.

Her heart felt as if it were going to break out of her rib cage, and she couldn't catch her breath. Nick wasn't doing any better in the breathing department. She wondered if a person could die of orgasmic bliss. Maybe they should call 911.

Rosalie thought nothing could shock her more than having an orgasm that wasn't self-induced, but two? Not that she was complaining. Who needed to breathe, anyway?

Nick pulled her back into his arms, and she nuzzled his neck. He smelled like a wonderful mix of hot, sweaty man, a deep woodsy cologne, and sex. She couldn't help but wiggle. Aftershocks buzzed though her body. He groaned. The next thing she knew, he'd rolled both of them over, as if she weighed nothing. Oh, shit, his hands were all over her big butt. She tried to push herself off him, but he tightened his hold.

"Oh, no, you don't. I'm not letting you go yet."

Rosalie was at a loss for words. He seemed to have that effect on her.

She closed her eyes and tried to catch her breath. She didn't want it to be over. She could wait an eternity before that awkward "was it good for you" conversation. This time, at least, she wouldn't have to lie.

"Lee?"

"Hmm?"

Rosalie thought women were the ones who always wanted to talk after sex. Leave it to her to find the one chatty man. He rolled them onto their sides and pulled his chest away from hers. They'd felt glued together with sweat. Rosalie lay with her eyes closed but felt his stare.

"Lee? Are you okay?"

"Fine." She opened her eyes, blinked, and saw concern on his face. She tried not to cringe when she thought about how she must look.

Nick pushed away and sat, running his hands through his hair. "It's a little late for regrets."

Whoa, where'd that come from? "What are you talking about?"

His back was to her, his shoulders rigidly straight. He took a deep breath and blew it out.

"Look, I'm sorry. I didn't plan to attack you the minute I walked through the door. I saw you, and all I could think of was being with you. All I felt was wanting you."

Rosalie sat, pulling the sheet around her and taking in the state of her bed. "I don't have any regrets."

"Yeah? Then why were you looking at me like you want to disappear?"

"I was thinking about how awful I must look. . ." God, she sounded like one of those needy women fishing for compliments.

Nick turned and tipped her face up, so she had no choice but to meet his eyes.

"You look beautiful—good enough to eat. But that will have to wait 'til later. Right now, I need sustenance. Are we going out or staying in?"

Rosalie shrugged, too stunned to answer.

"Do you like pizza?"

"Yeah, sure."

Nick reached across her for his cell phone. "Do you want a salad pizza?"

"A what?"

"You know, one of those pizzas with nothing but veggies and no cheese. It looks like salad on pizza dough."

"No. Why would I want that? I like mine with everything but green pepper, but I can pick them off."

"Everything? Even anchovies?"

"I love anchovies, but don't get them if you don't."

"No, anchovies are good. I've never met a girl who'd eat them."

"I have DiLorenzo's on speed dial, unless you want to order from somewhere else."

While Nick ordered, Rosalie slipped out of bed and did her best to fade into the wallpaper on the way to the bathroom. She closed the door and leaned against it, wondering what to do. Her only robe was in the closet.

Nick rapped on the door and then shoved it open, sticking his head in and smirking. "It'll be at least forty minutes—I told them not to rush. We have time for a shower." He slipped through the door, walked bare-assed to the tub, and started the water. "Come on, I've wanted to see you wet and soapy for a while now."

"Oh, yeah, it's been ages." Rosalie didn't hide the sarcasm.

He cut her off with a kiss, lifted her into the shower, and slid her down his body with a groan.

Chapter 6

ROSALIE STEPPED OUT OF THE BATHROOM AS NICK RAN FOR the front door, wearing only a towel. She'd never seen a better-looking man naked, not even if you count that picture of Keith Urban in *Playgirl*—which you couldn't, since Keith held his guitar in front of everything interesting. Besides, no sane woman would go for a man who was prettier than she was, not to mention thinner, which explains why he married Nicole Kidman.

The only things pretty about Nick were his eyes. A woman could wax poetic about their color or kill for his lashes—curled, dark, and so thick, they held water. Mmmm . . . That was only one of the wonderful tidbits she'd discovered. The other was that self-induced orgasms didn't register on the Richter scale compared to those given by Nick. Hell, orgasms induced by her battery-operated boyfriend, BOB, didn't even measure up to Nick-induced aftershocks. The real things rated at least a 6.7, and that was without doing the deed. It boggled the mind.

Rosalie pulled a T-shirt and flannel pants from one of the clean laundry piles, thankful for the time it would take Nick to deal with the delivery boy. She wasn't uncomfortable with her body, but she was uncomfortable displaying it to gorgeous men. Guys like Nick went for tall, skinny blondes, surgically enhanced to bring their cup size up to the highest letter they could recite without singing. Not that her cup size wasn't respectable—if anything, it was too respectable. The discomfort lay in the fact that her breasts were proportionate to the rest of her body. Nick was probably used to women who looked like swizzle sticks with boobs, and Rosalie was *so* not that.

Nick strolled in, wearing nothing but a smile and holding a pizza and beer. If he ever posed for *Playgirl*, hiding the goods would not be on his agenda. The smile turned into a flat line and a raised eyebrow.

"I thought you wanted to eat in bed."

"I do."

"So, why are you dressed?"

"Eating in bed doesn't mean I have to eat naked, does it? I eat in bed all the time, and I'm always dressed. I wanted to get comfortable. Besides, it's dangerous to eat naked."

"Dangerous?"

Nick pulled the sheet and blanket up to his waist and then covered the family jewels with a pillow. He admitted, if only to himself, that eating naked at Rosalie's was indeed dangerous, not to mention a team sport.

She picked a pepper off her slice and fed it to Dave, who lay between them. Dave smacked his dripping lips and groaned in pleasure, moving his head from Rosalie's thigh to Nick's. Dave's eyebrows rose in a silent plea without moving his head. His damn head must weigh 15 pounds, Nick thought, feeling like he had a cinder block on his thigh. No wonder Dave needed to rest it.

Nick picked a piece of Canadian bacon off his slice

and flipped it toward Dave, who raised his head to make the catch and swallowed the piece whole. Nick only heard the slap of jowls and the gulp.

"Don't feed Dave human food. It's not good for him." Rosalie licked her fingers and shrugged. "You forgot to get napkins."

Nick swallowed a groan, thankful the pillow hid his somewhat surprising erection. It had been, what, forty minutes? And one lick of her finger had the bad boy standing at attention. He cleared his throat and took a sip of beer. "You tossed him a pepper."

Rosalie sank back into the pillows resting against the headboard of her iron bed.

"Vegetables are okay. They're healthy."

She bit into the pizza and caught threads of melted cheese that stretched from her mouth to the slice between the fingers she had licked. Tilting her head back, she dropped them in her mouth. Nick had never before considered eating pizza erotic.

Dave raked his paw across the pillow on Nick's lap in an apparent plea for more.

Rosalie patted the pillow. "Told you it was dangerous. Do you want to put on your jeans?"

"Jeans wouldn't cut it. I'd need a cup at the very least." Besides, he doubted he'd be able to zip the damn jeans up now.

"Speaking of cups." Rosalie reached into the drawer of her bedside table and rummaged around. Did she have a cup stashed in there? Hell, it looked as if she had everything else. She searched the covers surrounding her and slid her hand under his pillow—not the one on his lap, damn.

"You're not lying on my remote, are you? I want to catch the score. Islanders are facing off against the Flyers tonight."

"You're more than welcome to look, but you'd better be careful. I guarantee you'll miss the game if you check under any more of my pillows."

Rosalie snorted and ran her hand under Dave, continuing her search. Dave groaned and rolled over onto his back, his jowls flopping open, exposing a set of impressive teeth. She scratched his belly and found his tickle spot. Dave rolled onto his side and kicked Nick with increasing speed. He not only kicked Nick, but sent the pillow on Nick's lap and the empty pizza box flying.

"Oops." She pulled the slice of pizza Nick was biting into out of his mouth, leaned over Dave, and bussed a kiss on Nick's cheek. "Sorry."

Rosalie didn't return his pizza, not that he cared. It wasn't as if he was still hungry—at least, not for pizza. She rolled on her stomach to search under the bed. Nick lay back and enjoyed the view of her rather spectacular posterior. If only she hadn't covered it in flannel.

All the movement proved too much for Dave. He extracted himself by walking over Nick and jumping off the bed.

For the second time that day, Dave knocked the air out of Nick. He tried to breathe as pain radiated through him. Dave was not only a guard dog, but also an excellent form of birth control. Permanent birth control.

"Damn, I can never find anything when I need it." Rosalie scanned the room and there, lying on top of the TV, was the remote. Of all the stupid places to put a remote control, that had to be the worst. Nick grunted. He must have seen the remote the same time she had. One of them had to get it. She turned to sweet-talk him into it, but his color had turned as white as newly fallen snow before rush hour, and his mouth hung open as he gasped for air.

"What's the matter? Oh, no! Dave didn't. Did he? He did. Oh, Nick. I'm so sorry. Here, let me see. . ."

Nick groaned again and held the covers tight over his lap. The look he gave her was anything but welcoming. Okay, that was the wrong thing to say.

Nick took a deep breath and released it. His color returned, though his mouth still hung open like a big fish on dry land.

She considered offering to kiss it and make it better. But the way he looked, even that wouldn't help.

The best remedy for an ailing man is chicken soup and control of the remote. In this case, Rosalie doubted chicken soup would cut it, but beer sounded like a good bet. She climbed out of bed, plumped his pillows, handed him the remote, and kicked Dave out of the bedroom before getting Nick a beer. If he didn't want to drink it, he could always use it as a cold compress.

Nick made an amazing recovery while they watched the game and seemed to like hockey as much as she did. Rosalie was thankful that Nick learned quickly not to crowd her. It was hard to cuss out a ref when you were tucked under someone's arm, and it was impossible to do hand gestures.

She turned off the set when the post-game commentary began. It had been painful enough watching the

Flyers annihilate the Islanders 5-1. No need to subject herself to more torture.

As if witnessing the slaughter hadn't been bad enough, Rosalie had another problem to deal with. It was ten o'clock, and Nick was still in her bed. The bed she slept in alone. She stretched and yawned, hoping Nick would take the hint and hit the road. Oh, God. What if he wanted to stay over? How could she ask him to leave without sounding as if she were asking him to leave? One more reason to go to a guy's place—she could leave when she wanted. Well, except with Nick. He'd insist on taking her home, and they'd be back in her bed. Together.

They both spoke at the same time. Whew, what a relief. Rosalie really didn't want to say, "Nick, it's been fun, but I'd like you to leave now so I can get to sleep."

"Sorry, Nick, you go first."

"No, after you."

Oh, no, you don't. "Um . . . I forgot what I was going to say. You go ahead." Ha.

Talk about awkward. There was nothing worse than the morning after or, in this case, the evening after a first sexual encounter. Both parties are über-polite until they get used to the idea that they've seen each other naked, or one of them leaves. Rosalie wasn't used to the idea and might never be, which meant it was time for him to go.

Nick smiled and took her hand. He looked as uncomfortable now as he had when Dave did the cha-cha on his privates.

"I have a staff meeting before we open tomorrow, so I have to take off. I'm sorry."

"No problem. I've got to get in early, too. I didn't accomplish much today." Rosalie tried to cover her feeling of utter relief better than Nick had hid his discomfort. He looked at her as if she'd grown another head. Gee, guess she'd failed.

Rosalie helped Nick find his clothes. She'd thrown his jacket on the floor beside the bed and thought his shirt might have gone in the direction of the treadmill, which, like all treadmills, had morphed into a large clothes hanger. His pants and boxers, thank God, were within his reach.

By the time Rosalie found his shirt, he'd buttoned his jeans. Somehow, she resisted the urge to run her hands over his chest and stomach once more. Who knew muscles could feel so good? The man could do an infomercial for a weight machine.

She tried to act as if they'd had dinner together without an appetizer of white-hot, multi-orgasmic sex. Because really, what could she say? Thanks for the orgasms? Having no set precedent for such a situation, she felt as if she were walking blindfolded though a minefield.

Nick finished dressing while she picked up the pizza box and beer bottles and took them to the kitchen. No, she wasn't practicing avoidance. She was keeping busy and straightening up the apartment like she did all the time. Right.

Nick never spent the night at a girlfriend's place because it was much more difficult to avoid making plans while in bed or in the shower together. There was always that question she'd sneak in when his brain was concentrating on sex. In between the "Oh yeah, baby," and "Damn, that was good!" she'd throw in something like, "Would you like to meet my parents for lunch?" and all he heard was "yada-yada-yada." The next thing he knew, her old man would be grilling him on his intentions and his portfolio (though not necessarily in that order); her mother would be saying how beautiful their children would be; and he'd find himself hurtling at breakneck speed down the aisle toward matrimonial hell.

Nick checked his reflection in the mirror. This nonrelationship with Rosalie was unlike any other he'd ever experienced. He'd never told a girl he couldn't spend the night without her trying to talk him into staying. He'd seen everything from pouting to bitter anger. Rosalie was the first to look relieved. Hell, truth be told, she looked as if she couldn't wait for him to go. He should be thrilled. Finally, a woman who followed his rules.

Yeah, this was good.

He scanned the items on her dresser: a shoe with a broken heel; jewelry—nothing expensive, more unusual, funky; a bra and a thong like the one she'd worn the other night; and perfume. He picked up the square, red bottle and sniffed. Her scent. Gold lettering caught his eye—*Trouble*. How apropos. Nick returned the perfume to its place, shook his head at the irony, grabbed his jacket, and left the bedroom.

Rosalie was waiting next to the bar separating the kitchen from the dining area, shifting her weight from foot to foot. Nick slid into his jacket and closed the distance between them. She had a recently ravished look that brought back memories of them doing several things he'd like to repeat.

He wrapped his arms around her and waited until her tension drained away. It took a moment, but she relaxed and leaned into him. He gave her a soft kiss, not a peck, but not a kiss that would keep him up the rest of the night, either.

"'Night, Lee. I'll call you tomorrow."

Tension returned to her body. Maybe she was afraid she'd never hear from him again. He tipped her chin up to look in her eyes. She moved away, her fingers busy twisting the drawstring of her pants.

"Um . . . I'm starting with a new client tomorrow. I'll be working late the rest of the week."

Nick stepped back. She wasn't worried she wouldn't hear from him again. It seemed if anyone had to worry the other wasn't interested, it was him. Not that he would. Still, he couldn't imagine why she wouldn't want to see him. He'd made sure she'd had a good time in bed. Maybe she was pissed about getting all dressed up for nothing, or because he hadn't told her how nice she looked. Or maybe she was telling the truth and had a busy week ahead.

"You know, you've never told me what you do."

"I'm a corporate turnaround expert. I go into failing companies, take over as their interim chief financial officer, and try to turn things around. It takes me at least a week to get up to speed.

"Okay, let's get-together on Friday night then."

"I'm sorry, Nick, but I've got a status meeting with my boss Friday afternoon that will probably run late."

Nick groaned. He had box seats for the Islanders at New Jersey Saturday. He would love to take Rosalie, but mechanics couldn't afford box seats. Besides, too many people knew him there. Someone would let the cat out of the bag. But it was an afternoon game, so it should be over by three or four. "How about Saturday night?"

"That sounds good. I'll call you."

She'd call *him*?

Rosalie looked around her new office at Premier Motorcars and picked through the unappetizing salad she ate at her desk. Why did she always relegate herself to eating salad when she started dating someone new? It was useless, because by the time dinner came around, she was starving and ate everything in sight. Even the fact she hadn't stopped at the store wouldn't help, since ordering in and eating an entire pizza in one sitting wasn't out of the realm of possibility. Why did she do this to herself?

She took another bite of salad, wondering what they used to make fake crabmeat and if it was naturally that shade of orange, or if she was ingesting carcinogenic dye in the name of losing weight. A soft knock sounded, and Gina poked her head in.

"Rosalie . . . can we have a minute?"

We? She pushed aside the lifeless salad and the spreadsheet she'd been studying, slipped on her jacket, and stepped into her pumps.

"Come in."

Gina walked in carrying a file, followed by Sam, her brother-in-law the cop. From the look of the two, Rosalie knew something was wrong.

"What's the matter? Is my family all right?"

"It's nothing like that. Everyone's fine." Gina was halfway to the desk before she realized Sam was still standing in the doorway. She laid the file on the desk, turned around and posed, hands on hips, head cocked. Rosalie could very well imagine Gina's expression. It had the desired effect. Sam, the big bad homicide detective, looked as if he wanted to run crying for his mommy. Rosalie knew the feeling well and had the urge to cross herself and thank God Gina hadn't pointed that look at her.

"Do I really need to be a witness to what is obviously a private family matter? I have a lot of ground to cover . . ." Sam was squirming, the poor guy. " . . . not that it isn't always a pleasure to see you, Sam."

"Sam." Gina stomped her foot and pointed at Rosalie. "Tell her."

"Tell me what?" Rosalie slid forward in her chair.

Sam closed his eyes and rubbed the bridge of his nose before letting out a sigh worthy of old Mrs. Goldstein, Rosalie's neighbor. All he was missing was the "Oy vey."

Sam straightened and stood, shoulders back, chest out, head held high. "Gina, give me a break here. I did what you asked. I'm done."

For the sake of all New Yorkers, Rosalie hoped his intimidation routine worked better on the perps than it did on Gina. She walked right up to him, grabbed his tie, pulled him into the office, and pointed to a chair in front of the desk. "Sit."

He sat.

The fear-factor wielded by the tiny woman was amazing. Sam stood over a foot taller and outweighed her by a hundred pounds, but she had him well trained. Rosalie expected Gina to pat his head and say, "Good boy."

It was time for diversionary tactics. Poor Sam looked as if he wanted to disappear, he was so embarrassed. "Gina, what's this all about?"

"Nick."

Whoa, hold on. "My Nick?"

"So he's your Nick now, is he?"

Uh, oh. Rosalie winced. Gina had turned on her.

"You don't even know his last name yet. Do you?"

Rosalie looked toward Sam and then scowled at Gina. It was a waste of time. Gina was the pushiest woman Rosalie had ever met, and she always spoke her mind, however inappropriate.

"Gina . . ." Rosalie growled. She didn't take the warning.

"I worry about you, Rosalie. I asked Sam—"

Sam guffawed. "You mean threatened—"

Gina speared him with a look of boredom and a wave of her hand. "Whatever."

She turned to Rosalie, sympathy rolling off her in waves. Oh, God. Gina was beginning to scare her.

"The only person working at Romeo's whose name is Nick and fits the description you gave me is Dominick Romeo. *The Dominick Romeo*."

Rosalie laughed as relief swept through her. "Right, I'm sure Dominick Romeo was driving around in a wrecker Sunday night on his way to a costume party at some chichi Westside Club and thought he'd stop to tow a car. Why not? It makes a great prop."

"Here's proof."

Gina picked up the file she'd placed on the desk and tossed it in front of Rosalie. She opened it. There were copies of several pictures of Nick, each with a different woman on his arm. In most of the pictures, he wore a tuxedo. Nick at the Tony Awards with a Broadway starlet, at a charity event with a blonde anorexic, at a benefit concert for hurricane victims with another tall, blonde, and busty Barbie clone.

Then she pulled out a piece of paper with notes scratched on it and stared at the underlined words. *1990 juvenile arrest—nonviolent crime. Record expunged.* Rosalie couldn't believe Gina had done this. And Sam. What was he thinking?

"You ran a check on him? Sam, how dare you invade his privacy like that? Isn't it against the law?"

Sam squirmed in his seat. "Gina was worried."

"Gina, I told you to leave it alone. Didn't I? How could you do this?"

"You're angry at *me*? I'm not the one lying to you."

Rosalie remembered Nick's scowl when she'd teased him about . . . well, being him. And the way he'd looked when he asked if she was out to land a rich guy. No wonder he'd let her think he was a mechanic.

"Now that I think about it, Nick never lied to me. He is only guilty of failing to correct my false assumptions. So, he's a sneak. But knowing his reputation and how women talk, can you blame him?"

Rosalie wasn't mad. Nick didn't seem malicious. He was trying to protect himself. It wasn't as if he knew her. How would he know she wasn't a money-hungry bitch? Especially after that crack she'd made about him being Brooklyn's version of Donald Trump, who could blame him?

She threw her salad in the trash and straightened her desk. "You know what? It doesn't matter. Our relationship is casual. What do I care if he's loaded? It's not as if I'm after him for his money."

Gina shook her head and laughed. "No, you're in it for the sex. I knew something was different about you on Wednesday. You did more than eat dinner and watch hockey with your Romeo, didn't you?"

Sam stood and backed away. "Um . . . okay, well, I guess I'll let you girls do whatever . . . um, my lunch hour ended ten minutes ago, and my partner . . . well, I gotta go."

Sam all but ran out the door, the lucky bastard. Gina stared at Rosalie as if she'd lost her mind.

"What do you want me to say, Gina? Do you want me to tell you I slept with him? Give you a blow-by-blow? Well, too bad. I don't have to explain my sex life to you or anyone."

"You're my best friend, and I worry about you. I know the type of guys you've gone out with. Dominick Romeo is way out of your league. Be careful, Rosalie."

Her head snapped up at that one. "Be careful of what?"

"He's a Romeo, *chica*. If he had a dollar for every heart he's broken, his net worth would rival that of Bill Gates. The man is notorious."

"You know me, Gina. I'm not looking for a relationship. I already told him that."

"You gave Dominick Romeo the talk?"

"Of course. Monday I told him I was interested in

good company—a monogamous, temporary relationship with no strings and no commitments. I said that if he was looking for more, he shouldn't waste his time with me."

"And you believe this load of crap?"

"What do you mean? Of course, I do. You know me. I don't have a problem keeping things simple. I don't like being tied down. I'm not the relationship type."

"Did you ever think that maybe that's because you've only dated losers? Seriously, Rosalie. Who could fall for a guy like Joey?"

"Hey, he wasn't that bad."

"Yeah, as long as you don't mind a total lack of substance and personality."

What could she say? Gina was right. Dating Joey was like dating an android.

"You know Lana, my friend who works at the Shubert Theater? She told me Dominick Romeo dated What's-Her-Name, that Broadway Babe. There's a picture of them in that file. Lana's roommate, Liz, is a wardrobe mistress there and said Mr. Romeo was a fixture in What's-Her-Name's dressing room. He was hot and charming, and Broadway Babe was walking around with her head in the clouds and a stupid grin for a few months. She started talking about the lease on her apartment coming up, and she was thinking of moving in with him."

"Gina . . . is this going to take much longer?" Just because she wasn't interested in being his significant other didn't mean she wanted to hear all the skinny on the women he dated.

Gina shot her a disgusted look. Rosalie mentally started filing her nails.

"No. Anyway, after the show one Friday, Romeo knocks on Broadway Babe's dressing room door and asks Liz to give them a minute. Liz took off, but she left her stuff because she still had to get the wardrobe ready for the Saturday matinee. . ."

"Gina. . ."

"Don Juan . . . I mean, Romeo, was there for awhile and left alone, which wasn't unusual. None of the cast goes out Friday night, because it's hard to stay up all night and do two shows Saturday.

"The point, Gina?"

"The point is, Liz went in to finish work, and Broadway Babe was lying prostrate with grief, crying so hard, she couldn't breathe. He'd dumped her. There she was, thinking everything was all hunky-dory, they'd move in together and get married or something, and he dumped her."

"That's too bad for her, but it makes no difference to me. Nick and I have a deal. We agreed not to do love and commitment. We're going to keep it light, have a good time, and when it isn't a good time, we'll walk away. No harm, no foul. There's nothing to worry about."

"Yeah, Rosalie, you keep telling yourself that. Remember, there's always a first time for everything, and since you've changed your MO, there's an even better chance you'll end up checking into Heartbreak Hotel."

"Changed my MO?"

"Your *modus operandi,* your usual way of doing things."

"I know what it means, Gina. What I don't know is how my MO has changed."

"You're not dating a loser this time. Romeo is a hot, rich guy who has a reputation for keeping his woman happy until he breaks her heart and moves on to his next victim."

"The same could be said for me. Well, except for the hot part, and the rich part, and maybe the happy part. But the breaking hearts and moving on parts are true enough."

Rosalie set aside the file of information on Nick and watched as Gina put her hands on her tiny hips and did her Wicked Witch of the West laugh. Gina knew Rosalie well enough to know she was dying to see what other juicy gossip was in that file, but she wasn't about to admit it.

"So, what are you going to do to the lying, scheming, dirty, son-of-a—"

"Enough already. I'm going to do nothing. It doesn't matter if he's Nick Romeo or Nick Cage. Think about it. His money has to complicate his relationships. Who could blame him for keeping it to himself? Think of all the women in New York whose only goal in life is to marry rich. He must feel objectified."

"Dominick Romeo, the poor little rich boy."

"Look Gina, he'll tell me when he's ready, or not. I'm not going to say anything, and if you ever meet him, neither will you. Do you understand me?"

"Fine, but don't expect me to join the Dominick Romeo Fan Club. I still object to what he's doing, even if you don't."

"Fine. Now, would you take off your overprotective best friend hat and put on your loyal and able assistant hat? If you do, we might get through the books before tomorrow's meeting." Rosalie blew her hair out of her eyes and shook her head. "I almost wish Nick would tell me who he is. I could really use his industry know-how."

Nick ended the call with his banker and beeped his assistant. "Lois, has anyone called?"

"Not since the last time you asked."

"I was on the phone—"

"And you told me to interrupt you if Ms. Ronaldi called. She did not."

"Did you get the reports from Saunders? They were supposed to be on my desk by noon."

"They were, and as far as I know, they still are. The third quarter reports are in the file labeled "Third Quarter Reports." And before you ask, the file you've been keeping on Premier Motors is in the folder labeled "Premier Motors." The takeover strategy and feasibility reports are on top. Is there anything else?"

"Yes, call the employment agency and get me an assistant without an attitude."

"As if anyone else would put up with you. If that's all, the other line is ringing."

Nick hung up the phone, focused on the paper in front of him, and realized he was looking at the report he'd asked Lois about. Damn, he was losing it.

He couldn't believe he was sitting around, waiting for Rosalie to call. The worst part was that he'd been waiting for three days and driving everyone around him nuts.

He returned the reports to their files and threw them in his briefcase. He was shrugging on his suit jacket when his cell phone rang. "Hello."

"Having a bad day, Nick?"

"Lee?"

"It's Rosalie."

"How are you doing? You sound different."

"I'm well. You?"

"Fine."

"Look Nick, my meeting broke for a minute, and I have to get back, but I needed to call—" She coughed and cleared her throat.

"About tomorrow night?"

"Well, yes, that, and you have my car. You said someone took it to Romeo's. I thought you would drive it over on Tuesday, but . . . well, I got sidetracked and forgot to ask about it."

"Sidetracked, huh? Is that what you call it?"

"Nick, tell me you have my car."

"I have your car."

"Good. Do you still want to get together tomorrow night?"

"Sure. Dinner and movie?"

"Could we do takeout and a rental? I haven't been home all week, and Dave is feeling neglected. Besides, I'm working on less than five hours sleep in the last two days, and tonight promises to be another late one."

"No problem. You pick the menu. I'll pick up a movie. What do you want to see?"

"Anything that's not depressing."

"Done. I'll see you about eight at your place. Don't stay out too late. You don't sound so good."

"I have a cough and a sore throat, but it's no big deal. I need sleep.

Nick heard someone call her.

"I'll be there in a minute. Thank you, Gina." She coughed again. Her cough sounded awful.

"Look Nick, I've got to run. See you tomorrow."

He heard the dial tone before he could say good-bye.

Nick stood in the drama section of the video store, trying to pick out a chick flick Rosalie might like. He grabbed the one with shoes in the title. Cameron Diaz was hot, and he'd never met a woman who didn't have a sick fascination with shoes that he'd never understand. He got the movie of that Broadway show what's-her-name had been in while they'd been dating. Damn, he hoped the movie was different from the play. He'd seen the play a dozen times. And a comedy—couldn't miss with Monty Python. He picked up a box of microwave popcorn, Goobers, and Raisinettes and drove the Mustang to Rosalie's.

Nick stopped to pick up a box of condoms and a bouquet of flowers in the market down the street from her place. All he needed was wine and takeout, and the evening would be complete. He rang Rosalie's apartment and saw Dave barking at the front window, but Rosalie didn't buzz him in. He checked his watch. He was right on time. Dave continued to bark. A man walked out the security door, and Nick caught it before it closed. He went down the hall and knocked on Rosalie's door. Dave whined, and Nick knocked again. He turned the knob. She'd left the door unlocked, so he poked his head in.

"Lee?"

The place looked as if someone had tossed it. That

didn't bother him, but Dave did. He sat beside the door, whining.

"Lee, it's Nick, can I come in?" No answer. What to do? Aw, the hell with it. He walked in, prepared for Dave to jump all over him, but Dave turned and ran to the bedroom. Nick followed and found Dave lying on the bed with his head on Rosalie's lap, and Rosalie sound asleep, looking like someone who'd been dead a week. She wore a ratty T-shirt and held a box of tissues under her arm. Used tissues littered the bed all around her. A bottle of cough medicine sat on the bedside table next to an empty glass. Dave whined again.

Nick dropped the bag and sat beside her. When he brushed the hair from her forehead, her eyelids fluttered open. She was burning up.

"Nick?" Rosalie coughed for a minute. Damn, she sounded like she had pneumonia. "What are you doing here?"

"We had a date, remember? DVDs and takeout? Sound familiar?"

"Didn't you get my message? I called your cell . . . hey, how did you get in here, anyway?"

"Dave let me in."

"Oh." Her eyelids closed.

"Lee, wake up." She didn't move. Nick picked up the tissues, tossed them in the trash can, and took her glass into the kitchen. She needed juice and something to bring down her fever. He opened the fridge and found it emptier than his. There was one egg, three beers, a yogurt, expired milk, and the usual condiments. He grabbed a beer, opened it, and took a long pull. He filled a glass with water, got the bottle of acetaminophen out of the cabinet above the sink, and wondered where she kept her thermometer. He checked the medicine chest, but all he found was Midol and girl shit. No thermometer.

Nick sat beside Rosalie and gave her a good shake. "Wake up. Time to take your medicine."

She opened her eyes. "I hate pills."

"I know. Take these anyway. You have a fever." He popped them in her mouth and handed her the water. "I'm going out to get dinner. Where are your keys? I'll need to get back in."

Rosalie took the pills. "I don't know . . . there's an extra set in the drawer next to the sink. But Nick, you don't have to do this. I'm fine. I need a little rest, that's all."

"Don't worry about it. You rest. I'll be right back." He kissed her forehead, and she mumbled something about being tired. He stood and looked down at her. What had he gotten himself into?

Rosalie awoke in the middle of the night, coughing. Nick sat, as he had all night, with her between his legs and her back leaning against his bare chest. He'd been going back and forth, trying to decide what he should do—take her to the hospital, or wait for morning and get her to a doctor. Her fever was high, and the medicine wasn't helping.

She coughed so hard, he worried she'd break something, and she wasn't breathing well. He rubbed her back. "It's okay." Heat radiated from her, and she wasn't due for more acetaminophen for an hour and a half.

"Lee, your fever's up. I need to take you to the emergency room. This isn't a cold."

"Nick? What are you doing here?"

"Taking care of you. Now come on, let's get you dressed. I'm taking you to the hospital."

Chapter 7

NICK STOOD AT THE PAY PHONE IN THE ER. HE COULDN'T use his cell phone in the hospital, and he wasn't about to chance a walk outside in case Rosalie's doctor came to tell him what was going on. He only had two numbers memorized besides his own—his mother's and his cousin Vinny's. There was no way he would call his mother for help with a girl. She'd be planning the wedding before he hung up the damn phone. Not that Vinny's wife Mona was much better, but maybe his luck would change and Vinny would answer.

"Hello?"

So much for that. "Mona, it's Nick."

"Nick? Who's sick?"

"How do you know someone's sick?"

"I hear a doctor being paged in the background."

"Oh, right. It's Lee. We're at Brooklyn Hospital's ER."

"Is she okay?"

"I don't know. The doctors think it's pneumonia. They're taking X-rays. Listen, let me talk to Vinny."

"He's not here. It's his week to take Nana to church."

"Shit, that's right, it's Sunday."

"What do you need, Nick?"

"Mona, have Vin go to my place and pack clothes for me, maybe enough for two or three days. Oh, and tell him to get my cell phone charger. It's on my desk in the study. He's got the key."

"Okay."

"And go to the store and get whatever I'll need for Lee. There's nothing but batteries in her refrigerator, so I need you to do major shopping. You know, get every- thing I need to make chicken soup and buy the basics so I can throw together quick dinners for myself. I need stuff for her fever, a thermometer, juice—what- ever, and bring it to her place. I should have her home in a couple hours."

"You're going to take care of her?"

Nick scrubbed his hand over his face. "I can't leave her by herself, can I?"

"No, but you could call her family. Let them take care of her."

No way. He'd heard how that mother of hers spoke to her. Rosalie didn't need to deal with that nudje when she was sick as a dog. "Look, Mona, it's not a big deal."

"I never thought I'd see the day when Nick Romeo would care for anyone other than himself."

"Hey, I care for people. Look at you and Vin."

"You have to care for us. We're family."

"I wouldn't be so sure about that."

"Don't try to pull that crap on me, Nicky."

"Mona, just get the stuff I need, will you?"

"Okay, I'll be there in a few hours."

He gave her Rosalie's address and hung up before she could start again.

Rosalie wanted to go home. She'd never been in a hos- pital before in her life, except for when she was born, and she didn't want to start hanging out in one now. She pulled the oxygen mask off her face to tell the nurse putting a clothespin-type thingy on her finger that she was leaving.

"Oh, no, you don't." He said in a Mike Tyson voice.

Leaving wouldn't be easy. Nurse Gus not only sounded like Mike Tyson; he was built like him, too. Rosalie didn't have the strength to fight him.

"You need the oxygen," he said as he repositioned the mask on her face.

"I need my clothes."

"We're going to take a little trip to Radiology for a few chest shots." He released a brake and rolled the bed through the curtained area. Rosalie moved her hand to hold the side-rail, and it hurt like a son of a bitch. Oh, my God! There was a tube stuck in the top of her hand. She'd forgotten about that.

Rosalie hadn't forgotten that Nick had brought her there. Where was he? "Nick?"

The nurse patted her arm but kept rolling her down the hall. "Don't worry; your man's still here. He's pacing the waiting room. He hasn't stopped barraging us with questions, not that we're complaining. He's a cutie."

Rosalie shot the nurse a you-haven't-got-a-snowball's-chance-in-hell look.

"Girl, jus' 'cause the store's closed don't mean I can't window-shop."

By the time she got back to the ER, Rosalie was ready for a nap. Who knew X-rays were so draining? Maybe it wasn't the X-rays. Maybe it was all that moving around while trying to keep her butt covered. Nurse Gus parked her bed in the little cubicle where the doctor was talking to Nick. Dr. Deena Jansen was your usual nightmare—

tall, thin, blonde, and gorgeous, with the best boobs money can buy. Did doctors give each other discounts? She could see it now . . . *"I'll trade you a boob job for an appendectomy and a tonsillectomy."*

"Hey, that's no fair. . ."

"What do you mean? You got two boobs. It's twice the work."

The doctor's husky voice drew Rosalie from her mental meanderings.

"We gave her a heavy antibiotic in her IV, so she doesn't need to start this. . ." she handed Nick a prescription, " . . . until tomorrow morning. We've also given her IV steroids, so start these . . ." another prescription changed hands " . . . first thing in the morning as well, six for the first three days, then decrease to five for three days, and so on. The breathing treatments are every four hours around-the-clock, but if she's asleep and not having trouble breathing, don't wake her."

Nick folded the pile of prescriptions and placed them in his wallet. "Thanks, doc."

They were talking about her as if she wasn't there. Like she was in a coma or something.

"Who gave you permission to talk to Nick about my condition?" Rosalie meant to sound forceful, but even to her own ears, she sounded weak.

Nick and the doctor, who looked curiously like a Barbie doll, turned and stared at her. The doctor gave Rosalie one of those condescending smiles they must practice in med school and patted her hand. "You did, Ms. Ronaldi."

The nurse put the sides of the bed down and giggled.

Rosalie had never seen a 250-pound man giggle, but Nurse Gus did. It wasn't pretty.

"Well, that doesn't mean I want you talking about me as if I'm not here."

Nick reached for her hand, which she moved before he could catch it. Rosalie folded her arms, forgetting the darn IV. Shit, that hurt! It tugged on the blasted tape holding the IV in place. Ow!

Nick patted her shoulder. What the hell did she look like? A freaking dog?

"I'm going home."

The doctor looked at Nick, and Nick nodded. Then Dr. Barbie cleared her throat. "I'm releasing you, but only because your fiancé said you'd get around-the-clock care. Frankly, I'd rather admit you, but he insisted that you'd refuse to stay."

Fiancé? Nick smiled and squeezed Rosalie's shoulder . . . then he added a wink for good measure. Rosalie bit the side of her cheek. Jeez, she was sick, not stupid. She got it.

"Fine. Nick's right. I wouldn't stay. So tell me what's wrong with me, what I need to do, and let me out of here."

Nurse Gus started futzing with the IV and then pulled the tape off. Ow! The next thing she knew, he was pulling a needle the size of a coffee stirrer out of her hand.

The doctor tore a sheet off the top of her chart. "You, Ms. Ronaldi, have pneumonia. Here are the instructions I gave your fiancé. He's already arranged to have the nebulizer delivered." She laid the instructions on the bed.

"Nebulizer?"

Nick patted Rosalie's shoulder again. "Don't worry, honey, I took care of it. Let's get you home."

Nick looked like a kid who'd gotten away with putting a tack on the teacher's chair. He knew he could call her anything and she'd smile sweetly as long as she got the hell out of there. But that was okay; let him have his fun. She was going to kill him for dragging her, kicking and screaming, to the hospital in the first place. What was it they said about revenge? It's better served cold? Oh, yeah, and it's sweet.

Nick turned and shook the doctor's hand. "Thank you, doctor. I'll take good care of her."

The doctor nodded. "You're welcome."

She held his hand a little too long. Oh, my God, she was flirting with him. She was holding his gaze and doing that licking her lips thing. *Hello! Remember me? The one who isn't in a coma?*

"It was a pleasure meeting you, Nick."

Oh, I'm sure. Look at her, tossing her hair. Rosalie couldn't believe it. Dr. Barbie actually did the hair flip. *He's engaged, remember?* She turned to Rosalie and looked at her, as if she'd gotten a whiff of something putrid.

"Listen to Nick, Ms. Ronaldi, or you'll end up right back in the hospital. Pneumonia is nothing to fool around with."

"Fine." Talk about bedside manner. Sheesh, Rosalie had seen icebergs with more warmth. Well, except when she was trying to steal someone's fiancé. Dr. Barbie left the cubicle, and Rosalie resisted the urge to stick out her tongue. What a bitch.

"You. . ." Nick turned to Rosalie "act like you've never seen a doctor before."

"I haven't . . . well, not for anything but checkups. I

don't get sick."

Nick did that eyebrow raise again.

Rosalie ignored the look he gave her. If she hadn't, she would have smacked him, and her hand still hurt too much from being used as a pincushion.

"Where are my clothes?"

Nick pulled a bag from beneath the bed and emptied it.

"Thanks." He untied the top of her hospital gown. "Nick, I can dress myself."

He ignored her, and she was too tired to fight. What the hell, she had already gone way beyond the total humiliation stage.

After Rosalie dressed, Nurse Gus dropped her into a wheelchair, and Nick kissed her forehead before he went to get his car. At least he didn't pat her again.

Rosalie fell asleep on the way home and awoke in Nick's arms. Her neighbors, Wayne and Henry, in matching smoking jackets, held the door while Nick carried her upstairs and into the building.

"Nick, put me down. I'm not an invalid."

Most women dream about a man picking her up and carrying her to the bedroom. With Rosalie, it had always been one of her nightmares. A guy would pick her up, groan from the weight, and end up dropping her as his back went out. She cringed, waiting for the nightmare to become reality, but Nick didn't even grunt. She thought that carrying something as heavy as her up steps would at least make him short of breath. Nothing. Either she'd lost weight, or he was in great shape.

"I'll put you down as soon as I can put you down in bed."

The coughing started again, damn. Rosalie decided that after she caught her breath, she'd thank him for last night. It was sweet of him to take care of her—unnecessary, but sweet. And it was nice of him to take her to the hospital. She'd been wrong, if you believed Dr. Hey-baby-wanna-date." Admitting it would kill her, but she would. Then Nick could leave. All she'd have to do was call China Wok for delivery and the pharmacy for her prescriptions. She'd be fine.

Rosalie awoke to the smell of chicken soup and Nick. A bed tray sat on her dresser. Hold on—she didn't own a bed tray. He pulled her up, shoved pillows behind her, and stuck a thermometer in her mouth. Where'd that come from?

Someone had cleaned off her dresser. Rosalie wondered where all her things were. She'd have asked if she'd had the energy—and if her mouth hadn't been full of thermometer. She was so tired. Nick took the thermometer out when it beeped and read it. He didn't say what her temperature was, and she didn't ask. What did it matter, anyway?

"What are you still doing here?"

"Feeding you and making sure you take your medicine."

He placed the tray on her lap, sat beside her, and spooned up what looked like homemade chicken soup.

Rosalie pushed his hand away. "I can feed myself."

"Fine." Nick crossed his arms and stared.

"What?"

"I'm waiting."

"Waiting for what?"

"You to feed yourself."

"I don't feel like eating."

"Okay."

Nick picked up the spoon again, and she pushed it away again. He got that annoyed look she used to find so sexy. Now it irritated her.

"Either you feed yourself, or I'll feed you. Your choice."

"You will not."

"Who's going to stop me?"

"Dave. That's who."

"I don't think so." Dave chose that moment to lie his head on Nick's lap and look up at the big galoot with adoring eyes.

"Traitor."

Rosalie ate a few spoonfuls of soup.

Nick shook Rosalie awake. He had removed the tray and was holding a weird-shaped piece of plastic with a tube coming out of it that attached to a box on the bedside table. The table, the surface of which hadn't been seen in ages, was now clean. What was going on? Were the good fairy maids coming in and working as she slept?

"Time to do your breathing treatment."

"Huh?"

"Put this in your mouth, close your lips around it, and breathe in and out until the medicine's all gone."

"You gotta be kidding."

He picked up the machine and set it on the bed next to her. "Nope."

He stuck the plastic contraption in Rosalie's mouth

and turned on the machine. It was loud. It buzzed, vibrated, and was almost as obnoxious as the taste of the vapor she had to breathe.

God, she'd died and gone to hell.

Nick watched Rosalie do her breathing treatment. She staked him with her gaze and looked as if she wanted to kill him. Thank God she was too weak to do much of anything. Hopefully, by the time she was well, she'd be thanking him instead of plotting his murder.

He checked the time. It was only one o'clock. Hell, he'd been there less than eighteen hours, and it felt as if he hadn't slept in weeks. He rubbed his eyes, and the image of Rosalie in that hospital bed with tubes coming out of her hit him. She'd had her eyes closed. The faded-looking shiners beneath were more pronounced in the hospital's florescent lighting. Her color had been pasty, and she had been so still. Damn, for a second he'd thought she'd died. He'd held onto the bed rail with a white-knuckled grip, afraid he'd fall over. When she'd moved, his sense of relief had been even more disturbing than the thought of taking a header.

And the doctor—she was a piece of work. Doctor Feelgood had ignored Rosalie until she spoke. He'd have hell to pay when Rosalie remembered he'd lied about them being engaged. She would probably think he'd lied so he could see her, not so he could get away from Dr. Look-at-me, Look-at-me. That was okay. What Rosalie didn't know wouldn't hurt her.

Rosalie finished the treatment and immediately fell asleep. The medicine worked wonders. Her breathing seemed softer now, quieter, but he still decided to keep her propped up. Mona had said it would help. He stood and returned to the kitchen to get something to eat, grateful that Mona brought over so many groceries, he could cook enough to feed himself, Rosalie, and ten of his closest friends.

After heating up the lasagna he'd made earlier, he sat down just as the cell phone in Rosalie's purse started ringing. He took a bite and burned his mouth. A few minutes later, her landline rang. Nick didn't want to answer it, but he didn't want it to wake Rosalie, either. The machine picked up.

"Rosalie, where the hell are you? Ma's already pissed as hell and making my life miserable, since you flushed your last hope of marriage down the proverbial toilet. Now you're skipping out on Sunday dinner? You better be dead, or you'll wish you were. She's . . ."

Nick picked up the telephone. "Hello?"

"Who's this? Where's Rosalie?"

"Hi, I'm Nick—and you are . . . ?"

"Rosalie's sister, Annabelle."

"Annabelle, Lee's here. She's sick in bed and won't be able to come to dinner."

"Lee? *Rosalie* doesn't get sick. Let me speak to her."

"I'm sorry, she's asleep. I'll have her call you the next time she wakes."

"How do I know you're not some kind of ax murderer holding her hostage or something?"

"If I were, would I answer the phone?"

"Good point. Okay, so you're not an ax murderer. Who are you?" She paused for a moment, "Oh, I know who you are."

"You do?"

"Yeah, sure, you're the guy who went to Fiorentino's to buy breakfast two days after she dumped Joey Manetti. You're the rebound guy."

"Excuse me?"

"Yeah, you're the guy she picked up to prove she could still . . . well, you know."

"Listen, Annabelle, for your information, I asked Lee out before she broke up with the idiot she'd been seeing. I am not a rebound guy."

"Sure. Whatever."

"Annabelle, tell your mother that Rosalie's not feeling well, and she'll call her later in the week."

"Fine, but Mama's gonna be pissed that you're there, and Rosalie's in bed, and she wouldn't talk to me."

"Then don't tell her. Say you called Rosalie, and she's sick. You don't even have to lie. Do your sister a favor, and don't tell your mother you spoke to me. Lee's feeling bad enough as it is. She doesn't need your mother coming down on her, too."

"Okay, but you tell her she owes me."

"Gee, Annabelle, you're all heart." Nick hung up the phone and hoped Rosalie was adopted.

Rosalie's first thought when she awoke was why wasn't she sleeping alone? Her second thought was, *who* was sleeping with her? She removed the hand that held her left breast—not through her shirt, either. And turned her head. Nick. Her brain began functioning, and it all came back . . . Nick dragging her to the hospital; Nurse Gus and Dr. Barbie; Nick carrying her to bed, forcing her to eat, making her do that awful nebulizer treatment every fifteen minutes, or at least, that's how it felt. Nick invading her life, spending the night, taking care of her—and Dave, the traitor. Oh, yeah, she remembered everything.

Nick's hand slid beneath her top again. The man was incorrigible, even in sleep. He did feel good cuddled against her, and at least he didn't snore. If he had, she'd have had to make him leave.

"I can hear you thinking." His voice was gravelly with sleep and rumbled over her.

"Why are you here?"

"Why do you ask that every time you wake up?"

"Because I wonder why you're here every time I wake up."

"We're on a date."

"I canceled."

"I never got the message."

"Obviously."

"Your fever's down."

"How do you know?"

"I'm holding you, and you don't feel like a damn radiator."

"So that's why you're spooning me . . . ?" She reached back and touched nothing but his bare hip " . . . naked? To check my temperature?"

"Would you believe me if I said yes?"

Rosalie would have laughed, if she hadn't started coughing. Nick tightened his hold on her. He splayed his hand over her chest, and the pressure actually made her feel a little better. Go figure.

"You poor baby." He checked his watch. "Yeah, it's

that time again."

"Oh, no, it's not."

"Lee, don't you think it's a coincidence you wake up every four hours, right in time to do a breathing treatment? Think about it. You can't breathe, so you wake up. When you can breathe, you sleep. The only way either one of us is going to get any more sleep tonight is for you to do your breathing treatment."

"You could always go home and sleep."

"Lee. . ."

Damn. "Fine, I'll do it, but only because I'm tired. Capisce?"

"Capisce."

Rosalie woke alone and got out of bed in search of Nick. Her legs felt like lead as she shuffled down the hall.

Nick was in the kitchen tasting something over a large pot on the stove. He turned, and Rosalie almost laughed. *He was wearing her Women Need Men Like Fish Need Bicycles* apron. When he spotted her, he ripped the apron off as if he was embarrassed and shoved it in the drawer behind him.

"I didn't know you cooked."

"I don't."

Rosalie made it to the stove and peeked into the pot. Red sauce bubbled over meatballs, sausage, and braciole. "It sure looks like cooking to me. You made braciole?"

Nick turned the cutest shade of red. "Yeah, so?"

Rosalie tried not to laugh; she'd never seen Nick embarrassed. She wrapped her arms around him and kissed his cheek. "Thanks."

"Yeah, well. I need to eat, too, you know." He sounded pacified. She hadn't meant to give him a hard time. Heck, she appreciated the effort. She'd never seen a guy cook on something that didn't require charcoal before—well, at least a guy who wasn't a chef. Actually, the whole cooking thing was sexy in a Bobby Flay or *Take Home Chef* kinda way. Rosalie sometimes fantasized that the hot Aussie, Curtis somebody, the Take Home Chef, would run into her at the market and come back to her place to fix dinner. Then, she'd remember what a mess her apartment was and thank God he hadn't, because it would be so embarrassing to have to get out of it on national TV. She supposed she could take him to her mother's but then her mother would wreck the whole show by telling him that he was doing everything wrong.

Rosalie shook her head and stepped away from Nick. "Isn't it Tuesday? Don't you have to work?"

He had his briefcase and papers all over the table.

"It's Wednesday, and I took time off."

"Nick, go to work. I'm fine. I don't need a nursemaid."

Nick led her over to the table and pulled out a chair for her. "I'm taking you to the doctor early this afternoon. Once we see how you're doing, we'll talk about it."

Damn, he was pushy. She sat, because, well, she was getting light-headed.

"What is this? The world's longest date? I'm not going back to the hospital, and the only doctor I know is a gynecologist. I don't think she'd be much help."

"I called a buddy of mine—Mike. He's a pulmonologist. Lungs are his specialty."

An hour after they returned from the doctor's appointment, Nick stormed into the bathroom like a boxer jumping into a ring. Rosalie almost put her eye out with the mascara wand. What was with him? Hadn't he ever heard of knocking?

She calmly put the mascara wand back in the tube. "Damn." She rubbed the big black mark under her eye with the corner of a washcloth. As if the rings under her eyes weren't dark enough.

Nick filled the bathroom with barely controlled rage. "You are the most hardheaded, stubborn woman I know."

"Yeah, and your point is?" Rosalie tossed the washcloth in the sink and walked past him into the bedroom. She began searching her drawers for a pair of stockings. There were no longer clean laundry piles lying around. Sometime while she was in her pneumonia-induced coma, Nick had not only washed, folded, and put away the dirty pile, but he had folded and put away the clean pile, too. Rosalie had no idea where her clothes were. She should have been embarrassed. Instead, she was annoyed.

"You're not well enough to work. Mike said. . ."

She turned and spoke through clenched teeth. "Mike doesn't have a meeting with the Board of Directors. My clients don't care if I have a cold. . ."

She'd thought she was on the mend; she thought she'd be fine to go into work for a few hours. But after dragging herself out of bed, showering, and dressing, all she had the energy for was sleep.

Nick stepped into her personal space and stared down

at her. She had to admit, his stare was pretty effective.

"You have pneumonia."

She ignored the urge to step back, did her teenage eye roll, and stood her ground. "Whatever. I have to make a report to the Board of Directors."

"Okay. You go in; you give them your damn report; and you come home. I'll drive."

They were nose to nose, and she was running out of steam. "What are you? My mother?"

"No, but I'll call your mother. . ."

"You wouldn't dare!"

"Wanna bet?"

"Fine, you drive me and bring me home, but then you're outta here. I appreciate your help, but, Nick. . ."

"Lee." His voice had gentled. Nick wrapped his arms around her and hugged her against him. Damn, he felt good. She rested her head on his chest and listened to his heartbeat while he rubbed her back. "I'm just going to drive you to work and back, and then I'm going to make dinner. No more chicken soup. You're up to real food. Besides, you're almost well enough to finish our date. I brought movies."

"You did?"

"Yeah."

Of all the businesses in trouble, why did Rosalie have to turn around Premier Motorcars? The one dealership Nick had spent his life coveting, the one dealership he'd been unable to buy, the one dealership he'd targeted for a hostile takeover. Damn.

Nick must have hid his shock well when he'd dropped

Rosalie off in front of the familiar building. She hadn't asked what was wrong or said anything when he offered to wait in the car. After he'd slid the Mustang into a parking space down the block, he was tempted to bang his head on the steering wheel. What a mess.

When Nick was eight-years-old, he'd wanted to see a Ferrari. He'd heard that people owned such things, but never having seen one in Brooklyn, he was skeptical. Supposedly, there was a car dealership in the City that sold cars worth so much money, the door handles were made of solid gold.

One hot summer day, Nick had stolen two tokens from his mother and hopped the subway into the City. He'd spent a couple of hours with his nose pressed up against the cool glass of the showroom, checking out cars he'd only seen before in his Matchbox collection. He'd been eyeing the solid-gold door handles when Mr. Lassiter snuck up behind him and put his hand on Nick's shoulder. Nick had thought for sure he was going to be run off. Instead, he'd been invited in. That's when he'd fallen in love for the first and only time.

Walking though the big glass doors of Premier Motorcars had been a life-altering moment. He'd only experienced a few—walking into Premier, getting arrested, finding Rosalie asleep in the emergency room and thinking she was dead. Nick shook his head, trying to erase that image. He didn't want to think about what it meant.

From the moment he walked into Premier, he'd loved everything about the business. The air-conditioning that sent a chill though his whole body; the sound of shoes

tapping across polished marble; the smell of the place—
a combination of coffee, cigarettes, leather, and new car.

That was the first time he'd looked under the hood of
a brand-new car. The fact that the car was a Ferrari had
only made the experience that much better. The owner
of the dealership, Mr. Lassiter, had even let him sit in the
driver's seat. It was the first time Nick's butt had ever
touched leather.

Mr. Lassiter had been good to him when he'd gotten
out of Juvie and asked for a job. Nick had nothing to feel
guilty about. He'd worked his ass off for the man and
would still be if he hadn't been replaced by Mr. Lassiter's
Ivy League son.

Jack Jr. was the stereotypical trust fund baby. He
worked as little as possible, drove expensive cars, and
spent money like it was going out of style. But that wasn't
enough for Jack. What the trust fund didn't buy him, he
didn't mind taking by force. Like most bullies, Jack only
preyed on people weaker than himself. One evening,
Nick walked into his office after hours and caught Jack
forcing himself on the new receptionist. When Nick
pulled Jack off her, her dress was ripped, and she was in
tears. Nick saw red. Jack Jr. had gone crying to daddy,
told him God only knows what, and the next day, both
Nick and the receptionist were out of a job.

Before Nick left, he'd warned Lassiter that Junior
would ruin him. Was it Nick's fault he'd been right? Anything Nick had done only hastened the inevitable. So
he'd made a few calls, mentioned a concern or two to a
high-ranking loan officer. So what? He'd done nothing
too underhanded, certainly nothing illegal, and there was

no paper trail. Unfortunately, no matter how much Nick told himself he had nothing to feel guilty about, he still heard Father Francis's voice in his head, telling him he was going straight to hell. And as if that wasn't bad enough, Rosalie now stood between Nick and the one thing he'd wanted since he'd had the innocence to dream.

Premier Motorcars.

Chapter 8

NICK TURNED OFF THE TV AND DVD PLAYER. HE AND Rosalie had been watching *Life of Brian*. No, *he'd* been watching—she'd fallen asleep ten minutes into the movie. One minute she was laughing that great laugh of hers, and the next, she was dead to the world. Good thing they'd been watching in bed.

It was almost eleven. Not too late to call Mike and find out how Rosalie was doing medically. He still couldn't believe she'd told him that her condition was none of his business. Hell, he was the one who'd made the damn appointment with Mike in the first place. If it wasn't his business, whose was it?

Rosalie was asleep on top of him. It took a minute for Nick to slide out without waking her. She was a piece of work. When she was awake, she was always so careful about not touching him. It was as if she were afraid they'd look as if they were together, which they weren't. He knew that, and it was obvious she knew that. What difference did it make if she touched him? The minute she fell asleep, though, she was all over him like cotton on silicone in a wet T-shirt contest.

Nick stood and reached for his sweats, tiptoed out of the bedroom, and shut the door. He didn't want Rosalie to know he was checking up on her. Nick called Mike's pager and punched in his cell phone number. Ten minutes later, his phone vibrated.

"Hello."

"This is Dr. Flynn. You had me paged?"

"Mikey, it's me, Nick."

"I thought that number looked familiar. So, how's our patient?"

Nick groaned.

"That good, huh?"

"She's impossible, Mike. Do you believe she went to work today?"

"No kidding. How'd she get there?"

"I drove her. If I hadn't, she'd have taken the damn subway."

"I heard from the dayshift nurse that Nurse Gus had to threaten to sedate her to keep her from climbing over the side of the bed to escape. He said you pulled a he-man stunt and carried her into the ER."

"She wasn't going to go in otherwise."

"Dr. Jansen asked about you."

"Dr. who?"

"The attending. Tall, blonde, gorgeous. You know—Pamela Anderson with a brain. She also asked how long you and Rosalie have been engaged."

"Hey, I had to tell her something. She was more interested in checking me out than in helping Lee."

"Yeah, I know. I got a date with her."

"Mikey, when are you going to stop picking up my throwaways?"

"When you stop throwing them back. I've been trying to get a date with Deena Jansen since she started her residency. Hell, if I'd known all I had to do was tell her I'm in tight with the great Romeo, I'd. . ."

"Christ, do you have to start that again?"

"No, I don't have to, but I will. By the way, you never did tell me what's with you and Rosalie. She's not your usual type."

"What do you mean?"

"She's normal—not like the shallow, self-involved, dimwitted women you usually date—the ones who think the earth and sun revolve around you. As a matter of fact, she didn't seem impressed with you at all."

"And you call that normal? That's what you think. Did you know she curses in three languages?"

"I caught that. She didn't think I spoke Italian. When I told her, she started with Greek."

"Make that four."

"She's got an amazing personality, a great job—"

"Yeah, you're not going to believe where I drove her."

"Premier Motorcars. I know. Nick, tell me you're not seeing her as some kind of kinky corporate espionage."

"What are you, nuts? No. I just found out about her connection to Premier today when I drove her to work. Christ, Mike, what kind of asshole do you think I am?"

"Hey, this is me you're talking to. The one who listened to you rant and rave about how you were going to take over Premier Motors if it was the last thing you did. You've wanted that place since we were kids. I know you, Nick. Nothing gets between you and what you want. Especially not a woman. Make sure whatever you do to her doesn't make her hate you so much, she won't date your best friend, okay? So, how long have you been seeing her?"

"A little over a week. Why?"

"I want to make sure my calendar is free when you throw her back. I'm looking forward to catching her.

She's got one hell of a body. Let's see, I give it another month and a half, which puts us into—"

"Hold on. What do you know about her body?"

"Enough to know I look forward to getting better acquainted with it."

"The only thing you're going to get better acquainted with is my fist, if you don't stop talking about her like that."

"Nick, man, I didn't mean—"

"It doesn't matter. Besides, she doesn't like doctors."

"All women like doctors. They just don't like seeing us professionally. Didn't you get the memo? Doctors are prime marriage material."

"No, I must have missed that one. Now you have two strikes against you in Lee's book. She's not into marriage, either."

"Right."

"Look, I'm calling because Lee wouldn't tell me what you said. And I want to make sure she's okay."

"Nick? You feeling all right? Suffered a recent blow to the head?"

"Oh, you're a laugh riot, Mike. Look, I'm staying at her place and taking care of her, and I need to know if she's well enough to, you know, resume normal activities."

"Oh, I get it. You want to know when you're gonna get laid."

"No. Well, okay, yes, that, too. But I also want to know if she should be going to work, and if I should be leaving her alone."

"Okay, look, I don't think I'd be breaking doctor-patient confidentiality to tell you that, no, she shouldn't be going to work yet—maybe late next week for a few hours a day. As for sex, well, I'd hold off on that, too. And, yes, you can leave her alone, if you think you can trust her not to go to work or have sex without you."

Nick waited for Mike to stop laughing. "You know, Lee could be right. Maybe you did get your medical license out of a box of Cracker Jacks."

Dave whined and stuck his nose in Nick's armpit, almost knocking the telephone from his hand.

"What was that?"

"Dave, Lee's dog. I have to go."

"You're taking care of the dog, too?"

"Yeah. What of it?"

"Oh, nothing. I'm picturing you walking a shih tzu, that's all. Thanks, you made my day."

"Yeah? Why don't you come over and make a house call? I'm sure Dave would love to take a chunk out of your ass. Dave eats shih tzus for breakfast. Don'cha, boy? Look, Mike, I've got to go. Give me a call sometime next week. We'll have lunch."

"Take good care of Rosalie. Oh, and give her my number when you dump her, will you?"

"Dream on."

Nick hung up and grimaced. Damn, it'd been over a week since he and Rosalie were together, and he knew he was a selfish bastard, but he'd been hoping Mike would say she was up for recreational activities. Christ, he wasn't sure how much longer he could go on sleeping with her body plastered against his. He hadn't been sleeping much at all, and tonight was going to be another long one.

Nick shrugged his coat on and stepped into his running shoes. Maybe a nice long walk in sub-zero temperatures would take the edge off. Lord knows, cold showers weren't cutting it.

"Come on, Dave, I'll take you out one last time tonight. But if you take another dump, you're on your own." Nick grabbed Dave's leash. "Someone should invent a way to attach a bag to your ass. The pooper-scooper law sucks."

At least Dave had the decency to look embarrassed.

Monday morning, Nick disengaged himself from Rosalie's grasp and slipped out of bed. It was only five-thirty, still fully dark, and Nick wondered if all those stories he'd heard about blue balls were true.

He'd been awake and trying to fall back to sleep for over an hour. He'd come to the conclusion that sleep wasn't going to happen. Typical. Maybe he'd go to the office and stretch out on the couch. Rosalie's couch was too close to Rosalie, and the way he felt right now, if he didn't leave, he'd either attack her or go crazy. She was too soft in all the places he was hard; she was too comfortable; she smelled too good; and damn, the way she wrapped herself around him was enough to tempt a saint. Nick was no saint.

He hit the bathroom, showered, and dressed in jeans and a sweater. He'd change into one of the suits he'd hauled to the office since staying at Rosalie's. It was faster than going home to change and then to the dealership. Sure, his secretary was giving him funny looks, but that was nothing new. Lois had been doing that for the last ten years. He was used to it.

Nick fed and walked Dave, made coffee for himself, and set the pot to brew automatically for Rosalie. It didn't take long for him to learn that coffee was necessary to Rosalie's survival, as well as everyone else's. Being around Rosalie before she had coffee was like waving a red cape at a Brahma bull—not a bright idea. The woman was downright vicious. Nick grabbed his briefcase, keys, and phone, and patted Dave's head.

"I'll be back with lunch. You take care of Lee for me."

He went to the door to get his coat and he the oddest feeling he should stay—an ominous feeling. Nick shook his head. Talk about melodramatic—he heard organ music playing in his head. Da-da-duh-dum. He was being ridiculous. Rosalie was fine. Her breathing was back to normal; she hadn't wheezed all night; and her cough was under control. In short, she was sleeping like a babe. A very sexy, hot, arousing, desirable babe. Damn, he had to get the hell out of there, or all his good intentions would disappear. She'd definitely be better off without him hanging around wanting to get her all excited and breathing heavy.

He adjusted himself, pulled his jacket on, and checked to make sure it covered his bulge. He didn't want Henry and Wayne getting the wrong idea if he passed them on the way out. Grabbing his briefcase, he took a deep breath, pushed the bad feeling aside, and left for work.

Nick crashed for a few hours in his office and spent the rest of the morning going through the motions. He knew that he spoke to people, had meetings, and made decisions, but he did it all by rote. His mind was on Rosalie. He couldn't get past the feeling that something was wrong.

"Earth to Nick."

Nick looked up from the ad copy he'd been staring at for the last half hour. Lois was looking at him as if she wanted to commit murder.

Nick had the urge to get out of his chair and step out of her reach. He'd hired her because she was a real hard ass. A single mom with five boys, only one of whom was still at home, the woman could give a Marine Drill Sergeant lessons on how to be one of the few, the proud . . . Hell, the Marines could use her as a secret weapon. She looked harmless enough, but as Nick had found out early on, she was more dangerous than a nuclear bomb. Until now, she had never directed her rage at him. It was okay if she directed it at the press or pushy salesmen, but he'd thought he was safe because he signed her paychecks. He'd been wrong.

"What's the matter with you?"

"Me?" Nick sputtered. "What do you mean? Nothing's the matter with me."

"Okay," Lois threw up her hands, "don't tell me. I don't care, but let me tell you something. You've been acting strange since the beginning of last week, and you're walking around here with your head up your ass. You came this close to losing our biggest client today. Mr. Ackerman was going to take his business elsewhere. Do you know how big a fleet his company has? How many cars, trucks, and vans he purchases from us annually? How much he spends on repairs and maintenance each year?"

"I do not have my head up my ass—"

"Oh, really? Is that why you slept through your breakfast meeting this morning? Do you realize that's the second time you've stood him up? You didn't even have the decency to cancel."

"A breakfast meeting? Damn."

"I just spent an hour on the phone placating him. Do you mind telling me where the hell your head is? Because it's not here. Hell, it's not even at Premier Motors. You couldn't find Premier's file when you were looking right at it, and you've yet to comment on the new interim CFO. What's going on with you, Nick?"

"Okay . . . you know that woman I've been seeing?"

"Rosalie Ronaldi? Yeah, what about her?"

"You remember when I told you how I got in trouble as a kid?"

"When you and a friend got arrested for grand theft auto? How could I forget?"

Nick rubbed the back of his neck. "Yeah, well, the friend happened to be Rosalie's big brother."

Lois shook her head and looked as if she was about to give him hell. He might as well get the inevitable over with. He braced for it, as if he were about to pull a Band-Aid off a hairy part of his body. It was going to sting . . . badly. He held up his hand to stop the onslaught until he was finished. "Wait, there's more."

"More? Spit it out, Nick."

"She's a turnaround expert, and she's turning around Premier Motors. She's the new interim CFO."

Lois crossed her arms over her abundant chest and gave Nick a look that had him saying Hail Marys under his breath. "You know, Nick, I thought you had your head up your ass, but now I know the truth. You can't have your head up your ass, because you *are* an ass. How dare you use that poor woman for your own purposes? That's just wrong in so many ways—"

"Whoa, hold on. I'm not using Lee—well, not without her consent, anyway. I didn't know she was the interim CFO. I didn't know she had anything to do with Premier Motors until Wednesday. What do you take me for?"

"A guy who'd keep his identity a secret from the woman he's sleeping with, because she'd probably never see him if she knew who he really was. I know you, Dominick Romeo. You're determined to acquire Premier Motors, and you're not above using others to forward your agenda."

"Okay, I'll admit I've skated on the edge of propriety when it comes to business dealings, but I've never done anything illegal."

"Last time I checked, corporate espionage was illegal, not to mention immoral. Hell, you could get Rosalie fired and blackballed. Who's going to hire a turnaround expert who gives information to the man planning a hostile takeover?"

"It's hardly hostile. I made them a very fair offer."

"That's not the point, and you know it. You need to choose between your girlfriend and Premier Motors."

"That's ridiculous. Rosalie is temporary, and Premier is business. I don't mix business and pleasure."

"How's it going to look when someone finds out she's sleeping with the man intent on taking over the company she's been hired to save?"

"That's not going to happen. I'm not going to do, nor have I done, anything to hurt Premier. I simply sat back and watched Lassiter run it into the ground, all by his lonesome. I haven't done anything to hurt Lee, either, but there's little chance of her turning around Premier Motors."

Lois looked skeptical.

"Besides, Lee and I will be history by the time I make my next offer to Lassiter, and I'll make sure she's not hurt by any of this."

"Oh, that's right. I forgot. You're the great and powerful Oz. You control everything and everyone. You know what, Nick? Since you're so good at it, next time you sleep through a breakfast meeting and destroy a valuable client relationship, clean up your own mess. I'm finished. And if Rosalie knew who you were and what you're doing, she'd be finished, too."

Nick had to hand it to her. Lois sure could dish it out. He'd never thought of how this might affect Rosalie, but hey, they were just sleeping together. They never talked business. Rosalie thought he was a mechanic. Why would she talk about confidential information with a mechanic? Sure, when she found out the truth, there'd be hell to pay, but until then, he was going to enjoy himself. Besides, it wasn't as if he needed to take advantage of Rosalie. He was the best in the business. What would be the fun of winning if he had to cheat to do it? Rosalie knew him well enough to know he'd never use her. Well, he hoped she did, anyway.

"Look, Lois. I promise, nothing's going to happen to Lee, so stop worrying. Have I ever broken a promise to you?"

"No, you haven't. But Nick, think about what you're doing."

"I will, and Lois, thanks for covering for me today.

I'm sorry I put you in an uncomfortable situation. It's been a hard couple of weeks." Nick checked his watch and stood, walking toward his private bathroom. "I'm on my way out. I'll be back first thing in the morning."

"Nick, it's not even noon, and you didn't wake up until nine thirty. Aren't you even going to tell me what you're doing sleeping in your office?"

"No, I'm not."

"Stop the buzzing, stop the buzzing! Who would come over this early in the morning?" Rosalie got out of bed and moved as quickly as she could—which she had to admit was a snail's pace—to the door, slapped the intercom button, and croaked, "What?"

"Rosalie Angelina Ronaldi, you open this door this minute, or I'm going to call your father and see what he has to say."

She buzzed her mother in and wondered if her cough medicine had enough codeine in it to make dealing with Mama bearable. Somehow, she doubted it.

Rosalie unlocked the door before Mama started ringing that bell, too. As if her head didn't hurt enough. God, she hoped Nick had made coffee.

Dave sat next to the door and whined. "I feel your pain, buddy."

Mrs. Ronaldi started talking even before she had the door open an inch.

"Rosalie, what is the meaning—my Lord, you look like something the cat dragged in. Can't you fix yourself up a little? It's noon, why aren't you dressed? Put some makeup on, for God's sake. What if Joey comes to see you? I told him you were sick. Such a nice boy, that Joey."

"Hi, Ma."

"What? You couldn't call me yourself and tell me you were sick? What's wrong with you? You know better than to make me worry."

"Sorry, I fell asleep."

"And get that mangy mutt away from me. I'll have black hair all over my outfit."

She took her coat off and handed it to Rosalie, who threw it on the couch. Dave, the traitor, ran into the bedroom.

"Well, at least you cleaned the apartment."

"I did?" Rosalie looked around. She could see all the counters and tabletops. Amazing. "Um, yeah, I did."

"I suppose you did that because Joey called and will be coming over?"

Rosalie poured two coffees and smiled to herself. Thank you, Nick. You're a prince among men—the prince of darkness, but a prince all the same.

"I don't know if Joey called, Ma, and I don't care. I don't want Joey to call; I don't want Joey to come over; and once and for all, I don't want to marry Joey. The only thing I want from Joey is for him to leave me alone."

After sliding the coffee cup across the breakfast bar to her mother, Rosalie opened a box of biscotti and stuffed one in her mouth. When she offered the box to her mother, the woman walked into the kitchen and took out two plates. Rosalie didn't see the point of dirtying a plate. If you ate over the sink, you never had to do dishes.

"You're sick. You don't know what you're saying."

Mama continued as she took the biscotti out of Rosalie's hand and set it on the plate.

"I'm sick, not crazy." Though she might be hallucinating. She couldn't believe how nice her place looked. Wow. She felt like someone on that show *Clean Sweep*. She was dying to open a closet door but afraid it might cause an avalanche if Nick had shoved everything in there, like she always did.

"You're coming home with me, so I can take care of you."

"No, thanks. Ma, I'm fine. Really. I feel a lot better."

Her mother eyed the refrigerator. Oh, no. If she opened the door before Rosalie blocked it and saw there was no food, Rosalie's position as failure of the Ronaldi family was cemented for eternity. Damn. It was hard to move fast when she couldn't breathe, and her mother beat her. As the door swung open, Rosalie closed her eyes, shook her head, and prayed for divine intervention—hell, any intervention would do, she wasn't picky.

"And I thought you couldn't cook."

"I can, too." She opened her eyes and did another double take. The refrigerator was overflowing. And not only with beer and batteries, which would have been typical.

"I don't consider boiling pasta and heating canned sauce cooking." Her mother quipped. "This lasagna looks homemade."

"A friend brought it over. Look, I'm being well fed, and I'm tired. I want to sleep, so thanks for coming, Ma. I'll call you tomorrow." She put her arm around her mother and was trying to usher her to the door when Mama turned and walked into the bedroom. Of course, she freaked when she found Dave sleeping on the bed with all fours in the air and a smile on his face—well, when his jowls flopped open like that, it looked like a smile, anyway.

"You sleep with that in your bed?"

Among other things. If she only knew. . .

"Get off!"

Poor Dave flew off the bed and out into the garden. Only the sound of the doggy door swinging back and forth penetrated the silence, until Rosalie heard the front door open.

"Lucy, I'm home."

Oh, no. It wasn't only the bad Ricky Ricardo imitation that was upsetting. Things were beginning to get dark and fuzzy. She sat on her bed and considered putting her head between her knees, but she wasn't sure if that was the crash position or what one should do when feeling faint.

"Lee, do you want to eat in bed?"

From what she could see through the gray fuzz, her mother was crossing herself and doing that breast-beating thing she did when she was über-upset. Yeah. She was mumbling that prayer to the Virgin Mother again.

"Lee?"

The bedroom door swung open and there was Nick in all his glory, though he looked kinda squiggy around the edges. Maybe she'd taken too much of that cough syrup. She could never get the spoon from the bottle to her mouth without spilling it all over herself, so she improvised and took a swig or two.

She lay down, faced the wall, and groaned.

"Mama, Nick; Nick, that's my mother, Maria Ronaldi. Mama was just leaving."

"Well, I never!"

"Yeah, Ma, I know. I'm a disappointment, a puttana, yada, yada, yada. I'll call you and give you plenty of time to yell all about it. But not now. I'm not up to it."

Rosalie felt as if she were floating away and far below her, she heard Nick's hushed voice. . .

"I think you'd better go now, Mrs. Ronaldi."

Chapter 9

NICK EYED ROSALIE'S MOTHER WHO, HE HAD TO ADMIT, was a beautiful woman in an old-world way. She was a hotter, Italian version of Mrs. Cleaver, without the pearls. Damn, he hoped like hell she didn't recognize him either as Richie's long-lost friend or as Dominick Romeo.

Mrs. Ronaldi stomped into the living room and turned, bringing Nick back to the present. She wore the same expression his Nana did before she gave someone the evil eye—an Italian curse. He knew it well. He'd been on the receiving end a few times, usually by a mother who didn't want him messing with her daughter, but as far as he could tell, the curses never amounted to much more than insomnia. He'd spent more than a few sleepless nights wondering what horror would befall him. It wasn't enough to make him change his ways, but it was enough to make him want to hold a crucifix in front of him for protection.

"Who do you think you are, telling me to leave my own daughter's apartment?"

"I'm the one who spent the last week taking care of her, the one who spent nine hours pacing the damn emergency room, the one who dragged her to the best pulmonologist in the state. Who do you think you are, upsetting her? Can't you see she's sick? She has pneumonia, for Christ's sake. Lee didn't look this bad when I carried her into the hospital."

"Lee?"

What was it about this woman that made him want to act like a caveman and pound something with a club? He settled for puffing up his chest and crossing his arms. "Yeah, Lee."

"Rosalie never said anything about going to the hosp—"

"I can't imagine why."

Nick spun around and plucked Mrs. Ronaldi's coat off the couch, put it on the stunned woman's shoulders, and herded her out the door.

"I'll have Lee call you when she feels better."

Nick let out a breath of relief when he got Mrs. Ronaldi out of the building and the security door closed behind her. She hadn't recognized him. Thank God.

When Nick returned, he found Dave at the front window with his paws on the sill, growling at the retreating Mrs. Ronaldi.

"Some watchdog you are. Where were you when the battle-ax was hounding Lee?"

Nick grabbed the bag of Thai food and brought it into the bedroom.

Rosalie still had her head buried in the pillows. She uttered a muffled, "Is she gone yet?"

"Oh, yeah. She's gone all right."

Nick sat on his side of the bed, digging through the contents of the bag. Rosalie groaned as she sat up and reached for both sets of chopsticks. She broke one set apart and rubbed them together to remove the splinters.

She looked better than she had when he'd first walked in. The death-mask look must have been from shock.

Obviously, introducing him to her mother had not been on the top of her list of things to do. Nick pushed the hair off her cheek, watched it curl around his finger, and decided not to think about why that bothered him. He pulled the silken strand down, let go, and watched it spring back while Rosalie stared at him wide-eyed.

"I told your mother you'd call when you felt better."

Dave jumped on the bed and laid his head on Nick's knee.

Rosalie bussed a kiss on Nick's cheek. "Thanks."

"For what?"

Rosalie set the first pair of chopsticks down while she concentrated on pulling the wrapper off the second set. "Oh, I don't know, making coffee, filling the refrigerator, straightening up the apartment. Where did you put everything, anyway?"

Nick dropped a couple of napkins on Rosalie's lap. "You know, there are these amazing things called drawers and cabinets, even closets."

"I have a fear of closets. When I open them, something heavy falls on my head."

Nick opened the box of pad thai and handed it to Rosalie. "No digging for shrimp this time."

"I'm not guilty of excavation. I told you, all the shrimp were right on top. Poor shrimp distribution was not my fault." She grabbed the first shrimp she saw and popped it in her mouth, before handing him his chopsticks.

Nick took a shrimp from the container. "The secret to proper closet usage is to hang the clothes, put the heavier things on the floor, and put the lighter things on the shelves—or invest in a cargo net." He popped the shrimp in his mouth.

"Why didn't I think of that? Where does one buy a cargo net?"

She opened another box and dug in. "Oh, man, how did you know I love red curry and roast duck?"

"The last time I ordered it, I didn't get so much as a bite." Nick passed her the spicy eggplant salad and grabbed the roast duck.

Rosalie ate a few bites and then opened the sticky rice with chicken. "I thought this was for Dave."

"It is."

"He's only supposed to eat vegetarian sticky rice."

"Oh, come on, Lee, the boy needs real meat. It's chicken. Chicken won't hurt him." He took the box and set it between Dave's front paws. Dave scarfed down the contents before Rosalie finished her argument. Smart dog.

"You're spoiling him. I know you gave him lasagna last night."

"What are you complaining about? I gave you some, too."

"No wonder Dave loves you. His emotions are driven by his stomach."

"Maybe it's because your taste in men has improved, which doesn't do much to recommend me. It sounds as if there was no way to go but up. Besides, I'm a loveable guy. I've never had to resort to bribery."

Rosalie gave Nick a doubtful look. Great. His own girlfriend . . . or whatever Rosalie was, doubted that he was loveable. It amazed him how one look from Rosalie could make his ego feel as battered and bruised as if it'd been run over and dragged for miles by a crosstown bus.

"How'd you sleep?"

"Fine, until Mama dropped by. What a way to start the day. Awakening with my mother at the door might be a marginal step above awakening with a horse head sharing the sheets, but only because it's less messy."

Nick swallowed hard and stared into the box of red curry and roast duck.

"Thanks for that mental picture."

Rosalie handed him a box of pineapple fried rice, took back the duck, and looked pleased with herself.

"You did that on purpose so you could steal the duck."

"It worked, didn't it?"

"If you wanted more, you could have asked."

"What's the fun in that?"

"Oh, and spoiling my appetite is a regular trip to Disneyland."

"Aw, poor baby." She took the box of rice from Nick, set it on her bedside table, and scooted closer, nudging Dave off the bed.

In less time than it took to register that he was in trouble, Nick was wading knee-deep in it. She had her arm around his waist, her breast flattened against his side, and her hand sliding down the center of his cable-knit sweater toward Old Faithful. She nibbled on his earlobe and whispered, "Feel better now?"

No, better would not be the word he'd use to describe how he felt. Horny, conflicted, frustrated—yes, those would sum it up. Nick could hear Mike laughing at him—again, not a good thing, when the object of your lust is sucking on your ear—though it did have the necessary effect on Old Faithful, which deflated almost as fast as it had inflated. Nick got up and stood at the foot of the bed. He had to get away from Rosalie or risk tossing Dr. Know-it-All's orders right out the window, along with the laugh track running rampant in Nick's head.

What was going on? When Rosalie touched Nick, he stiffened up—and not in a good way. Maybe all this togetherness had killed the sexual interest, on his part, anyway. Hers, like a creature in a horror movie, seemed to have awakened from the dead in attack mode, and all she got was a pat. She couldn't believe he'd patted her shoulder.

"Lee, why don't you try to get some sleep? You look tired."

"I'm not tired. I've been sleeping for over a week. I've never slept so much in my life."

"Do you want to watch TV? I got a few movies."

"No, I don't want to watch TV! Hell, for all the good this is doing me, I might as well go to work."

"You shouldn't go to work until late next week at the earliest. . ."

"Says who?"

"Says Mike."

"Oh, really? And how do you know what Mike said to his patient, since I, the patient, never told you? You wouldn't have by any chance wormed information out of my doctor, would you? What else did the good doctor tell you? And you better be straight with me, because I have no problem getting Mike on the phone and asking him myself, if for no other reason than to assure him, in no uncertain terms, he's seen the last of me—as a patient, anyway."

"What in the hell is that supposed to mean? Why would you see him at all if not as a patient?"

"Hold up here. You're the one in trouble, not me. Where do you get off being pissed?"

She started coughing, and not a little cough. She sounded like a freaking goose honking and felt the burn right between her breasts. Every cough felt as if it were cutting a hole in her. Of all the times to start a coughing jag. She was just getting warmed up for a good fight.

Nick hovered over her, pushing her back against the pillows and reaching for the damn nebulizer.

"See, Mike was right. You can't go getting all excited—look what happens."

He shoved a glass of water in her face, so she drank some, trying not to choke on it. He held the nebulizer out, and she pushed it away and took a blast of her handy-dandy inhaler. It tasted like garbage, but it only took seconds to get through, compared to the eons it took for a nebulizer treatment. There's nothing like a shot of Albuterol to set things right. Rosalie wanted him to leave once she started to breathe regularly. It wasn't as if she needed him. She was doing fine by herself.

"Look, you're off the hook. I'm able to take care of myself. You can go back to whatever it is you should be doing. I don't need a babysitter. I never did. Thanks for every—"

"Oh, no, you don't. You're not getting rid of me that easy. I'm not leaving, until you're able to throw me out yourself. Besides, we never did finish our date."

"What are you? A masochist? So far, this date can go in the annals of dating as the longest and most vile date imaginable. Hell, the only time you had any fun was when Dr. Barbie was flipping her hair and jiggling her artificial mammary glands in your face."

"You caught that?"

She couldn't believe it. The man actually looked guilty. As if he'd had anything to do with it—well, other than looking like an X-rated dream date with that whole just-got-out-of-bed sex god thing he'd cornered the market on. "Caught what? That she was throwing herself at you, or that they were fake?"

"Both, either—I don't know."

Damn the man. He made it so hard to hold onto the mad. It took all the fun out of fighting and left her with no outlet for all that energy, especially since she was in bed, and he wasn't. "I was sick, not dead. And it wasn't as if she was subtle."

"That's why I told her we were engaged. You're not mad about that, are you?"

"Not unless you believe it."

"Not a chance."

"Good."

"Fine."

Did he have to be so damned adamant about it? Plenty of guys had asked her to marry them.

Nick ran his hands through his hair and shook his head. "So, are we done fighting?"

She picked up the empty carton Dave had left on the bed. "I don't know. I'm still plenty pissed about you talking to Dr. Mike behind my back."

"Well, it's not as if you were forthcoming. Give me a break, would you? I've been sleeping with you every night, and every night you plaster that hot little body of yours to mine, and every night I lay awake thinking of all the things I'd like to do you."

"I do not plaster myself to you."

"Oh, yes, you do. You might be all cool and stand-offish when you're awake, but when you're asleep, you cling to me like a drunk's hand around a bottle of cheap whiskey."

"I'm not standoffish."

"Oh, come on. You're afraid to touch me because you think I'll make something of it, and all night long you shrink-wrap yourself to me. I haven't slept all week. So yeah, I guess I am a masochist."

"Then why did you jump off the bed? Oh, and then you patted my shoulder. Don't pat me. I'm not a damn dog."

"I jumped off the bed because Mike said I should wait until next week, and damn it, the minute you get excited, you start coughing up a lung. And that's just from getting mad at me. Can you imagine if you . . . well, I remember how heavy our breathing was after only one kiss."

"You asked Mike when we could have sex?"

"Well, not in so many words, but yeah. I'm sorry."

The look on his face was priceless. It was a fascinating combination of embarrassment mixed with total disappointment, guilt, and a heaping helping of chagrin. The man was irresistible. She couldn't help it. She had to laugh. It felt good to laugh a straight from the belly, tear-inducing laugh.

"Aye? Who needs Monty Python when you have me to laugh at, right?

"I'm not laughing at you. Well, okay, I guess I am, but only because you're so cute."

Nick sat on the bed and groaned. "Don't say that! It's the kiss of death. Don't you know you're never supposed to call a man cute? Puppies are cute; stuffed animals are cute; babies are cute. I'm sexy, hot, gorgeous—"

"Not to mention modest, unassuming, and unpretentious—"

"Right, those, too. How would you like it if I said you were cute?"

"Okay, I admit "cute" is the wrong word. How's irresistible?"

"Better." He pushed her hair behind her ear. "So, you think I'm irresistible, huh?"

Nick might have sounded appeased, but it wasn't long before he pulled the old you're-recovering-from-pneumonia-and-you-need-your-rest ploy. He tucked her in, pulled the shades, and tiptoed out of the room.

Rosalie fumed until she could no longer fight her ever-present exhaustion and drifted off to sleep. She was in the middle of a dream, one of those dreams when you know you're dreaming. The fact that she dreamed she was walking through an air tunnel seemed weird, but she went with it—that was, until her hair began being drawn toward the fan blades at the end of the tunnel like some kind of reverse blow dryer. That's when she decided it was time to stop dreaming. She awoke with a start and found that the noise wasn't a dream after all. It was real. She didn't know what it was, but she planned to find out.

Feeling like a naughty child, Rosalie snuck out of bed and opened the bedroom door a crack. When she saw the coast was clear, she stepped out.

Nick had his back to her, so she was able to stare for a good long time. She still couldn't believe her eyes. She tried to remember what time she'd taken that codeine-laced cough syrup. It had been well before lunch, before her mother had arrived. It was already after three in the afternoon. There was no way this was a drug-induced hallucination. Amazing. Rosalie tilted her head to the side and watched with abandon.

Nick was doing a really good impression of Superman, the man of steel. But instead of lifting a car off the ground with one hand to keep a baby from being crushed, Nick was lifting the end of Rosalie's long, extremely heavy sectional sofa to vacuum under it.

Yes, she was watching a man vacuum, which was enough to make her wonder if she'd been pulled into an alternate universe. Nick's arm and neck muscles bulged as he expertly maneuvered a vacuum that looked as if it came out of an episode of *Star Trek*. The thing was amazing. It was also purple. Really purple. Who made bright purple vacuums, and where in the hell did it come from? It did have some black on it, and it wasn't a girlie purple. But still, it was purple.

Nick vacuumed with such attention to detail and skill that it put her own vacuuming skills to shame. He was even careful to go over the indentations left by the feet of the couch several times to make sure he'd sucked up all the dirt while he held up a couch so heavy, it took three men to deliver.

It took a while, since there was no shortage of dirt—she hadn't vacuumed under the couch since she'd bought the damn thing five years ago. The clear plastic cylinder on the Trekkie-inspired vacuum was filled with a tornado of dirt and dog hair.

That vacuum was a far cry from the green Hoover up-
right she'd inherited from her grandmother—God rest
her soul. Rosalie crossed herself. The vacuum might be
old, but it was tough—even though the last time she
used it, the apartment filled with the scent of burning
rubber. Rosalie knew she had it somewhere in the apartment, she just wasn't sure where. Maybe she'd put it
down in her storage area in the basement? No, the last
time she'd seen it was in the den next to the ironing
board she never used. Come to think of it, she never
used the vacuum, either. Maybe because the to-be-
ironed pile was hanging on the handle.

Nick bent down and gently lowered the couch to the
floor, showing off his butt. He'd taken off the sweater
he'd worn earlier and wore only a white T-shirt. What
was it about men in faded 501s and white-white T-shirts?

Nick's T-shirts were as white as a movie star's teeth.
If she didn't know any better, she'd think his mother did
his laundry. But after watching him sort laundry while
she pretended to sleep the other day, she knew he definitely bleached the whites himself. She hadn't seen her
whites that bright since she'd taken them out of the shopping bags.

The man was a regular domestic god—he cooked, he
cleaned, and he looked sexy as hell doing it. No wonder
most Italian men watched while their women cleaned the
house. It was a total turn on—even watching Nick stir
the pasta sauce he made (which would give her own
grandmother's sauce a run for the money) made her hot.
Too bad he wouldn't touch her. She was going to die of
terminal horniness. Damn him.

The room went silent. Nick turned and caught her watching. Busted.

"What are you doing up? Did the noise wake you?"

"No, the noise didn't wake me. I could hardly sleep for the rest of the day, could I? Nick, what is that?"

"What?"

Nick lovingly ran his hand over the machine beside him. Rosalie couldn't believe she was jealous of a dumb vacuum. But sadly, it was the truth.

"This? It's the Animal. Isn't it great? It's specially made for homes with pets. It's got more power to suck up animal hair, and a HEPA filter to cut down on allergens—"

"Where did it come from?"

"I went out and picked up a few things when you were sleeping yesterday."

"You bought me a vacuum?"

"Well, yeah. But it's not like it's a gift or anything. I couldn't use that useless excuse for a vacuum I found in the den. What was I supposed to do? I didn't want to bring one of mine over, when there was a model that was perfect for what I need here."

"You have more than one vacuum? Why on earth would anyone need more than one vacuum?" Frankly, she didn't really see the need for the one she had. Well, okay, there was a need, but it wasn't as if the world would end if you didn't use the *right* vacuum.

Nick crossed his arms. "You have to have the right tool for the job. Have you ever tried to use a Phillips screwdriver instead of a regular slotted screwdriver?"

Rosalie was losing steam, so she walked around Nick, stepped over the cord for the Animal, and couldn't help but wonder when they started naming vacuums after WWF Wrestlers. She pushed the corner seat cushion into place and sat. "No, can't say that I have."

"It doesn't work. You can't make it work. And if you try, you ruin both the screw and the screwdriver." Nick smugly nodded his head, as if screwdrivers had anything to do with vacuums. When it came down to it, Rosalie didn't have the energy to care. She did make a mental note to find out how much he spent on the vacuum and pay him back. After all, he said it wasn't a gift. Of course, if it was a gift, she'd have to rethink her taste in . . . whatever he was to her—bed buddy? Sex buddy? As depressing as it was, Rosalie had to admit that lately, Nick had been more of a nursemaid—a sexy nursemaid, one that took the job way too seriously for her taste, but he sure beat Nurse Gus any day.

Nick sat at his desk bright and early on Monday morning and couldn't wipe the smile off his face. He'd had a great weekend. If someone had told him a month ago he could have a good time with a woman doing nothing in particular, and without so much as a kiss on the mouth, he'd have told him to have his head examined.

With Rosalie, everything was different. Maybe it was because he felt comfortable that she wouldn't go off on a marriage bender, or maybe it was because she didn't expect much. She didn't expect him to talk during a game and didn't ask him what he was thinking. She didn't expect him to care about things like the discontinuation of her favorite color of lipstick, and she wouldn't think it deserved national tragedy status. She didn't even freak out if he or Dave spilled food on the bed. She said that's why man made sheets washable. Go figure.

Being with her was easy, comfortable—just like her place. She wasn't the type to get pissed off if he put his feet up on the furniture; she didn't cling unless they were in bed; and he had to admit, waking up with her on top of him was nice. It would be even nicer if he could do something about it. He'd been good about following Mike's orders but tonight—well, tonight was the night. Rosalie had an appointment with Mike, and Nick was going to call his buddy and make sure he got the all clear for extracurricular activities.

Nick's intercom beeped. "Yes, Lois?"

"Dr. Flynn calling. He said it was important."

"Thanks, put him through."

"What's up, Mike?"

"That's what I want to know. Rosalie canceled her appointment."

"What?"

"You heard me. My receptionist said she wouldn't reschedule. She said she'd have to call next week to do it."

"When was this?"

"A half hour ago."

"Okay, thanks for the heads up."

"No problem. Is she doing well?"

"Yeah, she seems to be better every day."

"That's good, at least, but I need to see her."

"Oh, believe me, you will." Nick disconnected the call and dialed Rosalie's number. The line was busy. Who didn't have call waiting? He hung up and changed into his casual clothes.

It took Nick all of fifteen minutes to get to Rosalie's apartment. He let himself in and heard her before he saw her.

"Look, by definition, an emergency is something that isn't planned. I couldn't call earlier to make a reservation. I didn't know I needed one."

Nick crossed his arms and eavesdropped without guilt.

"I know he's giant. You must have more than one giant dog that boards with you. Okay, fine, how big is the large K-E-N-N-E-L? No, I don't know how long I'll—"

Nick heard her rummaging in the bathroom and moved closer to the bedroom door. Dave had his head and shoulders stuffed as far under the bed as caninely possible.

"I don't think it will be more than a week." She let out an exasperated breath and coughed.

That was it. Nick walked in and took the telephone out of her hand. "Thank you. We'll get back to you. Good-bye." He disconnected the call.

Rosalie blew the hair out of her eyes and glared. "What in the hell do you think you're doing?"

"I was going to ask you the same question."

"I'm going out of town on business. It's an emergency. I need to find a K-E-N-N-E-L for Dave."

"First off, you might as well stop spelling the word. Dave's not stupid. He knows you're going to send him to doggie jail, which is why he's hiding under the bed. Second, a kennel is unnecessary—"

"Oh, don't even go there. You have no right to tell me where I can and cannot go."

"I'm not. I was only saying—"

"Look, just because you've been helpful doesn't give you the—"

"I'll take care of Dave."

"What?"

"You heard me. I'm not letting you put Dave in a kennel. I'll take care of him." Nick moved in close. They were nose to nose. "When did you plan on telling me you were leaving?"

Rosalie backed into the sink. "I was going to call from the airport. How did you find out?"

"Mike called. He was concerned. You canceled your appointment without rescheduling."

"So you came all the way over here?"

"I called first. The line was busy."

"I spent the morning on the phone with Gina. I've got to go to Michigan and deal with a few things and have dinner with an old college buddy."

"You're having dinner with an old . . . buddy?"

"Yeah, is that a problem?"

Hell, yeah, it was a problem, but he wasn't about to tell her that. "No, no problem. Have a nice time."

"I will, but it's mostly business. I need to see if Leisure can give me any information."

"Leisure?"

"A nickname. Someone's been spreading a rumor that Premier Motors is having trouble with their financing. I'm hoping Leisure can help ferret out the culprit. My plane leaves in three hours."

Good luck with that. There was absolutely no way that information could be traced back to him. "It won't do any good to tell you that you shouldn't be traveling, so I'll ask if you've packed all your medicine."

"Yes, it's in my carry-on."

"Your nebulizer?"

"I've got my inhaler. I'm not taking the nebulizer."

"Lee."

"Do you know how heavy that damn thing is?"

"Lee."

"Fine. I'll probably die of exhaustion from carrying it and then you can live with the guilt."

"I'll have someone take you—"

"Oh, no. I'm not going to get into a wheelchair."

Nick held his hands up. "No wheelchair, I promise. They'll drive you to the gate in a golf cart. Give me your itinerary. I'll set it up."

"That's not necessary."

"Lee."

She pushed away from him and went into the living-room. Nick followed so closely, he bumped into her when she stopped to pull her itinerary out of her briefcase.

"You know I hate when you're pushy."

"I know." Nick smiled and pulled her into his arms.

God, he felt good. She rested her head on his chest and listened to his heartbeat. He rubbed her back, and the tension she'd been holding since he walked in drained away. She'd thought for sure he was going to do something stupid, like tell her she couldn't go. Then she'd have had to stop seeing him, and she really didn't want to do that.

Nick kissed her temple and gave her a good squeeze. "Better?"

She nodded. She couldn't very well tell him that dressing, packing, and working on the phone all morning had left her so drained, she only had enough energy left to crawl into bed and sleep.

"Are you packed?"

"Yes. I'm just waiting for a fax from Gina, and the limo will—"

"Call her and tell her to cancel the limo. I'm taking you to the airport."

"Nick."

He handed her the phone and called the airport on his cell.

Twenty minutes later, Nick and Rosalie left for the airport. She spent the drive fighting to stay awake while Nurse Nick gave her the daily lecture on taking her medicine, drinking fluids, and working no more than four hours a day. Yeah, like that was going to happen, but she saw no need to tell him.

They pulled up to the curb. Nick released the trunk, got out, and unloaded her bags. She checked her suitcase curbside, and Nick tipped the baggage handler before she could get money out of her wallet. She decided not to argue with him. She was way too tired.

Rosalie waited for Nick to say good-bye. She wasn't sure how one went about doing that. She'd never had a guy take her to the airport before.

"Try to sleep on the plane. You look exhausted."

Nothing got by him. "Okay."

"Call me when you get in and let me know how to get in touch with you."

"Why?"

"In case I need to get in touch with you. What if something happens to Dave?"

"Fine, I'll call."

"Fine."

He scowled at her. His jaw had a tick in it, and he raked his fingers through his hair. Why was an irritated Nick such a complete turn-on? Her body started buzzing; her hormones did the hula; and when she met his gaze, he had that stormy eye thing going on in a big way.

"Transportation is waiting for you by the ticket counter. They'll take you to your gate."

She nodded.

"You take care." He pushed a lock of hair behind her ear. Tingles shot through her body.

"You, too."

"Call me when you get to your hotel. You have all my numbers. I'll pick you up from the airport when you come home." He gave her his don't-you-dare-argue-with-me look.

"Fine, I'll call you with my return flight information." Rosalie waited for him to do something. He must have been waiting for the same thing. She decided to make a fast retreat.

"Well, I'll see ya." She picked up her bag and headed to the terminal.

A heartbeat later, he caught her arm. "Lee?"

She turned, and he was right there, against her. She lost her balance, and he caught her. He'd snuck up on her again. Damn him. She opened her mouth to yell at him, but he kissed her and stole her thoughts. She'd almost forgotten how fabulous a kisser Nick was. It had been so long since he'd done anything but pat her. He sure wasn't patting her now. No, he was nibbling on her lips, teasing her with the hot tip of his tongue, and making her want more.

A car behind them beeped, and the driver yelled, "Get a room!"

Nick gave her another hard kiss, winked, and let her go. "Later."

Later they'd get a room, or he'd see her later? His smile told her he knew that a room sounded really good—any room with him in it. But that wasn't going to happen. Damn him.

Rosalie walked into the terminal.

Motor City, here I come.

Chapter 10

NICK SAT IN THE MUSTANG AND WATCHED ROSALIE disappear into the terminal. Rosalie wasn't well enough to travel, but he couldn't tell her that. She'd been waiting to hear him say that—and one word from him was all it would take for her to end whatever it was they had. Not that she wanted to, which was why she hadn't planned to say good-bye before she left.

If Nick could kick his own ass around a city block, he would. He'd seen the exhaustion on her face; not that anyone else would notice it. She looked every bit the hot New York executive. Her head was held high, her chin raised in defiance of the world, and her long-legged stride ate up distance and walked over anyone in her way. The crease of her pants was sharp enough to cut, and her four-inch designer heels doubled as weapons. He tried to remember if the women in Michigan wore sexy pantsuits like hers. Not that it mattered. He had a feeling wherever Rosalie went west of New Jersey, she'd stick out like a sore thumb. She might as well have had *Made in New York* stamped on her forehead. It wasn't that she looked typical—she didn't. But she had that attitude Nick found only in New Yorkers.

The woman he watched walk away was quite a switch from the makeup free, sweatshirt and flannel pant-clad Islanders fanatic with whom he'd spent the weekend fighting over the remote and eating in bed.

Nick tried not to think about the fact that he was the reason Rosalie was leaving and having dinner with some college buddy named Leisure. The only female buddies Nick had in college were bed buddies—again, not something he wanted to contemplate. Damn.

He shook his head, put the car in gear, and headed back to Brooklyn feeling way too somber. But what did he expect? He had been looking forward to a night of slow, explosive lovemaking, not a run in the park with Dave.

Nick let himself into the apartment and tossed his keys on the table. Dave sauntered out of the bedroom and eyed him warily. The poor guy must still be wondering when he was going to jail. Nick followed Dave back to the bedroom, lugging the bag he'd packed when he'd stopped to pick up his mail. Dave resumed hiding under the bed.

"Come on out, Dave, you're going to hang with the big boys this week. Relax, I'm not taking you to jail." Nick kicked off his shoes and made room in the dresser for his things. He wondered if his clothes would end up smelling like Rosalie. She kept sachets in her underwear drawer, and their scent permeated the room. Everything smelled like *Trouble*. He didn't think it mattered what his boxers smelled like, so he neatly folded her undies and tucked his boxers in next to them. Too bad checking out her underwear didn't hold the same appeal without her in it. At least he'd been dead-on when he guessed her size. What could he say? It was a gift.

Nick finished unpacking and thought a run might bring him out of his foul mood, so he changed into sweats and running shoes.

"Come on, Dave. Let's go for a run. You need the exercise, if you're going to keep sneaking lasagna."

Dave was not a runner. Nick took it slow, but after only about a mile, Dave planted his ass and refused to move in any direction except toward home. Nick tugged on his collar, even tried cajoling him. Dave lay down and played dead until Nick bribed him with a foot-long from a street vendor to get him moving again. Dave walked all the way home with a limp. How he'd managed to make it look as if all four legs were in pain was a true Oscar-worthy performance.

Nick couldn't wait to tell Rosalie about their quasi-run. Well, all except for the part about the hot dog. She'd have a cow about Nick feeding Dave meat, so he'd leave that factoid out.

By the time they got home, Nick calculated Rosalie was checking into her hotel. Which hotel, he wasn't sure, and not knowing wasn't helping his mood. He'd run all the way to the apartment to check on her. He'd been worried sick, only to be smacked upside the head with proof of how little she cared. He should have at least rated a good-bye in person—not over the phone from the airport.

The words sounded familiar. He recalled his old girlfriend, Tonya, saying something similar when he'd had Lois call and cancel their date due to an unexpected trip. She'd said he'd hurt her. Damn, now he felt like a real schmuck about that. But he wasn't hurt—he was mad.

Nick showered with his cell phone within reach. The one that didn't ring. He ate leftover pad thai, minus every shrimp—Rosalie had been excavating again. She'd have made a great anthropologist.

The landline rang. As was his habit, Nick let the machine answer. When they heard Rosalie's voice, he and Dave ran to the phone. Dave almost knocked him over in his excitement, though Nick suspected the near tumble could well have been a payback for the run.

"Hi, sweetie! How are you?"

Nick picked up the handset. "Hi."

"Nick?"

"Yeah, who were you expecting?"

"Why did you pick up?"

"You called."

"I was calling for Dave."

"You called to talk to the dog?"

"I always do. He likes it."

"I can see that. I thought you were calling to talk to me."

"I never call you "sweetie." What made you think I called for you?"

"Gee, I don't know. Maybe because most people don't telephone dogs."

"Well, I do. It keeps him from walking around the apartment with my clothes."

Nick let that one go. There were some things better left unknown.

"How are you feeling?"

Rosalie groaned. "You know, I never thought I'd see the day when I missed a guy asking me 'what are you wearing,' but it sure beats the dreaded 'how are you feeling' question."

"Okay, what are you wearing?"

"Never mind. I'm feeling fine. Do you have a pen? I'll give you my cell number."

"You have a cell phone?" Well, of course she did. Now he remembered hearing her purse ring right before her sister had called.

"Doesn't everyone?"

Nick wrote down the number and bit his tongue to keep from asking why she hadn't given it to him a week ago.

"When are you coming home?"

"I don't know. I don't know what I'm dealing with yet. I'll call you."

"Get some rest. You sound tired."

"I know, I know, drink fluids, take my medicine, eat well. Did I forget anything?"

"Yeah, you did."

"What?"

"Tonight, when you're sleepy. . ."

"Yeah?"

"And you're lying in that big, cold hotel bed all alone. . ."

He heard her breath catch. "Uh huh. . ." came out as half word, half moan.

He took a deep breath and tried to sound normal, even bored. "Sleep well."

"Nick!"

"'Bye, Lee, I'll talk to you tomorrow." He disconnected the call and found a morose Dave watching. The reason it was called a hangdog expression was brought into crystal clarity. Nick knew how the dog felt.

"Look on the bright side, big guy. At least you're not in a kennel." Try as he might, Nick failed to see the bright side of his own situation.

Dave limped into the bedroom, lumbered onto the bed, and fell into a run-induced coma. So much for dogs being good company. Nick wandered around the apartment and, after about an hour, realized what was wrong. He was lonely.

Rosalie rolled over again and looked at the clock. It was only eight-thirty, and she'd been lying down for two hours. What a complete waste of time. How was she supposed to nap after what Nick had done to her? All he had to do was talk to her in that come-to-papa voice, and she turned to unset Jell-O.

Sitting up, she ordered room service. She wasn't hungry, but she needed to take her medicine. In her head, she heard Nick bugging her about the importance of taking medicine on a full stomach.

Oh, God, when had his voice replaced her mother's as her inner nag?

The phone rang, and she stared at it. It had to be either Nick or Gina. She wasn't sure she wanted to talk to either of them, but she knew wondering who had called would drive her crazy. She might as well answer the damn phone.

"Hello."

"Well, ain't that a fine how-do-you-do?"

"Gina? Why are you talking like a yokel?"

"I thought it might take some getting used to. I'm trying to help you out.

"You know, just because Michigan is west of the Hudson doesn't mean it's full of country bumpkins.

"Honey, as far as I'm concerned, there are three cities:

New York, Chicago, and LA. If you're not from one of
the above, you're a bumpkin."

"Thanks for the lesson. Now, have you called for a
reason?"

"Several."

There was a knock on the door. "Hold on, I think my
food's here."

"Okay, answer it, but look through the peephole first.
They do have peepholes in Michigan, don't they?"

"No, Gina, Home Depot only sells doors with peepholes in New York, Chicago, and LA. They don't have
mad rapists anywhere else."

"Funny, very funny."

She answered the door and let the kid set the room
service tray on the table. After tipping him, she followed
him to the door and locked up tight.

"I'm back."

"What'd you order? Something expensive, I hope.
Lord knows, they owe you for making you fly all the way
out there to clean up this mess. Oh, and it is a mess."

"I gathered. I ordered a steak. I couldn't remember if
Michigan was famous for steak or if that was Kansas.
Geography was never my strong suit."

"Don't ask me. If it isn't in one of the six boroughs, I
don't know much about it. Sure, I'd like to go to Hawaii,
the Bahamas, maybe Guadalupe, but aside from that, the
only place I want to be is New York."

"Gina, there are only five boroughs—"

"You forgot Florida. You've heard of the South
Bronx; Florida is the South Manhattan. Don't you know
anything?"

Rosalie cut into the perfect steak—so rare, you could save it with sutures—and took a bite, nearly groaning in ecstasy. She'd never known how good it could feel to be able to taste food again. A trickle of blood dripped onto her chin, and she laughed.

"What's so funny?"

"Oh nothing. You know how I like my steak rare—"

"Uh huh."

"Well, Nick would be calling me Vampira right about now. He says I'm the only person alive that likes steak more rare than he does. One night he was cooking and, well, we got distracted. We forgot about the steak until it was well-done."

"Eeww."

"I know. As far as I'm concerned, the term "well-done" is an oxymoron. Nick ended up boiling some pasta and making this amazing clam sauce. Dave ate the steak. Thank God, Dave wasn't picky."

"Listen to you. You miss him."

"I do not. I miss Dave, not Nick. Though it does feel strange being alone. Nick barely left me all week, and when he did, he seemed to have this innate ability to come back just as I was waking up. Hell, every time I awakened, he was there with liquids, food, or drugs— sometimes all three. It was amazing, really. He only got on my nerves when he shoved medicine down my throat. But then, that had more to do with the medication than with him."

"Oh, yeah, I can see you don't miss him at all."

"He's nice . . . and a really good sport. He didn't even mind when I called him Nurse Ratched. He gave me one of his don't-mess-with-me looks, but he wasn't very convincing."

"Sounds like a real prince."

"I admit, he's special. He'd have to be to like Dave— either that or crazy. It was cute, the way he got so perturbed over the thought of Dave in a kennel. As if I would put my baby anywhere but the Ritz Carlton of kennels. I doubt they offer daily massages in Sing Sing."

"I thought you were going to call him from the airport so he wouldn't give you a hard time about traveling."

"Yeah, that was the plan, but I called to cancel the doctor's appointment—"

"Oh, you had another appointment with that Barbie clone?"

"No. Nick made me see his friend, Mike. He's a pulmonologist."

"A what?"

"A lung doctor. And Mike called Nick, and Nick came running over like—"

"Like he cares about you?"

"No, he was more concerned about Dave going to a kennel than he was about me flying to Michigan."

"Somebody sounds jealous," she said in the singsong tone third graders use.

"Gina, is there something you need to tell me, or did you call to get on my nerves?"

"I emailed you the report I put together from the trash I got from Randi with an 'I,' Lassiter's assistant. After one look, you'll see why the Board of Directors hired us. Talk about a sloppy job. Giving you a hard time is just a bonus."

"Glad I could help."

"Hey, Dorothy, just because he cares about Toto doesn't mean he's not concerned about you. He did run all the way to your place to see you."

"And he did drive me to the airport—"

"What about the limo I sent?"

"I canceled it."

"Rosalie, you sound tired. Why don't you look at what we're up against and then go to bed? You're going to need all your strength tomorrow. All I can say is, it's a good thing you're there and Lassiter's here. Once you see what he did, you're going to want to murder him, and I'd sure hate to have Sam arrest you."

She groaned. "Okay, thanks, and email me those other numbers as soon as you get them."

"I will. Sleep well."

"Ha. Night, Gina."

She looked over the report and cringed. Damn that Lassiter. Gina was right. It was a good thing she wasn't in the office. The work she and Gina had done over the phone that afternoon had her feeling marginally better, but Gina was right, Rosalie would need all her strength to turn this company around. Too bad she couldn't bounce ideas around with Nick. Nick would probably take one look at the financials and know what needed to be done, instead of doing what she'd be doing—spending the next few weeks getting up to speed.

She ordered a wake-up call, did a breathing treatment, and crawled into bed. Nestled into the incredible pillows, she made a mental note to hit the hotel's website and buy a couple.

❖ ❖ ❖

Rosalie was falling out of bed. Yes, she knew she was too old for that, but for some reason, she must have been sleeping on top of the pillows. She felt herself falling and grabbed onto what she thought was the mattress, but it wasn't. The pillows did cushion her fall, but she doubted whoever was below her thought so.

Rosalie lay sprawled on the floor at six-thirty in the morning, with a rug burn on her knee. Gathering the pillows, she climbed back in bed. The rug burn hurt like hell and looked even worse. She grabbed her phone off the bedside table, scrolled down to Nick's number, and hit "Send." Nick answered on the second ring.

"Lee?"

"Hi."

"Did you just wake up?"

"Yeah."

"And the first thing you did was call me?"

It was a question, but it sounded more like a statement of fact. "No, it's not the first thing I did." She didn't think she had to tell him the first thing she'd done was pick herself up off the floor.

"Sure, if you say so. You sound sleepy and sexy as hell . . . the way you always do for the first ten minutes, before your brain starts screaming for caffeine. Did you call room service yet?"

Damn, she knew she'd forgotten something. "Of course. Um . . . how's Dave?"

"He's fine. He seems to be feeling better."

"Why, what was wrong?"

"We went for a run yesterday. You should have seen him. After a mile, he lay down and refused to go any farther. It took me almost an hour to get him to walk home, and then he looked as if he were limping on all fours. I've never seen anything like it. After we talked to you, he was out for the rest of the night."

"Outside?"

"No. Out, as in asleep on the bed. He takes over the entire bed, like someone else I know. But at least you don't snore."

"It's nice to know I'm a better sleeping companion than Dave. You'd better watch it. All these compliments are going right to my head."

She heard a siren and then Dave groaning.

"Dave, cut it out, I'm driving here."

"You're driving with Dave?"

"Yeah, we're going to work."

"It's against the law to talk on a cell phone and drive. Pull over."

"You know, Dave, when your mom calls, all she does is order me around. I don't think she's had her coffee yet. I'm pulling over. Happy now?"

"Are you talking to me or to Dave?"

"You."

"I'm thrilled. Let me get this straight—you're taking Dave to work with you? What are you, nuts? Dave isn't a Pekingese. He's not portable."

"Sure he is. He likes the car, but he refused to sit in the back seat, so I buckled him in."

"You put a seat belt on Dave?"

"Only the shoulder strap. I thought it would keep him from going too far forward. He should be safe enough, since the car has airbags . . ."

"You actually thought of his safety? That's so sweet."

"Lee, give me a break. Sweet is almost as bad as cute. We got six inches of snow last night, and the kids have a snow day. My secretary is bringing her son, Tyler, with her to work. I thought Dave would like to hang with us."

"You're going to let a kid and a dog follow you around?"

"Sure. Tyler's great. We shoot hoops and do guy stuff together."

"Ooh, the mysterious guy stuff."

"Yes, very mysterious. Even Lois doesn't know what we do. Ty took the blood oath right after I taught him how to pee standing up."

"What do you mean? I thought the big deal with guys was writing your name in the snow . . ."

"Sweetheart, he didn't know how to spell. He was only two. He's a bright kid, but not that bright. Look, I've got to run, or I'll be late, and I'm already on Lois's shit list."

"Oh, right. Um, give Dave a kiss for me."

"Not likely."

"Make sure he doesn't drink antifreeze or anything."

"I'll keep him in my office."

"Nick?"

"Yeah?"

"Thanks."

"Forget about it."

Not likely.

Rosalie disconnected the call on a sigh. Damn the man. There's nothing more attractive than a man who loves dogs or kids. Of course, Nick would do both.

Again Rosalie hung up before Nick could say good-bye. Damn. He didn't want her thanks. He only wanted her to come home.

Dave gave him a disappointed look.

"I miss her too, big guy, but there's no way in hell I'm going to kiss you. Maybe later, after Lois leaves, we can call your mom on the speakerphone. How does that sound?"

Nick wondered if he was losing it. As if it wasn't bad enough that he was talking to a one-hundred-fifty-pound mutt, he could have sworn Dave raised a brow as if to say, "You really expect me to answer? What do you think this is, an episode of *Lassie?*"

Only Rosalie would have a sarcastic dog.

Nick and Dave spent the next week and a half working long hours. Lois set up a dog bed for Dave beside Nick's desk, and when he had meetings, Nick used the conference room instead of his office. Ty came by every day after school and took Dave to the park for twenty bucks for the week. Dave loved Ty, and Ty needed more responsibility and something to occupy his time after school. Ty was about the same age Nick had been when he'd started down the road to Juvie. He sure as hell wasn't going to let Ty make the same mistake.

Nick leaned back in his chair and yawned. Christ, he'd thought he'd sleep better without Rosalie around to tie him in knots. It wasn't the case; if anything, his sleep problems were worse. He'd hardly slept at all since she left, and when he did manage to fall asleep, he'd wake up with his arm around Dave. Which was embarrassing as hell, even for Dave.

"Wake up!"

"What?" Nick's eyes shot open, and he found Lois leaning over his chair. "Christ, Lois, what are you trying to do? Give me a freakin' heart attack?"

"If you weren't sleeping on the job, you'd have heard your phone ringing. Maybe you need to set the ring tone louder . . . or get some sleep. You look like hell."

"What time is it?"

"Time for you to get out of the office. You're no good to me like this, Nick. I've run out of patience. Go home. Don't come back until you get a minimum of eight hours of sleep."

"But Ty is coming. . ."

"That's okay. I'm taking the afternoon off. I'll take him to the park. Dave can have the day off, too. Now both of you, get out of here."

Nick was too tired to argue, and she was right about him being no good to anyone at work. He hooked Dave's leash to his collar and headed home.

Rosalie opened the door to the apartment, stuck her head in, and waited for Dave to do his sorry impression of the Snoopy Happy Dance. But there was no Dave.

She wanted to cry. She was tired and cranky, and she wanted to see Dave and Nick. She couldn't believe she'd come all this way at this ungodly hour, and Nick wasn't even here.

Her eyes stung, not from tears, but because they'd been open for eighteen hours straight.

It wasn't that she missed Nick. How could she? He'd taken up residence in her brain. The only good thing about Nick filling her thoughts was that she no longer heard her mother.

Rosalie should have listened when Gina told her to fly back in the morning. But no, she'd wanted to go home. She'd wanted to sleep in her own bed and see her own dog. And yes, she'd wanted to surprise Nick. To think she'd done all that, and he wasn't even here!

As she lugged in her bags, Dave trudged out of the bedroom. For the first time all week, she felt like celebrating. He did full-body stretches on his way to greet her. It was a far cry from a Snoopy Happy Dance, but she'd take what she could get. He waited for his kiss and butted his head into her. She wasn't sure if it was a sign of affection, but that's how she chose to take it. Tossing her coat on the couch, she kicked her shoes off and followed Dave to the bedroom.

Dave crawled onto the bed and resumed sleeping with his big head resting on Nick's chest. Nick reached out, laying his arm over Dave's neck. Talk about a Kodak moment. Not to mention perfect blackmail material. Rosalie had a feeling Nick would do anything to keep Mike and Vinny from knowing he and Dave slept together. It was a shame she was too tired to find her camera.

She gave Dave's rump a pat and pulled him off the bed, careful to keep him from stepping on Nick.

Nick didn't even stir. Amazing. She stripped out of her clothes, slipped on a sleep shirt, and slid beneath the covers. God, it was good to be home.

Rosalie had read somewhere that a person could get addicted to their lover's scent. Even after years apart, if they smelled that person, they would have an intense physical reaction. She'd thought it was a bunch of romantic bunk before now. Of course, she was never one to awaken on top of her lover, with her head pillowed on the soft spot below his collarbone and her nose pressed against his chest. God, he smelled good.

"I can hear you thinking."

"You cannot. I think silently." She didn't move. She listened to the drum of his heart and the rumble of his voice and basked in the warmth of his arms surrounding her.

"Yeah, but it sets off an electric current I can hear. Welcome home."

"Thanks. Your hands are on my ass."

"I know." He gave her butt a squeeze. "It seems to be a bone of contention with you."

"There's nothing bony about it. It's big."

He increased the pressure, kneading the tension out of her glutes and hamstrings. "You've got the perfect ass. An ass a man wants to grab and hold onto for a long time. I've dreamed about your ass."

"Oh, yeah." She meant it to sound sarcastic but missed the bar. Even to her ears, it sounded like an invitation to proceed, which worked, too. She wanted to moan; it felt so good. Who'd have thought your butt could be a direct route to the state of arousal?

"Why didn't you call? I'd have picked you up."

Rosalie smiled against his neck. "I wanted to surprise you." His pulse thrummed with increasing speed beneath her lips, keeping time with hers. She licked a path to his ear and whispered, "But you didn't wake up." Rosalie nipped his earlobe and then pulled it into her mouth to soothe it as she slid her leg the rest of the way over to straddle him.

"Oh, baby, I'm up, and I'm lovin' my surprise."

When he said he was up, he wasn't kidding. His erection pressed against the fabric of her boy shorts, and the pressure sent her blood from heated to boiling. Her belly grew warm and heavy. She was melting from the inside out.

Rosalie pushed herself up to look into his eyes and fell into the swirling vortex she saw there. Hot and possessive need, raw and raging, spinning with a spark of something she couldn't name. So intense, it scared her as much as it excited her.

Panic skittered through her. She had the urge to run, but as if he'd read her mind, Nick tightened his hold.

Her breath came out in a whoosh. She wasn't sure if it was because he'd flipped them over none too gently, or because she feared being branded. His body was hard on hers, pushing her into the mattress. His kiss was a staggering embodiment of heat, lust, impatience, and latent anger. Whether the anger was aimed at himself or at her, she was unsure.

His stubble-covered face scraped her skin, his tongue swept into her mouth, and his power surrounded her. Like a swimmer in a riptide, she sank deeper. Resistance was futile and unthinkable.

Rosalie's brain was on sensation overload. There was no time to think, only to respond. His hands were everywhere—in her hair, on her face, and on her breasts. His rough skin abraded her sensitive nipples before his mouth soothed, laved, and then bit, sending shooting currents of heat skittering. Fires ignited in all the expected places and a few new ones.

He pulled the sleep shirt over her head and slid himself down her body. She spread her legs to accommodate him, but instead of stopping, he continued lower. His fingers slid under the waistband of her boy shorts, and before she knew his intention, he'd ripped them off.

Who would have thought the sound of ripping fabric would be such a turn-on? Her toes curled, her breathing rasped, and her heart pounded so hard, it was as if she'd overdosed on adrenaline. She wondered if her heart would burst.

"Nick, please. . ."

His fingers ran around her navel in concentric circles that got larger with every pass. Her hips had a mind of their own, rising to meet his hand. Her legs spread, and her heels dug into the mattress. She'd never felt so needy. When he put his mouth on her, she jerked in his grasp. Her hands held his hair, bringing him closer. His tongue, his mouth, his teeth, the rasp of his beard against her thighs, and the vibration of his groan sent her flying. When his fingers joined his mouth, she soared, screamed, and pulled the sheets from the bed, all the while fighting for breath as his mouth and fingers continued drawing it out, taking her higher and higher, until she imploded.

Rosalie was vaguely aware of Nick holding her close, kissing her, and murmuring something as her mind reconfigured after the devastating orgasm. He was smiling down at her and brushing the hair from her forehead.

She wrapped leaden arms around his neck and kissed him.

Gone was the rage, replaced by quiet tenderness, soft slow strokes of his hands, and the feel of his full-body kiss. She explored the muscles of his back, his arms, his sides, and his hips.

Her hips rose, and his erection slid into her. Hard, big, smooth.

"Lee, stop." Nick groaned and rolled off her. His chest heaved like a bellows.

"What? What's the matter?"

"Condoms."

"Damn, I forgot."

"Yeah, for a second, I did, too." He reached across the bed, pulled open the bedside table drawer, and tossed some on the bed beside her. She sat, ripped one open with her teeth, and reached for him, but he grabbed her hands.

"No funny stuff. I'm not sure how much more I can take."

"I'll be good. I swear."

"Yeah, that's what I'm afraid of."

She kissed him as she rolled the condom down. The kiss spun out as he pressed her down and covered her with his body.

Nick rose over Rosalie. She saw emotion swirl in his storm cloud-colored eyes, and for an instant, she knew with absolute certainty they were in the same place. They were suspended somewhere between like and love. A place she'd never been before. A place she didn't want to be. She told herself it was only a dream. But as he settled between her legs, grabbed her hips, and slid into her, slow and long, she knew that was a lie. No dream could ever feel that real, that good, or that scary.

Nothing she'd ever experienced had prepared her for

Nick. His eyes locked on hers. He thrust up and back, moving at a slow, easy pace, maddeningly controlled. His pupils darkened, and his breathing turned into gasps, his muscles bunched, and his jaw clenched.

Rosalie wrapped her legs around his waist and arched her back, and his control snapped. He plunged and bucked, and she met him thrust for thrust. Her orgasm built. She didn't want this to end. He moved to the side, changing the angle, and kissed her as she came apart, swallowing her cries.

Nick never slowed his pace as her whole body spasmed. He rode out her climax and brought her up again. He moved so perceptively, he seemed to know her body better than she did.

His face shined with sweat, his back was slick, and his muscles quivered. Watching him drew her closer to the edge. As a shower of mini-explosions shot through her, she wrapped her arms around his neck, pulled him down, and kissed him, sucking his tongue into her mouth as he sunk his body into hers. He came with a roar. He stiffened, shuddered and then exploded. He collapsed, his face pressed against her neck, but his body still tensed and thrust twice more before he relaxed.

He was heavy, but a good heavy. She kissed his neck and felt him twitch inside her. He slid off, rolled over, and threw his arm across his eyes. Rosalie snuggled against him and rested her head on his chest, listening to his heartbeat slow.

Nick had finally made love to Rosalie. He'd thought about it so many times, had planned how he'd take it slow, savor it, and not get her too worked up. He knew she wasn't one hundred percent better, and there'd be plenty of time later for extreme sex. He'd wanted this first time to last for hours. What a joke. He'd been lucky if it had lasted ten minutes, and that estimate was generous. He hadn't felt like this . . . well, ever. He was legendary for his control, but that control disappeared whenever Rosalie was within touching distance. One look from Rosalie, and he was fighting to restrain himself. Even trying to distract himself by naming the players from the Islanders last Stanley Cup win in '83 was a bust. All he could recall was Ronald Melanson, the goalie.

Making love to Rosalie had nearly done him in. Nothing had ever felt more right, and at the same time, more wrong. Until that moment, he'd never considered keeping things from her a lie. He knew now he'd blown it. Like a line of dominoes, each one pushing the next over, the consequences of his actions tumbled before him, and he was helpless to stop them. He should have come clean about who he was, and what he was, and what he wanted. A woman had a right to know her lover's name, rap sheet, and occupation. But he was already inside her, and God help him, somehow, she had gotten inside him. It was too late to say, "Lee, sweetheart, I have something to tell you. . ."

Chapter 11

NICK LAY WITH HIS ARM COVERING HIS EYES, AND ROSALIE snuggled against his side. He'd just had the most amazing sex of his life, and all he felt was guilt.

He'd wanted to hide his eyes from the depth of her stare, afraid of what she might see—their connection and his guilty conscience. If she'd continued, he'd have spilled his guts and told her how much he'd missed her, how he hadn't been able to sleep without her, who he was, and how he'd been trying for the last five years to take over the company she was working to save, the job her promotion depended upon.

Good thing he hadn't said anything. If he had, it would have been a monumental mistake—one that would either have given her the wrong idea or sent her running from the room. He thought the latter was more likely. And it was against the rules she'd set, and he'd agreed to. He had no right to change them. Even if he'd been straight with her, even if he'd never told her any lies, he still couldn't have told her he liked sleeping with her and that he missed her when she was away.

"Nick? Are you asleep?"

"No. Sorry, I zoned out." He pulled her closer and kissed what he thought was her forehead, though it was hard to tell with her hair falling over her face.

"Is something wrong?"

Christ, could he be a bigger schmuck? He'd had amazing sex with her and afterward all he could do was lay there and stew. Way to go, Romeo.

He pasted on what he hoped was a convincing smile, rolled over on top of her and, without meeting her eyes, gave her a kiss that she returned with enthusiasm and heat. Oh, man, the woman could get him hard with one kiss.

"Yeah, something is definitely wrong. I have to go to work, and I'd much rather spend the day making love to you."

"Mmmm, that *would* be nice, since I'm supposed to be traveling today and not expected at the office until tomorrow."

"Oh, really? Well, let me see what I can do about getting out early. You go back to sleep and take advantage of your day off."

"Okay. I guess I am a little tired." She yawned and snuggled down into the soft feather pillows.

Nick got out of bed and told himself he had it good. A beautiful woman wanted his body on a temporary basis, just as he wanted hers. They liked each other, and they had a lot of laughs. He should enjoy being together until it stopped being fun, her brother visited and outed him, or she found out who he was, whichever came first. He'd been upfront with her—well, about everything except who he was and what he wanted, namely Premier Motors. And really, was keeping something from someone a lie? He heard Father Francis' voice in his head telling him that a lie of omission was every bit as serious as any other lie.

He got into a hot shower and wished Father Francis would keep his words of wisdom to himself. He'd been wishing the same thing since he was a kid, and it hadn't worked yet. Father Francis was overperceptive and always had reason to say, "I told you so."

Nick took care of the three Ss, dressed quietly, fed Dave, and fixed Rosalie coffee. It was the least he could do for skipping what should come after great sex—the cuddling, the recap, and the stuff women want to hear. He set the coffeemaker to brew in a few hours, pulled out a bag of bagels, and set it out for her, hoping she'd take the hint and eat.

"Aw, the hell with it." He wrote a few things down, called for Dave, and they left for work.

Coffee. There was nothing like the smell of coffee brewing to put a smile on Rosalie's face first thing in the morning. Well, except for sex. Exceptional sex.

She found her sleep shirt thrown over the treadmill with the remnants of her favorite boy shorts. She stretched, feeling pleasantly achy and more relaxed than she could ever remember. It sure beat the disappointment that had always followed a first time before—not that there had been many, but she was beginning to see a definite pattern evolving.

Making love to Nick was different. It required no learning—it came naturally. Even kissing was seamless. There were no bumping noses, no clinking teeth, and no cold fish lips. It was a choreographed dance of mouths and bodies, the likes of which she'd never experienced before. It made a girl wonder what else she'd been missing all these years.

In the bathroom, Rosalie was surprised to see guy stuff on the counter. At least, Nick was neat. There was no gross shaving cream mixed with hair in a ring around her sink and no toothpaste spit on the faucet. He didn't have much. His razor, deodorant, shaving cream, and after-shave were on the other side of the double sink from the tumble of baskets filled with her assorted accoutrements.

She didn't know why she hadn't noticed his things before. Maybe this was the first time she'd felt well enough to concentrate on anything more than breathing and moving at the same time. Plus, Nick was unobtrusive. In the bathroom at least . . . come to think of it, unobtrusive is not a word she'd use to describe Nick. His things were unobtrusive, but Nick? No way.

Rosalie took a sniff of his aftershave. Without Nick, the scent wasn't the same. Not that it was bad, but being on Nick made it so much better. His toothbrush hung next to hers. His tube of toothpaste, squeezed from the bottom, stood beside hers in the water glass.

She braced herself for the panic, but it didn't come. At least *all* his stuff wasn't there. She puttered around the bathroom for a while, put on one of those green-goop masks she never took the time to use, and while that set, went in search of coffee.

The scene that greeted her in the kitchen made her laugh. The mask was drying and felt tight; when she laughed, it cracked. She probably looked like *The Bride of Frankenstein.* A sticky note attached to a bag of bagels said "EAT," another note on the coffeemaker said "DRINK," and one attached to the phone said "CALL ME." The phone rang.

"I thought I was supposed to call you."

"Most children do call their mother, but no, not you. I have to find out that you have pneumonia from a *cafone* as he throws me out of my own daughter's apartment. He's an animal!"

Note to self: Always check caller ID before answering the phone. "Good morning, Ma. I'm fine. And how are you?"

"Who does he think he is, and what's all this about you having pneumonia? How dare you not tell me? I thought it was a cold. Then I called and called, and you didn't answer your phone. I kept getting the message machine that always hangs up on me before I finish. I had to call your office and hear that you were out of town from your girl."

"Ma, Gina is my assistant, not 'my girl.' I left town unexpectedly, and only got back late last night. I still haven't had my coffee. Is there something you need?"

"Rosalie, what are you doing with your life? You had a good man who wanted to take care of you, to marry you, to make babies with you. And what do you do? You break his heart and take up with a good-for-nothing *cafone*. Do you want I should die of a heart attack before I ever hold a grandchild?"

"Ma, isn't it a little early to start planning your heart attack? You're barely middle-aged."

"Your sainted grandmother, she died at sixty-two."

"Yeah, but she got hit by a bus. That doesn't count."

"Her vision went with age. She never saw it coming. God rest her soul."

"So make an eye doctor appointment. Think of it as preventive medicine. Besides, Annabelle is getting

married. You'll have grandbabies before you know it."
Then maybe you'll stop bothering me. "Why don't you
call Richie and ask him when he's going to start
producing the next generation of Ronaldis?"

"Men can have babies anytime. Look at Charlie
Chaplin. Women, the eggs get stale and then they don't
work so good."

Rosalie couldn't believe she was having this conversation. But then, most conversations she had with her
mother left her asking one question: Why?

"Ma, why don't you and Papa take a vacation? You
can go down to Florida and visit with Aunt Anna, go on
a cruise or something. Get out of the cold."

"What? So you can run your life into the ground? No,
I stay where I'm needed."

"Driving me crazy is not a necessity. It's an option."

"Besides, your father, he's working late a lot. He's got
a big project, and well, he's busy."

"What do you mean, he's busy? He does home
remodels. No one works late on a home remodel.
Owners don't want to listen to hammering while
they're eating, not to mention when their children are
sleeping. Are you sure you heard him right?" By now,
the mask was flaking off her face, and pieces were
floating around her like green snowflakes. Her skin felt
so tight, it hurt.

"Look, Ma, I've got to go."

"Okay, Rosalie. I'll see you on Sunday. Are you going
to bring the *cafone*?"

"His name is Nick, and he's not a *cafone*. But no, I'm
not bringing him."

She didn't argue, which was unlike her, and she let out a plaintive sigh.

"Watch yourself with this Nick character. He's a good-looking man, but he's got the devil in those eyes."

Her mother would be singing a different tune if she knew who the *cafone* with the devil in his eyes actually was. "Ma, we're only dating. It's nothing serious. I'll see you Sunday."

Rosalie went to chisel the mask off her face, hoping there would still be skin left when she finished, and couldn't help thinking about Nick. At first, Nick keeping his identity under wraps had seemed okay. She understood that he was protecting himself by not telling her who he was. He didn't know her then, but it wasn't as if he didn't know her now, after everything they'd been through. You can't spend twenty-four hours a day together for an entire week and not know each other. Rosalie was sleeping and having the most intense, incredible sex with a man who didn't trust her enough to tell her his real name.

Nick had meetings, signed contracts, and worked with his accounting department, the sales manager, the service manager, the parts manager, and the auto body manager. He felt as if he was hyperaware, hypersensitive, and moving at hypersonic speed.

Lois kept shooting him strange looks, but she hadn't said anything. What was there to say? She couldn't complain that he was too productive, when she'd been giving him a hard time about not working enough. He didn't know how he could have been expected to work while

Rosalie was sick. He hadn't been able to think of anything else. Now that she was back in town and healthy, who could blame him for trying to finish up early? All he could think of was going home and making love to her again.

Dave groaned and rolled over with all fours in the air. Nick had learned that was a sure sign Dave wanted a belly rub. He slipped off his loafer and rubbed Dave's stomach with his foot while he finished making notes about the year-end reports. As the numbers stood, this had been his best year and that was saying a lot. Previous year earnings had been up almost ten percent over the year before.

His phone vibrated. He checked the caller ID and recognized Rosalie's number. It was after eleven. At least she'd slept in.

"Hey, you're up."

"I am. Thanks for breakfast."

"You're welcome." He had to bite his tongue to keep from asking how she was feeling.

"My dog is missing. Do you happen to know where he is?"

"I brought him to work. He likes it here, and I didn't want you to have to get up and take him out."

"Are you going to bring him back, or is he to become a permanent resident of Romeo's, like my car?"

"Think of the hassle parking is when you don't have a driveway. The savings in tickets alone—"

"Fine, I give up. As long as it's safe, and I can get to it."

"It's safe, and I can guarantee you access twenty-four/seven."

"And Dave?"

"What can I say? He likes coming to work. I like

having him around, and Ty likes walking him. He's getting good exercise, and he loves Ty."

"Fine, but you'll bring him home later, right?"

"Of course. Besides, I have unfinished business with you. I'm going to be here another few hours, but I should be back by four. Are you up to taking a run to Chinatown? We can walk around and grab dinner. I promise to have you home and in bed early."

"You do, huh? Well, okay. I haven't been to Chinatown in eons. Maybe we can stop in Little Italy for dessert."

"Sounds good. We'll see you in a few hours."

Nick ended the call with a smile on his face and tackled the rest of the pile that filled his in-box.

"Lee? We're home."

"Hi, big boy! Come to Mama."

Nick let Dave off the leash, and the dog ran to Rosalie. If only she greeted him the same way. Nick waited for Dave to get his fill of kisses and "Did you miss me's?"

Rosalie gave him a shy smile. "Hi."

All he got was a "Hi?" What's wrong with this picture?

Nick shrugged out of his jacket, threw it on the couch, and moved within touching distance. "Try to contain your excitement. No need to gush all over me."

Rosalie held his gaze, tipping her head back until they were a hair's breadth away from touching. "I wouldn't want you to get a big head."

"No chance of that as long as I'm with you." Nick gave her a slow smile and cupped her cheek before kissing her, an easy brush of lips that had her reaching up and wrapping her arms around his neck. Never one to resist a willing woman, he pulled her closer and kissed her again and again. "Hi, yourself."

He stepped back before he forgot his plan to take her out. "Are you still up for Chinatown? If not, we can go someplace around here."

"Oh, no, you're not skipping out on our date."

Nick picked up her coat, held it out for her, and wrapped a colorful scarf around her neck. "Do you have your gloves?"

"Nick, one conversation with my mother a day is my limit. I've been a grown-up for a long time."

"Point taken. Are you feeling up to taking the subway in, or should we drive?"

"Subway works for me."

There was something about riding a subway with a guy that was so high school. The whole experience made Rosalie feel young and pretty. Especially when that guy was holding the overhead handle with one hand and had the other wrapped around her waist, her back pressed against his front. His bedroom voice whispered in her ear. His breath fanned her cheek, and naughty thoughts ran through her mind. She wished they were in an empty car instead of a standing room only tin can during rush hour.

Nick growled at a man who bumped into her when the train lurched forward. She had nothing to hold onto and didn't want to touch the guy in front of her, so she turned and held onto Nick.

Rosalie had never ridden the subway without holding onto either a pole or the overhead strap. No, that wasn't true. She had when she was a little kid, and she'd gone into the city with her father. He'd let her stand and hold onto his leg. She remembered feeling as if nothing bad could ever happen when she was with her dad. She was getting that same feeling with Nick.

All of a sudden, the train felt too crowded, the temperature too hot, and Nick's arm around her too stifling. At the next stop, when she tried to move away, he tightened his hold. She pushed his arm away, stepped back, and grabbed a pole as people shuffled out.

She didn't know if it was the crowd, the heat, or what. She did know she wanted off the train. Nick's stare burned through her. Intense. Demanding. She felt it as sure as the cool metal she was clinging to. She studied the signs above the windows and then glanced outside. Finally, Canal Street. She caught her breath and waited for the doors to open. Nick's hand slid across the nape of her neck. His thumb caressed her skin.

"You okay?"

She swallowed hard. "Fine."

And like that morning when she'd asked him the same question, they both knew the answer was a lie.

In temporary relationships, while you might be unable to hide that something was bothering you, you had the option to ignore it entirely. The lie was tantamount to an unanimous vote to adopt the "Don't ask, don't tell" policy.

If Nick had wanted to tell her why he was near panic that morning after they'd made love, she'd have been glad to listen. Rosalie asked once, but it would be against the rules to bring it up again. She knew he was fighting the urge to break the rule, but he knew damn well if he did, it would leave him open to having to answer her question from that morning.

Rosalie climbed the stairs to Canal Street, and the comforting smell of Chinatown wrapped around her like a Polar fleece blanket, soft and warm. The sound of a mother scolding her daughter in Chinese, kids playing stickball in an alley, and the squawk of live chickens floated over the hum of street traffic. She took a deep breath. The smell of Chinese food made her mouth water, and the cold air erased the last of her unease. Nick held her hand and stuffed their joined hands into the pocket of his jacket.

They walked down Canal toward Bowery, checking out the shops that carried everything from Chinese herbs and live chickens to knockoff purses and top-of-the-line electronics. When they came to Mulberry Street, Nick stopped.

"What do you feel like eating, Chinese or Italian?"

Now as an Italian, Rosalie ate Italian food all the time, but it was also her absolute favorite comfort food. She'd been in Michigan for over a week, and they wouldn't know good Italian food if it sat on a plate and served itself. She felt as if she was going through withdrawal.

"Italian."

Nick smiled. "A girl after my own heart. Come on, I know this great little place down off Prince Street. You'll love it."

He was right. The place was great. There were six or eight tables, and the owner sat at a corner table, drinking coffee and chatting with the clientele. A wall of old brick ran the length of the restaurant on one side, a golden painted plaster wall on the other. Ornate artwork hung everywhere, giving the room a relaxed, cluttered, homey look. Rosalie sank into the chair Nick held, took the menu from the waiter, and perused it while Nick ordered wine.

The food was exceptional, the atmosphere relaxed, and before she knew it, two hours had passed.

They were sipping their second cup of demitasse when she asked, "What exactly do you do with Dave when you're at work?"

Nick laughed and sat back in his chair, rocking on two legs. "Lois bought him a bed, so most of the day he sleeps. He's got Lois conned. She keeps dog biscuits in her drawer, and every once in awhile, he walks into her office and puts his head on her desk and does that eyebrow thing that turns her into putty."

"He can spot a sucker a mile away."

"Ty comes by after school and walks him, or maybe it's the other way around. They hang out at the park or run parts down to the body shop and pretty much wear each other out. By the time we get home, Dave is so tired, he eats, does his thing, and then crashes."

"Does his thing?"

"Yeah, you know, his thing. The thing the law requires us to pick up."

She laughed. "Oh, that thing."

Nick's eyes twinkled. He leaned forward to say something under his breath. When he did, the man two tables away came into view, kissing his girlfriend. They were so caught up in each other, they were oblivious to anyone else in the room.

Papa?

The shock must have shown on her face, because Nick turned to see what she was staring at.

"Lee? What's wrong?"

Jesus, she felt like Cher in a bad remake of *Moonstruck*. It was not a great feeling. Part of her wanted to flee out the back door and forget she'd ever seen him. Another part of her wanted to stop by their table, take the bottle of champagne he'd ordered, and crack him upside the head with it.

Rosalie knew her mother could be difficult. But she'd been there for him day in and day out, no matter how he'd treated her, no matter how he'd ignored her. She'd cooked for him, cleaned for him, and had done whatever he'd told her to do. She didn't deserve a lying, stinking, cheat for a husband.

"Nothing. Look, Nick, I see someone I know. Would you mind getting the bill? I'll go talk to them and meet you outside. Okay?"

She moved to stand, but Nick grabbed her hand, holding her in place.

"Oh, no, you don't. Who is that guy?"

"No one worth knowing. I'll see you outside." She pulled her hand away and picked up her purse. Nick was out of his chair and holding her coat for her before she could pick it up herself. She slid into it and started toward Pop, but Nick wrapped his arm around her, effectively shielding Pop from her, or her from Pop, she wasn't sure which.

"Nick, the bill."

"It's covered. Come on."

They walked right past her father and his girlfriend and out the door. A waiter ran after them.

"Sir, your change."

Nick waved him off. "Keep it."

Nick didn't ask questions, and he didn't expect explanations. He tucked her under his arm, walked down the street to a nearby pub, and led her to a booth.

"Here, sit. I'll be right back."

A minute later, he set a scotch down and squeezed into the booth beside her.

Johnny Walker Black rolled over her tongue and slid down her throat, warming her from within. "I've never drank Scotch with you. You guessed my drink?"

She kept her eyes on the glass. In the restaurant, she'd felt only anger. Well, anger and a good bit of righteous indignation. Now she felt sorrow and pity, but most of all, sadness.

"Hey, I'm not blind. You have two bottles in your kitchen. So, that man you'd stared at with murder in your eyes. He's your father?"

"Yeah, how'd you know?"

"It was the family resemblance, and the only thing I could come up with that would cause you to shoot daggers at a man his age."

"You know, growing up, I always resented my mother. I looked down on her. I never understood why she let him control her. He gave her an allowance like a child, told her what to wear and what to buy, and then at the end of the day, he'd ignore her while he sat by the TV, reading the paper and drinking his wine."

"Lee, you don't know what goes on in a marriage. . ."

"'Someday you'll fall in love and want to take care of your husband the same way,' she'd say. 'He'll take care of you, too. You'll see.' I saw, all right. A long time ago. But I never expected to see it in person."

Nick picked up his phone and looked at the screen. "Drink up. It's time to go home."

Rosalie finished her drink and followed him out of the bar. He opened the door to a waiting car.

"Lee, this is my friend, Jim. Jim, this is Lee. Jim's giving us a ride home."

She got in the Town Car and slid across the leather seat. She didn't care how they got home. All she knew was that she wanted to be there yesterday.

Staring out the window as they drove over the Manhattan Bridge and down Flatbush Avenue, she wondered why she was so upset. It wasn't as if she'd never known. She'd heard the loud fights and louder silences. She'd felt the tension that had loomed like a ghost—a presence without a name.

They pulled up in front of the apartment, and Nick opened the door. Cold wind blew into the warm interior and made her eyes water. The temperature was dropping, like her mood. Nick helped her out of the car.

"Come on, let's get inside."

He unlocked the security door and the apartment door while she took her coat off. Rosalie walked in, threw the coat on the couch, and collapsed. There, on the coffee table, was the family picture they'd taken at Christmas. They were all smiling—Rosalie, Richie, Annabelle, Mama, and Papa—the perfect, happy family. What a crock.

Without saying a word, Nick took Dave outside. When they returned, she was still staring at the picture. Nick took the frame out of her hand and put it on the table. "Not all men cheat."

"Really? Name one who doesn't."

"Vinny. He'd never cheat on Mona. They love each other. They're happy."

"Look at the photograph, Nick. Looks are deceiving. You said yourself, you never know what goes on in a marriage."

"No, you don't. But I know Mona."

"What? Mona wouldn't put up with a lying, cheating husband? What choice would she have? Does she know how to support herself and her kids? Her only option would be to leave her home with no money, no security, no skills—and do what? Work as a waitress in someone else's restaurant?"

She was on a roll now. "It's amazing how easy it is for men. They marry a sweet young thing. They say, 'Oh, no, you don't have to work, I'll take care of you.' There's Cinderella, thinking she married a prince, when the poor thing is oblivious that she's sold herself into slavery."

"Oh, come on, Lee. Look at you. You don't need a man to support you. If you got married, you'd never be in a position where you couldn't support yourself."

"Exactly."

"So why are you so against marriage?"

It sucked when someone argued logically. What could she say? He was right. She would never allow herself to be in a position that would make her dependent on anyone for anything.

He thought he'd won. He looked all smug and triumphant.

"So, Nick? Since you're such a fan of the institution, how come you're not married?"

"I'm not the one who has a problem."

"I don't have a problem."

"No, you're right. You don't have a problem," the sarcasm in his voice made her want to smack him. "You're living under the misconception that marriage means the loss of independence."

"Yeah, well, we all have our own little versions of reality, don't we? Most men think all women want someone who'll pay their bills, buy them jewelry, and give them a nice place to live while they spend their time shopping and getting their nails done. And in certain cases, they're right, but you can't paint all women with the same brush."

"What do you want, Lee?"

How had he done that? One minute they were arguing, and then he said five words. Five words, and she went from mad to aroused. It was as if he'd flipped a switch. And he knew it.

All of a sudden, he was standing close; so close, the heat radiating off him warmed her; so close, she saw the storm forming in his eyes; so close, she touched him.

One touch, and she stopped thinking and started feeling. The warmth of him heated her, the strength of him supported her. His mouth, his hands, and his body were her escape.

Nick couldn't figure out why he'd been arguing with her

about marriage, of all things, but at that moment, it had seemed important to inform her that all marriages didn't sentence women to lives of indentured servitude.

He'd almost come out and said that if he ever got married, which he wouldn't, he'd want an independent woman. One who was sure of herself and her place in the world. He'd want a woman who had a full life, independent of his. He didn't think marrying someone made a person responsible for their spouse's happiness, but should add to their spouse's happiness.

Take him, for instance. He'd been happy when he met Rosalie, but being with her made him happier. She added to his life, to his happiness, and he'd stay with her until she didn't.

She looked mad, sad, and so damn beautiful. He wanted to make her forget about her cheating father, to stop her from thinking about it, to shut down her mind and give her pleasure. There was only one way he knew how to do that.

He made love to her.

Nick stayed awake long after Rosalie had fallen asleep, listening to her breathing. He'd never really thought about his happiness before—well, not as it related to any one person. Rosalie made him happy, and he hoped he made her happy, but he wasn't sure. He didn't know what she wanted from him. Other women he'd dated had a shopping list of things that would make them happy, and weren't shy about sharing the information. Not Rosalie. She never said what she wanted. The one time he'd tried to help her out with her car, she'd refused. At first, he wondered if she was playing a game. Play hard to get and whet a guy's appetite. Now that he knew her, he knew better.

Nick had never lost the upper hand in a relationship. He'd never wondered if a woman wanted him. He'd never wanted a woman more than the woman had wanted him. Until Rosalie. It wasn't a comfortable situation, but it was improving. At least, she'd stopped asking him to leave.

Chapter 12

ROSALIE HAD JUST GOTTEN OUT OF A STATUS MEETING with her boss and didn't want to go back to the dealership. She was tired; she was cranky; she was starving; and she still had two hours and thirty-eight minutes until she could go home. Gina and the back-office gang had passed her around like a hot potato, each hoping they wouldn't be the one dealing with her when she finally blew. Who could blame them? It was as if she was looking down from above, watching herself get through the day and doing everything wrong, and she could do nothing to stop it.

What the hell was she going to do on Sunday? How was she going to sit across from her father and pretend she didn't know what was going on? She should have gone after him with the champagne bottle when she'd had the chance. If she had, this whole mess would be over and done with. Holding onto anger was so not her.

Rosalie stared at the couch. A nap was tempting. She wondered if anyone would notice. She could still be getting over the crud, or depression could have set in. Whatever the reason, the only thing that sounded the least bit appealing was sleep.

A knock snapped her out of her musing. The door opened a few inches. A hand stuck through the crack, waving a tissue.

"Is it safe to enter?"

No matter how bad things got, Gina could always make her smile. "Come on in."

"What has that prick done to put you in such a mood?" She heard Gina ask from beyond the door. The door swung open, and a huge flower arrangement with legs appeared. The legs Rosalie guessed were Gina's; the flower arrangement looked like something you'd see in a really expensive hotel. The kind of flowers that looked so perfect, you had to touch them to see if they were real. Of course, when you did, everyone knew you'd grown up in a house with fake flowers and plastic fruit.

"What does the card say?" It never occurred to her that Gina hadn't already read it.

"'Nick.' That's it. Do you believe the nerve of that man? You come to work in the mood from hell; you have everyone from the mailroom on up walking around with wastepaper baskets on their heads to protect them from the fallout; and the only clue to the puzzle that is Rosalie Ronaldi's bad mood is 'Nick'? What did he do? You can tell me. I'll call Sam, and he can go over there and rough him up."

"Sam's a cop. Cops don't rough people up."

"You're right, I'll have to handle it myself. I told you he was trouble."

"Down, girl. It's not Nick. Nick's been, well . . . you know."

"No, I don't know. I wish you'd tell me, so I can deal with it and go on with my terribly uneventful, boring, and tedious life."

"Gina, I'm sorry. I can't talk about this. It's family stuff and—"

"Did something happen to Richie?"

"No. He's fine. I'm sorry about today."

"That's okay. It was almost worth it to see the big boss confused. He had the nerve to ask me if women could have PMS twice in one month."

"He didn't!"

Gina set the flowers on the credenza and took a seat across from the desk. She kicked off her shoe and pulled her leg underneath her.

"Okay, if Nick The Prick didn't hurt you, then what happened?"

"Gina, would you please stop calling him that? He's been—"

"What?"

Damn, why had she opened her mouth? "Great."

"If I had to venture a guess, I'd say you must be pretty great, too, to rate those flowers. It looks like he signed the card himself."

She tossed the small envelope on Rosalie's desk.

"How can you tell?"

"Puleeze, do I have to teach you everything? Look. It's written with a masculine hand, and you know the only people who work in flower shops are women and gay men."

Rosalie opened the envelope, and sure enough, there was Nick's name scrawled in his writing. She opened the top drawer of her desk and tucked the envelope inside.

"Uh, oh. I knew it!"

Gina launched herself out of the chair and planted her hands on the desk.

"You're saving the card. You're falling for him."

"I am not. I save all my cards."

"Okay, then show me Joey's card from the last time he sent flowers. When was that? Oh, right, your birthday."

There wasn't one other card in the drawer. Damn.

"You can't, because you threw it in the trash along with the flowers a few days later. No great loss there. They were cheap flowers."

Rosalie tossed Nick's card into the trash. "There, are you happy now?"

Gina inspected her manicure. "Not especially. I'll leave you now, so you can drool over your flowers in private and dig the card out of the trash can. If you change your mind and want to talk about whatever it is that caused this lovely mood, you know where to reach me."

What could she say? If she thanked Gina, she'd be admitting that she'd drool over the flowers and dig the card out of the trash. Not that Gina ever doubted it, but still, a girl had her pride. "Thanks for the offer. If I need to talk to someone, you'll be the first person I call."

Gina rose, slipped on her stilettos, and sashayed through the door. "Have fun going through your trash."

The door closed on Rosalie's response, which was probably a good thing.

After waiting to see if Gina would come back to catch her in the act, Rosalie took her time drooling over the flowers. But not even flowers could cheer her. She should be handling this better. It wasn't as if she hadn't suspected her father was screwing around, but seeing proof was a different story.

Rosalie picked up the phone and dialed. "Hi, Ma."

"Rosalie? What's wrong?"

"Nothing. Why?"

"You never call unless something is wrong. Are you sure you're okay? You don't sound like yourself. Did that *cafone* do something to hurt you? I told you, he had the devil in his eyes. I don't know why you don't find a nice steady man like your father. You could call Joey—"

"Ma, stop. I'm not going to call Joey. I only want to find out how you and Papa are."

"Tell me what it is. You never call without a reason."

So much for subtlety. "Okay, Ma, you caught me. I've been thinking that you and Papa should take some time and do something together. I have a friend with a time-share in Florida. On Sanibel Island. She's offered it to me any time I want. Do you and Papa want to go down for a week or even a long weekend? I can arrange the whole thing. What do you think?"

"Rosalie, I told you, your father's working on a big project. He's not going to want to go out of town."

"Maybe he will, if you ask. When was the last time you two did anything remotely romantic? Why don't you go to Florida and invest time in your relationship?"

"Ever since you met that *cafone,* you're talking and acting nuts. You know, I saw on Oprah—"

"Ma, there's nothing wrong with me. I only wanted to do something nice for you and Papa. Talk to him. Maybe you can talk him into slowing down enough to go for a long weekend. Try. Okay?"

"Sure, okay. Rosalie? You sure you're all right? Is something wrong?"

"I'm feeling run down and tired. I guess it's harder to get over pneumonia than the usual crud. I'm not supposed to be working full days yet. Maybe it's catching up with me. I'm not sure I'll be up for Sunday. I'll call you."

"You want I should bring you some chicken soup?"

"No, Ma, but thanks. I have soup at home."

"Okay, cookie. I'll talk to you soon, then."

A tear escaped, and Rosalie brushed it away. Her mother hadn't called her cookie in years. "'Bye, Mama. I love you."

She hung up the phone and looked at all the work she'd been avoiding piled on the desk.

Her phone beeped. "Ro, a man is on line one. He said his name is Nick. Just Nick."

"Thanks, Gina." She took a deep breath. "Hello?"

"Hi. How's your day?"

"Not so good, but the flowers are beautiful. Thanks, Nick."

"I thought you might need some cheering up. Plus, it gives me an excuse to pick you up from work. I'm parked across the street, whenever you're ready."

"I was wondering how I was going to get the flowers home. It would have been a shame to leave them in the office, but I wasn't looking forward to the subway ride."

"I can come up and carry them for you."

"No. I mean, thanks, but that's not necessary. I'll be down in a little while, all right? Let me clean off my desk and check my schedule for Monday."

"Okay. I'll see you in a few."

She hung up the phone and beeped Gina. "Can you come in here for a minute? I need to go over next week's schedule before I leave."

"Sure thing, boss, but isn't it a little early?"

She strolled in with her notepad and a printout of the calendar.

"You have lunch with Mr. Lassiter, Sr., on Monday."

"Okay. E-mail him the report so I don't have to shock him into a three-martini lunch."

"Good idea. You have a meeting with Mr. Hunter, the senior loan officer, at three. His office. He's making you dance."

"I'll remember to wear my tap shoes. Is there anything I need to look over before Monday morning's staff meeting?"

"I have a file on my desk that will fill you in on everything you missed this last week."

"Fine. I'm going to take off. Have a good weekend."

Gina picked up the flowers. "I'll help you downstairs with these."

"No, thanks, I've got it." Rosalie threw the strap of her briefcase over her shoulder and took the flowers from Gina.

"You won't even let me catch a glimpse of your Romeo, will you?"

"Not if I can help it."

"What if I promise not to say anything?"

"As if that were possible. Come on, Gina. Just because you promised not to say anything about who he is doesn't mean you won't say something else equally horrible. You're passive-aggressive." She didn't mention the fact that sometimes Gina was not quite so passive.

Gina crossed her arms and pouted—a pout that would have had every male on the planet rushing to do her bidding.

"It's not going to work."

She humphed and blew her straight black bangs out of her eyes. "Fine. Here. Give me your briefcase, and I'll leave it at the security desk."

Nick had had a lunch meeting with his bankers in the financial district, so it wasn't a big deal to stop by and pick up Rosalie. Of course, he had to go all the way uptown to the New York Athletic Club on Central Park South to change clothes. Okay, so he was pathetic; it wasn't as if he didn't know he was pathetic.

He couldn't stop thinking about how she'd looked the night before when she caught her father with his mistress. She'd been an amazing mixture of a scared little girl and a pissed off, indignant woman. For a minute, he'd been afraid she'd go after her father, which would have been very bad on several levels. It would have been the last time he'd have been able to take her to his favorite restaurant in Nolita, plus it would have cost him a fortune to get her out of jail and defend her for murder. After he'd shuffled her out of the restaurant, he'd thought for sure he was in for an evening of weeping. He'd been wrong again. Rosalie hadn't shed one tear. After the blood returned to her face, she'd pulled herself together, and though she'd been quiet, she'd never shown weakness. It was scary. She had a way of putting up an impenetrable wall that, even when they'd made love, he hadn't been able to breach. It bothered him. Not that making love to her was a hardship, but it would be nice to feel as if it meant something to her other than a physical release.

Nick scrubbed his hands over his face and laughed out loud. He felt like an ass. He had exactly what he wanted. He'd finally found someone who wasn't falling all over herself to trick him into marriage, and it was denting his ego. Ain't that a kick in the pants? Damn, he'd thought he knew himself, then one woman walked into his life and turned everything upside down.

A flash of red caught his eye. She'd stepped out of the revolving door, and all he could see were her legs. The wind had whipped down the street and blown open her long, red cashmere coat. He couldn't complain about the view but wondered what she was thinking. She was getting over pneumonia, and she didn't have the sense to button her damn coat? Was she asking for a relapse? The flowers covered the rest of her. Maybe he had overdone the flowers. He'd never even asked the florist the price. Damn, he had to remember he was supposedly living on a service manager's salary. He was sure a greenhouse full of flowers would set a service manager back a year's poker money.

She rested the vase on her hip to scan the street, and when she saw him leaning against the car, a smile took shape before she consciously shut it down. It wasn't much, but it was something. Maybe she wasn't as immune to him as she acted.

Nick nodded at her and jaywalked through the throng of cabs waiting at the light.

"Here, let me take those." Nick took the flowers from her with one hand and pulled her in close for a kiss. "Button up. It's cold as hell out here."

Rosalie raised an eyebrow but said nothing. She made fast work of the buttons while groaning her displeasure. He figured he'd gotten off easy.

"I'll be right back. I need to run to the security desk for my briefcase."

"Okay. I'll put these in the car."

He was contemplating where to put the arrangement when she came up behind him and wrapped her arms around his waist.

"How are you going to get that monstrosity in there?"

"I'm going to have to push your seat forward as far as it'll go and set them on the floor in the back."

"You know, everyone I saw while I was carrying these down from my office looked at me with such pity. A couple of them even asked if you had done something awful and were groveling."

Nick handed her the flowers and bent down to move the seat. He looked up and smiled. "Yeah? What did you say?"

"I told them no. Now they all think you're compensating for something."

He shook his head, took the flowers from her, and wedged them into the backseat. "Great."

She reached out and squeezed his shoulder before she gave him a nudge. "Oh, come on, Nick. You have to admit, the flowers are a little over the top."

He slid the seat as far back as he could without breaking the vase and stood, pulling her into his arms. "All right. I went a little overboard, but it was worth it. You look happy."

"I don't know about happy, but I did have a good laugh."

Nick helped her into the car. He got a bonus on the flowers as she tried to pull her skirt down in the legroomless front seat. A good deed rewarded.

He climbed in beside her and laughed. "You know,

the show I'm getting here," his hand traced the hem of her skirt, which barely reached the top of her thigh-high stockings, "was worth every penny those flowers set me back. You have the most amazing legs."

"I don't know about amazing, but they're long. And right now, they're practically wrapped around my neck, so would you mind driving?"

"You expect me to be able to drive after putting that image in my head?"

Rosalie had to hand it to the man; he sure knew how to make a girl feel wanted. He had no problem driving. He drove the car and drove her crazy at the same time. Whenever his hand wasn't on the gearshift, it was on her thigh, tracing slow and lazy circles above her stocking but never moving closer to the one place she ached for him to touch. By the time they pulled up in front of her brownstone, she was ready for bed, but the last thing on her mind was sleep. All thoughts of her crazy family, her bad day, and her worse mood had slipped into oblivion.

Nick killed the engine and reached across her to get her door. They were face-to-face, and she fought the urge to nuzzle his neck.

Nick stilled for a moment before he continued. "I'll get the flowers. I need them to hide behind, if you get my drift. Bending down to get them might be a problem, though."

"Oh. . ." She reached over and ran her hand down the length of his fly. "Oh, my." It hadn't occurred to her that he might have been . . . uncomfortable, too.

"What? You think I can spend twenty minutes with you in a car in your sexy stockings and fuck-me shoes,

with my hand up your skirt, and not have a hard-on?
Sweetheart, I can barely be in the same room with you
and not react like a kid at his first porn flick."

She opened the door, hoping the cool air would dissi-
pate the heat building up in the car. "I'll get the flowers.
You can use my briefcase." She cleared her throat, trying
to rid her voice of its sudden huskiness. "I hope we don't
run into Henry and Wayne."

Nick pressed closer, and the timbre of his voice made
it clear the cool air wasn't doing the job. "If we do,
they'll know I'm not compensating for anything."

There was no chance of that. They spent the evening
making love. Nick wasn't one of those once-a-day-if-
you're-lucky lovers. No, he was the good-for-two-in-a-
row, every-few-hours kind of lover she'd only read about
in romance novels. Nick proved those guys did exist.
Thank God and Nora Roberts.

Saturday, they only ventured out once for food—if
you called Bosco Chocolate Syrup food. Nick had the
kitchen well stocked with all the other essentials—ice
cream, strawberries, and whipped cream. They'd had
Bosco but had run out. Who knew she had such a taste
for chocolate—especially after she learned it wasn't just
for ice cream any more?

By Sunday morning, Rosalie had exhausted the
poor guy into what looked like a coma. She and Dave
took pity on him and went without him on their weekly
excursion to the dog park and then to Fiorentino's
Italian-Jewish deli and bakery. A perfect combination.
Where else could you buy cannolis and knishes? She
bought bagels, lox, and cream cheese with chives, plus

dessert to go with a box of coffee, and headed home with plans to kiss Nick awake.

Nick rolled over and groaned at the sunlight streaming through the windows. His stomach muscles were sore. He'd never had enough sex to wear him out—until now. Either he was getting out of shape, or he'd never stayed long enough for round two. Or three. Or four. Damn. If he'd known that spending the weekend with a woman would be this good, he would have done it a while ago. But he'd never spent time with a woman who didn't get on his nerves before. Rosalie had her idiosyncrasies, an aversion to all things closet-related being at the top of the list, but they were more cute than annoying.

The bed dipped. He reached behind him and wrapped his arm around her waist. Oh, man. The waist wasn't Rosalie's. It was smaller and bonier. He let go, rolled over while grabbing the sheet that rode low on his hips, and sat up in a split second.

"Who the hell are you?"

The black-haired, dark-eyed pixie looked him over. Nick fought the urge to pull the sheet up higher.

"So, you're Nick, just Nick, eh?"

"Yes. And you are?"

"Gina."

She stuck her delicate, manicured hand out to shake his, forcing Nick to switch the hand that held the sheet around him before shaking. If she hadn't looked so serious, he would have laughed at the absurdity of the situation.

She wore a tight, long-sleeved T-shirt tucked into spray-painted-on jeans, with a big belt that accentuated her small waist and anything but small bust. Damn, a few weeks ago, waking up to a woman who looked like Gina would have been a dream come true. Now, it was a nightmare.

Nick cleared his throat. "Do I know you?"

"No. But I know all about you, Nick, just Nick, so I'm not going to waste time with the niceties."

"I think that's pretty clear, considering the way you barged in here."

Gina rolled her eyes heavenward, as if she were praying for patience. "Whatever. Rosalie is entirely too nice and trusting, and you've got her eating out of your hand. I'm looking out for her, and I thought you should know I'm keeping my eye on you. You hurt her, and I'll cut your privates off with rusty nail clippers. That way it's slow, painful, and guaranteed to cause lockjaw. Any questions?"

"Yes. Would you mind waiting to threaten me until I'm dressed?"

"No, I don't mind." Gina sat and waited.

"Are you going to watch?"

"As if you have anything I haven't seen before." She turned her back and crossed her arms while she tapped the toe of an extremely dangerous-looking black boot with a heel thin enough to double as a weapon.

"Where's Lee?"

"She took Dave to the dog park. They'll be at least a half hour. They left a few minutes ago."

"She knew you were here?" Nick asked.

"Of course not. I waited for her to leave. She'd kill me if she knew I came to meet you."

"You mean you came to threaten me."

"Exactly. Are you going to get dressed, or are you going to sit there looking pretty? I need a cup of coffee."

"I do not look pretty. And the last thing I want is to be in bed, naked, with you. I'll get dressed as soon as you leave the room. You're welcome to help yourself to coffee. I'm sure you can figure out where everything is, since you figured out how to get in here."

"That was easy enough. I buzzed Henry and Wayne. They let me in. Rosalie never locks her door when she's not going out for long."

Gina turned and glared at him. "I'll go make coffee, but only because I'm dying for a cup. I don't like you. Am I making myself clear?"

"Crystal. I don't like you, either."

She nodded and left the bedroom, shutting the door behind her.

Nick got up, threw on sweats and a T-shirt, brushed his teeth, and was out before the coffee was ready. He hoped she made it strong. He was going to need a lot of caffeine to take on this pint-sized bulldog.

Nick reminded himself that this was his turf. He was going to make sure Gina knew it. He grabbed two mugs out of the cabinet and peered into the fridge. "Do you take milk or half-and-half?

"Black."

"Sugar?"

"No."

He poured coffee and set a mug in front of her at the breakfast bar.

"So, Gina. You work for Lee."

"I work with Rosalie."

Nick took a sip of coffee and leaned against the counter. "Yeah, right." He meant for that to zing her. It didn't. "You don't need to worry about Lee. We're playing by her rules, not mine."

"Rosalie never played with fire before, rules or no rules. I don't want her getting burned."

"She's a big girl. She can take care of herself. Besides, I'd never hurt her."

Gina gave him a long, long, long look—one that he was sure would make a weaker man squirm like a worm on the end of a hook. He stood stock-still. Damn, for a tiny thing, she sure packed a punch. Nick couldn't afford to lose, so he stared her down, using his height advantage, though truth be told, it didn't seem to have any effect on her.

He couldn't help but admire her. It took balls of steel to walk in on a sleeping, naked man twice her size and threaten him. Especially a man she'd never met before.

She was all that and looked as dangerous as a crate of dynamite near a bonfire.

Gina broke eye contact and checked her watch. "Okay, as long as we understand each other, I'll go. Remember what I said about rusty nail clippers."

"How could I forget?"

"I trust we'll keep this little tête-à-tête between us?"

"Fine."

"I still don't like you."

Nick smiled for the first time since he saw her. He knew she was kidding. Not about castration—she was dead serious about that—but she was kidding about not liking him. It would take a bigger woman than her to resist a Romeo. Hell, the only woman who had was Rosalie. For kicks, Nick winked at her to piss her off. "I still don't like you, either."

Gina laughed. "Behave, Nick, just Nick. I would really hate to have to hurt you." She picked up a black leather trench coat and slid into it.

"I'd tell you to behave," Nick smiled, "but I think there's little chance of that."

"You're pretty perceptive. It's been . . . interesting."

She gave him a quick salute and walked out as silently as she'd entered.

Chapter 13

ROSALIE HAD MISSED GINA'S VISIT BY MOMENTS. NICK didn't know if he was pleased that she hadn't caught Gina or not. He hated keeping things from her, but at this point, what difference did one more little lie of omission make?

Rosalie closed the door behind her, and Dave ran to him, dragging his leash. Nick bent down to unhook it and was putting it away when he caught Rosalie smiling at him. It wasn't the usual pasted-on smile. She smiled her genuine smile, the one that slipped out when she didn't have her guard up. The one that made him feel— what? Good? Yeah, the one that made him feel good.

He found himself smiling back. He hoped he didn't look as idiotic as he felt, standing there with a shit-eating grin on his face, but how could he help it? She looked, well . . . adorable. He'd be happy to spend the day doing nothing but looking at her. Her cheeks and nose were pink from the cold, and her hair was windblown. She was wearing his old bomber jacket, which was huge on her, and holding an armload of bags and boxes.

"I hope you didn't make breakfast. I stopped at Fiorentino's. Mrs. F. must have been in the back. I think we're safe from my mother's wrath."

She dumped the bags on the table, spun around, and ran into Nick. He caught her arms to steady her.

She blew the bangs out of her eyes and tipped her head back to meet his gaze. "You always do that to me."

"I know." He kissed her, warming her lips under his. "How was your walk?"

Rosalie unzipped her coat and threw it on the back of the chair. "Good. We ran into Tommy and Jasmine. Have you met them yet? Dave has a crush on Jasmine, a cute little basset. It's hysterical."

Nick took the coat and hung it in the closet while he listened.

"She has him totally wrapped. He drools all over her, literally. We had to towel her off. It was gross." She pulled out plates and a cup, poured herself coffee from the insulated box, and topped his off. After adding creamer to both cups, she set them on the table. "I think Jasmine watches for us out their front window. We take them to the dog park and let them run around together."

Nick took juice from the fridge, got glasses, and handed her one. Rosalie dug through the bags, bit into the first chocolate-covered doughnut she found, and continued talking with a full mouth. "Do you want a bagel and lox, or pastry?"

He had to laugh. She had chocolate all over her mouth. Hell, she even had a spot on her nose. He handed her a napkin. "Bagel first, dessert later."

"Spoilsport. What do you have planned today?"

"I was going to see if Dave might want to try running again."

Dave stretched out under the table, rolled over, and groaned.

Rosalie laughed. "I wouldn't count on it."

"It looks as if I'll have to go it alone then."

"I think he's more the walking type. The only time he runs is when there's food involved."

"Tell me about it." Nick went back into the kitchen and got silverware. "The Islanders are playing Montreal. It's a home game. I thought we could watch it. How about you? Any plans?"

"I'm supposed to go to my parents' for supper. You know, the weekly torture. I could get out of it."

"Is that what you want?" Nick passed her a plate, sat down, and cut his bagel.

"I don't know. It's not like I'm going to be able to avoid my father forever. I might as well face him sooner rather than later. Things like this tend to get more and more ominous the longer they're avoided."

"It sounds as if you're trying to talk yourself into going."

"I guess I am. I don't know how I'm going to sit across from him and act as if I hadn't caught him playing tonsil hockey with the *puttana.*"

"Do you want me to go with you?" Nick heard himself ask the question, but it took a second to register that he actually had. The look on Rosalie's face took away any doubt. She couldn't have been any more shocked than he was.

"What, are you nuts? No, I don't want you to come with me! That's all I need. They'd take one look at you, and my dad's screwing around would be the least of my worries."

Nick called himself every name in the book. He should have been relieved that he didn't have to do the "meet the parents" thing. But did the thought of him meeting her family have to horrify her so? It wasn't as if he hadn't already met her mother, though he'd been angry, and he was sure he hadn't shown her his best side. Hell, who was he kidding? He'd thrown her out of the apartment.

Rosalie went on fixing her bagel as if she hadn't insulted him. He watched as her comment registered, and she thought about what she'd said. She looked up from her plate guilty as hell.

"Gosh, Nick, I didn't mean it the way it sounded. It's my family, they're . . . well, if you don't want them to start planning a wedding, you'll stay clear. Besides, they already think I'm some kind of *puttana*. God, it's like a cosmic joke, isn't it? Bringing you home with me will only make matters worse."

"Stop already. You're right. I don't know what I was thinking." He got up and drained his juice in one gulp. "I'm going for a run."

He went into the bedroom to put on his socks. Ignoring her, he passed the table on his way to the door and stepped into his running shoes. He bent down to tie them.

Rosalie came up behind him and touched his shoulder. "Nick?"

He stood and took his Polar fleece jacket off the hook next to Dave's leash. "It's fine, Lee. Forget about it. I'll be back in awhile."

Running had always been like therapy for Nick. An escape. Only now, he didn't do it to escape arrest; he escaped his world and all its problems. He concentrated on breathing, the slap of his shoes against the pavement, and the feeling of freedom when he hit the zone.

Somehow, running had a way of making things clearer. After many a run, he'd found that somewhere beneath all the everyday problems and trials that kept him occupied, he'd already made the important decision he'd been mulling over. He just hadn't recognized it. Today was different. The only thing he saw was how close he'd come to getting his ass caught in the string of lies he'd so neatly woven. The string was beginning to resemble a noose.

If Rosalie had taken him up on his offer, what was the chance that someone wouldn't have recognized him? They'd either see him as Rich's ex-con friend who, in their eyes, led their son down the path to military school. Or they'd recognize him as Dominick Romeo of Romeo's Auto Mall, et al. Add the name of a car company to the end of Romeo's, and it would name at least one of his dealerships.

Hell, he was lucky Gina hadn't recognized him. Of course, most people were used to seeing him in a power suit, not bare-assed naked and covered only by a thin sheet.

He considered coming clean and telling Rosalie the truth about everything. His history with her brother, and his interest in taking over Premier Motors. But what good would it do—other than to clear his guilty conscience? Rosalie would find out the truth in her own time and then it would be over. She'd kick him to the curb, and who could blame her? He'd do the same if he were in her shoes.

Nick jogged in place as he waited for a break in traffic. He ran across the street, but his thoughts followed him.

It wasn't as if he wanted to be with Rosalie forever,

but taking his best guess as to when the noose would tighten, he wouldn't have the time he needed. He wanted more. He couldn't afford to do anything that might risk what little time he had left.

No matter how he envisioned the end of this thing with Rosalie, he was always the one who got screwed—the one who hadn't had enough. Enough what? Enough time? Enough fun? Aw, hell, enough of Rosalie? The only variable was when he'd get screwed. Not if, or how, but when.

He picked up his pace as he hit the park. There was nothing to stop him—no streetlights or old ladies pulling their grocery carts, no mothers with kids in strollers or women with little yappy dogs. No one he couldn't run around.

He'd told Gina he wouldn't hurt Rosalie. Another lie. He'd gladly deal with Gina and her rusty nail clippers to avoid the look of betrayal he knew he'd eventually see on Rosalie's face. He imagined her expression wouldn't be much different than the one he'd seen the other night when she'd caught her father cheating on her mother. Christ, how did he ever get to be such a total asshole?

"Dominick!"

Nick heard his name and slowed when he spotted his mother and grandmother walking toward him on the path. Nick bent over and rested with his hands on his knees, cooling down and waiting for them. He pulled his T-shirt from beneath his Polar fleece jacket and wiped his face with it. So much for his run.

"Mama, Nana, hi." He bent down for his kiss. His mother first and then Nana, who kissed both cheeks and gave him a pat for good measure. At least she'd

given up pinching. Nick's grandmother—all five foot,
two inches and a hundred and nineteen pounds of
her—was tough as nails. Back when he was a kid and
Park Slope was one of the toughest neighborhoods in
New York, he'd seen her take down men three times
her size with just a look. She bragged about her weight
as often as possible—it was the same her whole adult
life, except for when she was pregnant—and the fact
she still had great legs—something she mentioned
more often than any grandson wanted to hear. Nick
might not have liked it, but he had to admit that for a
woman pushing eighty, she looked damn good. She
took great pride in the fact that she still caught old
men's eyes. Nick even heard that Father Francis had
been caught checking out his grandmother, which was
yet another thing he could have lived a long and happy
life without knowing. Nick shook his head. He didn't
have a large family, but the few family members he had
were colorful.

She held his face close to hers. "What? You forget
how to shave? And your hair, it's too long."

"Nana, I'll shave and shower after I get home."

"And you'll go to the barbershop Monday?"

"Soon. I promise."

Short hair was a big thing for his grandmother; Nick's
grandfather had been a barber. There were pictures of a
kind, white-haired man giving Nick his first haircut, and
every one after that until the day his grandfather died.
Nick had memories of going to the barbershop his grandfather owned with Uncle Giovanni and watching his
grandfather cut hair, shave men with straight-blade

razors, and sing along with the opera playing on an old plastic art deco radio.

Nana let go of his face, and with a frown on hers, crossed herself and patted the black shawl she still wore bobby pinned to her head. "You going to church?"

Nick's mother gave him a thorough once over before taking her mother's arm. "Not today, Mama. Remember, I told you that Nick is taking care of a sick friend? That's why he couldn't take you to church this morning."

Nick kicked the dirt. Another lie. If his mother knew how he was taking care of Rosalie, she wouldn't be quite so understanding. He wondered if his mother knew more than she was letting on. She inexplicably knew more than she should be capable of finding out, something that wigged him out on a regular basis.

Even after working two or three jobs at a time for most of her life, she was still a beautiful woman. When she was younger, she was a dead ringer for Gina Lollobrigida, which was why Nick's father married her. Even now, she was stunning—her dark brunette hair had been replaced by silver, but that did nothing to dim her beauty. Nick knew that every strand of silver was due to him. Before he'd gotten into trouble, her hair was the deepest brunette with just a touch of gray. When he came out of Juvie, her hair was pure silver; there wasn't a strand of brown to be found. Nick didn't think it was a coincidence. He'd never forget the hell he put her through when he was a kid, and all she'd done to try to get him out of the trouble he'd run headlong toward. Nick owed her the world and now he was lying to her.

"Is your girlfriend feeling better?"

"Yeah, Mama. She is. Thanks for asking."

"Good, so you'll bring her over to the house for dinner then."

"Mama, we're friends. We don't take each other to meet our family . . . we're not serious."

His mother raised her eyebrow but didn't say what she was thinking. The lecture he had coming to him was written all over her face.

"It's complicated, Mama."

"Fine, you come over and tell me all about it. It's been too long since we had a talk. Now that your *friend* is feeling better, you having a meal with your family won't be a problem, will it?"

"No, it's no problem." Nick took his grandmother's arm. "Come on, it's getting cold. Let me walk you home."

Nick walked, holding his grandmother's arm and slowing his steps to match hers, and caught his mother's eye over his grandmother's head.

"Mona tells me your girlfriend Rosalie was very nice when you brought her to the restaurant."

"Of course, Lee's nice. Why would I go out with a girl who's not nice?"

"I don't know, Dominick. It seems to me you've gone out with a lot of girls who weren't nice. Mona said your Rosalie is different from the rest."

"Yeah, she's different, all right."

Nick was never so happy in his life to see the brownstone he'd bought for his mother and grandmother. He took his mother's key, unlocked the door, and helped his grandmother in. The smell he'd always considered the smell of home assaulted his senses, and he waited for that feeling of comfort and belonging to waft over him. It didn't. All it did was make him miss Rosalie's place. The sound of Dave running up to greet him, the smile Rosalie shot him before she caught herself, the smell of Rosalie that permeated everything in the apartment.

"'Bye, Mama." He kissed his mother and gave her a hug. "I'll call you soon about dinner." Nick turned to his grandmother. "'Bye, Nana. Save me some of whatever it is you got in the oven."

"Ricotta pie. You come back and have some with me tomorrow, no?"

"I'll try, Nana. *Ti amo*." Nick kissed her cheek, winked at his mother, and took off for home. Running the whole way.

How far can one man run? It'd been an hour, and Nick still wasn't back. Why had she opened her big fat mouth? Damn, it wasn't that she didn't appreciate his offer, but what the hell was he thinking? Did he think no one would recognize him? He was a freaking genius when it came to business, but as a liar, he sucked. Being a lousy liar wasn't a bad thing, but it sure made keeping him thinking his little secret was still a secret a pain in the ass. Why did she bother? Maybe she should bring him home and let Annabelle squeal with delight. Annabelle was, Rosalie was sure, the founding member of the Dominick Romeo Fan Club.

Rosalie knew she shouldn't be the one feeling guilty; she hadn't meant to hurt him. He'd made the mess to begin with. If he'd only come clean. . .

The door swung open, and Nick walked in. She

wasn't even going to think about the feeling of utter relief that washed over her when she saw him. She also chose to ignore the urge to run to him and wrap her arms around his unbelievably sexy, albeit sweaty, body. He pulled off the Polar fleece jacket, revealing a wet T-shirt clinging to his chest. To think she used to drool over the pond scene in *Pride & Prejudice*. Even Colin Firth, with his soulful eyes, sexy voice, and to die for English accent, had nothing on a sweaty Nick.

He walked into the kitchen and pulled a water out of the fridge. He held her gaze but said nothing as he twisted the cap off, and without breaking eye contact, drank the whole thing. He tossed the bottle in the recycling bin, walked toward her, and lifted her off her feet.

She found herself clinging to him as he walked backward to the bathroom, all the while kissing her in a way that made all thought impossible. Well, not all thought, just all thought that wasn't explicitly sexual.

"Nick, I need my car." Rosalie checked her watch. Shit, she was already late.

Nick rolled over in bed looking so damn appealing, she was tempted to call her mother and tell her she'd had a relapse.

"No, you don't. Take mine."

"I can't take yours."

"Why not? Don't you know how to drive a stick?"

"I know how to drive a stick; that's not the issue. The problem is that it's your car."

"Yeah, I think we've established that."

"What if you need it?"

"Why would I need it? I'm not going anywhere."

"You're not?"

"Not unless you want me to."

Oh, nō, she wasn't going to touch that one with a hockey stick and protective gear.

She fluffed her wet hair. If she were any later, she would risk a slew of questions. She had to leave right that minute.

"Where are your keys?"

"In my jacket pocket—the one you had on this morning. It's in the closet."

"I didn't put it in the closet."

"I know." He climbed out of bed and wrapped his arms around her, pulling her into a tight hug. "Drive safe. Call me if you have any problems or need anything."

"Right. Um, okay. 'Bye." She didn't know what came over her, but she kissed him good-bye, an honest to goodness "See you later, honey" kiss. Now, a different person would be fine with that, but neither of them were into domestic scenes. Still, it wasn't as if he hadn't kissed her, too.

Focusing on the kiss the whole way to her parents' house helped her keep from overanalyzing the symbolism of driving his car. She knew he probably had a lot of cars, literally parking lots full, but still, she'd never dated a guy who let her drive his car.

She parked on the street two houses down from her parents' and took a deep breath before climbing the steps. The door opened before she hit the top.

"Where did you get that car? It's hot. Is it the rebound guy's car?"

"Hi, Annabelle. I'm fine. How are you?"

"You know, busy. I'm making wedding plans and trying to spend time with Johnny, but he's been working a lot. This is his busy season."

Rosalie pictured Johnny rubbing his hands together with one of his smarmy grins on his face. It was not pretty. The man was so pale that he looked like a corpse. Actually, now that she thought about it, he kind of looked like a cross between Count Dracula and Danny Aiello— only heavier and with bad teeth. "I didn't realize morticians had busy seasons."

"Oh, yeah. I swear, they practically pray for a flu epidemic. It's kinda sick when you think about it."

"Now there's an understatement."

"Anyway, he says he'll get them all in the end. Everybody dies."

"And on that happy note, where are Mama and Papa?"

Rosalie set her purse on the table by the door and checked out the hair situation, hoping it had dried on the way over. She'd had the heat blasting. Damn! She looked like the recipient of a botched home permanent or a poodle way overdo for a trip to the groomer. She had a feeling the day would head downhill from there, which was a scary thought.

"Ma and Aunt Rose are in the kitchen. Johnny and Papa are watching TV."

"Hockey?" She hung her coat on the hall tree.

"No, synchronized swimming. Of course, hockey. They're watching the pregame stuff; you know, the male version of *Oprah*."

They walked through the empty living room and into the dining room. Rosalie gave herself a mental head slap. She should have asked Nick to tape the game for her. "Yeah, I like the part where Dr. Phil discusses their feelings about the fight in last night's game. Stay tuned for a very special Sports Talk—The Cause of Unnecessary Roughness."

They passed the dining table. There was no food out, but at least it was set.

"Rosalie, is that you?" She heard her mother call from the kitchen.

"Yeah, Ma," she answered and whispered to Annabelle, "Are you helping Mama?"

"As little as possible. She's in a mood."

"There seems to be a lot of that going around."

"She and Aunt Rose have their heads together, and you know what a nightmare it is when the two of them are in cahoots."

"Yeah, if only they'd use all that power for good instead of evil."

Her mother yelled again. "Rosalie? Come in here. What? I have to do everything myself? I didn't spend eighteen years teaching you to run a house for no reason." She rushed into the dining room, set the antipasti down, wiped her hands on her apron, and gave Rosalie the once-over. "You've still got bags under your eyes. You need more sleep. And for Pete's sake, do something with that mop."

"What does it matter what my hair looks like?"

"What? You need a special occasion to look presentable?"

Rosalie had a bad feeling. Whenever her mother brought up her appearance, there was a reason—one having to do with her lack of a wedding date, a marriage partner, or interest in either. "Ma? What did you do?"

"Nothing. I did nothing."

"You tell me what you did, or I'm leaving right now."

Mama turned and went back into the kitchen. Rosalie followed, with Annabelle on her heels. God forbid Annabelle should miss the show.

Mama checked the roast in the oven. "Come. Time to eat. If we don't sit down, my roast is going to be overcooked."

"I'm not moving until you tell me what is going on."

Mama did the breast-pounding thing again and said a prayer to the Virgin Mother under her breath. Aunt Rose arrived carrying an empty beer bottle. She must have been upstairs in the den telling Papa and Johnny to come down. She looked at Mama, then at Rosalie. "What happened? Someone die?"

Annabelle got a wineglass, filled it, and leaned against the counter. "Not yet, but there's still time. Mama was just going to tell Rosalie that Joey Manetti is coming to dinner."

Before Rosalie could lay into Mama, Papa came in. "What's going on here? Rose told me supper's ready. There's no food on the table. What am I to eat? Plastic?"

Annabelle laughed. "There's enough of it out there. The tablecloth, the seat covers . . ."

Rosalie looked at Mama and then at Papa. She couldn't decide which one she wanted to strangle first. "Hi, Pop. What's new?" He was waiting for his kiss. He wasn't going to get one.

The doorbell rang. Mama had the dish towel wrung tight between her hands. "That's Joey. Annabelle, get the door and keep your mouth shut. Rosalie, you be nice to Joey. He's a guest."

Annabelle grumbled about always missing all the good stuff and stalked off. Rosalie took a deep breath and tried to keep her voice down. "Mama, how dare you invite Joey over. You know I'm seeing someone else."

Papa looked at Mama. "Maria?"

"A *cafone*. You're seeing an animal."

"I'm seeing a nice man who treats me well and respects what I do, unlike Joey. He even takes me out to nice places. As a matter of fact, Thursday night he took me to Pane e Vino in Nolita. You and Papa should go when Pop isn't too busy . . . working."

Papa's eyes bulged. Blood drained from his face. He grabbed the chair beside him. Rosalie wondered if he was going to fall over. That might have gotten her out of dinner, especially if he'd hit his head on the corner of the table and required stitches.

Mama was too busy wringing her hands to notice Papa's shock. Who would have thought olive skin could change color so quickly? Papa turned the color of that grayish stuff Rosalie used to fill nail holes in the wall. It was probably a good thing Mama was stewing in her own juices. If she'd seen him, she'd have called 911. He looked about ready to pass out, but Rosalie couldn't summon any pity. The way she looked at it, he was lucky Nick had kept her from going after him with the champagne bottle.

Aunt Rose didn't miss a thing, though she kept her mouth shut, which, when Rosalie thought about it, was even scarier than if she'd screamed and smacked someone upside the head. She surveyed the situation and, as usual, took charge. They didn't call her "The Colonel" for nothing.

"Maria, you go make nice with Joey. I don't know what you were thinking inviting him, but now we have to make the best of it."

Mama shot one last scathing look at Rosalie and rushed out of the room.

Papa took a deep breath and straightened. His face, which had been gray a second ago, turned red. Rosalie hadn't seen him look like that since the day after she'd gotten her learner's permit, took the car out by herself, and hit a police cruiser.

Rose pushed past Rosalie to get to the stove. "I'm going to take the roast out of the oven so it doesn't end up tasting like cardboard. Paulie, take this pasta to the dining room and sit down." She handed him the bowl. "We don't need you getting in our way. Rosalie, you stay and help make gravy."

Rosalie shut her mouth and did as she was told while Aunt Rose pulled the roast out of the oven and placed it on a plate before deglazing the roasting pan with wine.

She took a deep breath and continued. "It isn't easy being your mother. She don't know what she don't know, and she don't know you. You go your own way; you always did. She tries to make you go her way. She thinks what she's doing is right. She does her best. She worries about you."

Rosalie gathered the ingredients for gravy. "I know."

Aunt Rose continued to scrape the drippings with a wooden spoon. She pulled the spoon out of the pan and pointed it at Rosalie, swinging it back-and-forth, splattering everything in the area. "When you go out there and eat, be polite and forgive your mama for what she's done."

"Okay." Man, the way that woman wielded a spoon, who needed guns?

"And leave your papa alone. You already said what you needed to say."

She handed Rosalie the spoon to continue with the gravy and picked up a knife.

Rosalie took a deep breath and a step back—the woman was a menace with a spoon, with a knife she was downright terrifying. "Aunt Rose, I know."

Rose crossed herself and looked up to heaven. "Yeah, so do I."

"You know?"

Aunt Rose nodded as she scraped the knife against the sharpening steel. "When men get to be a certain age, they do something stupid. Some buy an expensive sports car; some buy a toupee. Your father, he has all his hair, and he can't afford a second car."

"But Aunt Rose. . ."

She pointed the knife at Rosalie and shook it. "You stay out of it, Rosalie. No good can come from getting in the middle of something that has nothing to do with you."

"But Mama—"

Aunt Rose made a slashing gesture with the knife, effectively cutting off the rest of the argument. Rosalie stepped back. Aunt Rose looked as if she'd been one of The Three Musketeers in a past life.

"Your mama made her own bed years ago. She's content to sleep in it. Who are we to judge? Wait until you're married, you'll see."

"Oh, yeah, like that's going to happen. I'm never getting married."

"That's what you think. I see the man you'll marry. You'll be married within the year."

"I see you're crazy. Why would I do something stupid like that?"

"*Amore, Putto, Cupido.* You can't run from your fate, and you can't stop it. Love dumbs you up, takes your eyesight, and changes you. You could get a little dumber. You're too smart for your own good. You always were. You take after me."

Good Lord, Rosalie hoped not. She watched Aunt Rose slice the meat in perfect thin slices and stayed well away from her. "Yeah, well, you're wrong, old lady."

"You think calling me what I am is going to change your stars, you're the crazy one." She picked up the roast and carried it into the dining room. Rosalie was left stirring the gravy and contemplating slipping out the backdoor.

"Okay, Rosalie." Annabelle strode in. "Things are getting tense out there. Mama's wringing her hands, and Pop looks as if he wants to kill someone. Joey's nervous. Even Johnny's starting to shake. You better get out there."

"What the hell am I supposed to do?"

"I don't know. You're the smart one in the family. You'll think of something."

"Bring out more wine. That might help. And for God's sake, take that knife away from Aunt Rose. We don't need weapons at the table."

"Good point."

Rosalie filled the gravy boat, grabbed the ladle on her way to the dining room, and took a deep breath. Someday she'd laugh about this. Not now, but someday.

"Gravy's done." Rosalie set it on the table.

Joey jumped out of his chair. "Hi, Rosalie. It's nice to see you."

He pulled out the chair for her; of course, it was the chair next to Johnny the Octopus. She looked up into Joey's eager face and mentally winced. What was she supposed to do? Lie and say it was nice to see him, too? Nope, she couldn't stomach it.

"Thanks." She smiled and sat. "Hi, Johnny."

Johnny never stopped stuffing his face full of pasta. He nodded with spaghetti still hanging out of his mouth. God, how did Annabelle put up with such a pig?

Aunt Rose gave Johnny the evil eye. "Johnny De Palma. What? Were you raised by wolves? Don't your people say grace?"

"Sure. Before we eat. But I'm already on the second course."

"We wait until everyone is seated to say grace and eat nothing until the food is blessed."

Johnny looked around and saw he was the only one eating. He shrugged and put down his fork and spoon.

Grace was said, and Joey stuffed his face after a fast "Amen," not even bothering to make the sign of the cross. Mama passed Rosalie the pasta, *puttanesca*. How appropriate that she'd made a dish that, if translated into English, would be whore's pasta. Rosalie assumed it was a not-so-subtle hint. She put about one-tenth of what she wanted on her plate. It was all she could do to ignore the urge to eat right out of the damn serving bowl. The pressure was killing her.

Rosalie watched Joey, who sat across from her, between Papa at the head of the table and Annabelle. She didn't know how she'd spent two years looking at Joey's face. Not that anything was wrong with it, but it was suddenly annoying, and that was before he opened his big mouth.

Aunt Rose told her she was getting dumber—ha! Joey was living proof that Aunt Rose was wrong. The smartest thing Rosalie had ever done was refuse to marry Joey. Of course, since meeting Nick, the title "the idiot" had replaced Joey's name in her thoughts. She could see Nick in thirty years asking, "You remember the idiot you used to date before you met me?"

Rosalie dropped her fork and spoon at the same time. The clatter made everyone jump. Oh, God! What was she thinking?

"Sorry." She reached across the table—she knew it was bad manners, but hey, these were desperate times—grabbed the wine bottle, and filled her glass.

Damn, why couldn't her family get with the program and serve wine like the rest of the world? In wineglasses with stems. Italian wineglasses were what everyone else refer to as juice glasses. They don't hold enough to deal with a dinner like this. Maybe that was why Italians had the world's lowest rate of alcoholism—stingy wine glasses.

Rosalie downed her wine and would have refilled the thimble-sized glass, if Aunt Rose hadn't been staring. Rosalie heard Aunt Rose's voice in her head. "Drink all the wine you want, little girl. It's not going to change your stars. It's only going to show you how dumb you can be. *Salute*."

Hearing Aunt Rose's voice as clear as if she'd spoken was enough to cause nightmares. She gave Rosalie a knowing smile.

Johnny nodded toward Joey. "Hey, Joey, what are you doing here?"

Johnny must have swallowed the huge amount of pasta he'd stuffed into his mouth. Either that, or he was talking with his mouth full, which would have surprised no one.

"I thought Rosalie dumped you. Are you trying to get her back?"

Joey wiped his mouth before answering. "She didn't dump me. We've decided to take a break."

Rosalie didn't correct him. She hoped he was only saying that to save face and wasn't delusional. But in either case, it was no longer her problem.

Johnny laughed. "It sounds like a permanent break to me. The guy she's dating let her drive his brand-new Mustang. You see what I'm saying?"

Johnny turned his eyes to Rosalie and used the tip of his knife to pick his teeth. Ewww. He put his knife down and sat back in his chair. "How long have you and what's-his-name been seeing each other? Since the day after Joey proposed, right, Rosalie?"

The pig put his hand on her thigh and squeezed. Rosalie stifled the urge to stab him with her fork. Instead, she broke her roll in half and dug an elbow into his ribs. Oops. She heard a pleasing grunt and smiled a feigned apology as she whispered under her breath, "Move your hand, or I'll mail it back to you." She should have left the damn carving knife on the table.

Annabelle was too busy watching Joey to notice her fiancé's behavior . . . well, other than his lack of tact, which only pleased her.

"Who I date, and when, is none of your business," Rosalie said.

Annabelle smiled sweetly, which was the equivalent of a warning flare. "That's right. Rosalie can sleep with whoever she wants."

Johnny raised his glass with one hand and stroked Rosalie's thigh with the other. "Here, here."

Joey choked. Mama started thumping her chest and praying to the Virgin again. Papa drank his wine, slammed the glass down on the table so hard the dishes rattled, and then refilled it. Annabelle smacked Joey on the back as Aunt Rose smacked Annabelle upside the head and cursed her in Italian.

Rosalie took advantage of the chaos to bend one of Johnny's fingers back until she felt a crack. She didn't know if it was his knuckle cracking or his finger breaking. She didn't care. His face turned red, and he started cursing, too. She calmly rose from the table, went to the front door, gathered her purse and coat, and left the asylum.

Nick vacuumed the living room, trying to calm down. Cleaning usually relaxed him—today, it wasn't working. There had been half a dozen calls for Rosalie from hysterical family members in the last hour, and Rosalie still wasn't home. Something had happened at dinner.

Something bad. With every phone call, his worry increased until he was sick with it. The last call came from someone named Aunt Rose. Nick shook his head, wondering what the hell the message meant.

He turned off the vacuum and listened to the message again.

"You, the one who Maria calls the *cafone*, you take good care of my Rosalie. She needs you, but she don't know she needs you. Oh, and you're a good man—stupid, but good. What can I say? All men turn stupid some time—this is your time. At least you won't be buying a toupee in thirty years, you already got a sports car, and you're no cheater. I can die knowing my Rosalie will be happy."

Nick wondered if insanity ran in Rosalie's family. That would explain the phone calls. He continued pacing. Dave lay on the couch following Nick's progress, letting out a whine every now and then, as if commiserating.

Nick needed to find Rosalie. Doing nothing but vacuuming was driving him crazy. He went to the closet, got his jacket, and was putting it on when the front door opened. A weary, haggard, and demoralized-looking Rosalie stepped inside. Christ, she was gone an hour and a half, and she looked as if she'd been tortured for a week.

"What took you so long to come home? You scared me. I thought . . . hell, I don't know what I thought." Nick drew her close and held her. "What happened?"

He slipped the coat off her shoulders and let it drop to the floor. Ignoring it, they went to the couch and sat.

Nick pulled her onto his lap. He still wore his jacket but couldn't figure out how to take it off without letting go of her. She'd tucked her head under his chin, her face resting against his neck, and she had yet to say anything. A quiet Rosalie was disconcerting.

"Lee, are you okay?"

She nodded against his neck. He felt her chest expand as she took a deep breath, as if she was trying to calm herself.

"Where were you?"

"Green-Wood Cemetery. I took a walk."

"In this cold? Are you nuts? You're frozen."

"I had to get out of there, and I was so mad, I didn't want to drive. I turned into the cemetery, parked your car, and took a walk. Then all I wanted was to come home."

"What happened?"

"God, what didn't? Ma invited Joey to dinner—"

"The idiot?"

She nodded, her cold nose moving up and down against his neck.

"Before he showed up, my mother . . . God, Nick— she knows. How could she know and stay?"

"Sweetheart, you don't know—"

"I know. Aunt Rose said. I don't know how Mama can still live with him."

"You talked to your aunt about your father's affair? You told her?"

"Papa was there when I told them I was seeing someone else and that we'd gone to Pane e Vino in Nolita on Thursday night. Papa looked as if he were about to have a coronary. He knows I know. Then it kept getting worse.

It was awful. When we sat down to supper, Johnny rubbed Joey's nose in it because I drove your car. He kept putting his greasy hand on my thigh, and then Annabelle said I could sleep with whoever I wanted—"

"Wait a minute. Who put his hand on you?

"Johnny."

"Who the hell is Johnny?"

"Annabelle's fiancé."

"I'll break his fuckin' neck."

"Not necessary. I broke his finger. Well, it could have been his knuckle. It was hard to tell."

He patted her ass. "That's my girl."

"All hell broke loose. Johnny cursed. Joey choked. Mama prayed. Aunt Rose smacked Annabelle. Papa rattled the dishes. And I left."

"You're home now. I've got you. It's going to be all right."

"You feel so good." She snuggled closer. "Where were you going? You have your jacket on. And why is your prized vacuum out?"

"There are a ton of crazy messages from your family. I knew something was wrong. What can I say? I vacuum when I worry. Not that it helped. I had to do something so I was going to find you."

"I don't need a knight in shining armor, Nick. I take care of myself."

He tried not to laugh. Sure, she took care of herself, but she'd been clinging to him since the second she walked through the door. She'd come home, because she had to see him. She'd die before she'd admit it, but she needed him, even if it was only to hold her. Maybe old Aunt Rose wasn't crazy after all.

"Did you eat?"

She shook her head. "Not a bite."

"Good, me, either. I'll throw together a quick meal."

"Great."

"What do you feel like?"

"Anything but *puttanesca.*"

Nick raised an eyebrow at that but thought it best not to ask any more questions.

She gave him a squeeze and a slow, thorough kiss before sliding off his lap. "I'm going to take a hot shower. I'm still cold to the bone, and I want to wash off the icky feeling of Johnny's sweaty hand. God, he's such a pig. I might have to burn this skirt."

"You sure you don't want me to pay him a visit? I'll teach him to keep his hands to himself."

She patted his cheek. "That's a sweet offer. Cro-Magnon, but sweet."

Nick wrapped his arm around her waist as she slid back on his lap. He held her hips as he moved beneath her and whispered in her ear. "I know how much you like it when I play 'caveman.'"

He nipped her earlobe, and she groaned. "Oh, yeah. Let me get a shower; you get your club. I'll meet you in the cave in a half hour."

"Take your time. I have to hunt for food first."

"It's a date."

Chapter 14

IN THE THREE MONTHS SHE AND NICK HAD BEEN TOGETHER, they'd fallen into a comfortable routine. Nick took Dave to work with him most days, and he cooked dinner most nights. Rosalie almost always helped Nick with the dishes. Sometimes, if Nick worked late, they'd go to DiNicola's for a bite. And today Rosalie was, as usual, running late for her Monday morning staff meeting. Shoot.

"Nick, I can't find my black bra. Do you know where it is? It was right here the last time I looked."

The bras that were always hung to dry on a hanger on the shower curtain rod had suddenly disappeared.

Nick stuck his head in the bathroom and smiled that smile. Every time he did that, she ended up late for work. Of course, she walked around all day with a smile on her face. Still, her constant tardiness wasn't setting a good example for the staff.

She should have known better than to walk around with nothing on except her stockings and thong. She was beginning to think she subconsciously planned for him to find her in compromising positions. They both enjoyed the outcome, but why couldn't he ever catch her when she was running early? Probably because they didn't get out of bed until she was already running late. Damn it.

Nick turned the corner and leered. Rosalie crossed her arms over her chest. "Don't look at me in that tone of face. I'm late. Where is my black bra?"

Nick leaned against the doorjamb and smirked. "Do you want the thin one that shows your nipples or that shiny one that accentuates your cleavage?"

Rosalie uncrossed her arms, looked down, and saw that the thin one might cause undue attention. "The shiny one."

"They're both put away where they belong."

"What are you talking about?" Rosalie took the hanger off the rod and held it out to him. "This is where they belong."

"No, sweetheart, that's where you hang them to dry. Then you're supposed to put them away in something called a drawer."

"Why? They were fine hanging right here, and I always knew where they were. See? Now I have to look in two places."

"You know, it's a good thing you're so cute when you say things like that. If you weren't, you'd drive me crazy."

"Don't even go there. You're the one who has me wondering if I'm on the fast track to Bellevue. You're always putting stuff where I can't find it. I spend my life looking for things I swear I'd put down a second ago."

She walked past Nick into the bedroom and started searching for the drawer he'd designated as the bra drawer.

"Come on, don't tell me you miss coming home to a place that looks as if it has been tossed."

"Okay, I won't."

Rosalie slammed a drawer that contained Nick's boxer shorts. Nick opened the one next to it and pulled out her black satiny bra that matched her thong . . . well, except for the little red bow on the back. The one he was tracing with his fingers. She slapped his hand away. "Stop it, Nick. I have a staff meeting, and it'll look really bad if I'm late . . . again."

"It's not my fault you can't resist my body."

"Don't you have a car to fix or something?"

He wrapped his arms around Rosalie and kissed her shoulder, watching the reflection in the mirror of his dark hands moving over her much lighter stomach.

"Okay, get dressed, and I'll drive you to the express train. Hurry, Dave's already got his leash and is waiting by the door."

"You're bringing Dave?"

"Yeah, of course. Don't worry; I'll make him ride in the back until I drop you off."

"You're all heart." Rosalie slipped a silk shell over her bra and stepped into her skirt. She caught his eye in the mirror as he helped her into her suit jacket.

She stepped into the shoes she'd spent twenty minutes searching for. She still hadn't gotten into the habit of looking in the closet. Who would have thought to look for her shoes where they belonged? Nick waited by the front door, holding her coat. Her briefcase and purse sat on the table beside the door for her to grab on the way out. Odd, since she'd thrown them on the couch Friday.

Nick took Dave's leash out of his mouth and snapped it to his collar. "Get used to it, buddy. No matter how great they are, women always leave a guy cooling his jets by the door."

"Men." Rosalie walked out, leaving Nick to lock up, and waited for him by the car, tapping her foot the whole time. He opened her door. Rosalie moved to get in, but Dave snuck past her and jumped in the front seat.

"Dave, get in back until we drop your mom off. Go on, move it."

Dave whined, moved between the seats, and lay down in back. Nick handed her in before taking the driver's seat.

He started the car and pulled into traffic. "What do you want to do for dinner tonight?"

"I have a late meeting with my boss to give him a status report on Premier Motors. I don't know how long that will take. I'll call you on the way out of the office, okay?"

"Sure. If you want, take the express, and I'll meet you back here. Let me know."

He pulled up to the curb by the station. They kissed each other good-bye, and Rosalie got out. Dave jumped in the front seat. They were getting better at the whole "'Bye, honey, see you tonight" kissing thing. She waved as Nick reached around Dave and buckled the seat belt. The lunatic.

Rosalie pressed the intercom button, waited for the beep, and spoke. "Gina?"

"You rang?"

"Is the computer tech still working in your office?"

"No. He works normal hours. It's after closing time. He's long gone."

Rosalie had been so preoccupied when she'd returned from her meeting downtown that she'd walked past Gina's desk with a mumbled greeting and hadn't noticed.

"Would you come in here, please?"

A moment later, Gina sashayed in, steno pad in hand, zebra-print stilettos on. The stilettos matched the belt that turned a plain black wraparound into a dress worthy of a sex goddess—which explained why the computer tech had been in Gina's office for at least three hours. Not that Rosalie cared, since Premier was paying the guy by the job, not by the hour, and Gina wasn't one to let work slide. Still, it was painful to watch her toy with a man like a cat with a mouse before making the kill.

"So, did you put the poor guy out of his misery and agree to go out with him?"

Gina sat, kicked off her left stiletto, and curled her leg beneath her. "What? Oh, Gary. We're meeting for drinks after work tomorrow night." She examined her manicure. "But I don't know. He's really not my type."

"He's breathing, isn't he?"

"Ha, very funny. What's put you in attack mode today?"

"I'm sorry. You're right. I'm in a bad mood, and I'm taking it out on you. The meeting didn't go well. All I got were more questions I couldn't answer. I keep hitting brick walls. Missing files, incomplete accounting information, and huge holes in the information I've been getting from Mr. Jack Lassiter Jr. Not to mention the rumor that Premier is in worse shape that it actually is. Maybe I'm paranoid, but I can't help feeling as if I've stepped into the middle of a dastardly plan."

"So what role do you play? Dudley Do-Right, or maybe you're the love interest, Nell?"

"Gina, be serious. We've got a real problem here."

"I am being serious. Think about it. Who would make

the best Snidley Whiplash?" She tapped the side of her head. "Think, think, think. I'd say Jack Jr., but really, I doubt he's smart enough, and why would he want to hurt the company his family started? He'd be cutting off his nose to spite his face. Now, if we were looking for the source of the rumors, you'd have to look for a high roller, someone who has firsthand knowledge of the financial workings of car dealerships. Someone who'd be hot to take over this dealership, if Premier should fold. Hmm . . . maybe you could ask Nick, just Nick. Oh! Or . . . maybe it is Nick, just Nick. Say, does he have a mustache and a funny yet evil laugh?"

"Come on, Gina. Talk about grasping for straws. Nick knows how much this job means to me. He'd never hurt me like that.

"Rosalie, you're thinking like a girlfriend, not a businesswoman."

Rosalie shook her head no, but Gina was right. Damn, how embarrassing.

"A man would never look at this situation and think of the CFO's feelings. He'd see it as business—which would give him free rein to destroy anything and anyone in his way."

Well, yeah. But that doesn't mean he'd target the business his girlfriend is supposed to be saving—even if it is the most prestigious car dealership in Manhattan. Damn, this was so not looking good. What car guy wouldn't want to own the Ferrari dealership?

"You can be sure Nick the Dick would see you as his lover in the bedroom, his adversary in the boardroom, and never the twain shall meet. How do you think he got to be so successful? By being a nice guy and making sure he didn't hurt anyone's feelings? Wake up and smell the exhaust fumes."

"Drop it, Gina. It's not Nick." Oh, man, it better not be Nick, because if it was, she'd kill him.

"Fine. But you have to admit, it makes sense. Who else would have that kind of clout? Nick Romeo deals with every automobile financing company known to man, and every bank either has a piece of his business or would do anything to get it. One well-placed word from a player like Nick Romeo, and a schmuck like Junior would be persona non grata. Hell, some would deny Lassiter credit, just to score points with Nick Romeo."

"Okay, Gina. Let's just say you're right. How could Nick control what goes on inside Premier?

"Maybe he can't. Maybe there's more than one culprit. Maybe they're working together. Stranger things have happened."

"Then it's definitely not Nick. He's not much of a team player." Well, at least, not in his personal life.

"The only employee who has a grudge against Premier that I know of is Jack Jr., which is a given. You take over a man's job, and he's going to get his feelings hurt. Junior couldn't have been happy to be demoted. If he wasn't the son of the founder, he'd be out of a job."

Rosalie fought off a sudden chill as she pictured Jack Lassiter, Jr. "The guy creeps me out. He gives off really bad vibes."

Gina nodded. "Yeah, he's your typical past-his-prime playboy who hasn't come to grips with his thinning hair, his expanding waistline, and his several chins. He's still a legend in his own mind. He's got a wife, a mistress, and he's looking to cheat on both."

"He hasn't made a play for you, has he?"

"Of course, he has. And he did it less than an hour after we got here. But you know me; I handled it.

"Oh, I have no doubt of that."

"So far, all I've learned about Jack Jr. is that compared to him, a pet rock would look like a member of Mensa. I copied all the files I could off his secretary Randi's computer our first day here, before he had time to tell her to clean the hard drive. After he left that first day, it took me all of fifteen minutes to pull up every deleted memo, letter, and financial record on his computer."

"Gina—"

"You don't think I *need* those computer geeks we hire, do you?"

"Geez, Gina." Rosalie didn't know whether to be angry or impressed.

"What can I say? I have a thing for men with pocket protectors. Bad hair and glasses turn me on. I have X-rated dreams starring Bill Gates. It's a sickness."

"What did you find?"

"Oh, you know, the usual. There were a ton of poor management decisions, but that's not news. If not for idiots like him, we'd be looking for work. Junior was robbing Peter to pay Paul when it came to making the minimum inventory and parts purchases to keep from losing the several dealerships they still have. But that's typical of any company with a poor debt-to-income ratio. There's hanky-panky with the sexatary—expensive lunch dates, which, upon closer inspection, turned out to be room service meals. The room rates were expensed as parking costs, which, when you think about it, makes a sick kind of sense."

"There was nothing else?"

"I'm not sure. There's a steady stream of cash flowing to one particular body shop, without much of a paper trail. I'm looking into it."

"Talk to his secretary. She can't be all that happy her married boyfriend/boss has been demoted, especially if you let it slip that he's been chasing you around the desk for the last three months. All the perks she's gotten from dating him have been taken away. After seeing Jack Jr., why else would anyone sleep with him, especially someone who looks like Randi? Let me know what you find out."

Gina nodded and made a note on her steno pad. "What about Mr. Lassiter Sr.? Where does he fit in?"

"I'm not exactly sure. I would think he has a good picture of where the company stands, since he's one of the Board members who hired us. Premier's precarious financial position couldn't have come as a shock. My guess is, the old man hired us to pick up the pieces of a failing company and get it moving in the right direction before he goes for a quick sale."

"If Lassiter's looking for a quick sale, why wouldn't the saboteur simply buy the company? Why take the time and trouble to put them out of business?"

"Good question. Maybe it's personal." Rosalie made notes. Missing/incomplete information; rumors→ Nick? "Okay, so who's the source of the rumors, or is it two individuals we're up against?"

Gina sat back down. "I don't know, Rosalie." She

snapped her fingers. "Damn, I left my crystal ball at home today. Perhaps we can look in it tomorrow, and it will give us all the answers. Or, maybe you can get information from Nick, just Nick."

"I can't. He doesn't know I know who he is."

"What? You've been sleeping with the man for the last three months, and neither of you have come clean yet?"

Rosalie put her elbows on the desk and dropped her head in her hands. "No."

"That's one more strike against him. He may be keeping his identity from you so that you won't suspect him."

"Yeah, I thought of that, too."

"Well, are you going to finally confront him?"

"No. I'm not going to say anything unless he does first."

"Wow, that's real mature."

Rosalie sat back and firmly put on her woman-in-charge persona. "Gina, if he's the one who's the source of the rumors and possibly has ties to someone inside, do we really want to let him know we're on to him?"

Gina blew her hair out of her eyes, stood, and locked gazes with Rosalie. "Is that the only reason you're not confronting him? Or are you waiting for him to confess all and beg for forgiveness?"

Well, yeah, that, too, but she'd take that little factoid to her grave. Rosalie stared Gina down until her assistant gave in, looked away, and strode out the door without another word.

Rosalie picked up the phone and dialed Nick.

Nick closed his cell phone. Rosalie was late. She didn't

know when she'd be home, and she sounded stressed and exhausted. Nick rubbed Dave's head, which was resting on his lap, and looked around the apartment.

"Come on, boy. Let's go get something for dinner. We'll surprise your mom when she gets home." Dave waited by the door with his tail wagging.

They headed to Vinny's restaurant and went in through the back door.

Vinny turned around, eyeing Nick and Dave. He pointed at Dave and wagged his finger. "You keep that mutt outta my kitchen."

"You know, Dave has better manners than you do. Don't talk about him that way." Nick widened his stance, because Dave had begun leaning on his leg. He'd learned from experience that, unless you were prepared, when Dave leaned all the way—you fell over. "Dave, down."

Dave gave him one of his you-gotta-be-kidding looks.

"You want a meatball, you behave."

Dave lay down at the threshold to the kitchen, and Nick stepped over him.

"I need dinner, something nice. It sounds as if Lee's had an awful day. I'm not sure when she'll be home, so it has to be something that will keep."

Vin flipped something in a frying pan and set it down on the stove. "What do I look like, the freaking Barefoot Contessa? I hear she lives in the Hamptons; you want I should give you directions? Oh, right, you know how to get there. You got a freakin' house out there. So why are you here bugging me?"

"Come on, Vin, I just want to . . . I don't know . . . make Lee feel better, you know?"

"I know you got it bad. That's what I know."

"Cut it out, Vin."

"Cut it out, Vin," he parroted back. "Nino, I need two chicken *cacciatores* to go, give them extra pasta, and throw in a half-dozen meatballs for the mutt. Oh, and box up a few *cannolis* while you're at it. Nick and I are going to step into my office."

Nick looked over at Dave, who had fallen asleep. "Nino, keep an eye on Dave for me, okay?"

"Sure, sure. I keep an eye on everything. I cook, I clean, I dog sit. Go. Go!"

Nick followed Vinny to his office off the kitchen. Vin sat behind the desk, spun around in his chair, and reached for a bottle of Jack Daniels. "You want whiskey or wine?"

"Neither. What do you need, Vin?"

"I'm just looking out for my baby cousin—"

"Come on, I'm no baby, and you know it."

Vinny poured a glass of Jack for himself and rolled it around the glass, sniffed it, then took a sip. "Ah . . . Okay, here's what I need to say. I think you're getting in over your head with this girl. You're going to end up with a broken heart if you don't watch out."

"Oh, right. Have you ever seen me get attached to a woman?"

"No, but then you've never come to the restaurant wanting to bring a woman a nice dinner because she's had a lousy day, either. Matter-of-fact, if some chick you were seeing had a lousy day, you were either the reason her day was lousy or running as fast as you could in the opposite direction."

"Lee is different. She doesn't try to trick me, and she's not after my money. She's not one of those women who make you prove you care by expecting you to jump through hoops like a toy poodle. Lee is fun and nice, and she's low maintenance. When I do something for her, she's floored. When she smiles, it means so much more because it's real. She's real."

"Like I said, you got it bad."

Nick shook his head. "You've been drinking too much. Lee and I have a good time together. So what? I like her."

"Oh, how the mighty have fallen." Vinny took a sip of his drink and leaned back in his chair. "Now listen up, I'm only going to say this once. That way when you're in bad shape after having your heart stomped on and shoved down your throat, I won't have to kick you when you're down." He leaned forward, as if he were about to pass along a golden tidbit of age-old wisdom. "Dominick Romco, what did I tell you? You never listen to me. See, I told you she'd break that heart of yours. I told you this would happen, remember?"

"Vin, you are as bad as Nana. Next, you'll be saying I should get married and bring you bambinos to rock to sleep."

"It'd be nice to have a baby around. I love kids, you know that."

"You're scaring me, Vin. Do yourself a favor and get rid of the bottle. Go to a meeting." Nick backed out of the office, afraid Vin would throw something at him.

"Ha, ha, very funny. You are so fucked, my friend."

"Whatever. Put the bill on my tab. I'm out of here."

Vinny's off-key rendition of the wedding march followed Nick down the hall toward the kitchen.

On his way out, Nick stopped by the wine cellar and grabbed a nice bottle he was sure Vin would curse him out about later. Served Vinny right for giving him shit about Rosalie.

Nick drove back to the apartment, discounting everything Vinny had said. Hadn't Nick sworn off marriage? He'd told Vin a million times that he was putting an end to the Romeo line. Hell, he'd even made Vin and Mona the beneficiaries of his estate, and their kids after them. He had no intention of repeating Romeo history.

Sure, Nick liked Rosalie more than all the others put together. That was true, but only because she was different. They were a pair, neither of them wanting to turn into their parents. Not that Nick remembered his father, but he'd heard enough about the bastard to know he'd become a carbon copy . . . only he warned the girls not to fall for him, and he took off before he married them. Oh, yeah, and he used birth control.

When Nick got to the apartment, he struggled with the four freakin' locks on the damn door while juggling the bags containing dinner. He heard the phone ringing. Thinking it might be Rosalie, he pushed the door open and hurried in.

The machine picked up "Hey, little sis, I thought you'd be home by now. How ya doing, kiddo? Ma said something about a boyfriend? He better be treating you right, but Lord knows, he can't be any worse than that jackass Joey. Ma hates the new guy, which is a good sign. I'll be down the middle of next week for spring break. Can I use your car again? I have to go to Jersey to see the Delgatos. You remember Tom, right? Anyway, if I don't hear from you, I'll call when I get in. Love you, Ro. 'Bye."

Nick dropped the bags on the table. Christ, Rich was coming home. It felt as if someone had punched him in the chest. He sank into a chair, trying to breathe and control his urge to pound something. He wasn't ready. Goddamnit!

Chapter 15

Rosalie GOT OFF THE TRAIN AT THE SAME STOP WHERE Nick had dropped her off that morning, and Nick was nowhere to be found. Great. She'd called him like he'd told her to. Maybe he hadn't gotten the message. It wouldn't be the first time. Thinking she'd never survive a long walk in heels that were already killing her, she caught a cab home.

When the cab pulled up to the brownstone, the apartment was dark. Dave nudged the curtains open. His reflective leash hung from his collar. Rosalie's heart stopped. Something was wrong. She threw a twenty at the cabbie and ran up the steps, cursing the time it took to get through the security door. The door to the apartment stood open. Nick never left the door open. She took a deep breath and barreled inside.

"Nick?"

The place was completely dark. He sat at the table, wearing his jacket, his head in his hands. His elbows rested on his knees. Dave circled his chair and whined.

"God, Nick. What's the matter? What happened?"

He looked up, startled. "Lee. I thought you were going to call."

"I did. Are you okay? Why are you sitting here in the dark? Did something happen?"

Nick stood, his movements jerky and arthritic. He moved like an old man did after sitting for too long.

He waved his hand toward the bags on the table. "I got dinner. What time is it?"

"Nick, what's wrong with you?"

"Nothing."

His eyes changed. They went blank. She'd never seen him look at her like that. She stepped back, feeling as if she'd been slapped.

"Fine." She threw her briefcase down and cursed silently. So he'd reinstated the "don't ask, don't tell" policy. As if her day hadn't been bad enough, she had to come home to this.

Rosalie went into the bedroom, shut the door, and sat on the bed trying hard not to cry. She was mad, that's all. He'd told her to call him. She had, and he'd left her standing on a street corner in the dark. Then he'd dismissed her when she wanted to know what the hell was wrong with him. She had every right to be pissed. God, she hoped this didn't have something to do with Premier.

Rosalie took a deep breath that sounded suspiciously like one taken between sobs. She'd be damned if she'd let him hurt her. Well, no more.

She changed out of her suit and threw it on the treadmill just to piss him off. Dressed in her ugliest nightshirt and ratty sweats, she checked her face in the mirror and practiced her I-could-give-a-shit look before leaving the bedroom.

The table was set, the plates filled, and the wine poured. Nick shrugged. "I thought you'd be hungry."

"Yeah, I am."

He held the chair for her, and she sat, wondering what the hell was going on, but unable to ask.

"There's *cannoli* for dessert."

"Oh."

Rosalie ate but didn't taste anything. Conversation was nonexistent. After they did the dishes in silence, she did work she didn't need to do while Nick watched TV in the bedroom. Dave went from room to room, looking as confused as she felt.

Nick took Dave for a walk at about eleven. When they returned, he stood beside Rosalie.

She looked up and met his shuttered eyes. "What?"

"Are you coming to bed?"

"No." She shuffled through her paperwork. "I've got work to finish before tomorrow."

He watched her for a minute, as if he wanted to say something, but turned away and walked quietly into the bedroom. After a few minutes, she saw the light go off. The silence was deafening.

Nick peered over the edge of a freshly dug grave. He pulled the collar of his overcoat together and wondered what he'd done with his cashmere scarf. The wind cut through all the layers he wore and chilled him bone deep. Rosalie stood more than an arm's length away, staring at him as he looked down into the depths of the empty grave. Her sadness smacked into him like a cold wave. A tear ran down her cheek, and he reached for her. He wasn't sure if it was to comfort her or himself. His hand found nothing but air, as her image began to fade.

Nick awoke with a start. Breathless. His heart raced, and he jerked. Rosalie, whose sleeping body lay draped over his, grumbled something. She took a deep breath and snuggled closer, using his shoulder as a pillow. Her soft, steady breathing warmed his neck. He pulled her closer and held on, telling himself it had just been a bad dream. He was still able to reach out and touch her. He could make love to her. She was still his.

For now, at least.

He ran his hand down her bare back and remembered how she'd looked that morning—sexy, confused, and indignant. No one could do indignant better than Rosalie. Sometimes, he ticked her off, just because it was such a turn-on. There wasn't a time Rosalie hadn't made every nerve in his body stand at attention. He wanted her. Even when she looked like death. Even when she was dressed in her rattiest, form-camouflaging rags. Even when she wore ugly clothes like those she'd worn earlier.

He rolled them over and stroked her smooth skin while she slept. Even asleep, she was the most sensual woman he'd ever known. He took her already-tight nipple into his mouth and slid between her legs. Her hips moved beneath him, rubbing against his arousal. Rosalie sucked in a breath and pulled his head closer to her breast.

"Nick" she sighed. He couldn't tell if she was awake yet. He didn't care. Nick needed her—right now. She'd wake up eventually, and he was going to make sure she'd awaken with a smile on her face.

"Oh, God, yes." Rosalie was almost afraid to open her eyes and discover it was an extremely vivid dream. A delicious, head-swimming, pulse-racing, breath-catching dream. She wrapped her legs around the sex god, who in her dream looked exactly like Nick, and felt him shudder.

Stubble scraped against her breast, and a chill came over her when the cool air whisked over her damp nipple.

"Open your eyes, Lee. Look at me."

Darn it. She wanted to keep on dreaming. She didn't want to take the chance that she'd see a blank stare. She was already exposed, raw.

She wiggled, increasing the pleasure, but not enough. Satisfaction was out of reach.

A soft kiss from familiar, insistent lips slid over her mouth. She heard a groan, then nothing but cool air washed over her body.

"Come on, sweetheart, I need you to look at me."

She really hated it when he called her sweetheart in that deep, sleepy, "do me, baby" voice of his.

"Please, Lee."

The bed dipped beside her, and she rolled toward him. She opened her eyes, and her Nick stared back at her. He sat stroking her bare body. His gaze branded her and pulled her into a swirling vortex, surrounded by pulsating body heat. She held onto him as he stretched out over her. His body touched hers as she arched her back and flipped them over. A look of surprise, then pleasure came over his face.

She straddled his hips. "I want to make love to you this time."

Rosalie held his gaze as she slowly slid her body onto his, her breasts rubbing against the coarse hair of his chest. He hissed before he lifted his hips to drive himself deeper into her. They clung to each other. She felt possession and possessed. When they moved, their gazes locked, their bodies entwined, and they jumped off the

edge of a cliff. Fear, sorrow, and a hailstorm of feeling
pelted her. She saw desperation and need in his eyes.
She'd never seen Nick vulnerable before. The man making love to her was stripped bare.

Rosalie held him, made love to him. Took what he offered and gave all she had. She opened herself up and
invited him into her heart, her soul. Why, she didn't
know. Maybe because he'd asked. Maybe because he'd
met her halfway. His kisses breathed life into her. Their
bodies moved as one, and they came apart together,
clinging to each other and holding off the dark cloud that
loomed over them.

Later, Rosalie awoke alone to the alarm clock. When
she reached for Nick, she felt only cold sheets. He was
long gone. She wondered if it had all been a dream. The
way he'd looked. The way she felt. The way they'd made
love. A shiver of apprehension ran through her. She
reached over to the dresser and pulled open a drawer. A
pile of his boxers lay neatly folded next to her thongs.
Relief rushed through her. For a moment, she'd thought
maybe last night had been his way of saying good-bye.
She laughed at herself. She was being ridiculous. He'd
had a bad day and was a little quiet. It wasn't the end of
the world.

She stretched and called for Dave. When Dave didn't
jump up on the bed, she smiled. He'd taken Dave to work
with him. She bet he'd even buckled the big guy in.

Nick hadn't fallen back to sleep after he and Rosalie had
made love. He'd spent the rest of the night holding her
and memorizing the way she felt against him. The enor-

mity of what had happened still had the power of a fist in the gut. Their lovemaking had always been incredible, athletic, and rang bells he'd never heard before. Last night had felt like the beginning of the end. It was as if she'd known it, too. It was more tender, more touching, more intense. Hell, it was so powerful, the memory alone brought tears to his eyes. He'd never felt anything so deeply, and he knew he'd never feel that with anyone else. Only Rosalie.

"Nick?" Rosalie called his name and saw that he was somewhere else. Again. "Nick?" She reached across the pizza box and gave him a shake. His eyes focused as he came back from wherever he'd been—probably the same place he was since his strange behavior had begun Monday night. She knew that something was up with him, something he wasn't sharing. She'd asked once, but it had come across loud and clear that the subject was off-limits. She just hoped he wasn't feeling guilty about screwing her, her career, and Premier Motorcars over.

"Yeah. Um . . . what did you say?"

"I asked if you wanted a beer." He looked more sad, preoccupied, and restless than guilty. His gaze shot to the pizza between them as, if he'd never seen it before.

"Yeah, a beer would be good."

Rosalie got an IPA for him—one of those disgustingly dark beers she could stand a spoon in—and a Hefeweizen for herself. She sat down, put the beer on the coffee table in front of him, and gnawed on her crust while she watched him peel the label off his beer bottle.

He'd hardly touched the pizza. This distance between

them was driving her nuts. He'd been acting as if he wanted to be somewhere else. Maybe it wasn't guilt at all. Maybe he was moving on. Hell, from the looks of it, he'd already moved on—in spirit, if not in body.

Rosalie tried to take a deep breath, but her lungs refused to work. Could she be coming down with pneumonia again? It felt as if a lead weight had landed on her chest, making it almost impossible to breathe.

The pizza in her stomach suddenly felt as if it might make an unscheduled appearance. She tossed her napkin on her plate. "Are you done here?"

Nick made no response.

"Okay, fine." She got up and collected the pizza box and plates, and put everything away in the kitchen. He didn't seem to notice.

"I'm going to take Dave out." Rosalie threw her coat over her shoulders, grabbed Dave's leash, and stepped into her shoes, not stopping to put Dave's leash on until they were outside. She took a deep breath and then another, trying to calm her racing pulse. She'd had it. Nothing she'd done reached Nick—hell, one time, she'd even sat on him, and all he'd done was hold her and stare off into space. He didn't laugh anymore. He didn't play. It was as if he'd had a personality transplant. He still held her at night, and they still made love, but that was different, too. It was serious, sad.

Rosalie took Dave for a long walk. She walked until Dave tugged her back in the direction of home. He was done, and unless she wanted to carry him, she was, too.

When they returned home, she tossed her coat on the couch. Nick watched her. He didn't get up and hang her

coat, and he didn't tease her. He just watched. She cleared
her throat and shifted from foot to foot under his scrutiny.
"I've got a long day tomorrow. I'm going to bed."

"I'll turn in, too," he said and rose from the couch.

Nick followed her into the bedroom. She undressed
while he brushed his teeth, and he was in bed by the time
she was done in the bathroom. Rosalie climbed into bed
and fought the urge to cuddle up to him, fought the urge
to smack him, fought the urge to cry.

Nick was miserable, and worse yet, he knew he was making Rosalie miserable. At dinner, he'd been unable to eat,
trying to decide what to do. He wasn't ready to leave. She
was lying beside him in bed, and for the first time since
they'd been together, she wasn't on top of him. He missed
the way her hair caught in his five o'clock shadow. He
missed the way she felt against him. Hell, he even missed
that little noise she made when he moved and jostled her.

It seemed to take hours, but she'd finally fallen asleep.
He heard it in her steady breathing. She rolled on top of
him, and he was able to relax for the first time all day.

When he'd met Rosalie, his relationship with her
brother was an inconvenience. Not telling her about it was
simpler than digging up the whole mess. Nick was almost
sure she wouldn't hear about the hints he'd dropped about
Premier Motors. There was nothing in writing. So, okay,
he felt guilty about it, why, he wasn't sure. It wasn't as if
he knew Rosalie was the rumored interim CFO. But, his
luck being what it was, he'd be better off confessing all
right now, before Rich came home. For reasons Nick did-
n't want to examine too closely, he wasn't ready to cut

Rosalie loose. So, he'd take his chances and tell her everything. Even if she tossed his ass out, it would be better than this incessant waiting.

Nick just wasn't sure how to go about telling her. He'd never seen the point in explaining his actions to a woman before. It had always been easier to leave. Vinny had been married to Mona since Nick was a kid. Knowing Vinny, he'd become such an expert at doing the explanation mambo, he could be an instructor on *Dancing with the Stars*. It was going to be as embarrassing as hell, but Nick would have to ask for advice. He hoped Vin didn't make the experience too humiliating.

At least now he had a plan. He'd come home tomorrow and begin the weekend doing the ol' explanation mambo, which would lead to Rosalie getting fighting mad, him apologizing, and if he were lucky, the two of them having make-up sex. If he wasn't, at least he'd put an end to this torment.

Nick ran his hand over Rosalie's hair and let the ends curl around his fingers while his other hand skimmed over the thigh she'd thrown over his and headed for her ass. He fell asleep in that position—with one hand in her hair, the other on her ass, and a smile on his face.

Nick got up early and stopped at Vinny's on the way to work. He parked down the street and walked Dave a few houses up the road. Before they made it to the top of Vinny's stoop, Nick saw the error of his ways. This was not a good time. Every light in the house was on, and Mona was already yelling at the kids. Nick turned around and would have made a clean escape, if Dave hadn't lifted his leg on the fire hydrant in front of the house. Before he could pull Dave away, Vinny stepped onto the porch to pick up the morning paper and gave Nick the once-over.

"Who died?"

Nick opened his mouth and closed it. He shook his head and turned to walk away. A big beefy hand reached out and grabbed his collar.

"Oh, no, not so fast. You don't show up on my doorstep at six a.m. and walk away without a word. I smell woman trouble. Come on, let's go to the restaurant."

Nick sat at the bar with one hand wrapped around a coffee cup and the other holding up his head while Dave lay behind the bar and snored.

"You're an idiot." Vinny stood behind the bar, leaning on the counter, took a sip of coffee, and topped off Nick's with a shot of Jack Daniels. "Let's recap. This whole thing began when you picked up Rosalie in the wrecker on your way home. The next day you brought her here. Am I right?"

Nick nodded and took a swig of his spiked coffee.

"So that kiss I walked in on—you know, the one so hot I could have brought in a brass band and neither of you would have noticed—that was your first kiss?"

Nick nodded.

"Is she always that hot?"

Nick shot Vinny a warning look, and then, disgusted with himself, he nodded.

Vinny added a shot of Jack to his own coffee, drank it, and sat down. "Damn, if that was your first kiss . . . You say you took her home and never really left. It's been what, three months?"

Nick nodded again.

"So you dropped the bombs to the lenders about Premier before you were practically living with Lee—and way before you found out she took over the joint."

"Yeah."

"And you say she still doesn't know who you are. She still thinks you're a mechanic."

Nick didn't bother nodding this time. He was starting to feel like a freaking bobblehead doll.

"Nick, I never thought I'd say this, but you don't know jack about women." Vinny held up his hands in surrender. "I know, I know, you've been with half the female population of Manhattan, but I've been married to Mona for eighteen years. Let me tell you, there's not a man alive who can keep his identity a secret from the woman he's sleeping with—not a smart, Italian woman, anyway. Rosalie knew who you were within forty-eight hours of your first date. No nice Italian girl sleeps with a guy unless she knows his first, middle, and last names—at least, not more than once."

Nick had to admit, Vin had a point. Rosalie had never asked his full name. He'd thought she was too embarrassed. What was she supposed to do? Roll over and say, "The sex was great, and by the way, what was your name again?" He'd never questioned it because, well, he was a guy, and it served his purpose.

"If she's known all along, why didn't she say something? Why wasn't she mad? Why'd she make me lie to her?"

Vinny poured another shot into both their coffees and shook his head. "Women."

"Christ, I'm a fucking idiot. Here I thought I was pulling the wool over her eyes, and all the while, she was the one keeping *me* in the dark." Nick stared into his cup. "I've only driven the Viper once since I've met her. I've been running around, changing clothes everywhere I go, so she won't see me in a fuckin' suit. I never introduced her to my mother, Nana, or the rest of the family. Shit. If she knew, then how come she never asked for anything? She gets pissed if I pay for pizza twice in a row."

"Don't ask me to figure out women. You can ask Mona if you want. But if you tell her I knew anything about this stunt you pulled, I'll have to kill you."

"Hey, I'll admit I'm stupid, but even I'm not that dumb. Besides, you'd never get the chance to kill me. She'd do it first."

Vinny sat back with a shit-eating grin on his face. "So, you're in love with Lee?"

Nick looked up and shook his head no.

"You like her?"

Nick liked Rosalie a lot. He nodded.

"Okay, so you like her. She's a hot piece of ass."

Nick was on Vinny so fast, he made his own head spin. He reached across the bar, grabbed his cousin by the shirt, and lifted him off his feet. Dave woke up and started barking. Vinny only smiled and patted Nick on the shoulder.

"Yup, you love her. No guy moves as fast as you did to protect the honor of a girl he's not in love with. Now, put me down, and I'll tell you what you have to do.

Nick put Vinny down and gave him his best scowl.

Damn. Nick should have known Vin would be anything but helpful.

"Okay, first thing you need to do is spill your guts. Just remember, never, ever, say anything about the fact that she was the reason you did wrong. You've got to suck it up and say the dreaded words. You might want to write these down and practice in front of a mirror." Vinny handed Nick a bar napkin and a pen.

"It's all my fault. I was stupid, and I wasn't thinking. You're absolutely right. I don't want to lose you, and I'll do anything if you'll give me another chance."

Nick stopped writing; he couldn't believe what he was hearing.

"Why are you looking at me as if I grew another head?"

"You actually say shit like this?"

"Nick, you'll learn that it's a lot less painful to just get it over with quickly. In her eyes, you're always wrong. Until you grovel, life as you know it will never be the same. There will be no sex, no peace, and if she's like Mona, no sleep until you crawl on your belly like the snake that you are—that, my friend, is a direct quote.

"The absolute worst thing you can do is tell her that if it wasn't for her, you wouldn't have been forced to lie this whole time. You need to tell her exactly what she wants to hear.

"It's not going to be pretty; expect yelling, tears. You may even have to duck if she loses it and throws something at you. You've got your work cut out for you, so you better get your ass in gear."

Vin took a bar rag and started polishing the bottles. "After you grovel, you're going to need to buy out a flower shop. Call Carmine's, have him make you up a nice expensive bouquet and keep them coming. Hit the chocolate place on Avenue M. They sell Godiva. Buy twice as much as you think one person can eat in a year. Women have bitchfests when their men do something stupid. They get together to discuss us, compare notes, and sympathize. She has to have enough chocolate to share."

Nick didn't grovel. He didn't bother telling Vinny that, because obviously, Vin had enough experience groveling to teach a class in that, too. Nick knew what Vinny didn't—once you grovel, they know they've got you hooked. Vinny was a perfect example. Mona'd had Vinny by the shorthairs for years.

"Why should I grovel? I didn't do anything wrong—except for not telling Lee who I was in the beginning. But if you're right, she's known all along."

"You're telling me that you're not gonna take the hit? What are you, nuts? You finally find the right girl, and you're gonna let this blow up in your face? You're gonna lose her."

"What are you talking about?"

"Nick, you've been putting pressure on Premier since the day you were canned because of that no-good Jack Lassiter, Jr. Have you done anything since you found out about Lee's involvement?"

"No." Nick fanned the napkins he'd been writing on and sat up straighter. "But that doesn't have anything to do with her."

"Sure." Vinny took another sip of his drink and sat back looking smug. "You go right ahead and keep telling yourself that. But if you're stupid enough to believe it, you're more of a putz than I thought you were."

Nick finished his Jack and coffee, stood, and whistled for Dave. He'd been calling himself enough names lately; he didn't need Vinny's help.

"Look, Nick. Think about what I said. If you're not ready to cut her loose, then don't. Try confessing your sins. Pretend you're talking to Father Francis. Who knows, maybe she's nothing like Mona, maybe she'll go easy on you."

Who knew that this would be so complicated or would smack so much of commitment? All this talk about love was enough to make him rethink the whole thing. But damn, the thought of the alternative was worse. Shit.

Rosalie's intercom beeped and pulled her out of the quagmire that was her relationship with Nick. She'd spent the last week wondering what was wrong with him, and she'd made the decision to find out what it was, even if she had to break every rule in the book to do it. Gina's voice filled her temporary office.

"Rosalie, there's a strange man on line one. He says his name is Leisure, and you'll know what it's regarding. He's even more cryptic than Nick, just Nick. Is he as good-looking?"

A smile crossed Rosalie's face. Is Leisure good-looking? She pictured her friend in her mind. Hmm. "Yeah, I guess he is, but I never thought of him like that."

"What? Is he your cousin or a priest or something?"

"No, just a good friend. I'll take the call. Thanks, Gina."

"I live to serve."

With the smile still on her face, Rosalie punched the flashing button on her desk phone, slipped her pumps off, leaned back in her chair, and settled in for a good chat. "Leisure. Hi. How's it going?"

"Are you alone, Rosalie?"

Rosalie dropped her feet to the floor and back into her shoes. Sitting forward, she grabbed her pen and pulled out a fresh yellow pad. "Yeah. Why? What's wrong?"

"You remember that issue you asked me to look into?"

"The rumors about Premier Motors?"

"That's the one. Well, it took some doing, but I got my hands on their file. It looks as if your suspicions were correct. There are notes about a telephone conversation regarding Lassiter, Premier, and their fiscal position. Are you still seeing Dominick Romeo?"

"Yeah." Rosalie cringed, dreading the answer but asking anyway. "What does Nick have to do with this?" She heard the blood rushing though her ears, and her face and hands got clammy. She waited for the answer for what seemed like an hour. "Leisure, you're scaring me. Tell me what you've found, and stop being so damned cloak-and-dagger about this."

"It's him, Rosalie. Dominick Romeo is sabotaging Premier Motorcars. He gave a laundry list of reasons we should no longer extend credit to Premier, Lassiter, and any customers he might have.

"Honey, if word gets out that you're associated with him, you can kiss your job—hell, your career—good-bye."

"I can't believe it's Nick. I mean, the thought occurred to me . . . but—"

"I don't know what to tell you, Rosalie, other than I've got notes in front of me regarding a conversation between Dominick Romeo and the senior VP of finance, as well as the fallout of said conversation. Your boyfriend implied that if we continued to handle Premier, we would lose his business. I don't need to tell you that Dominick Romeo's chain of dealerships means more to us than one dealership, even one as large as Lassiter's. And, if what Romeo said was accurate—and by virtue of your presence at Premier Motors, all evidence points to its validity—Premier is on precarious financial footing. Now just remember. You didn't hear any of this from me."

Rosalie's mind was spinning as she thanked Leisure and hung up the phone. She tried to rub the tension out of her neck, but the effort wasn't helping. Neither was Nick's name written in three-inch block letters on the yellow pad in front of her. Rosalie calmly took a red Sharpie out of her top desk drawer, pulled the cap off the marker and drew a thick "X" through the name. Then she picked up the phone and made a call. "Yes, this is Rosalie Ronaldi. I need to speak with Mr. Lassiter. It's urgent."

Nick sat at his desk twirling a pen between his fingers, back and forth, back and forth.

Rosalie would be home in a couple of hours. After checking the clock for the hundredth time that day, Nick paced his office, trying to come up with the right words to tell her the truth. He stuck his head out the door. "Lois, is Ty back with Dave yet?"

"No, they're at the body shop. Do you want me to call for them?"

"No, that's okay. I'll wait."

"Nick? I don't mean to pry—"

"Sure you do." He leaned against the doorjamb. "What is it, Lois?"

"I was going to ask you the same thing. What's wrong?" She held up a stack of letters he'd gone over earlier. "You were supposed to sign these. What did you do? Take them out of your in-box and stick them in your out-box?"

"I don't know. I thought I had signed them. Here, I'll take care of them now." He moved toward her desk. She dropped the letters, rolled her chair back, and stood.

"Nick, I don't care about the damn letters, but if there's something wrong. . ." She came around the desk toward him, giving him the concerned-mother routine.

"Nothing I can't handle."

She nodded, picked up the letters she'd dropped, handed them to him, and looked doubtful. "Maybe you should take Dave and Lee to your house in the Hamptons for a week. You haven't taken any time off in ages, except when Lee was sick, and that was no vacation. The beach in winter is so relaxing."

"I don't think so, Lois."

"Ty and I can take Dave, if that's a problem."

"No, Dave's not the problem, but thanks for the offer. I wasn't thinking when I started bringing Dave to the office. He's not going to be with us much longer. I know Ty loves him. I'm sorry."

"Something's wrong with Dave? Oh, God." She stepped back and covered her mouth with her hand.

"No." He reached out and squeezed her shoulder. "Dave's fine. It's Lee. Things aren't going well."

"They aren't?" She covered his hand with hers. "Oh, Nick. Are you sure you can't work things out? I thought everything was different with Lee—better."

Nick shrugged off her hand and went back into his office. He heard footsteps behind him. He should have known better than to think Lois would let this drop. Damn, he was not in the mood to discuss his private life with his secretary.

"You know, if you tell her everything, there's a chance she might forgive you and take you back. Personally, I'd start with telling her who you are. I mean, allowing her to believe you're the service manager is almost understandable, especially with your track record with women."

Nick chose not to mention that he suspected Rosàlie knew who he was from the beginning. "What's that supposed to mean?"

"Nick, as long as I've known you, you've only dated plastic, shallow, money-hungry women. They've never lasted more than a month. I'm sure if you come clean with Rosalie before you get caught in your lies, she'll understand why you didn't correct her false assumption. Especially if you tell her the truth."

"The truth?"

"Yes. She was the first genuine woman you've met in years, and you were afraid she wouldn't agree to see you if she knew your history with her brother."

"I was not afraid."

"Fine. Call it whatever your fragile male ego can live with.

Now, the rest is going to be more difficult. You need to make sure she understands that you'd fallen in love with her long before you were aware of her position with Premier."

"What?"

"You heard me. Telling her that you love her will take the sting out of it."

Great, first Vinny, now Lois. "But I don't."

"Don't what?"

"I don't love her."

Lois looked up at him. "Oh, God. What is it with men?" Then she nailed him with her 'don't mess with me' glare. "You honestly believe you're not in love with Rosalie?"

"Lois, you know me. I don't do love."

"You don't, huh? I guess you bring Dave here for your health. And Ty—you don't love him? He means nothing to you?"

"Hold on. Ty has nothing to do with this."

"There's your mother, your grandmother, Vinny and his family, me and Tyler, Dave. Don't you see? You take care of the people you love. You're not good with the words, but your actions—they tell the real story. I knew you were in love with Rosalie as soon as I heard you had taken her to see Mike. When was the last time you made a doctor's appointment for one of your girlfriends?"

"Lois, I like Lee. She's a friend." Nick twirled his pen through his fingers. "But I don't love her."

A knock on the door interrupted Nick's explanation, which was a good thing, because he'd run out of reasons he didn't love Rosalie—he just didn't, that's all there was to it.

Lois shook her head and reached for the door. Good, she was finished telling him how he felt. Women. They think they know everything. Before she opened the door, she turned. Shit.

He took a deep breath and waited for the final blow.

"Nick, I'm warning you. If you let Rosalie go, you'll spend the rest of your life regretting it. Don't you see how lucky you are? This could very well be a once in a lifetime chance at true love. Don't let it go without a fight, because you're too stupid and closed-minded to admit the truth. You are not your father. Get over it already."

Nick was happy to hear the door slam behind her. Thank God that was over. He signed the letters, threw them in his out-box, and waited for Ty to bring Dave back. He wanted to go home, spend the night with Rosalie, hold her, make love to her, and ignore the internal countdown to his own personal D-day.

When Rosalie entered the apartment, everything looked the same as it had that morning, but it felt different. It felt like it had before she'd met Nick, only cleaner.

She shrugged off her coat, threw it on the couch, and sat on it. Nick had his running shoes placed neatly by the front door. The Frisbee he'd bought for Dave leaned against the wall in front of them. Nick's Polar fleece running jacket dangled on the hook next to where Dave's leash usually hung. His cell phone charger was on the buffet. He'd put it next to hers and neatly stowed all the cords. Everywhere she looked, Nick was there.

Rosalie had come home early, because she needed to

change for her meeting with Mr. Lassiter Sr. She'd never been to the Harvard Club, but knew her dress-down, Friday business-casual garb wouldn't exactly blend. She started stripping on the way to the bedroom and threw her clothes on the bed. Opening the closet, she picked out her best suit with the matching silk shell. Nick's clothes hung beside hers. His shoes were placed on the floor like little soldiers all lined up. She pulled on her skirt, stepped into her lucky shoes, turned, and faced the bed. The book Nick had been reading lay on the bedside table on his side of the bed. Oh, God. When had that become his side? When had they chosen sides? Rosalie slipped the shell over her head and shrugged into her jacket before sinking onto the bedspread of the expertly made bed. She opened the drawer, and sure enough, everything in there was Nick's. He'd moved in. They were living together. When had that happened?

She was living . . . Hell, who was she kidding? She was in love with a man who'd spent their entire relationship lying to her. All this time, she'd kept telling herself he was lying about his identity because of his money, when from the get-go, she'd been nothing but a cog in the wheel of a master plan to take over Premier Motorcars. Shack up with the interim CFO and have all the information you need at your fingertips. God only knew what he'd learned. All those nights she'd brought home her computer, her files, Premier's financials. How could he do this to her?

Nick came home and vacuumed the living room. He'd had a miserable day at work, trying to figure out what to say to Rosalie.

He considered kidnapping her. He could get her in his car with Dave and come clean going eighty miles an hour down the Long Island Expressway. But with his luck, they'd get stuck in Friday traffic, and he wouldn't put it past Rosalie to get out and tell him to go screw himself. No, that wasn't a good plan. Even if she did calm down by the time they got to the beach house, the glitz of the Hamptons might be too much of a shock.

Maybe he should take her to his brownstone. At least it was close to what she knew. No. He didn't want to look like he was trying to buy forgiveness, and his place was a little over-the-top. He should never have let what's-her-name decorate it. Sure, he'd hired her to decorate before he slept with her, but as soon as they'd started sleeping together, she acted as if she were decorating her future home. At least she had good taste. Expensive, but good. Now, instead of a home, he lived in a showplace. Not that he spent much time there.

He looked around Rosalie's apartment. Here, he felt comfortable, at home. That settled it. He'd stay put and talk to her. He'd tell her everything, and if he lived through the aftermath, maybe she'd forgive him. Then they could . . . what? He didn't know. Keep doing whatever it was they were doing.

Dave kicked his food bowl. The poor guy was hungry. Nick looked at his watch. Shit, it was six-thirty. No wonder Dave complained. Nick fed the dog and checked the answering machine and his cell phone for messages. Nothing.

He went to vacuum the bedroom and saw the disaster. Rosalie had come home and gone out again. She usually left him a note or told him what was going on, but for some reason, she hadn't.

He settled in to wait for her. She was always home by eight.

Nick put away the clothes Rosalie threw on the bed and started cleaning the bathroom. He checked his watch. It was almost nine.

Worry set in. He chided himself about it, but he couldn't shake the feeling that something was wrong. He called her cell phone and left a message on her voice mail.

Nick opened the refrigerator and grabbed a beer. He took the bottle opener out of the drawer and his favorite mug out of the freezer and poured the beer before making himself a sandwich. He ate his sandwich at the counter and began cleaning the kitchen. After a few minutes, Dave whined, went through the living room, and lay down beside the door. Even the dog knew something was wrong.

It was ten when Nick started fighting panic. He'd run out of things to clean. If something had happened to Rosalie, no one would know to call him. He went to her desk where she kept her address book and thought about calling her parents, but what would he say? "Hi, Mr. and Mrs. Ronaldi, it's Dominick Romeo. Yeah, that's me, the one who got your son arrested. Well, I've been seeing your daughter, and she's missing. Do you know where she is?" That would go over real well.

He'd call her friends, except for one problem. He didn't know any of her friends. How could he have been with her for so long and never have met her friends? The only one she had spoken of was Gina. That was it. He'd call Gina. Gina knew him.

Nick didn't know Gina's last name, so he went through every name in Rosalie's address book until he came to Gina's. He felt three times a fool when he dialed the number, but it was either that or start calling hospitals.

"Hello?" barked the man who answered. Man, if his voice matched his body, Nick wouldn't want to run into him in a dark alley.

"Hello. I'm sorry to bother you so late, but is Gina there?"

"Who wants to know?"

"Dominick Romeo. I'm a friend of Rosalie Ronaldi's. Is Gina there?"

"Yeah, hang on." Nick heard him knock on a door, then the sound of a hand going over the mouthpiece.

"Hello?"

"Gina?"

"Yeah, who's this?"

"Gina, it's Nick. I'm sorry to call so late, but Lee isn't home, and she's always home by now. I'm worried about her. Do you know where she is?"

"Did you try her cell phone?"

"Christ, Gina, of course I tried her cell. Voice mail picks up. She always leaves a note when she goes out. She didn't leave one tonight. She didn't call to say she'd be late."

"Okay, calm down. She probably went out with friends or something. Did you try her parents?"

"No. I don't know them, and I don't know any of her friends. You're the only one I've met. Did she say anything to you at work about having plans?"

"No, but she acted a little strange."

"Define 'strange.'"

"She left early, and she didn't say where she was going. Did you two have a fight or something?"

"No. Things have been tense, but she seemed fine."

"Tense? Why tense? Nick, I told you what I'd do to you if you ever hurt her, remember?"

"Gina, I don't have time for threats. Are you going to help me find her or not?"

Gina said something in Spanish and then schooled her tone. "I'll call Rosalie's sister on her cell. I think I have the number somewhere. I'll call you back."

"Thanks, Gina. I'm at home."

"Whose home? Yours or Rosalie's?"

"Rosalie's."

Nick hung up and waited.

At midnight, Nick sat on the sofa, imagining Rosalie dead. He could hardly breathe. Gina had called him back after talking to Annabelle and Rosalie's parents, and he knew no more than before.

Nick had called every hospital in Manhattan and Brooklyn, but none had a record of anyone fitting Rosalie's description. Gina called every half hour, and every time the phone rang, he answered, thinking it was Rosalie. Every time it wasn't, he felt as if someone had kicked him in the gut. The minutes dragged like hours, the hours like weeks.

A little after three, Dave barked. Nick heard the snick of the lock, then Rosalie walked in. She didn't see him at first. She tottered in as if she were walking barefoot over broken glass, throwing her coat in the vicinity of the couch and her handbag on the table. When she flipped the light on, she saw him. He heard her gasp.

She'd been out with God knows who, while he'd been calling hospitals, picturing her floating in the East River, dreading the phone ringing, and praying it would. She was alive, thank God. Relief rolled over him, and then anger filled the void. He wanted to kill her for putting him through eight hours of hell. He wanted to hold her and never let her go. He wanted to handcuff her to him, so he'd never again have to wonder where the hell she was. Oh, yeah, and he wanted to punch something.

He rose, his body feeling as if Rosalie had thrown him out of a speeding truck and backed over him a few times for good measure. He went to the closet, got his jacket, and passed her on the way to the door.

"Nick." She reached out and touched his arm.

One look, that's all it took. She dropped her hand to her side and stepped back. Nick walked out without a word.

He stood on the sidewalk, fighting for breath. He hadn't known a body could hurt so much without being hit by a bus or shot. Pulling his cell phone off his belt, he punched in Gina's number. Hell, he'd called her so many times that night, he'd memorized it.

"Nick?"

"Yeah, she's home."

"Is she all right?"

"She's fine, as far as I could tell."

"Where the hell was she?"

"She didn't say."

"Did you ask?"

"No."

"Let me talk to her."

"I can't. I left."

"Where are you going to go at three in the morning?"

"Home, I guess." Christ, he'd just left his home. His home was with Rosalie.

"Nick, are you okay?"

"Yeah, I'm fine. I wanted to let you know she's okay. I've got to go." He hit the end button.

Nick walked. He didn't know where he was going. He didn't care. All he knew was if he was still moving, it meant he was still alive.

Nick looked as if she'd stabbed him, and then he looked . . . gone. She'd barely made it to the bathroom before tossing her cookies. The phone rang; the answering machine answered. She heard Gina's voice. She didn't care.

Rosalie's meeting with Mr. Lassiter had been illuminating. She hadn't known what to think, so she spent the rest of the night sitting in a pub and trying to make sense of what she'd learned. She had no trouble believing the story of Nick in Juvenile Hall—it explained the bad boy persona he wore so easily. Rosalie knew about Nick's mother and grandmother, but the news about his father . . . well. He'd never mentioned a father or the lack thereof. After spending time with Mr. Lassiter, Rosalie had no problem seeing a young Dominick Romeo looking up to the man, but she did have trouble believing that Nick was ever a rival or jealous of Jack Jr. No, there was more to the story than that—not that she'd probably ever hear the truth.

Rosalie picked herself up off the cold tile floor, rinsed

her face, and brushed her teeth. Damn it, why did she have to fall in love with Nick? Nick, who lived with her but wouldn't tell her his last name. Nick, who lay next to her night after night but was a world away. Nick, the guy she'd made a deal with and was stupid enough to fall for while she'd been busy having an affair.

The phone rang again. She ran to pick it up. "Nick?"

"No. It's Gina."

"Oh."

"She says, 'Oh.' I've been worried sick since ten o'clock, and she says, 'Oh.'"

Rosalie ignored the cursing and the mention of her name in the same sentence with the devil and something else she didn't understand, but figured it couldn't be good.

"Do you have any idea how frantic Nick was? Do you know what you did to him? He was calling hospitals, chica. He thought you were dead. How could you do that to him?"

"Well, it wasn't as if he was totally innocent. He lied to me."

"Yeah, and you knew it all along. Before it was okay, but now it's a federal offense?"

"Oh, God, Gina. I fucked up."

"You sure did. Now what are you going to do about it?"

"What can I do? I tried to stop him before he left, but the look in his eyes . . ."

"Rosalie, are you crying?"

"I love him, Gina. My timing is impeccable. I figure out I'm in love, right after I break the rules. The rules I made. How stupid can I be?"

"Pretty stupid."

"I wanted to beg him to stay. I started to, but then . . . he looked at me. He's gone, and I don't think he's ever coming back."

"What were you thinking?"

"I found out all this history with Mr. Lassiter. Nick worked for him since he was a kid. He kept his whole life from me. I got scared. He'd been acting strange, distancing himself. I thought he was—"

"You thought he was about to dump you, so you dumped him first."

"I'm always the one who does the distancing."

"Well, bully for you, you did it again. See if that keeps you warm at night. Use your head, Rosalie. Call him, say you're sorry, tell him how you feel."

"I can't. We made a deal, Gina."

"Then you're right, he won't be coming back. You and that stupid deal. The two of you deserve each other. I'm going to bed. I'll see you on Monday."

The sound of beeping signaled her to disconnect the call. She had a feeling she wouldn't be getting any "poor baby's" from Gina over this breakup, either.

Chapter 16

"YOU SHOULD PUT SOME PREPARATION H ON THE BAGS under your eyes. You look like hell."

She'd already tried the Preparation H trick. God forbid, Gina found out she was commenting on the results. Rosalie kept her voice even. "Good morning, Gina. And how was your weekend?"

"Better than yours, I see. So, when did you finally stop crying?"

"I did not cry." Bawled was more like it. She didn't think she'd ever cried herself to sleep, woken up, and done it again before. And she knew for a fact, she'd never done it for an entire weekend.

"Have you heard from Nick?"

"No." Rosalie didn't think Gina meant listening to the messages he'd left on her cell. They went from curious, to concerned, to worried, to frantic. She couldn't help herself. She'd listened to them over and over all weekend, just to hear his voice.

"When are you going to call and tell him you love him?"

"Never. Don't you get it? We made a deal. It's against the rules to. . . to. . ."

"Fall in love? Care about each other? Or maybe, it's against the rules to be human and screw up. At the very least, you should call and tell him you're sorry for scaring the living piss out of him."

"I can't." Rosalie double-timed it to her office and slammed the door. At least she'd made it before she embarrassed herself . . . well, okay, before she embarrassed herself further. She sat on the leather couch and willed her tears to disappear. If she started crying again, who knew when she'd stop.

It was two o'clock, and Rosalie wasn't hungry. Gina had buzzed her an hour earlier, saying she was going to lunch. She could have asked Gina to pick something up for her, but she couldn't look at food without getting sick. She'd never felt like this. She hurt all over. She couldn't eat. She couldn't sleep. Every time she dozed off, she'd awaken falling off Nick's side of the damn bed.

Even Dave was upset. He'd walked around the house all weekend with a pair of Nick's boxers in his mouth, whining. He'd hardly eaten, and he'd spent most of his time staring out the window, looking for Nick and ignoring her.

Nick had finally hit rock bottom, or at least, he hoped he had. He went to the office, packed up Dave's dog toys, bones, and bed, and tossed them in Rosalie's Volkswagen before he returned it to her place.

There he was, for the entire world to see, driving around in a Barbie mobile, and he couldn't care less.

Going back to the apartment and packing his belongings would likely kill him. He'd sat around all weekend, trying to figure out how to put things back together with Rosalie, but when it came down to it, he had no options. He'd made a deal with her—no strings and no commitments. It would last until one or both stopped having a good time. Obviously, she'd learned the truth, and she'd moved on. If she hadn't, she would have called him, yelled at him, hit him, something that showed she cared and wanted him to come back. Right?

He parked the yellow Beetle in front of the brownstone and found Dave looking at him through the window. Something white hung from his mouth. God, Nick missed that dog. That morning, when he'd gone to the office without Dave, Lois had looked at him as if he'd kicked her. She'd gotten up and hurried out of the door. If he hadn't known better, he'd have sworn she was about to cry. Christ. As if he didn't feel bad enough, he had to be responsible for making the Rock of Gibraltar cry.

Nick got out of Rosalie's car, gathered Dave's things, and brought them into the apartment. Dave jumped on Nick and greeted him as though he'd been gone a lifetime. Damn, Nick was going to miss the big guy, but that was only a miniscule fraction of the hole left in his life by Rosalie. Nick carried in the empty bags he'd brought from his place and started packing. He took his hanging clothes and put them in a garment bag, emptied his drawers into a suitcase, and packed his shaving kit. He dumped the drawer of his bedside table into another bag, tossed in the book he'd been reading, and searched the rest of the apartment, gathering his things. Nick decided to leave the vacuum and food processor he'd bought for the apartment. Not that he thought Rosalie would ever use them, but Nick knew he'd never be able to see them without thinking about Rosalie and Dave. Life was hard enough; he didn't need any more reminders of all he'd lost. Dave followed him around the apartment with what Nick realized was a pair of his boxers. He tried to take them away, but Dave wouldn't let go.

"You drop my drawers, or I'm not taking you for a walk."

Dave dropped them, but only to go out. When they returned, he picked them right back up again and settled into the corner where Nick had placed Dave's bed.

"Look, buddy. I have to go. You take good care of your mom for me. Okay?"

Nick set Rosalie's car keys on the kitchen counter, right beside the set of apartment keys he'd been carrying. He took one last look around, grabbed his bags, and stepped into the hall, letting the door slam shut behind him. There. He couldn't go back inside if he wanted to. And by God, he wanted to. He saw Dave watching him drive away in the Mustang he'd left parked in front of Rosalie's apartment when he took his middle of the night walkabout.

Home, sweet home. Nick parked in front of his brownstone. He knew it wasn't far enough away from Rosalie, but then, he doubted Alaska would be. He put his car in drive and headed for the Long Island Expressway.

He called Lois. "I'm going away for a few days. I've got my cell if you need me. Oh, and if you hear from Lee, call me right away. Okay?"

"Where are you going, Nick?"

"I'm going to the beach house for awhile. I need to get out of town."

"You didn't dognap Dave, did you?"

"No. Why would I do that?"

"If you had, Lee would come after you, and maybe you'd both get your heads on straight and work things out."

"Lois—"

"Don't you 'Lois' me, Dominick Romeo. I've watched you date and dump a plethora of women over the last ten years. You never had feelings for any of them until Rosalie. If you're not smart enough to recognize love when it runs over you and fight for it, well then, you don't deserve it. So go to the beach house and lick your wounds. But let me tell you something, Nick, wounds that deep don't ever heal."

"She left me, Lo. She doesn't want me."

"Are you sure of that? Did you ask her? Did you talk to her at all?"

"I've got to go. I'll call you in a few days."

"Stop at the grocery store before you start drinking. You'll be in no shape to drive afterward, and I'm not driving all the way out there to feed you."

"If she calls—"

"I know. I'll get in touch."

Rosalie worked until eight. She was avoiding going home. She'd called her neighbors, Henry and Wayne, earlier. It sounded as if they knew Nick had left, and they said they'd be happy to take care of Dave. She would have worked later, but by eight, she was dead on her feet. All she'd eaten was . . . nothing. Unless you counted the milk in her coffee—she'd had a lot of that.

When Rosalie left the building, she scanned the street, hoping she'd see Nick's car. She didn't.

When she got off the train at her stop, she looked for Nick. He wasn't there.

When she got home and found her beloved yellow Beetle parked in front of her apartment, she fell apart. Right there, on the front stoop of her brownstone, she lost it. Nick was gone. He'd come back, but only to return her car. Oh, God, she'd thought it hurt when he walked out. She'd thought maybe, after he cooled off, he'd come home and at least have a fight with her—give her a chance to explain. She thought he cared enough to yell at her. But he didn't. He'd returned her car.

"Rosalie? Is that you, darlin'? Wayne, come out here!" Henry sat beside her on the stoop, put his arm around her, and pushed her head against his chest.

"Henry? What is it? I've got dinner . . . Oh, my Lord, Rosalie. Is she hurt? What happened?" Wayne always reminded her of a hummingbird. He was small, flighty, and never stopped moving, but was amazing to watch. She didn't have to open her eyes to know he was in a full dither.

"I don't know. Dave was going berserk, and I looked out the window. Wayne, be a love and pick up her things. She must have dropped her purse. There are tampons and God only knows what rolling down the sidewalk."

Rosalie tried to pretend that nothing had happened—that Nick was inside waiting, that her car was still gone, that she still had a life—anything to get a grip, but it didn't work. When she opened her eyes and saw her car, reality crashed into her again.

She tried, but she couldn't stop crying long enough to tell them what had happened. She could only point to her car and do that weird hiccup thing she did when she cried so hard, she couldn't stop to breathe. Henry tightened his hold and pulled her up with him as he stood.

"I'm taking you inside. Come on darlin', I've got you."

They led her up the steps and into their apartment, handed her tissues, and let her cry while they commiserated the way best girlfriends would.

When she'd run out of tears, they treated her like a sick child. They plied her with tea, made her nibble on toast, and before she knew it, Henry was leading her to their guest room.

"You'll stay with us tonight. You're in no shape to be alone. Wayne, be a love and go over to Rosalie's and get her a lovely nightgown. She needs to feel pretty. Don't forget her toothbrush. Come on, darlin', let's get this suit jacket off you."

Wayne came back a minute later with only her toothbrush. "Henry, she didn't have one decent nightgown. Obviously, she sleeps *au natural*, because I don't think she would be caught dead in some of the nightshirts I found in her bureau. Rosalie, darling, we really must do something about your lingerie. You need at least a few peignoirs. We'll do a shopping day this weekend. A little retail therapy might be just what the doctor ordered. I know when Henry and I went through a rough patch—"

Henry groaned. "Wayne, not now. Can't you see she's overcome with grief?" Henry left the room and returned with a T-shirt and sweats. "Here darlin', try these."

A fresh rush of tears began. She couldn't believe she was crying again, and in front of people she'd see every day for the rest of her life. Next, she'd start collecting cats—well, only after Dave passed. He went nuts if you even mentioned the word C-A-T in his presence.

Oh, God, she was going to turn into one of those old women with sixty cats, and she'd live here until the SPCA came to take the cats and Social Services put her in a home for crazy, old people.

Henry sat beside her and wrapped his arm around her shoulders. "Damn it, Wayne. See what you did. She's started the waterworks again, and I just got her calmed down."

Wayne left the room in what looked like tears, but it was hard for Rosalie to tell, since she was crying, her eyes were puffy, and she had a tissue covering her red nose.

"I swear. Wayne is such a drama queen. Rosalie, you go ahead and change while I calm Wayne down. I'll be back in a minute to tuck you in, okay?"

Rosalie slept for the first time since Nick had walked out on her. She knew that wasn't precisely the way it had happened, but he'd been the one who'd left. He was the one who had to come back. Right?

She awoke the next morning thinking that she was cuddled up to Nick. When the fog in her head cleared, she found it wasn't Nick at all, but one of those long body pillows. She'd barely kept herself from falling apart yet again. She stretched, and when she saw the time, she screamed. A second later, Wayne knocked and poked his head in.

"Don't worry. We called Gina and told her you were sick and that we were taking care of you. She's not expecting you in the office today."

Rosalie lay back against the pillows. "Thanks, Wayne. For everything."

He came in and waved away her thanks. "Oh, stop, don't you worry about it. You just take care of yourself. When that man of yours comes back, you two will work everything out. You'll see."

"I don't think—"

"I know. I heard it all last night. You didn't see how he picked you up and carried you in when you were sick. It was so romantic. He held you like you were the most precious thing in the world. And the way he looked at you—doll, if he looked at me that way, I'd melt, that's what I'd do. I'd melt. You listen to me; Nick will be back. It might take a while on account of all that macho mojo he's dealing with. His type needs a way to come back without looking like they're whipped. Do you know what I mean?"

"I don't know. I guess."

"I'll be happy to have him back myself. He is a fine specimen. I swear—all the good ones are either straight or taken."

"Wayne." She picked up a pillow and threw it at him.

He caught it. "I know. I'm bad. Let's pretend I was talking about Henry. He's definitely taken."

"How do you know so much about macho mojo?"

"Ha! I have to deal with that every day. Henry might be gay, but he's definitely all man when it comes to that macho stuff. Straight guys don't have that market cornered, girlfriend. Thank God." He stopped and sniffed the air and then checked his watch. "I made fresh scones. They smell like they're ready to come out of the oven.

You lie back and relax. I'll bring them to you along with your coffee."

A minute later, Wayne brought in a tray and set it on her lap. She picked at a scone. The only good thing to come out of the whole disaster was that she couldn't seem to eat. The one time she'd tried last weekend, she had to make a run for the toilet.

At least she was losing weight. Nick had always fed her; it was as if he wanted her to get fat. She'd comforted herself with the fact that sex burned a lot of calories. Now she was losing weight without even trying. And sadly, without sex.

After breakfast, she got up the nerve to go home. When she saw what awaited her in the apartment, she was too depressed to shower and dress.

Nick had left the keys to her car next to the keys to her apartment on the kitchen counter. No note, no nothing. He'd just packed all his things and left. The only traces that he was ever there—except for the neatness of the apartment—was his food processor, his beloved vacuum, and a dog bed and basket of dog toys he must have had at his office. When she saw those, whatever control she'd had over her emotions took ahold. Nick would make someone a great father some day. Which meant that he'd also make someone a great husband, and oh, God, she wouldn't be that someone. She didn't know why that bothered her so. She'd always sworn she'd never marry, but the thought of Nick married to someone other than her made her crazy.

Rosalie sat in front of the TV watching QVC and buying stuff she didn't need. She had ordered a pair of earrings and had just disconnected the call when the phone rang. She quickly muted the TV, praying it was Nick.

"Hello?"

"Hey, Rosalie." Not Nick; it was Richie. "I called you at work. Gina said you were sick. What's the matter?"

"Hi, Richie. It's nothing, just um . . . cramps." She'd learned a long time ago when something was wrong that you didn't want to talk about, all you had to do was tell the guy you had cramps. Once they found out it had to do with plumbing of the female variety, they got off the topic so fast, if they were in a car, they'd have left skid marks. It worked every time.

"I'll call Pop and ask him to pick me up at the airport. I'm coming in tonight."

"No, don't. I'll pick you up. It'll be good for me to get out. What time are you arriving?"

Rich gave her his flight information and saved her from her shopping spree on QVC. It was just as well. She was buying things she'd never use. How much cubic zirconia could one person wear? Especially someone who didn't wear much jewelry. She'd most likely end up giving it to Mama and Annabelle next Christmas.

Rosalie was a little late picking up her brother. She would have liked to blame it on traffic, but the truth was, she'd lost track of time. He waited outside baggage claim looking pissed. She pulled up in front of him and unlocked the door.

"Sorry I'm late." she said as Rich opened the door.

"Christ, you look like shit."

"Thanks, Richie, it's great to see you, too. Next time you need a ride, call someone else, okay?" She hit the trunk release, hoping he'd stow his bags and get off the topic of how terrible she looked, but he didn't take the hint.

"I mean it. What? Are you sick or something? Is it contagious?"

Frustrated, she got out of the car and grabbed one of his bags herself. The jerk.

"No, I'm not sick. I got dumped, okay? I really liked the guy, and well, I did something stupid, and he dumped me."

"I'm sorry, Ro. Do you want me to go beat him up? What's his name?"

"Dominick Romeo, and no, I don't what you to beat him up. Stay out of it, and whatever you do, don't talk to Mama about this."

"Nick Romeo? What the hell were you doing dating Nick Romeo?" He stashed his laptop and garment bag and got into the driver's seat.

Rosalie couldn't help herself. The tears started flowing.

"Oh, God. Please don't cry. I hate when girls cry, even you."

"Thanks, that's so touching."

"Yeah, you know me, Mr. Sensitivity. So, how's that cute little secretary of yours? Does she ask about me?"

Rosalie buckled up and checked to see if he was serious. He sure looked serious.

"Whoa, are you talking about Gina? You know she'd fillet you if she heard you called her a secretary—she's my assistant. Why would Gina ask about you? You met her, what, once?"

"Yeah, but we spent some quality time under the mistletoe at the Christmas party you dragged me to. Then we ran into each other on New Year's Eve—"

ROMEO, ROMEO313

"She never told me that."

Richie waggled his eyebrows.

"You didn't sleep with my assistant, did you?"

Rich pulled into traffic and adjusted the mirrors. "I don't kiss-and-tell. I told her I was flying in tonight. You're going to lend me your car, right?"

"You're not going to do anything weird or gross in it, are you?"

"What do you think? I'm a professor, for Christ's sake. I don't have to use backseats of cars anymore."

"Yeah, but Gina's living with her sister and her brother-in-law the cop while they're saving for a house. It's not like you're going to her place. And I'd be willing to bet you still can't sneak a girl into your bedroom at *Chez Ronaldi*."

"I'm not going to discuss my sex life with my little sister."

"Fine, I'll keep out of your personal life, if you keep out of mine. Deal?"

"Sounds to me like you no longer have a personal life."

"Yeah, thanks for pointing that out."

"Hey, what's a big brother for?"

Nick sat on the cold, hard sand staring out at the waves. The tide was coming in, and soon he'd have to get his ass up, or he'd turn into a human icicle. He couldn't muster the energy to care. He watched as the waves came closer and closer to his feet. God, he was a sorry case. He knew he was lame when he started playing chicken with the surf in winter.

He stood and checked his cell phone for the millionth time. She still hadn't called. With every hour that went by, his hope waned and the pain in his heart increased. It was as if someone were cutting it out. He had heard people say they were heartsick, and he thought it was a euphemism, but this pain was definitely real. No amount of drinking, no amount of running, and no amount of denying made it go away.

He'd reconsidered groveling, but if Rosalie had wanted him back, she would have said so. Contacting her was against the rules. Why did he have to fall flat on his face in love with the one woman in the world who didn't want him?

Nick knew he had to make a clean break. He just hoped that he never ran into her. If he did, he'd probably end up on his knees, begging her to take him back—rules or no rules. It was hard enough dreaming about her every night. That same fucking dream over and over and over. He awoke alone in a cold sweat, breathing like a freight train.

No wonder he had avoided love all these years. It sucked. It hurt. And once it had you in its clutches, it wouldn't let you go.

Rosalie tore the last four days off her *Far Side* desk calendar, taking note of the tax-day cartoon.

"Rosalie, do you want to go to Katz's for lunch? It's supposed to reach seventy degrees today, and they're working at that new construction site. Maybe the guys will take off their shirts. You need eye candy."

"It's against OSHA regulations for construction workers to work without a shirt, pants, and hard hat, Gina. No matter how hot it is."

"Really? Are you sure? When I walk by, the guys are always taking off their shirts."

"Yeah, well, it has more to do with you than with the temperature outside."

"Hmm." She shrugged and sat on the corner of Rosalie's desk. "Come on, we haven't gone to lunch since before you and he-who-shall-not-be-mentioned split up. It's been over a month.

"What's going on? You haven't been eating, you're losing weight, and I know you're not pregnant. You're not, right? You'd tell me if you were, wouldn't you?"

"I can't believe you'd ask that. We always have our periods at the same time."

"Well, yeah, but the last time I had mine, you never asked to borrow a tampon. What's up with that? You always forget or run out."

"Nick put all the stuff lying all over the apartment away. Who knew I had, like, four boxes of tampons scattered around? I had to bring one into the office. There was no room left in the bathroom cabinet."

"Makes sense, especially since you seemed to have PMS from hell, though it was hard to tell if it was the breakup, or PMS, or a combination of both that made you act a little insane."

Rosalie shook her head and wondered if every assistant talked to her boss like this.

"That still doesn't explain why you're not eating. You've lost so much weight, even your skinny clothes are hanging on you."

"I've lost weight. So what?"

"So, you look like hell. You look worse than you did

when you had pneumonia, and believe me, you looked like shit then."

"I did? Why didn't you say something?"

"Me? I didn't think it was my place—"

"As if that ever stopped you. Gina, since we're having this little heart-to-heart, tell me something. How'd it go with my brother?" Her jaw dropped. Yeah, Rosalie had gotten her good. "You know, Rich, the tall, good-looking Italian guy you went out with three times the week he was here over spring break."

"Yeah, I know who you mean. So, we went out a few times. It was nice."

"Nice? It sounds as if Rich thought it was more than 'nice.' He's been calling and asking about you." Gina gave her that shrug that meant she didn't want to talk about it. "So, you're seeing my big brother, huh?"

"We hung out together when he was in town. It's nothing serious. He lives in—where is it—Maine, Vermont, New Hampshire? Somewhere like that."

"He lives in Vermont but teaches in New Hampshire."

"Yeah, well, he went back home. We had a good time during his visit. Now it's over, and he's doing whatever he does out there in the sticks."

Gina rolled her eyes, and Rosalie pretended not to notice. She paged through the notes on her desk.

Gina slid off the desk and sprinted out, pulling the door closed behind her. Rosalie waited a second to make sure she wouldn't reappear. When she thought the coast was clear, she retrieved the bottle of Mylanta she kept in her bottom desk drawer, took a healthy swig, and chased it down with cold coffee. Yuck.

By four o'clock, Rosalie was ready to leave. She needed to go shopping. Gina had a point. Even her skinny clothes were hanging on her. Doing the whole safety pin on the waistband thing was getting tedious, not to mention dangerous. As much weight as she'd lost everywhere else, though, none of it was in her chest. She'd always heard women complain that when they lost weight, their bust size decreased, but now that she was thinner than she'd been since college—okay, maybe high school—she still had big boobs. It shouldn't have surprised her; it was all a part of the cosmic joke that was her life.

Rosalie buzzed Gina and waited for her to answer. Gina didn't. Strange. She checked the phone and saw that Gina wasn't on the line. She waited while she cleaned off her desk.

A few minutes later, she heard noises in her outer office, and then Gina buzzed her.

"Rosalie, you have a visitor."

She didn't have time to deal with one more problem today. All she wanted to do was hit the sale at Macy's. As it was, she'd have to head uptown during rush hour, which was not fun. The subways started to resemble sardine cans by four-thirty, and cabs were scarcer than straight men on Fire Island.

She checked her schedule and saw no appointment. Of course, when she wondered who it could be, the first person who entered her mind was Nick. The thought of him hadn't stopped throwing her for a loop. She wondered how long it took for a broken heart to heal. Since she'd never had one before, she hadn't a clue. It wasn't as if she could ask someone, either. It was too embarrassing for words. She'd waited and waited for the pain to go away. She'd waited to be able to sleep without waking up because she'd reached for Nick and he wasn't there. She'd waited to be able to eat more than a little pastina with butter, or half a slice of toast, or a pint of Ben and Jerry's. She knew it wasn't exactly a low-cal diet, but she was losing weight. Go figure.

Rosalie slipped her shoes on and buttoned her suit jacket as she rose. The jacket covered the slightly—okay, maybe a little more than slightly—large skirt.

There was a knock on the door and then Gina stuck her head in, with a huge smile on her face and no lipstick. Odd, that. Gina always wore lipstick—bright, red, and glossy. A large hand pushed the door open from above her head. Way above. A large male hand. Rosalie's breath caught, and she held onto her desk. Nick?

Gina flew through the door, followed closely by Rich. "Hi, Ro. Still looking like shit, I see."

"Richie? What are you doing here?"

Gina sidestepped him and tried to back out. Rich caught her around the waist. How he did that, with him being so tall and Gina so short, was interesting to watch. Rosalie guessed that being a knuckle-dragger was good for something.

She swallowed her disappointment and wished for another swig of Mylanta. Then she remembered, too late, to check for a Mylanta mustache. Damn.

Gina pointed at her. "See, I told you. She walks around half the time with white stuff around her mouth from drinking bottles of stomach medicine."

"I do not."

Gina teetered to the desk and picked up the wastepaper basket. She pulled out two empty bottles. The cleaning people obviously hadn't come for a few days.

"You see why I called you?" Gina told Rich. "She's turning into a Mylanta-holic, and she's so thin. It's unnatural."

Rosalie was irate. "You called my brother and told him about me?"

"Well, what else was I to do? It was either Rich or your mother, and I thought you would be less likely to kill me if I called Rich. You don' eat, you don' sleep, you don' do anything but mope. This is an intervention. I saw it on *Montel* one time when I was home sick. It's like they bring together all the people that are important to—"

Rosalie shook her head in disbelief. Gina's accent was stronger than Rickie Ricardo's on *I Love Lucy*. She even had the hand gestures going.

"Gina, I know what an intervention is. Thank you. But I'm not an alcoholic, drug addict, or compulsive shopper. I don't need an intervention."

"Oh, yes, you do," Rich piped up, throwing an arm around Gina and pulling her to his side. "Don't blame Gina for caring about you, little sister."

"Rich, look, I'm sorry you were dragged all the way down here for nothing. I'm fine."

"Yeah, you look fine—if you're into cadavers."

"I don't need to defend myself to you. I tried to be polite, but now I'm out of here. Have a nice time in the city, Rich. Call me when you learn to mind your own business. And Gina, I'll talk to you about the meaning of the word 'privacy' tomorrow." Gina shot her a look.

Rosalie smiled, happy to have the opportunity to get back at her nosy assistant. "Yes, I know you don't like working late on Fridays, but it was the only time I could set up an appointment with Lassiter's secretary without anyone else finding out about it. Besides, you owe me. Good-bye."

Gina chased after Rosalie until she was out of the department. It sounded as if Rich had stopped her. It was a good thing, too. Rosalie didn't know what she would have done if Gina had caught up to her. She was holding her temper by a thread that was unraveling real fast.

The next day, Rosalie and Gina discussed their game plan.

Gina sat across from Rosalie's desk taking notes. "Okay, we're supposed to meet Randi, Jack's secretary, in an hour and a half. We've got a lot of ground to cover."

Rosalie nodded. "If all goes well with Randi, we should be able to take this to the Board on Monday. They can decide if they want to get the police involved. We have evidence of Jack's embezzlement for the last fiscal year. Depending on what gems Randi sees fit to share, since she's the one who overheard Jack proposition you. Oh, nice job with that."

"You know what I always say—"

"Men are pigs?"

"No, never marry the man you fool around with. He cheats on his wife."

Nick had the TV on with the hockey game playing in the background. It was a Friday night home game, but he didn't have the energy to go, and he always went to home games. Before Rosalie, he'd loved the game; now, it had turned into a sick form of self-inflicted torture. He couldn't watch without thinking of Rosalie, imagining what she'd say about a call, the names she'd call the refs, or the way she'd bounce on the bed when the Islanders penetrated the blue line or rushed the goal. Watching her through a power play was a thing of beauty. Her cheeks would pink with excitement, and she'd look the exact same way she did when she was turned on.

Shit, he did this to himself every time. He'd watch hockey, thinking of her the whole time, and all he'd have to show for it was a broken and bleeding heart and a hard-on—one that seemed to become nonexistent around every other women.

He'd tried jumping back into the dating scene. He'd had tickets to a fundraiser at the New York Philharmonic and had asked a gorgeous woman he'd met while she was doing a commercial for Romeo's. She was nothing like Rosalie, so he figured he'd be fine. He'd go out, have a good time, and sleep with Bridget. Or was it Barbara? Hmm . . . maybe Brenda. No, it was Brooke. That was her name, Brooke. He'd sleep with Brooke and get Rosalie out of his system. He'd taken her out and made small talk—very small talk. It wasn't as if there was anything wrong with her. She was nice, intelligent, and beautiful, but she wasn't Rosalie. He went as far as her front door.

The whole time he was out with Brooke, he'd felt as if he were cheating. Stupid, he knew, since Rosalie was the one who'd stepped out on him.

God, every time he thought about the last time he saw Rosalie, the pain knocked the wind right out of him.

The doorbell rang, and Nick grabbed his wallet to pay for the pizza he'd ordered. He'd only wanted the pizza to go with the beer he'd bought. He'd given up Jack Daniels since that week in the Hamptons. He'd begun to worry about his drinking.

God, he was a mess—a fact that Lois reminded him of on a daily basis. He hadn't been this miserable since his first week in Juvie. He never thought he'd survive that, but at least in there, he knew his release date. He had no idea how long this pain would last.

Nick opened the door and pulled a fifty out of his wallet. He looked up just as a fist crashed into his face.

Chapter 17

WHEN NICK ANSWERED THE DOOR, HE EXPECTED TO SEE the pizza boy, not Rich Ronaldi. And he never expected to be cold-cocked. Before he recovered, Rich followed through with a punch to the stomach, slammed the door shut, and was all over Nick.

"You lying, filthy son of a bitch."

Rich was a good fighter, Nick remembered. They danced around the foyer, catching punches and each landing their fair share.

They were evenly matched—two guys of approximately the same age, height, and weight who hadn't been in a fight since their teens.

It felt good to punch someone after years of just wanting to. Even the pain felt good—okay, maybe not good, but deserved. Rich had every right to beat the shit out of Nick. Hell, he'd had a right fifteen years ago, but they'd been arrested before Rich could break Nick's neck for sleeping with his girlfriend.

Still, the fact that he had it coming didn't mean Nick had to be a punching bag. Nick gave Rich a kidney shot.

The doorbell rang and worked like the bell in a boxing match. Nick and Rich stopped fighting, and both went to neutral corners.

Nick answered the door, picked up his wallet lying open on the floor, and paid for the pizza. If the delivery boy noticed anything strange, he never let on. Nick handed him a fifty and told him to keep the change, grabbed the pizza, and closed the door, wondering if he'd have time to put the pizza down before Rich went after him again.

Nick cleared his throat. "Do you want to call it a draw and eat?"

Rich nodded. "Yeah, I'm too old for this shit. But you'd better tell me why you were screwing with Rosalie and lying to her."

"I'll tell you everything. Don't hit me again until after I finish. Fair enough?"

Rich shrugged. "Okay. But it better be good." He followed Nick to the kitchen.

Nick slid the pizza onto the granite counter top, went to the refrigerator, and pulled out two beers. He handed one to Rich and put the other on his eye. The damn thing was still watering. He was glad it was red and swelling. Otherwise, the pizza boy would have thought he was crying. As it was, he was going to have one hell of a shiner.

Rich looked around Nick's kitchen and whistled. "Shit, this place has changed since the last time I was here."

"Yeah, I'm not living in the basement apartment anymore. I bought the building and turned it back into a single family."

"How are your mom and Vinny?"

"Good. I bought Mom a brownstone a few blocks away. She doesn't have to work any more, so she's enjoying herself. She's got Nana living with her. Vinny and Mona still have the restaurant, and they've had three kids. They're good. I hear you've done well for yourself—a professor at Dartmouth—who'd a thunk, huh?"

Rich nodded. "I bet if you asked one of those cops who arrested us how we'd turn out, he'd have said we'd both end up at Rikers Island doing hard time."

"No chance of that. One stint in Juvie, and I'd had enough to know I never wanted to be behind bars again."

Rich closed his eyes and shook his head. "Shit, Nick, I'm sorry about that. I asked my parents to help—"

"You what? After what I did, you asked your parents to help me out?"

"The only reason you got into trouble was because you followed me. You were the kid brother I never had. And I should have taken better care of you."

"Hold on. You're Rich Ronaldi, right? The Rich Ronaldi who caught me sleeping with his girlfriend the day we got arrested?"

"Hell, you were what—fifteen? And you were bombed. Sophia and I'd been fighting about something—I don't remember what—and she used you to get back at me. I knew how it was. I just never expected her to tip the cops off after I dumped her."

Nick sat on a bar stool. "That makes sense. Sophia was the snitch. I always wondered how we got caught." He opened his beer and took a long pull.

"You didn't know?"

Nick wiped his mouth on his sleeve and shook his head. "No. I pleaded guilty and was sent to Juvie. I guess in the end, it was the best thing that could have happened. I learned enough to know I wasn't cut out for crime. I didn't like doing time." He opened the pizza box, grabbed a slice, and pushed the box over to Rich. "Vinny helped me out, got me through high school. I got a job as a mechanic, put myself through Columbia, and opened my own place. I've been lucky."

"Yeah, now you're a big shot. I come back every now and then. I heard about how well you were doing. I would have looked you up, but I didn't think you'd appreciate a visit from me."

Nick shook his head. "Christ, I feel like we're in one of those reunion shows on that women's channel. What is it?"

Rich nodded. "Lifetime."

Nick raised an eyebrow.

"Hey, I have girlfriends."

"Yeah, well, don't expect me to say how much I've missed you and give you a hug or something. It's not going to happen. I am happy to see you, though."

"Yeah, same here. Except for all the shit I heard from Gina about you and Rosalie. I had to pound you for that."

"Understood. But in my own defense, Lee's the one who wanted no strings and no commitments. I was just following her rules, and I thought it'd be over long before you came to town for spring break." Nick took another bite of pizza and talked with his mouth full. "My relationships usually don't last a month before the woman starts making wedding plans."

"Why did you lie to Rosalie about who you are?"

"Gee, I don't know, Rich. I figured you'd have a problem with your little sister seeing the person who got your ass thrown in jail. My mistake."

"Anyone would be better than that asshole, Joey."

"Gee, thanks."

"Don't mention it. Besides, you had nothing to do with our arrest."

Nick shot Rich a you-gotta-be-kidding look.

"Okay, you had something to do with it, but only because you were a normal, horny fifteen-year-old and acted like one. Hell, you should never have been there in the first place, and you wouldn't have, if it weren't for me."

"Oh, come on, Rich. Let's face it; we were both looking for trouble, and we found it together. I knew what the hell I was doing. Though maybe not when I did Sophia. I can't remember that."

"Wow, that sucks—too drunk to remember your first time."

"How'd you know it was my first time?"

"Come on, Nick. This is me you're talking to."

"Right. I could never pull one over on you." He took a long draw on his beer.

"So, are you going to do the right thing and marry Rosalie?"

Nick choked and coughed. Marriage? He couldn't breathe. Rich smacked Nick on the back. It took him a minute to catch his breath. "Why would I need to marry Lee? Hell, why would she need to marry me?"

"Gina called me and asked me to fly down. She said Rosalie's sick."

"Sick? What's wrong with her? Is she back in the hospital?"

"Calm down. No, she's not in the hospital, but I'm worried. I've never seen Rosalie so skinny. She looks like hell, and Gina says the sight of food makes her queasy.

Gina doesn't think she is, but it sure sounds to me like she's pregnant."

"Pregnant? Did you say you think she's pregnant, as in, having-a-baby pregnant?"

"Yeah, that's usually how it goes. A woman gets knocked up, then nine months later, she has a baby."

Oh, God, a baby. He was going to be a father. Nick sat down, before he fell down. He hoped to heaven he'd be a better father than his old man, not that he could be worse. "You didn't ask her?"

"Hell, no, A guy can't ask his little sister that. He goes to the boyfriend, beats the shit out of him, and makes the boyfriend ask."

Nick nodded. It made perfect sense to him. "Christ, a baby."

"Yeah, a baby. What the hell are you going to do about it, Nick?"

Nick smiled so big, it cut his face in half. He was elated. A baby. Man, that was it. Screw the rules. A baby took precedence over the rules any day. He and Rosalie were having a baby. How cool was that? He pictured a little girl with Rosalie's curly hair and smile and a little boy who looked just like him. Damn, he'd get her back for sure now. They'd get married. She and Dave would move into the brownstone. They'd have to get rid of the furniture, though. No kid of his was going to grow up in a fuckin' museum. No, they'd do it up just like Rosalie's place, only bigger . . . and neater.

Rosalie couldn't go on eating pizza and takeout every night. When they were together, he'd always cooked for her. She needed to eat healthy stuff. He'd have to find out what to feed a pregnant woman. God, a kid—they were going to be a family. A real family. Like they were before, only now, they'd have a dog and a kid. Shit. They'd been a family before, but he'd never seen that. They spent time together. They had fun, even when they weren't making love. On Saturday mornings, before he went into work, they'd hang out in bed, drinking coffee and sharing the paper. They didn't talk. They didn't screw. They were just together. It was comfortable. That wasn't something he could see himself getting sick of. Vin was right. He'd found the right one, and he'd been too stupid to see it. He was a putz.

"Nick. You there?"

"Huh? Oh yeah. What did you say?"

"I asked, what you were going to do about Rosalie and the baby."

"I'm going to stop being a putz."

"Does that include doing the right thing and making an honest woman of her?"

"You let Lee hear you talking like that and she's going to kill you, you know."

"You see her anywhere within earshot?"

"No, but that's going to change, real soon. Well, if I can talk her into it. God, what if I can't?"

Rich put his arm around Nick. "I don't think you'll have too hard a time convincing her. When I came down for spring break, she told me she'd just gotten dumped. . ."

"I didn't dump her; she dumped me. She's the one who stepped out. . ."

"Look, I'm just telling you what she said. Don't argue with me."

"Fine. What the hell did she say?"

"She said that she really liked you, but she did something stupid, and you dumped her. She looked like she'd been crying for a week."

"When did you come down?"

"Let me think. The eighteenth, I think. It was a Tuesday."

"She went out on the Friday before. She never told me where she was going. I was waiting for her, expecting her to be home for dinner."

"What do you mean, home for dinner?"

"I'd been staying over at her place."

"She let you stay? As in an overnight stay? She never let anyone spend the night. I used to tease her, because she'd been with asshole Joey for two years, and she'd never woken up with him, except during conversations. She used to tell me that after sharing a bathroom with me, she'd never share a bathroom with another male."

"She never had a problem sharing a bathroom with me. We used to have a lot of fun in the bathroom—"

"Stop. You're talking about my sister here. That's way too much information."

"Look, all I'm saying is that we were practically living together. Hell, there was no practically about it. We *were* living together for a few months. I only stopped by here to pick up my mail. That Friday, I was waiting for her to come home. I'd planned to tell her the truth about who I was, and how you and I knew each other—tell her about my rap sheet."

"What rap sheet? You were a minor. You have no rap sheet. Hold on. You'd better not have a rap sheet. You said you cleaned up your act."

"I did. But Lee deserved to know the truth about everything, and I'd planned to tell her, but she didn't come home."

Rich tossed his bottle in the recycling bin and went to the refrigerator to get two more beers. He handed one to Nick.

Nick popped the cap and shrugged. "I knew things were tense, but I thought we were doing okay. I knew you were coming home, and if she found out about me before I had a chance to explain, she'd dump me faster than week-old garbage. Instead of spilling my guts, I spent the night calling hospitals. I thought she was dead or something. I went out of my mind with worry."

"Where did she go?"

"She didn't say. What the hell was I supposed to do? We'd made a deal when we started seeing each other. No commitments, no strings. She'd said we'd be together until it stopped being fun for one or both of us, and I guess it had stopped being fun for her, because she stepped out on me. She was the one who moved on. I was just the last one to find out about it."

"Shit, Nick. I'd have left too, but she did say she'd gotten scared and done something stupid."

"Then why didn't she tell me that she screwed up? She never called me, not a word, nothing. God, Rich, I waited for her to do something."

"Maybe she was waiting for you to do the same thing? Maybe because of that deal of yours, she figured since you left, if you wanted to see her again, you'd contact her."

"I sure as hell will now."

"Listen, buddy, you'd better check the attitude at the door if you want to get anywhere with my sister. Baby or no baby, she doesn't take crap from anyone. She doesn't need a man to have a baby. Sure, she'll never live it down, and my mother will disown her, but I don't think that'll bother Rosalie too much."

"I'll carry her to the church if I have to. It worked when I took her to the hospital. She ended up thanking me for that one. Just wait, you'll see. She's going to marry me. And damn soon, too."

The doorbell rang and rang again before Nick could reach it. "Coming! Jesus, what is this? Grand Central Station?" He opened the door to Lois and Tyler. Ty ran to Nick and clung to him, something the kid hadn't done since he was about eight. Ty was shaking.

Nick caught Lois' eye. Shit, she looked scared, and Lois never looked scared.

Nick rubbed Ty's back. "What happened? What's wrong?"

"Tyler, tell Nick what you told me."

Rich cleared his throat and stepped into the foyer. Nick nodded to Rich but didn't let go of Tyler. "Rich Ronaldi, this is my assistant, Lois, and her son, Tyler."

Lois shook Rich's hand. "Ronaldi as in Rosalie's brother?"

"Yeah, I am. It's nice to meet you. I can see you need some privacy, so I'll just be going—"

Lois shook her head. "No, you need to hear this, too. I called the police—"

Rich held his hands up. "Whoa, it was just a fight—"

"Not about you. Tyler, tell them what happened."

Tyler stepped back and looked at his mom. Lois laid her hand on Ty's shoulder. "I was at Gianelli's body shop today," he said.

Nick bent down and looked Tyler straight in the eye. "Yeah?"

"I was dropping off a driver's side mirror, but the guy working on the car wouldn't sign the order, so I had to wait for Mr. Gianelli to sign it."

"Okay."

"I was leaning against the wall next to Mr. Gianelli's office. It wasn't like I was trying to listen, I swear, but Mr. Gianelli was yelling, so I couldn't help it."

"Who was he yelling at?"

"Some guy he called Jackie. And Jackie sounded scared. He said that they were in more trouble than just losing the money from Premier Motors. He said Rosalie Ronaldi and her assistant Gina were on to them and that the bitches. . ." Ty ducked his head " . . . sorry, Mom. He said they were talking to his girlfriend, and she knew everything. He'd be finished if it came out. He'd not only lose Premier Motors; he'd lose everything. His wife and his home, and he'd spend the next fifteen years in jail.

"Mr. Gianelli said he'd take care of them. All three of them. Isn't Rosalie Dave's owner?"

"Yeah, buddy, she is."

"I got out of there and ran all the way back. I'm sorry I didn't get the order signed."

Nick grabbed Tyler and hugged him close. He and Lois never lost eye contact, and volumes were spoken with one long look. Nick rubbed Ty's back, still not letting the boy go. "Did anyone see you standing there?"

"I don't think so."

Nick tried to rein in his emotions before he let Tyler go. He felt so many things at once—relief that Ty was safe, anger about what the boy had heard, thankfulness that he'd heard it before it was too late. Those were understandable, but nothing could have prepared him for the cold terror he felt knowing Rosalie was in danger.

Lois hugged her son. "We just got out of the police station and came right here. I don't know if they took us seriously. I'm worried, Nick."

It was Friday night. Rosalie should be home. He called the apartment. The machine picked up. "Lee, it's Nick. I need you to call me. It's urgent. Please." He left the same message on her cell, and at her office. Then he called Gina's cell, thankful he still had her number memorized. The call went straight to voice mail.

"Shit." Rich grabbed his jacket. "I remember Rosalie saying something about working late."

Nick grabbed his jacket on the way out. "We'll start at her place, and if she's not there, we'll try Premier Motors. Let's go."

Chapter 18

NICK AND RICH JUMPED INTO THE MUSTANG AND SPED TO Rosalie's. Henry and Wayne opened the security door for them and unlocked Rosalie's place. Dave was all over Nick before he grabbed his leash and went to the door to stand guard. Rosalie was gone, and so was her briefcase. The place looked the same as it had before Nick had moved in, with one exception—there were tissue boxes everywhere. Some held tissues; others served as tissue garbage cans.

"Do you know where she went?" Rich asked. "It's important."

Wayne tapped his pointer finger on his top lip. "She called and asked if we'd take care of Dave. She said she was going to be late."

Nick smiled. "Thanks. Look, is it all right if we take Dave with us?"

Rich stepped up. "Why?"

Nick attached Dave's leash. "Dave is a regular attack dog if he thinks Lee's in danger."

Rich smiled. "Works for me. And since she's my sister, I say we take the dog. You boys have a problem with that?"

Henry dropped the protective neighbor facade. "She's in danger? We're going, too."

Wayne started dithering. "We are? Don't you think we should wait here in case she comes back?"

Nick thought, what the hell. "Wayne, you stay here. Call Henry if she returns. Henry, you're in the back with Dave. Let's roll."

The Mustang broke the land speed record all the way to Manhattan. Nick parked illegally in front of Premier and had Henry stay in the car as the lookout, with instructions to text message a warning should anyone suspicious come by. He took Dave's leash and motioned Rich to follow.

It had been years since Nick had worked at Premier, but he knew the only way to get in without anyone noticing was through the back. He ran down the alley and swung himself onto the delivery bay. Nick had wondered if he'd have to haul Dave onto the platform, but the pooch made the jump without a moment's hesitation. It was as if Dave sensed Rosalie was in danger.

It was like old times. Nick and Rich used the same hand signals they'd used as kids. Strange, after twenty years, they'd fallen back in synch, as if they'd never been apart. As the three of them skulked to the backdoor, Nick cursed under his breath. The door had been left open. That door was never left unlocked. Ever. Someone had already broken in.

Nick fought the urge to scream Lee's name. He kept telling himself it hadn't been long since the threat was made, and Gianelli would most likely try to intimidate her first. But no matter what he told himself, it didn't stop the terror from threatening to overtake all rationality; it didn't stop the worst-case scenarios from running though his mind; it didn't stop the copper taste of terror; it didn't stop the regret. He should have seen this coming; he should have taken care of her; he should have done whatever it took to get her back; he should have said the words. He'd never told her he loved her.

Dave nudged Nick out of his terror-induced lightbulb moment. Shit, he was such a putz. Hugging the wall, Nick slid down the hallway, pausing to grab the fire extinguisher. He handed it to Rich and motioned him to stay.

There were two ways into his old office. He just hoped his old office was Rosalie's new office. Rich would cover the back entrance, and Nick would take Dave through the front.

Rosalie knew no father would be happy to learn that his son was a lying, cheating embezzler, but she hadn't expected Mr. Lassiter to deny the evidence. This was exactly what he was doing. She gripped the phone a little tighter and took a swig of Mylanta.

"Mr. Lassiter, I'm sorry. This is not something that can be hushed up. The Board hired me; I have a meeting with them Monday morning. I'm sharing this with you today as a courtesy."

She heard someone clear his throat and looked up to find two goombata entering her office. One man took the phone out of her hand and hung it up. The other swiveled her chair around to face him.

The big goombah in front of her looked like he was a few biscotti short of a full box. He pasted on a fake smile as Rosalie stood. "Hey, you don't belong in here. Who are you, and what do you want?"

He put his hands in the pockets of his jacket, opening it far enough to show a leather shoulder holster. Oh,

God, this so couldn't be happening. All the blood drained from her face, and most likely her brain, too, because she couldn't think straight. That alone was enough to piss her off.

"Now Ms. Ronaldi, there's no need to get excited. My name is Gino, and this here," he pointed to the guy on the other side of her desk, "is my associate, Dante."

Rosalie ignored the dumb schmuck with the gun and took a good look at Dante. She couldn't believe her eyes. "Dante? Dante DeEsposito?"

Sure enough, the man before her was none other than her old boyfriend. The boyfriend who'd joined the seminary after she turned down his marriage proposal. The first man she'd ever slept with.

"I guess the whole priest thing didn't work out, huh, Dante? What'd you do, leave the seminary and transfer to Cosa Nostra University?"

Gino snorted at that. "Ha, the seminary. Good one."

Dante cleared his throat. "Gino, you never told me we were coming to see Rosalie Ronaldi. You said she was some chick named Rose."

"What are you talking about? She's a chick, and her name is Rose. You gotta problem with that?"

"Yeah."

"So do I."

Rosalie heard Nick's voice and closed her eyes. She was almost afraid to look at him. He looked great for a guy who'd been in a fight recently. Damn, Rich, too. Nick was going to have one hell of a shiner in the morning. Leave it to Nick to pull off looking hot with his eye almost swollen shut.

"What is this—ghosts of boyfriends past meets the Godfather?"

Nick walked around the other side of Rosalie's desk, rolling her desk chair out of the way, and pulled her to his side. "What are you talking about, boyfriends?"

Rosalie motioned to Dante. "Ex-boyfriend number one, Dante DeEsposito, meet ex-boyfriend number four, Dominick Romeo, and this," she pointed to Gino, "is a co-worker of Dante's named Gino." Rosalie watched Nick and Dante stare each other down and measure each other in the great alpha male tradition. What a joke. Nick's hold on her tightened, and though it felt really good, she had this overwhelming urge to smack him.

Nick nodded toward Dante. "You're the one who ran off to join the seminary?"

Dante shrugged "Not for long." His chin rose in a Sicilian acknowledgement as he looked over Nick. "You're *the* Romeo?"

Nick made the same tough-guy movement. "You're Tony Gianelli's muscle?"

Gino seemed to be blind to the male posturing going on right in front of him—the man had obviously suffered too many blows to the head.

"So you both banged little Rosie here, huh? My turn now?"

Ooh, that was so not a smart thing to say. Dante took a menacing step toward Gino, while Nick pulled her behind him.

Dante grabbed Gino by the collar, and Gino threw his hands up in surrender. "Just kidding, Dante. Leggo of me."

After a small shake, Dante put him down. Gino straightened his shirt and tucked it in over his protruding belly. "As I was saying," Gino continued, "Mr. Gianelli sent us to introduce ourselves and talk to Rosie here about a little problem we're havin' concerning one of her co-workers, Jackie Lassiter."

The tension in the room ratcheted up enough that Gino even seemed to notice. He cleared his throat. "See, we don't want no trouble, and we're sure you don't neither. We just come here to give you a friendly warning."

Rosalie tried to push Nick to the side, and when he didn't budge, she went around the desk and got right into Dante's face. "You call this a friendly warning? You have some nerve, coming into my office after all these years and threatening me. Does your mother know what you do, Dante?"

Gino again must not have been listening, because he picked up the conversation where he'd left off. "Yeah, real friendly-like. You see, Mr. Gianelli ain't too happy that you and that cute little secretary of yours are sticking your noses in business that don't concern you." Gino shook his head. "Not happy at all."

Nick was about to blow. Not that she wasn't at least as pissed off as he seemed. Shit, it wasn't everyday your ex-lover came to threaten you and did it in front of the man who recently stabbed you in the back.

"Well, you can just go back to Mr. Gianelli and tell him where he can stuff—"

Nick turned when he heard Dave bark and then growl. Rosalie shot him a what-the-hell-were-you-thinking-bringing-him-here look. Dave strolled in growling, teeth bared, ridge of black hair on his back standing up. Dave glommed onto Gino—the one with the gun—and began herding him toward the open doorway.

Gino paled. "Mr. Romeo, Dante and me, we don't want no trouble."

Gino moved a hand slowly toward his holster, and Nick felt like growling, too. "If you don't want trouble, you better keep your hands where Dave can see them. Once you do, I'll tell Dave to play nice."

Dante nodded to Gino, and Gino held both his hands up high. Dante looked right over Rosalie's head and spoke to Nick as if she weren't there. "You named your dog Dave?"

Nick bit back a smile when Rosalie poked Dante in the chest. "No, *I* named Dave. He's my dog."

Rosalie was so mad, she was shaking. Nick wasn't sure who she was madder at, Dante and Gino, or him.

Nick took a step toward her but didn't take his eyes off Dante. "If you don't want any trouble, then why are you here threatening my fiancé?

Rosalie turned away from Dante and glared. "Nick—"

Then all hell broke lose. Rich skulked in and hit Gino over the head with the fire extinguisher. Gino's body crumpled to the floor. He was down for the count.

Nick turned to pull Rosalie away and when Dante reached into his jacket, Nick saw red.

"Gun!"

The next thing he knew, he was tackling Rosalie to the floor, holding her down. He covered her body with his as Dave barreled into Dante, knocked him to the floor, and planted his paws on Dante's chest. Dave stood there, growling and frothing at the mouth.

When Nick was sure Dante wasn't moving and Rich had collected all the guns, he helped Rosalie up and pulled her into his arms.

Rosalie, shaking, held onto Nick, wondering if she could have imagined this whole fiasco. No, she blinked a few times, and Nick was still there. Unless her imagination came equipped with Touch-a-Vision and Smell-a-Vision, she was holding the real thing. Nick, who'd put himself between her and a guy with a gun. The dumb ass had tackled her, trying to protect her. He could have been killed.

Rosalie pulled away and took a good look at him. He was fine—well, except for the black eye. His eyes were so much bluer than she remembered, even the one that was almost swollen shut. She felt the familiar sting of tears, so she did the only thing she could to keep them from falling. She hit him.

"Who the hell do you think you are? Superman? You idiot. You could have been killed!"

Rich put his fingers between his teeth and whistled.

Rosalie faced her brother. "What?"

"Where's Gina?"

Rich was definitely frazzled, but curiously, not the least concerned about his little sister. Hmmm. "She went home with Sam and Randi."

"Who the hell are they?"

"Sam is her brother-in-law, the cop. We thought Randi, Jack Lassiter's secretary and mistress, might need protection until we could take all the evidence to the police."

Nick turned on her. "Oh, yeah. You thought Randi needed protection, but you didn't?"

Rosalie planted her hands on her hips and stuck out her chin. "You're the one who almost got killed!"

Nick looked as if he was going to throw an embolism.

That's when the sirens drowned out his mumbling and the cops stormed the room. After a few very uncomfortable minutes while New York's finest sorted out the good guys from the bad, things calmed down. Rich turned over the guns; Gino got a trip to the hospital to make sure he didn't have a concussion before going to jail; and the police put out an APB on Jack Jr. and Tony Gianelli. Everyone was taken to the police station for questioning. Well, everyone except Dave. Dave got to go home with Henry.

"Would you hold on a minute, Dave?" Rosalie called out. "I'm moving. I'm moving already. You know, it's not like you can't go out in the garden and take a leak. Why do you have to get me out of bed at the crack of dawn?"

She rolled over and couldn't believe it was nine o'clock and that Dave hadn't gotten her up earlier. Some mother she was. She went to the bathroom, brushed her teeth, and got ready for their trip to the dog park. She'd gotten a ride home from the station and hadn't seen or heard from Nick since they walked into the police station. If not for the bruise on her hip, she'd swear the whole thing had been one crazy dream.

Dave was whining at the door. The last thing she wanted to do right now was walk Dave, but no matter how depressed she'd gotten over the last month, Rosalie never missed their Saturday romp. She suspected that was the only reason Dave hadn't turned her in to the authorities.

Rosalie pulled on a pair of Nick's sweats that he'd left in the laundry, a bra, and a sweatshirt. She finger combed her hair, put on her dog park shoes—the ones she didn't mind stepping in shit in—and shoved her wallet in her jacket pocket. She'd grab a coffee at Fiorentino's on the way to the park.

Rosalie stepped into the hall, and Dave pulled her away before she could properly close the door. Not that she cared. She managed to get to the security door without falling. The sun shone in, nearly blinding her. She had no idea it was such a gorgeous day. She'd gotten out of the habit of opening the curtains in the morning. If she didn't open them, she had one less thing to do at night. Why bother? It wasn't as if the weather made a difference to her lately. Nothing did. It was spring. It rained. End of story.

Taking the sunglasses out of her jacket pocket, she slid them on. As she pushed the door open, Dave ran out and pulled on his leash, spinning her around. She tripped down the step, right into the arms of a very strong man.

Nick.

Dave was jumping on and around them, pushing in between them, and generally being a total pain in the ass.

"Dave, calm down. Sit." Nick didn't take his eyes or hands off her when he spoke. Dave sat, but he didn't look happy about it.

"You okay?"

"Uh, huh." My, what witty repartee.

"If I let go, you're not going to fall over, are you?"

"No."

"Okay." He let go, and she noticed he held a bouquet of crushed daisies. She widened her stance and held onto the handrail next to the steps just to make sure she wouldn't fall over.

"I brought these for you." He handed her the flowers. She leaned back against the handrail and avoided his hand when she accepted them. She didn't want to chance touching him; just seeing him was enough to affect her equilibrium.

Nick stepped back. "They looked better before we smashed them."

"Thanks."

Nick turned to Dave. "How's my boy? I got something for you, too." Nick pulled a pig's ear from his pocket.

Dave jumped on Nick, but he must have been prepared, because he didn't even step back. Dave gave him a big swipe of the tongue, which pretty much covered his whole face.

"Damn it, Dave. How many times do I have to tell you? I don't kiss guys—not even you. I thought we got that straight."

Dave didn't take his scolding seriously and continued to lick Nick's face. After Nick had sufficiently hugged and patted the huge mutt, he pushed Dave down. Dave settled for sitting beside Nick and leaning against him, the pig's ear hanging out of his mouth.

"Well, at least someone missed me."

Rosalie met his eyes and didn't know what to say. Did he want her to say she missed him?

He pulled her sunglasses down. "Lee, are you in there?"

She nodded.

"Good. You're late getting out this morning. I thought I might have missed you. Are you okay?"

"Um, yeah, I'm fine. Nice shiner. I could kill Rich. I told him to stay out of it."

Nick touched his left eye. "It's not as if I didn't deserve it. Rich and I have history. I had it coming to me long before I met you. We fought; we talked; we worked things out. It's all good . . . except for a few bruises. Then Lois came over with Ty and told us about Tony Gianelli." He stuffed his hands in his pockets. "Listen. I was thinking that I could take Dave to the park while you try to salvage the flowers. I'll pick up breakfast on the way back and we can talk. Okay?"

"Sure." She handed him the plastic bags she had in her pocket.

He took them and gave her a smile that didn't reach his eyes. "Ah, I'd almost forgotten about that part of walking Dave. It's the only thing I haven't missed."

Nick kissed her cheek and breathed in the scent of her. God, she smelled good—she looked awful, but she smelled like a dream. He'd even bought a bottle of her perfume to sniff every now and then. It didn't help. It wasn't the same. In a little over a month, she looked as if she'd lost twenty pounds. If Rosalie was pregnant, she sure as hell wasn't glowing.

She pushed her glasses back in place and handed him Dave's leash. Nick wished he could still see her eyes. Her eyes were so telling. A minute ago, she'd looked as if she might cry.

Nah, Rosalie was not the crying type. She was more the

get-pissed-instead-of-hurt type; she sure showed that yesterday. Dave pulled Nick down the steps, giving him an easy out.

As he turned to walk toward the park, he thought about his plan. It was going well so far. She'd agreed to talk with him, and he'd kissed her cheek without getting punched. That was something, anyway.

She didn't look especially happy to see him—not that she looked unhappy, either.

Before they reached the park, they were joined by Jasmine, the basset Dave had a crush on, and Tommy, the basset's owner.

The two guys did the usual nod and let the dogs set the pace, which was slow for Dave—Jasmine had short legs.

Tom cleared his throat. "I haven't seen you around for a few weeks. Were you out of town?"

"No, Rosalie and I stopped seeing each other."

"So, you back together?"

Nick wanted to know why the hell Tommy was so interested. "Yeah, we are."

"Good. I saw her last week at the park with Dave, and it looked like she was crying."

"Lee was crying? In public?"

Tommy nodded. "It looked that way. She was sitting on that bench over by the pond, and Dave was practically on her lap. I thought she was hurt or something. She said nothing was wrong, and she looked embarrassed as hell. So I left."

"Thanks, Tom. Look, I've got to go. I'll see you around. Come on, Dave, let's go home."

Nick loved the idea that Rosalie cared enough to cry over him. Why else would she have been crying? It didn't matter if Rosalie was sick or pregnant. Nick would do whatever it took to get her back. If they had a baby, that'd be great. Nick had begun to get used to the idea of having a family.

When he started worrying about being like his old man, he reminded himself of what Lois kept telling him. He'd been a part of Tyler's life for the last ten years; he loved him like a son; and he'd never leave him, no matter what. Ty could always depend on him. So why would it be different with Nick's own kid, or his wife? All those lectures Lois had given him had finally sunk in. Nick made a mental note to give her another raise and pick up that new Xbox for Ty.

Dave seemed to sense the rush, so he took care of business quicker than usual. When they got to Rosalie's door, Nick didn't know if he should knock or walk in. He couldn't remember ever knocking on Rosalie's door, and he didn't want to start now.

He walked in, startling her. She spilled ground coffee all over the counter. It looked as if she'd tried to fix herself up a little. She'd changed her clothes, though what she'd put on was hanging on her. She was bony. What had happened to his Lee?

He saw why Gina had called Rich. He tapped down the worry. He'd take care of her, and she'd be fine. But damn, if she was pregnant, she was one sick pregnant lady.

Nick set the bags down on the table. He'd stopped at Fiorentino's and gotten all her favorites. He knew the way to Rosalie's heart was through her stomach. At least it used to be.

Chapter 19

It was weird seeing Nick in her apartment again. She'd imagined him there so many times, and now that he was, she couldn't stop wondering if she was dreaming. The only thing that clued her in was the slight irritation she felt when he walked in without knocking, as if he owned the place. Of course, if he had knocked, it probably would have made her cry.

He subtly checked the apartment out. She'd kind of let the place go. It wasn't as bad as it had been before, but it was well on its way. Mail covered the table. One of the two things Nick had left behind, the vacuum, served as a coatrack holding her collection of outerwear. She'd kicked all her shoes off under every available piece of furniture. The thought of putting them in her closet only served to remind her of Nick, and she was depressed enough as it was. Hell, she'd been spinning around the toilet bowl of depression for the last thirty-five days, six hours, and eighteen minutes—not that she was counting.

Dave was doing a happy dance, jumping all over the apartment in glee. His tail banged the walls and closets like a drum. The traitor.

Reaching into the cupboard above her, Rosalie snagged the pain reliever and took one. Okay, she downed three and tapped a Pepcid out of its bottle. Her stomach was doing flips. She didn't know if it was because Nick had walked back into her life or because he'd brought food. In any case, she didn't trust her stomach.

"Should you be taking that?"

She turned and found Nick standing right behind her. She stepped away and wedged herself into the corner of the cupboards. "It's over-the-counter."

"Yeah, but is it safe?" He looked at her funny, like he was examining her.

"Safe enough."

Nick didn't seem to believe her. Too bad. He'd lost the right to make her take medicine, or not take it, when he walked out on her. She popped the pink pill in her mouth and crunched on it, just to piss him off. It worked—the crunching, not the pill. Her stomach was still roiling.

Nick stepped aside, swept the coffee she'd spilled off the counter with the side of his hand and into the sink, and finished setting up the coffee machine. That was fine with Rosalie. She always did like his coffee better than hers.

He nodded toward the bags. "I brought your favorite—chocolate-covered donuts. Go ahead and dig one out. I know you want to."

"Maybe later." Like when hell froze over. She swallowed back the nausea and rubbed her stomach. Nick stared, giving her the weirdest look. "What?"

"Nothing. Um, are you actually going to have breakfast before dessert?"

"I've been watching what I eat. That's all."

"Good. I've been reading about how important it is to eat healthy." He poured her a glass of orange juice he'd picked up and slid it down the counter. "Folic acid."

Whatever the acid was in OJ, it didn't sit well, either. She didn't mention it. It wasn't his business.

Taking the juice to the table, she set the glass down at his place. God, he still had a seat at the table, a side of the bed, keys . . .

"Hey, how did you get in the security door? Did you make a copy of my keys or something?"

Ooh, she saw steam shooting out his ears. Now all he needed was to blow his top. She had no idea what possessed her, but she intentionally pissed him off. It didn't make sense. She was happy he was there. Happy, confused, insecure—oh, and let's not forget, scared spitless. She wasn't sure what she was more afraid of—that he'd leave again, or that he'd stay and leave later. The only thing she knew was that she wanted him to stay forever. She never again wanted to go through what she had in the last thirty-five days, six hours, and twenty minutes.

Rosalie watched Nick trying to control his anger. His mouth moved as he counted to ten, and his teeth clenched. The tic in his jaw was going double time. Good. It was nice to see that she could still get a rise out of him.

"Henry and Wayne let me in. They seemed happy to see me."

"Oh." Okay, now she felt like a heel. "I'm sure they were."

"You don't look so happy."

She gathered the mail that she'd thrown all over the table and tossed it on the couch. She didn't turn to look at him. She was already on the verge of losing it.

"Nick, what are you doing here?"

She waited for his answer, listening to the Felix the Cat clock ticking. Every roll of Felix's eyes and swish of his tail seemed to take a lifetime. Her heart pounded— the part of it that wasn't broken, the part that kept her alive. Blood rushed through her ears. She held onto the back of the chair and prayed she wouldn't pass out.

He'd moved so quietly, Rosalie didn't know he was behind her until his hands cupped her shoulders and slid down the length of her arms. He pried her hands off the chair back and pulled her against him. A war waged in her head. Part of her wanted to stay in his arms, absorb the heat of his body against hers, and melt into his embrace. The other part wanted to run like hell. God, it hurt so much, thinking this might be the last time she ever touched him. At least when he'd walked out the last time, she hadn't known he wouldn't come back. If he left now, she'd know. And she wouldn't be surprised if it killed her. Rosalie honestly didn't think she could go through it again.

"Don't do this, Nick." She pulled away, but he didn't let go. He turned her around to face him and held her there.

"Don't do what? Don't love you? I tried that. It didn't work. Lee, I know I hurt you. I know I fucked up. I should never have kept things from you. But when I met you and found out that you were Rich Ronaldi's sister, I didn't think past—"

"Getting into my pants?"

"Well, yeah. Lee, I'm thirty-two-years-old, and I've never had a relationship last more than a month. I've never been in love before. I never wanted to be."

"Do you think this is what I wanted?"

"No. But I didn't know that then, and I thought once you found out who I was, you'd never want to see me again."

"Oh, yeah, you being The Dominick Romeo must have women running in the opposite direction. It must be tough. Maybe you should change your name to Dr. Hannibal Lecter. That might help."

"I was your brother's best friend until I slept with his girlfriend and got both our asses arrested. I didn't think he'd be real happy with me seeing his little sister."

"Hold on. You slept with Rich's girlfriend? Rich is three years older than you, and he was only seventeen when he was arrested. You slept with someone when you were fourteen? What did you do, play spin the bottle and tell ghost stories as foreplay?"

"I was fifteen, and to tell you the truth, I don't remember. I was drunk. I never would have touched Sophia if I was thinking clearly."

"Neither would Rich. She was such a slut. I was ten, and even I knew she would do anyone."

"Gee, thanks."

"Don't mention it. So this is why you didn't tell me who you were? It had nothing to do with Premier Motorcars?"

"I didn't know you were involved with Premier until I drove you there that day you insisted on going to work sick. I swear. Before that, I thought it was nice to go out with someone who didn't expect to be taken to a four-star restaurant on every date."

"We'll get to Premier in a moment. As for the four-star treatment, I can see that. I figured you didn't want me to know who you were because most women try to land you for your money."

"Well, yeah."

"But after you got to know me, why didn't you come clean?"

"I wanted to, but then I found out you were working with Premier. I thought if I came clean, you'd be so pissed about me lying, you wouldn't want to see me anymore. I figured I might as well wait until Rich came back for spring break. That way, I'd have as much time with you as possible. By the time I found out Rich was coming home, I couldn't stand the thought of losing you. I knew I had to tell you."

"So, why didn't you?"

"I was going to, but you didn't get home until three in the morning. Do you have any idea how worried I was?"

"Do you have any idea how much it hurt when I realized I was living with a man who cared so little about me, he'd never told me his name? And that's before I figured out I was sleeping with the enemy. You were trying to ruin the company I was trying to save."

Nick shook his head. "No. I'm sorry. God, Lee, it was never that. I just didn't want to lose you, and as for Premier, I did nothing to hurt the company after I found out you were the new CFO. I hardly had to do anything before then, except wait for Jack Jr. to flush Premier down the toilet. I should never have let him near you. God, Lee, I don't know what I'd have done if anything had happened to you."

Nick clung to her and kissed her. A sweet kiss on the lips. God, she'd missed him.

The coffee machine beeped, signaling it had finished brewing. She was dying for a cup. She also had to get away from Nick. She couldn't think when he was touching her. She went to the kitchen and poured a cup of coffee.

"Is that decaf?"

"What would be the point in drinking coffee, if not for the caffeine?"

"You should be avoiding caffeine. It's not good for you. It increases your blood pressure and your heart rate. Did you know that it's been linked to miscarriages?"

"So?"

"So, pregnant women shouldn't be drinking caffeinated anything. Ever since I got here, you've been popping pills, and now you're drinking coffee. Are you trying to lose our baby?"

Rosalie spun around, coffee sloshing over the rim of her cup onto the floor. "Oh my God! You came here because you think I'm pregnant?"

Her skin got all clammy, and a wave of nausea rolled over her. She ran to the bathroom. She'd never been one to be sick, especially in front of anyone, but Nick followed and rubbed her back while she threw up what little she had in her stomach.

Rosalie sat back and leaned against the cool tile wall, fighting tears. Nick handed her a wet washcloth. She wiped her face. God, it was happening again. He was going to leave.

"All better?"

She shook her head. "You need to leave, Nick."

"How could you think I'd leave you? We're having a baby, for God's sake. My baby. I'm not going anywhere."

"Don't you understand? There is no baby. You're off the hook. Go. Get out."

"What?"

"You heard me. There is no baby. Now would you please go? Please?" She couldn't stop the tears. Rosalie pulled her knees to her chest and buried her face in her arms, sobbing—waiting for him to leave again.

"Don't tell me you lost the baby. Lee?" He sat beside her on the floor and pulled her into his lap. "I'm so sorry, sweetheart. But it's going to be okay. You'll see. I read that twenty-five percent of the babies conceived are lost early. A lot of times, the woman doesn't even know it. We can try again real soon."

What, was he dense? "Nick, I didn't lose a baby. There never was a baby. I was never pregnant."

"Then what's wrong? Why are you sick?"

"What do you care? You don't love me. You only came back because you thought I was pregnant."

"Bullshit. If that were true, why would I still be here? I love you. Now damn it, Lee, tell me what the hell is wrong with you."

"Nothing." She pushed herself up and threw the washcloth on the counter. He stood beside her, looking at her in the mirror. Fine. She needed to brush her teeth. Let him watch. After everything Nick had seen, seeing her spit shouldn't bother him. She put a little toothpaste on the brush, hoping the taste wouldn't start her heaving again.

"I'll go make you some tea and toast. You need to eat, and we need to talk without you getting sick."

"I'm not hungry," she said around the toothbrush in her mouth.

"Do you realize that the only time you've ever *not* been hungry has been when you were sick?"

After rinsing out her mouth, she wiped herself with a towel. "Do you realize the only time I've been sick has been when you were here?"

"Well then, I guess we better move to my place." He picked her up, carried her into the bedroom, and set her down on the bed.

"Nick, I told you, I'm not sick, and I'm not pregnant—"

"That remains to be seen."

"What is that supposed to mean?"

"It means that suffering from a broken heart does not make one lose over twenty pounds in a month."

"How would you know?"

"I haven't lost twenty pounds, and I not only lost you, but I lost Dave. And I love that dog."

"Well, if it's any consolation, he's been miserable without you, too."

"You lie down while I make some breakfast. I'll be right back."

Nick dialed his cell phone on his way to the kitchen, made an appointment while he poured himself some coffee, and disconnected the call as he filled the kettle for Rosalie's tea. After rummaging around the near-empty cupboard, he found tea bags and opened the fridge to get the bread. There was nothing but batteries and condiments in the refrigerator. It was worse then it had been when they'd first started dating. Then at least she'd had milk, eggs, and beer. There was nothing in the freezer, either. She was going to have to eat a dry bagel. That was close enough to toast.

A few minutes later, he was back in the bedroom, and Rosalie looked as if she was sleeping. He sat beside her. Her eyes opened, and she greeted him with a suspicious look. "Hey."

He put the tray between them. "Here, eat slowly. This will help while we talk."

She looked wary. He'd thought they'd gotten beyond that. Hell, he'd told her he loved her—a sentiment she hadn't returned.

He pointed to the bagel and handed her the tea. "Take a bite; it'll make you feel better."

She took a sip of tea instead. She never did what he told her to do. He loved that about her . . . almost as much as he hated it.

"I was thinking of what it was like when we were together. You know—you, Dave, and me. It was good, wasn't it?"

"Nick, I'm sorry. I'm not interested in going back to whatever it was we had. I don't want that anymore. I've changed."

He leaned forward with his elbows on his knees, raked his fingers through his hair, and then stayed that way, holding his head, staring at the floor. "What do you mean, you don't want that? Are you talking about the deal, or are you talking about me?"

"The deal. I'm talking about the deal. You . . . we, well, it was good except for the lying. You really suck at lying."

"It was just good?"

"Hold on. You're the one who said it was good. What do you want me to say? That it was magnificent?"

He sat up straighter and smirked. "Yeah, magnificent works. I'd go with magnificent."

"So would I, but you said it was good."

"You're right. I'm really screwing this up, aren't I? This isn't the way I envisioned it at all."

"Envisioned what?"

"Seeing you again." He moved his food to the side and took her hand in his. "I thought it'd be like one of those sappy movies. You know, you'd see me, and you'd be happy. I definitely didn't expect to have to tackle you to the ground and hold you down, not to mention having to pick you up off the bathroom floor after you—"

"I get it. You don't have to draw a picture."

"I thought I'd tell you I loved you; you'd say you loved me, too; we'd have make-up sex; and then we'd get married. End of story."

"Hold on. I got you through the make-up sex. But marriage?"

"Yeah. I thought you, me, and Dave, we'd be a family. Like the people you see in the park. You know, the mom and dad, a dog, and two point five kids. Like one of those Rockwell paintings."

"Kids? Nick, I told you, I'm not pregnant."

"So we'll get married and work on that part of it."

She put her hand to his forehead. "Are you sick? What's come over you?"

"You. You make me happy. You drive me crazy. You fill my life. I want you to be a part of it, and I want to be part of yours. I want to take you home, introduce you to my mother and grandmother. I want to meet your family and friends. I was miserable without you. I felt as if I were in prison serving a life sentence. I never want to live like that again. I need you, Lee. Marry me."

It was a good thing Rosalie was in bed; if she hadn't been, she'd have fallen over. Marry Nick? "You mean marriage, as in wearing white, a church, a reception—that kind of marriage?"

Nick crowded her against the pillows.

"I'm talking about spending the rest of our lives together. Being a real family. Going to sleep with you every night. Waking up with you every morning. Making love to you. You know, love, honor, and cherish? Yada, yada, yada?"

Pushing him back, she slid out of bed and started pacing. By the time she'd walked around the bed once, he'd moved a pile of stuff that had been on the dresser and put the tray there.

"Why is it that men always remember the first three—love, honor, and cherish—because that's what they expect from their women, and the rest is 'yada, yada, yada?' That's the part about not screwing around. That's the part men forget."

Nick looked pissed, and when he got pissed, he tended to loom over her. "Lee, I'm not your father. I don't cheat."

"No. You lie."

Nick put his hands on her shoulders and slid them down her arms, linking their hands and pushing them behind her back, which also served to pull her against him. "I'm a terrible liar. You said so yourself."

"True." Lord, he felt good. It amazed her how all she had to do was get close to Nick and she felt better. Like how, when she came home from a long trip, she'd be too stressed and too tired to relax, but then she'd open her front door and her spirits would magically lift. Being with Nick was like that.

"And you love me."

"Uh, huh." Oh God, how was she supposed to think with him nuzzling her neck? Somehow, his hands had moved to her butt, and she'd wrapped her arms around his neck.

"And if you say yes right now, we can get to the make-up sex."

"Nick. Even Joey offered me a ring."

"Sweetheart, would you work with me here? You know, I've never done this before."

"Sorry."

"Sit down."

"Why?"

"Would you please, for once in our relationship, just do as I ask?"

"Are you going to start expecting me to do what you tell me to? Because, if you are—"

"Lee, please, you're killing me here."

"Fine." She sat.

"Good." Nick got down on one knee and pulled a little blue box out of his pocket.

Rosalie wondered if she was seeing things. She didn't know about every girl, but every Italian, Brooklyn girl, by the time she had her first Barbie doll stuffed into a wedding dress, dreamed of three things when it came to marriage. First, that she wouldn't look fat in white. Second, that she'd get married in St. Patrick's Cathedral. And third, that her engagement ring would come from Tiffany & Company.

Rosalie knew at least one of her childhood dreams had come true. And luckily, it was the only one she hadn't given up hope on or outgrown. There was no way she could pull off wearing white without looking like the Pillsbury Doughboy, and she'd given up on the whole St. Patrick's Cathedral bit when she learned the true story of Cinderella and Prince Charming. But Tiffany's still had the power to make her heart sing, and she'd recognize a Tiffany's box at a hundred yards.

Nick cleared his throat. "Lee, I promise to love, honor, and cherish you for the rest of my life. I promise never to screw around with anyone but you and always bring you chocolate. Will you marry me? You know you want to."

"Oh, Nick, you got me a ring."

"Why are you so surprised? I know I've never done this before, and I didn't say everything I should have, but even I know that when you ask the woman you love to marry you, you have to give her a ring." He laughed and kissed her, and then he held out the box. "Aren't you going to open it?"

Okay, Rosalie admitted to herself that she was a total sap, but she couldn't help it. She cried. She'd never cried happy tears before. She was smiling and crying at the same time. He wanted to marry her. He'd bought her a ring and everything.

Nick opened the box, and she couldn't breathe. It had to be the most amazing, most beautiful ring she'd ever seen. It looked like a square diamond, but it wasn't an emerald cut, because it was rounded, too. A platinum band embedded with diamonds surrounded the center stone. The shank held graduated diamonds. Oh, and there was even a matching wedding band.

He slipped the ring on her finger and then he kissed her hand. "Do you like the ring? Because if you don't—"

Rosalie wrapped her arms around him and held him tight, breathing in the scent of him and feeling whole for the first time in a month. He was a part of her. Sure, Nick drove her crazy sometimes—he was her other annoying, sexy, pushy, gorgeous, loving, giving, and funny half. "I love the ring, and I love you. I'm so happy—scared to death, but happy."

"Sweetheart, I was scared when I thought I'd lost you. When I heard someone wanted to hurt you, I was terrified. . ." his hold on her tightened so that she could barely breathe " . . . and when I walked in on those two guys threatening you, there are no words to describe how I felt."

Okay, things were getting way too depressing here, not to mention painful—if he squeezed her any harder, she'd break a rib.

"I don't understand what caused your one-eighty about marriage. You were always so against it. What happened?"

"Does it matter? I want to get married now. Right now. Today. That's all that counts."

"No, it's not. You can't pull that "don't-ask, don't-tell" crap with me any more. It's time you declassified your life—to me, anyway. When I ask questions, I want answers, even if the answers make you uncomfortable."

"Okay. I never wanted to marry because I thought the

Romeo men were a curse to women. It runs in the family—my father, his father, and his father before him. They met a woman, married her, knocked her up, and took off, never to be heard from again. I thought it was hereditary. I wanted to put an end to the Romeo line once and for all."

"That's ridiculous. What are you, *stunad*? The only reason your father and his father and his father before him did what they did is because they were assholes. You're not."

"No, apparently, I'm just stupid. Thanks, I think. You know, I could say the same thing about your reason for not wanting to get married."

"Sure you could, but you won't, because you don't want to fight with me."

"Good point. Get your shoes on. We're going out."

"Hey, what happened to the make-up sex? I was really looking forward to make-up sex."

"Oh, really? Well, I'm not in the mood. Come on. I want to take you home."

"Nick, what are you talking about? We are home. Can't we," she kissed his neck, sliding her chest against his to reach his mouth, "you know, stay home?"

He gave her one of those smiles that made her insides melt.

"You'd like that, wouldn't you?"

She was getting breathless thinking about how much she'd like that. "Oh, yeah."

"Fine, we can stay home as long as you want—right after you see a doctor. I called Mike. I need to make sure you're okay."

"I'm not sick."

"I'm not going to be satisfied that you're healthy until I hear it from a doctor. Either you get your shoes and a jacket on, or I'll pick you up and carry you out."

"Fine."

"Good."

Slipping on her Crocs, she grabbed her jacket, which hung on the vacuum, picked up her purse, and walked out the front door. "Why didn't you have Mike meet us here?"

"I didn't want him to interrupt anything."

"Well, thanks to you, there was nothing to interrupt."

"Oh, pardon me. I didn't consider a marriage proposal nothing."

"That's not what I meant, and you know it."

"Sweetheart, I know exactly what you meant. And I love that you can't wait to jump my bones. But there are some things more important than sex. Not many, but your health is one of the few. Just think, the sooner you get a clean bill of health, the sooner you can ravage me."

"Okay, let's go. But I better follow you over in my car."

"Why?"

"'Cause your head is so big, I don't think there's room in there for both me and your ego."

"There will be plenty of room. I'll put the top down. It's a beautiful day."

Chapter 20

WHEN NICK SAID HE WAS GOING TO TAKE ROSALIE TO HIS home, she figured it would be nice, but she never expected a freaking mansion. It was huge and stately, and everything a person could want in an upscale boutique hotel, but it wasn't exactly homey.

She fell in love with the original stained glass, the intricate woodwork, and the paneling—old-world mahogany, not Home Depot.

The decorating, however, gave her pause. It was so totally un-Nick. It looked fine for a guy who lived on a diet of ballet, champagne, caviar, and classical music, but not for Nick, who lived on beer, pizza, hockey, and rock with a little Sinatra thrown in for good measure. Not that Nick couldn't do the ballet, champagne and caviar, and orchestra thing on occasion, but he wouldn't be comfortable living in it, and neither would she. No wonder he'd moved in with her. Rosalie cringed at the thought of what Dave's tail alone would do to this place.

Nick stood beside her in the entry. "You hate it."

She must not have hidden her feelings well. Damn, why did he have to be so perceptive? "I don't hate it, but I'm having trouble seeing you here." She spun around, taking in the chandelier, the chichi knickknacks in the living room, the ornate Victorian dining room, the hunting club study/library. "The person who decorated it must not have known you at all. Are you comfortable living here? I'd be afraid to sit down."

"Lee, the only place I've ever felt comfortable was with you. Don't you see? You're my home, my love, my family. You're what I've been searching for my whole life. I sleep here when I'm not with you, and I use it as my mailing address, but I don't live here. I never have."

Nick wiped tears she didn't realize she'd been crying off her cheeks and kissed her. She snuggled closer in his arms. "So, where did you live before you moved here?"

"Nowhere."

"Where did you grow up?"

"Here. In the basement apartment. My mother used to manage this brownstone when it was a tenement. Park Slope has changed a lot in the last ten years. Growing up, I used to dream of buying the place and restoring it."

"And you always get what you want. I know."

The doorbell sounded. It was like being in a bell tower on Sunday, only louder and longer. "What? A simple ding-dong isn't good enough? Rich people even have ostentatious doorbells?"

"I didn't pick it out. The decorator did."

"I don't think I'd like this decorator of yours."

Nick choked and didn't grin. But he looked like he wanted to. "I'm sure you wouldn't."

He answered the door. It was Dr. Mike. Rosalie groaned.

Mike walked right past Nick without acknowledging his existence. "Rosalie, how's my favorite patient?"

Nick cleared his throat. "You're not even going to say hello?"

Mike got in Nick's face. "You deserve to be shot. I was in bed . . . in bed with a woman, and we were just getting to the good stuff when you had me paged. You said it was an emergency."

"It is."

Mike looked at Rosalie. "Do you feel as if you're dying, Rosalie?"

"No."

Mike turned back to Nick. "See, there's no emergency."

Nick seemed to grow in stature. He puffed up and looked scary. "Lee's sick. In my book, that's an emergency."

Mike looked Rosalie over. "You have lost a lot of weight. Have you been dieting?"

She shook her head. She really didn't want to talk about her stomach in front of Nick. Mike must have gotten the hint.

Mike took her arm and steered her toward the main staircase. "Since I'm here, I might as well take a look at you. Come on. Let's go up to one of the bedrooms. He's got a million of them."

Nick sputtered. "Bedroom? Why do you need to go to a bedroom? You're not taking Lee into a bedroom."

She turned around on the steps and glared at him. "What is your problem? You're the one who dragged Mike all the way over here. Where do you want him to examine me? In the kitchen?"

"Why not? All he's going to do is look down your throat, right, Mike?"

"Nick, I'm a doctor. Rosalie's a patient. Grow up."

Nick followed them up the stairs. When they got to a guest room, Mike led her inside and shut the door on Nick.

"I'll be right out here." She heard Nick yell through the heavy door.

Mike sat on a comfortable chair and nodded toward the other. "I think we should make him stand out there for a good long time. It'll serve him right for dragging me out here under false pretenses."

"I'm sorry about that. I told him I wasn't sick."

"I understand why he's concerned. You don't look well, Rosalie. What's the problem?"

"My stomach has been bothering me. I think it's stress."

"Bothering you how, exactly?"

"You know. My stomach hurts; I'm nauseous a lot; I don't have much of an appetite."

"How long has this been going on?"

"A little over a month."

"Is it getting better? Worse?"

"You're not going to talk to Nick about this, are you?"

"No, but if that's an engagement ring on your hand, you probably should. Could you be pregnant?"

"Not unless it's the second Immaculate Conception."

Mike looked questioningly at that. "Contraceptives aren't one hundred percent reliable."

"I know, but abstinence is. I haven't seen Nick in a month, and I had my period after we stopped seeing each other."

"You stopped seeing each other a month ago, and now you're engaged?"

"It's a long story. What else do you need to know?"

"I'm going to take your blood pressure, listen to your heart and lungs."

"Fine." He did his thing and didn't say much, so she figured everything must be normal. He took her temperature with one of those ear things. Again, he said nothing. He looked in her ears, down her throat, up her nose. "Are we done yet? I told you I was fine."

"Lie down on the bed and show me where it hurts."

Rosalie kicked off her shoes and lay on the bed. She pointed just below the breastbone. "Here."

"Unzip your pants for me, and pull your shirt up to right under your bra."

She did, and he did the usual poking and prodding thing on her stomach, and even listened to it with the stethoscope, a very cold stethoscope.

"Well, your uterus isn't enlarged, so it doesn't look as if you're pregnant."

"I told you that. Geez, Mike. You charge for this?"

Rosalie zipped up her pants and pulled her shirt back down. He offered her a hand up.

"Have you been vomiting?"

"A little."

"Is there blood in the vomit?"

"No." Okay, now she was beginning to worry.

"What have you been eating?"

"Not much."

"Do you drink a lot of coffee?"

"Yes."

"How much?"

"Three or four Venti, triple shot lattés a day."

"No more coffee. I want you to see a gastroenterologist friend of mine. I'll call and set something up right away."

"Why?"

"Well, my dear, it sounds to me like you have an ulcer. Do you take painkillers? Ibuprofen?"

"Yes."

"Not any more. Acetaminophen, if you must. I'll give you a prescription for something that will help decrease the acid level in your stomach, and I'll call and get you an appointment for Monday. You'll have to take a few tests. No canceling."

"Is this serious?"

"It can be. Ulcers are caused by bacteria, but stress, poor diet, and irregular and skipped meals are contributing factors."

"What am I going to tell Nick? He's going to freak."

Mike patted her on the back. "Well, if I were you, I'd start out by telling him I cured your pneumonia."

"Yeah, great."

"Why don't you go calm the bear while I pick up my things? I don't know who pissed him off and gave him that black eye, but I don't want one of those."

"He's harmless, and he's happy . . . well, except for the whole Premier Motors fiasco. Mr. Lassiter called me last night and told me they'd made a deal. Nick's always wanted Premier, but he never wanted to get it this way."

"Yeah, Nick's a good guy. He'd never hurt Mr. Lassiter if he could avoid it. But it sounds to me like he had no choice. Congratulations on your engagement. I wish you two all the best. I suppose I'll have to start finding my own dates now. Damn, that takes time."

"Excuse me?"

"I have, on occasion, comforted Nick's old girl-friends after he dumped them. Unfortunately, none were of your caliber."

"Is that a compliment I heard?"

"Yes, it's a definite compliment. Nick's a lucky man."

"Thanks, but I'm pretty lucky, too."

Nick knocked on the door. "What's going on in there? Lee? Sweetheart—"

She opened the door to a frantic Nick.

"What's taking so long?" He wrapped his arms around her and looked over her head at Mike. "Is she okay?"

Mike closed his little black bag and walked past them down the hall. "Your fiancée will tell you everything you need to know."

Rosalie smiled. "Thanks, Mike."

He jogged down the steps. It looked like he was in a hurry to get back to whomever he'd been dragged away from. "You're welcome. Consider it an engagement present," he called back. They heard the front door slam behind him.

Nick looked at her expectantly. "So?"

"Mike thinks I might have a little ulcer."

"A little ulcer? A little ulcer! *Madònne*, what's wrong with that head of yours?"

"Nick, it's okay. Mike gave me a prescription to calm my stomach, and I'll go to the doctor he recommended on Monday. I promise. So don't break my chops, because he says stress is a contributing factor, and you're stressing me out."

"I'm sorry. I really thought you were pregnant." He actually looked disappointed.

"I told you I wasn't."

"Yeah, but what do you know? You thought you had a cold, and you had pneumonia."

"I'm never going to live that down, am I?"

"Nope, I'll remind you of that for the rest of your life."

"Nick? Can we go home?"

"Sure, sweetheart, anything you want."

Oh, God, he used his deep, sexy, "do me baby" voice, and she almost climaxed right then and there. She made Pavlov's dogs seem unresponsive.

"You know," he pinned her against the wall. "I have a Jacuzzi."

"You do, huh?" He had a hell of a lot more than a Jacuzzi, but she wouldn't mind getting all that in a tub of hot bubbly water.

"It's great for relaxing—a great stress reliever." His fingers slipped under her shirt and over the skin of her stomach. Her breath rushed out with a whoosh. Her stomach muscles clenched—hell, so did all her muscles down there.

Nick kissed her neck. "I want you so bad. I've dreamed of being with you every night." His hands moved upward, over her rib cage. "I'd wake up alone and. . ."

His hold on her tightened as quickly as the mood changed. The desperation in his voice shocked her as much as it mirrored hers.

"I know. Me, too. I haven't had a good night's sleep since you left."

Nick took her face in his hands and placed his forehead against hers, his eyes shut tightly. "You're not keeping anything from me? You're really okay? Mike didn't say anything—"

"Nick, I told you everything. I'm fine. Promise." She kissed him—a kiss of understanding, forgiveness, love, hope, and relief. It blossomed from comforting to exciting, needy, and giving, to tender and demanding. There was no more pretending, no more doubting, no more hiding from each other or themselves.

Rosalie touched him with shaking hands. She was nervous. For the first time, she was unprotected, armed with only love and trust. She realized how a first tandem skydiving jump must feel—falling through the sky tied to one person and a parachute, with no control of either.

It was the scariest thing she'd ever done—and the most exciting. Every touch was magnified, every breath deeper, every look more intense, more meaningful. Their clothes shed like layers of armor until they lay naked on the bed, bursting with urgency and heat. Mutual desire was a palpable thing, heady and strong. The scent of Nick, the feel of him beneath her and within her, was familiar and new at the same time.

Nick held her in a vise like grip, as if he was afraid she'd disappear. His eyes were closed tight, concentration evident. She was on intensity overload. She needed him with her. Leaning forward, she kissed his mouth and cheeks. When he opened his eyes, tears appeared. She couldn't tell whose they were. Maybe both of theirs.

Their gazes locked, and the connection was complete—mind, spirit, body, and soul. Her climax raged through her like a wildfire, white-hot and all consuming. Nick groaned her name. His orgasm went on and on, fueling, feeding, and increasing hers.

She collapsed. She knew she should move, but she hadn't the energy to do anything but breathe and wonder at the enormity of it all.

Making love, true love, for the first time must be akin to a blind person seeing for the first time. Only one aspect of the person's life would change, but that change would color every other facet of his being forever. And no matter how long his vision lasted, he'd always have the memory of the first sight, the first light, the first person he laid eyes on. Nick would always be her first.

When they'd returned to Rosalie's apartment, her answering machine had been blinking. Rosalie had refused to listen to the messages. She'd said she wanted one day where no one could intrude on them. Since they weren't at cross-purposes, Nick hadn't argued with her.

The next morning, Nick held Rosalie while she slept. He couldn't imagine anything more perfect. Her left hand lay on his chest, her engagement ring catching the morning sun shining through her bedroom window. He'd wanted to take Dave to his house and stay there, but Rosalie had refused. She'd said Dave would wreak havoc and destroy everything. Like Nick actually cared about any of that stuff. But he cared enough about Rosalie to drop the subject when he saw it upset her. He'd woken up every half hour to make sure she was there. And yet, he'd still slept better than he had since he'd left.

Nick slid out from beneath Rosalie. He'd spent a lot of time forcing the issue of announcing their engagement to her family. Rosalie thought they should wait until after her sister's wedding. What Annabelle's wedding to that creep Johnny, the one who'd put his hands on Rosalie, had to do with them, Nick wasn't sure. The only thing

Nick was sure of was that Johnny's hands would be broken if he ever looked sideways at Rosalie again.

Nick watched Rosalie dress for dinner at her parents' house. He bit his tongue when he saw her take off her engagement ring and put it in her jewelry box. He took it out when she was in the bathroom and slipped the box into his jacket pocket. They were engaged, so in his mind, wherever she went, so did his ring. She'd want to put it on after they announced it. At least, he hoped she would. Damn. Nick knew she was dreading the Ronaldi family dinner he'd invited himself to. She wasn't feeling well—he'd only allowed her one cup of coffee instead of the usual pot—and he knew how scary she was without her daily overdose of caffeine. She was not in the best frame of mind.

It wasn't until he was standing beside her outside the opened front door of the Ronaldi house, watching all hell break loose, that Nick questioned the wisdom of escorting his fiancée to her family's home without invitation.

Rosalie hadn't even finished crossing the threshold before trouble began. Everyone was in the living room. Mr. Ronaldi was sitting on the Barcalounger with his newspaper; Rich was standing at the top of the steps; and an older woman Nick thought must be Rosalie's Aunt Rose stood next to a younger, anorexic version of Rosalie, who Nick was pretty sure was Annabelle.

Mrs. Ronaldi made the first move before Rosalie even got her jacket off. "Talk some sense into your sister, Rosalie. Tell her she can't cancel the wedding three weeks before the ceremony."

Annabelle shook her fist at her mother. "Ma, Johnny

was screwing Wanda Rigoletto at the funeral home beside a corpse. How can I marry him now?"

Mrs. Ronaldi waved her hand as if swatting a fly. "Men will be men. You don't cancel a wedding because he had one last fling."

Nick slid his arm around Rosalie. It looked as if she was about to blow. She shook with anger.

"Ma, what are you? Crazy? You don't expect Annabelle to still marry him, do you? Johnny De Palma is a disgusting pig. Why she wanted to marry him in the first place is a mystery. I think Annabelle has finally come to her senses." Rosalie shook her head with disgust. "If Annabelle was the one screwing around, you'd call her a puttana. When Johnny does it, you say men will be men? You know, Ma, I don't get you. If he's cheating now, he'll cheat later. But I guess that's okay. It doesn't matter if we marry the scum of the earth, as long as we're married and have babies. Right, Ma?"

Mrs. Ronaldi crossed herself. "You! What do you know? You work, work, work. You're so busy in your big office, you don't see what's important. You have no husband, no family. You'll die old and alone. If I rely on you, I'll go to my grave with no grandchildren."

Nick cleared his throat and pulled Rosalie closer. He wasn't sure if he was being supportive or proactive. "Mrs. Ronaldi."

She ground her teeth together, trying not to look as if she minded being interrupted. She wasn't much of an actor.

Nick threw in one of his dimpled grins. No woman had ever been able to resist him when he grinned—no woman except Rosalie. "I don't think you have anything to worry ab—"

Mrs. Ronaldi cut him off. "Who are you to tell me anything? What do you know?"

"I'm sorry, I don't think we've ever been properly introduced." He held his hand out toward her. "I'm Dominick Romeo. Since we're practically family, you can call me Nick."

Annabelle pointed to Nick. "I thought you were Nick, the rebound guy."

"No, I'm Nick, the fiancé guy."

A chorus of gasps followed Nick's announcement. Rosalie said nothing, but the hard elbow in his ribs conveyed her displeasure.

"What in the hell is this world coming to?" Annabelle screamed. "Rosalie lands Dominick Romeo, the car baron, and I can't even keep a freaking mortician? I'm the pretty one! I'm the one who everyone wants to be seen with!" Annabelle stomped her feet, turned, and ran from the room, crying.

Mrs. Ronaldi sputtered, "The animal? The animal is Dominick Romeo? My Rosalie is marrying Dominick Romeo?" She crossed herself, beat her breast, and said a prayer under her breath. Nick didn't know if she prayed for protection, or if she said a prayer of thanks.

Rosalie wanted to kill Nick. But she couldn't complain about the reaction. She should have sold tickets, or at the very least, videotaped it.

Rich smiled, nodding his approval. Annabelle had shown her true colors—as expected. Aunt Rose ran to

Rosalie and kissed both of her cheeks. "*Bene, bene, porta fortuna.*" Then she grabbed Nick, held his face in her hands, and looked him over. "So, you not so stupid after all, eh?" She kissed him on both cheeks and gave him a little smack. "No more acting stupid. We already have enough of that in this familia. *Capisce?*"

Nick winked at Aunt Rose. "*Capisce.*" He took both her hands in his and kissed each one. "*Grazi, tante, grazi.*"

Rosalie watched as Aunt Rose stood speechless, a first in Rosalie's experience. The old girl blushed. *Madònne*, she'd seen everything now.

Rich kissed Rosalie on both cheeks, "Congratulations, Ro. I'm so happy for you. Nick's a great guy."

"Thanks, Richie."

He and Nick did the whole guy hug thing, clapping each other on the back and generally acting macho.

It was good to see Nick and Rich together. They'd obviously come to terms after the fistfight and were acting like old friends, which she guessed they were.

Papa hefted himself out of his chair, stood beside Mama, and cleared his throat. "You happy, Rosalie?"

"Yeah, Pop, I'm very happy."

Pop moved forward and shook Nick's hand. "Welcome to the family. Rich, hurry down to the corner, buy champagne. We will celebrate."

Rich grabbed his coat and ran out. Mama and Aunt Rose scurried off to get champagne glasses.

Nick pulled Rosalie closer to his side, nuzzled her ear, and whispered, "So, are you still angry I spilled the beans?"

"Yes, no . . . I don't know. I thought Mama was going to have a coronary."

"Your sister's a piece of work. And for the record, you're the pretty one."

"Okay, you're forgiven. You don't need to suck up any more."

"Oh, yeah, I do."

"Why?"

"You'll see."

Nick pulled the Tiffany box from his pocket, opened it, and slipped her engagement ring back onto her finger.

A few minutes later, the doorbell rang. Rosalie answered the door, and Gina shot forward and hugged her. "Rosalie, Nick, congratulations! I'm so happy for you."

Nick hugged her. "Thanks, Gina. How've you been?"

"Better than you."

"Not now, you're not. It's good to see you again."

Rosalie scoffed. "Hold on, what's all this buddy, buddy stuff?"

Nick winked at Gina. "We've met before. I knew you'd want Gina here to celebrate with everyone, so I gave her a call."

Rosalie raised an eyebrow. There was something they weren't telling her—not that she cared too much. It was sweet of Nick to ask Gina to join them. Lord knew, she'd been nervous enough about bringing Nick to meet the parents. Why Nick had insisted on making the big announcement now was beyond her.

"Ma, Gina's here. We're going to need another plate at the table," Rosalie called to the kitchen.

The front door opened and hit Gina in the back. Rich stuck his head in. "What the . . . Gina?"

Gina's smile disappeared. "Rich. What are you doing here? I thought you'd flown back to Maine or New Hampshire or wherever."

Rich swallowed hard. "No, I, um . . . changed my flight. I'm taking a few days to settle a couple of things in the city."

"Here." Gina handed Nick the bottle of champagne she'd brought. "I can't stay. I wanted to stop by to say how happy I am for both of you. Rosalie, I'll see you in the office Monday. 'Bye."

She blew by Rich and out the door. Rich shoved the champagne he'd bought into Rosalie's arms and took off after Gina.

Nick smiled. "Do you think we'd get away with it if we took off, too?"

"Not a chance. Now that they've heard the news, they're going to want details. I told you we should have waited."

Nick kissed her, and the bottles clinked together. "I've waited long enough. No more. I want to get married right away."

"Hold on. It takes a long time to plan a wedding, unless you want to run to Vegas. But if we did that, we'd have a very short marriage. Mama will kill both of us if we don't get married in the church."

"So, we'll get married in the church. Soon."

"Nick, you have to reserve a date, then there's a reception hall, catering, flowers, a dress. There's a lot more to it than walking down an aisle and saying 'I do.'"

"Annabelle's not getting married. She had a date reserved with the church, reception hall, everything, right?"

"Of course, but—"

"So, we'll have a wedding instead. It's perfect. You can keep what she has or change it to suit you. Lois will help plan everything. So, when are we getting married?"

"Two weeks from Saturday?"

"That long, huh? Well, I guess I'll have to wait. See? You didn't think I could compromise."

"You're crazy. I can't put together a wedding in less than three weeks—"

"No, but Lois can. Don't worry about it."

"Don't worry about it? Don't worry about it? Are you crazy?"

"Not crazy, determined. And you know me; I always get what I want."

Rosalie, not being much for weddings in the first place, had no problem handing over the reins to her mother and Aunt Rose along with Nick's mother and grandmother. All Rosalie and Lois were responsible for was picking out the wedding gown and bridesmaids' dresses. Rosalie figured the fact she had agreed to get married in the first place would have stopped her mother from complaining, but of course, she was wrong. Her mother was against her first choice, but Lois and Nick's mother and grandmother were able to calm her down. At any rate, Rosalie was happy that the women in both families got along well, which allowed her to concentrate on brokering the deal between Premier and Romeo's.

In the end, Nick paid a pretty penny for the dealership of his dreams, but no more than Premier was worth. He seemed to get a kick out of hard-nosed negotiations with his fiancée—not that Rosalie didn't enjoy arguing for money and then going home and having make-up sex every night, either.

Nineteen days, two hours, and thirty-six minutes later, not that she was counting, Rosalie walked down the white rose petal-scattered aisle of St. Joseph's on her father's arm. Nick looked shocked. She didn't know why. She'd told him she wasn't wearing white. She refused to spend her wedding day looking like the Michelin Man. She guessed he hadn't expected scarlet. What could she say? Scarlet was her color. With her dark hair and olive complexion, well, she looked amazing. At least she'd allowed her mother to talk her into a traditional bouquet of white roses and lilies, the only traditional thing about her ensemble. She could see Nick loved her dress. The mermaid cut hugged her curves. Subtle beading made the gown shimmer without looking too fussy. She still hadn't gained back all the weight she'd lost during the month they were apart, and she couldn't eat. For the first time in her life, she looked slim.

A smile spread across Nick's face—that special smile he saved for her, the one that made her breath catch.

Nick took her hand, and all her nerves disappeared. After promising to honor, cherish, and supply her with a lifetime of love and chocolate, Nick got what he wanted.

But then, so did she.

The End

Acknowledgments

MY LOVE AND ETERNAL GRATITUDE GO OUT TO MY HUSBAND and partner in crime, Stephen, and to my children—my cohorts and the best things I've ever had a hand in creating: Tony, Anna, and Isabelle.

My parents, Richard Williams and Angela Feiler, and my stepfather, George Feiler, for their support and for teaching me that no matter how hard life gets, there's always something to laugh about.

My dear friend Kevin Dibley who gave me much needed information on dating in the twenty-first century and allowed me to explore the male psyche.

My favorite doctor, Dr. Michael Tolino, for helping me with all things medical and for not getting angry with me when I forget to tell him the person in need of medical assistance isn't a real person, but a character in my book.

My critique group—The Goddesses—Gail Reinhart, Peggy Parsons, and Kay Parker.

The members of The Valley Forge Romance Writers—never have I met a more helpful, caring, and supportive group of women. I thank you all.

My agent, Kevan Lyon, for all she does.

And lastly, to my editor and friend, Deb Werksman—you're the best.

About the Author

Robin Kaye was born in Brooklyn, New York, and grew up in the shadow of the Brooklyn Bridge next door to her Sicilian grandparents. Living with an extended family that's a cross between *Gilligan's Island* and *The Sopranos*, minus the desert isle and illegal activities, explains both her comedic timing and the cast of quirky characters in her books.

She's lived in half a dozen states, from Idaho to Florida, but the romance of Brooklyn has never left her heart. She currently resides in Maryland with her husband, three children, two dogs, and a three-legged cat with attitude.